Campbell Armstrong was born in Glasgow and educated at Sussex University. He and his family now live in Ireland. His bestselling novels *Jig*, *Mazurka*, *Mambo*, *Agents of Darkness*, *Concert of Ghosts* and *Jigsaw* have placed him in the front rank of international thriller writers. His latest novel, *Silencer*, is now available as a Doubleday hardback.

Also by Campbell Armstrong

JIGSAW

and published by Corgi Books

HEAT

Campbell Armstrong

CORGI BOOKS

HEAT
A CORGI BOOK : 0 552 14169 0

Originally published in Great Britain by Doubleday,
a division of Transworld Publishers Ltd

PRINTING HISTORY
Doubleday edition published 1996
Corgi edition published 1997

Set in 10/12pt Monotype Plantin by
Kestrel Data, Exeter, Devon.

Corgi Books are published by Transworld Publishers Ltd,
61–63 Uxbridge Road, London W5 5SA,
in Australia by Transworld Publishers (Australia) Pty Ltd,
15–25 Helles Avenue, Moorebank, NSW 2170
and in New Zealand by Transworld Publishers (NZ) Ltd,
3 William Pickering Drive, Albany, Auckland.

Reproduced, printed and bound in Great Britain by
Cox & Wyman Ltd, Reading, Berks.

For Aidan, Connor, Neil and Owen

1

BUCKINGHAMSHIRE, ENGLAND

The resort hotel, surrounded by a golf-course and tennis courts, was located in a secluded green valley of the kind reserved for the sporting pursuits of the rich. Horses were available for guests who wanted the experience of hacking country lanes, and there was a high-tech indoor gymnasium. Since Frank Pagan played neither golf nor tennis, and thought horses petulant creatures given to treacherous inclinations – and pumping iron, in his book, was an overrated activity with high cardiac arrest possibilities – he wasn't altogether at ease in these expensive, rustic surroundings.

But he had more pressing reasons for his lack of comfort. Sixty-three of them, to be exact. Sixty-three men and women.

He stood on the balcony outside his room and surveyed the area as far as the wooded horizon. It was glorious weather, the last day of an August that had been sunny and hot throughout. A few figures in the distance trotted after golf balls; on one of the tennis courts a middle-aged Australian woman scampered across red clay with racket outstretched to make a return to her partner, a taut, leathery man from Dallas.

Sixty-three reasons, Pagan thought.

He continued to observe the view. Cloudless sky, copper sun, a golf ball in high flight. A horse whinnied nearby. These were peripheral details to him. His concentration was elsewhere. He was thinking of the hidden figures in the landscape, the men and women who strolled among clumps of trees and communicated with one another by means of cordless phones, the casually dressed characters that drifted with apparent aimlessness around the edges of the tennis courts or wandered the foyer downstairs or strolled the corridors. These were the palace guard, the security forces he'd assembled to protect the sixty-three counter-terrorist specialists from around the world gathered here for this conference. The guards, members of Special Branch, equalled the specialists in number – and still Pagan, in his wary vigilance, wasn't sure this was enough.

He checked his watch. Five forty. There had been two seminars during the course of the day, one on the subject of electronic surveillance chaired by the expert from Dallas, the other concerned with ways of more efficiently sharing computer information to track the movement and identities of terrorists. Pagan, his attention inclined to wander, had sat through the meetings with the same discomfort he felt now on the balcony.

The safety of these international experts was his responsibility. And safety, as he knew, was a porous concept. It was an imperfect world, and you could take all the precautions you thought necessary – and still you were never sure you'd covered every contingency. The thought nagged him. But what could he do? Lock all the participants in their rooms for the three days of the conference? Shackle them to their beds?

He stepped back into his room, leaving open the balcony door. Dinner was at seven thirty, and after dinner, God help him, he was scheduled to give a speech. He dreaded public speaking because he was essentially a private man. But whether he liked it or not he was the star here, the principal speaker; the guests wanted to hear what he had to say on the subject of terrorism.

No, that wasn't entirely true: they wanted to hear about one terrorist in particular.

He sat on the bed, which was covered with sheets of paper on which he'd scribbled notes. He reckoned he'd speak for twelve minutes, fifteen maximum. The idea made him nervous. All faces turned in his direction, all attention focused on him. He was more accustomed to watching than to being watched. He picked up one of the sheets and looked at what he'd written . . . *After her disappearance in Venice last March, all of my department's time and energies have been concentrated on finding her* . . .

Finding her, he thought. The phrase, so flat and bone-dry, gave no indication of the amount of effort that had been expended. It suggested nothing of the intensity of the search, the hundreds of sightings that had turned out to be cases of mistaken identity. The long days spent perusing reports that had come from around the world – from the Far East, Europe, and the United States.

Finding her. There was a sense in which she'd become mythical. She'd entered a realm of invisibility.

He gathered a few crumpled sheets together and walked inside the bathroom and looked at himself in the mirror. He wondered how other people would see him when he rose to give his speech. He wanted to project confidence and optimism; to flash the occasional generous smile expected of people making after-dinner speeches. A joke to tell, perhaps. Something to lighten the atmosphere.

He ran a hand over his short hair, uttered aloud a few sentences in a brisk way. *We don't give up. That's the secret. We keep trying. We keep trying to imagine ourselves in her place, the kinds of things she's likely to do, the places she might visit, the old acquaintances she may be tempted to contact* . . . He studied his reflection, leaned forward and looked directly into his grey eyes and thought they were the colour of a wintry afternoon in London.

We keep trying, he thought. Because that's all we can do. Because the rest is thin air.

The chef was manic and operatic, didn't like a single member of his staff, considered them idiots incapable of performing even the simplest of tasks without his supervision. His nickname among the staff was Mussolini.

He'd discovered a human hair in the white wine sauce for the *écrivisses cardinalisées*, which caused him apoplexy. He stood in the centre of the stainless-steel kitchen with the offensive, spidery strand dangling from his fingers.

'And whose – whose is this? From whose scalp did this fall?' His eyes popped.

The kitchen hands, the choppers, the peelers, the under-chefs, everyone stopped what they were doing.

'It is black,' said the chef.

The staff was silent. The chef strutted back and forth like a detective about to interrogate the various suspects in a drawing-room murder.

'It comes from somebody with black hair,' said the chef.

Seven of the twelve kitchen staff had hair that colour. The chef realized he didn't have time to question them all; he was under pressure, he was always under pressure; he had a dinner to prepare for more than sixty people and already he was concerned about the *filet de boeuf en croute* because he considered the pastry-chef, a plain bespectacled woman whose only distinction was her total lack of personality, another potential incompetent. In fact, he had all kinds of concerns beyond a single human hair that had found its way into the wine sauce. The *soufflé au bleu* required his personal attention if he wanted to avert a disaster. And the *mousse aux marrons* – that was a production number all by itself.

He glared at the staff. 'Later, we will explore the matter of this hair more thoroughly,' he announced. He clapped his hands quickly several times. 'For now, back to work. All of you. Work work work! And no hairs! No more hairs!'

He wandered the kitchen, surveying his domain. He studied the pastry-chef a moment. She was rolling out sheets of brioche dough. She did this with a certain facility, admittedly, but the chef never allowed himself to think well of the accomplishments of other people. He watched her work. If she was aware of him, she gave no indication. She continued to roll the dough, her manner one of absorption.

He shook his head and walked away. He didn't like her wrist movements. It was always the same; there was always a fault to be found, if you looked for it. It was what the chef enjoyed most about the human race: it was superbly flawed. So why did he bother to sweat over the perfection of food, when the pigs chewed and swallowed it without appreciation? Because he was an artist. And an artist, as the whole world knew, did everything according to his own vision, appreciated or not.

At six thirty Robbie Foxworth, Pagan's assistant, joined Pagan in his room. Foxworth was already dressed for dinner: tux, cummerbund, bow-tie. He'd combed his red hair back with some kind of gel that glistened. He surveyed the bundle of sheets on Pagan's bed and said, 'Ah, this must be the speech.'

'You want to make it on my behalf, Foxie?'

'I don't think so,' said Foxie. 'These good people are expecting the great Frank Pagan, not his lieutenant and general gofer. Why? Are you nervous?'

'Am I ever nervous?'

'If you were, you'd hide it anyway, and nobody would ever know.'

Pagan fumbled with his tie and the bow slackened and fell apart, and the ends flopped. 'Can you do this for me, Foxie? I never got the hang of these things.'

Foxworth gathered the ends, tied the bow deftly. He knew about dinner-jackets and bow-ties. He'd gone to the kind of expensive school where one learned such things at an early age. He had also learned good manners and the need for self-discipline and how to comport himself with a certain dignity. His father had been a somebody in the Foreign Office, and the Foxworth family could trace its lineage back to the time of the Norman Conquest.

Pagan, who came from an altogether different background, South London, father a bricklayer, looked at himself in the dressing-table mirror and saw a stranger in a tuxedo. 'I always feel ridiculous in a monkey suit.'

Foxie said, 'You look fine, Frank. Suave's the word.'

Pagan adjusted his cummerbund slightly. He stepped out on to the balcony. The golf-course was

12

empty now, and so were the tennis courts. But the watchers were still scattered here and there.

Foxworth, who'd spent much of his life studying the often inscrutable nuances of Pagan's behaviour, detected an uneasiness in Frank that had nothing to do with the prospect of an after-dinner speech. 'You're bothered by something,' he said.

Pagan stared off into the distance. Birdsong and sunlight. All the open spaces. The copse of beech trees behind which the sun would eventually wane. 'I'm not sure,' he said.

'You've got security men coming out of the wood-work, Frank. Everything's covered. The hotel staff have been checked. Nobody can even get past the gatehouse without a special ID card. It's under control. Relax.'

Pagan wasn't always easily reassured. In every land-scape something always lurked; especially his inner terrain, where there were shadows, and tangled shrub-bery, and menaces too vague to name. He said, 'I could have done without this conference.'

'It was arranged last year,' Foxie remarked. 'How would it have looked if you'd cancelled it?'

Pagan shrugged. 'Sixty-three of the best counter-terrorist professionals in the world could have stayed at home, and I wouldn't have this headache.'

Foxie moved on to the balcony now. He sniffed the rich scented air of summer. 'Tranquillity,' he said, and gestured out across the view. 'Not even a breeze. All you have to worry about is this bloody speech, which I assume you've rehearsed and committed to memory.'

Pagan smiled. 'I need a joke, Foxie. One good joke to put in the speech. You know any?'

'My repertoire's a bit thin. Besides, I never remember jokes.'

Pagan stared across the golf-course and said, 'What the hell. I'm bad when it comes to telling them.'

'There you are then,' Foxie said, closing the subject.

'In any case,' Pagan added, 'I don't feel the topic of my speech merits much in the way of mirth.' He looked at Foxworth and suggested they have a pre-dinner drink from the mini-bar.

The pastry-chef spread a glaze of beaten eggs across the surface of the dough with a simple steady motion of her hand. Then she sealed the dough around the meat. The chef watched her.

'Two hundred degrees Celsius in the oven. No more, no less,' he said. He noticed she didn't have black hair. More mouse-coloured, and tucked in under her white cap.

'After fifty minutes, place foil over the tray. Ten minutes later, remove the tray from the oven.'

The pastry-chef checked the oven gauge, opened the door, slid the large tray inside.

'Fifty minutes,' the chef said.

The pastry-chef, whose English had a foreign inflection, said, 'Fifty minutes, of course.'

'Exactly fifty.' The chef tapped his wrist-watch. 'Precision is the key to everything.'

'Yes,' said the pastry-chef.

In his room, Pagan sipped his second Scotch and soda. The first had softened his mood somewhat. The second would help increase the illusion of relaxation. Foxie sat on a chair by the open balcony door with a glass of white wine in his hand. He was something of a connoisseur when it came to wines, and the one he was drinking was causing him to grimace. He held the glass up to the light, seeking impurities.

'Nasty stuff,' he said. 'Tastes of cardboard.' He set the glass down and looked at Pagan. 'What's the gist of your speech, Frank?'

'I thought a little background first,' Pagan answered. 'The explosion. Her associations with certain arms dealers. A mention of her freelance work in the Middle East.'

'Your audience will already know all that.'

'It does no harm to refresh their memories,' Pagan said. 'Then I'll cut to the chase. How we came close to capturing her in Venice. The steps we've taken in trying to find her ever since. A general review of procedures.'

Foxworth said, 'You don't have an ending, that's the problem.'

Pagan shrugged. 'Only a beginning and a middle.'

A beginning and a middle, and perhaps something of a mild fixation in between, Foxworth thought, although he didn't say so. He would never have uttered the thought aloud. When it came to the subject of the woman, you had to be careful what you said around Pagan. He was sensitive in ways Foxworth had never seen before, as if the woman were silver paper pressed upon an exposed nerve in his teeth, something that caused him a flash of pain. Perhaps pain wasn't the word. Something else. Foxie let his line of thought fade away. At times it served no purpose to explore Frank Pagan's psyche, which was a well-defended fortress.

The telephone was ringing on the bedside table. Pagan reached for it.

When he heard the voice on the other end of the line, he felt the mellow effects of the Scotch dissipate immediately. He was at once jolted into sharp attentiveness.

She said, 'I want to see you.'

15

'Where are you?' he asked.

'Don't ask unanswerable questions, Pagan. You should know better. I just think we should sit down and talk. It's been a while.' She laughed, and although it was a light sound, almost musical, it chilled him. 'Leave the hotel now.'

'I can't leave now,' Pagan said. He was conscious of Foxworth's puzzled expression.

'Forget the dinner, babe,' she said. 'Forget the big speech. Drive to the village of Stratton. There's a pub called The Swan. Go inside. Wait for me there. If you're alone, I'll contact you. If you bring backup, even one, you don't see me.'

Pagan said, 'The Swan. In Stratton.'

'Only if you leave now. Waste time, I'm history.'

'I'll be there.' He set the receiver down.

Foxworth asked, 'Well?'

'I have to go.'

'You can't go. You've got people who've travelled thousands of miles to hear you speak, Frank. For God's sake. You've got Australians, Americans, Kuwaitis—'

'Don't remind me,' Pagan said. 'Just handle things for me. That's all I ask. Make some kind of excuse.'

'Such as?'

'Think of something.'

'Frank—'

'I'm going, Foxie. Enjoy the dinner, explain I was unavoidably called away – I might be back in time for dessert.'

Foxworth sighed, ran a hand across his face. 'I don't have to guess who called, do I?'

'No,' Pagan said. 'You don't.'

'And she's going to meet you in Stratton. At The Swan.'

'That's what she says.'

16

'Why the hell is she in this neck of the woods at this particular time?'

'That remains to be seen.'

Foxworth stood up. 'It smells, Frank. There's a bad odour. I don't like it.'

'I'm used to bad odours,' Pagan replied. He walked toward the door. 'Don't mention this to anyone. One other thing. Make absolutely sure the security level is intensified. I want the grounds searched. The corridors. The rooms. The wine cellar. The kitchen. Everywhere. If anyone asks about all this activity, you know what to tell them.'

'I believe the phrase is precautionary measures,' Foxie said.

'Big precautionary measures,' and Pagan was gone from his room at speed, a flash of black and white, a man in a hurry so purposeful and concentrated it might have been interpreted by a casual onlooker as a sign of dementia.

Stratton was twelve miles from the hotel and the road was narrow, curved. Pagan drove quickly, without care. He swung into the bends, meadows passed in a green visual haze.

She calls unexpectedly. She calls out of nowhere. What was he supposed to do? Ignore her? He'd lived so many months with her in his mind she had the status of a constant imaginary companion – except she wasn't a figment, she was real, cruelly so; and, yes, beautifully so.

He reached Stratton, which resembled a postcard of the kind tourists buy as souvenirs of Merry Olde England. A few thatched cottages, a small central square, a modest pencil of a monument to the men who'd fallen in two world wars.

The Swan was located on one side of the square. Pagan parked, went inside the pub. There was no sign of her – but he hadn't expected any. She wasn't going to be sitting on a stool at the bar with a gin and tonic in her hand, just waiting for his arrival. She'd be in the vicinity, of course, making sure he'd come on his own. She wouldn't take chances. When she was certain he was unaccompanied, she'd telephone the bar and arrange another meeting place. She was happy with labyrinths. She lived her life inside them. Intricacies appealed to her, elaborations were amusing.

I want to see you, she'd said. And he'd jumped, as she'd known he would. He'd lunged, as he always did when it came to her.

He walked to the bar, ordered a Scotch, waited.

I want to see you. Why? he wondered.

For the first time since she'd phoned he had the uneasy sensation that perhaps this was a ruse, a ploy of sorts. She wanted him to come to The Swan in Stratton because – because she didn't want him to stay at the hotel. Why?

Sixty-three counter-terrorist specialists. That was quite a number assembled under one roof. And each one of them was her enemy, or at least a potential enemy. He ran his fingertips round the rim of his drink, listened to the whisper of flesh on glass. He didn't like the drift of his thoughts, but then he brought to mind the presence and experience of the security force and it eased his concerns a moment.

I want to see you.

Seven months on from their last encounter, she turns up out of some mystifying heaven with a command. He sipped his drink, but he wasn't in the mood for alcohol. He watched the door, glanced at the other few occupants of the room – a couple of German tourists,

18

two Americans in tartan caps they must have purchased during the ten-minute Scottish leg of their thirty-six hour whirlwind experience of that quaint museum known as the UK. Nobody else.

He set down his glass. Waited. He wasn't good at waiting. He found himself staring at the telephone at the end of the bar. He imagined her somewhere nearby, watching him. He'd come to imbue her with extraordinary powers – the ability to be present without being detectable, the capacity for disappearances that amounted to sorcery. He thought of the London underground train, the bomb she'd placed in a carriage last February, and for a second he was haunted by the post-explosion smells of the dark tunnel – charred plastic, cindered clothing, human flesh. These came to him even now in bad dreams from which he woke sweating.

The telephone rang. Pagan didn't even wait for the barman to pick up. He did it himself, hastily grabbing the receiver.

She said, 'I've changed my mind.'

'What do you mean you've changed your mind?'

'I don't need to see you.'

'I've been waiting here—'

'Alone with your thoughts,' she said.

'You said you wanted to see me.'

'You're so very obedient, Frank. I like that.'

Obedient. He wondered about the ramifications of that word and decided he didn't like them.

She said, 'You'd jump through hoops of fire for me, wouldn't you?'

He made no reply.

'Go back to the hotel, where you're really needed. I'll be in touch.' She hung up.

Pagan replaced the receiver and went outside

19

quickly. Where you're really needed. What was that supposed to mean? He didn't want to think, didn't want to analyse the statement. He drove numbly and at speed. When he reached the resort he skidded past the gatehouse and headed up the gravel driveway toward the hotel. The building, a neo-Gothic stately home converted to a luxury resort a few years ago by a Japanese consortium, came in view. He parked his car and hurried up the steps and moved in the direction of the dining-room.

He shoved the doors open. He wasn't prepared for what confronted him.

2

LONDON

The first day of September was hot. Richard Pasco arrived at Heathrow airport where he was met by a young man called Ralph Donovan. He judged Donovan, blond and blue-eyed and glossy with good health, to be a junior spook, a messenger boy from Langley.

Donovan was cheerful and attentive, helping him through immigration. Pasco had trouble with the leg; he'd never become accustomed to the crude steel prosthetic that had been fashioned for him in Russia. It rubbed against the stump of flesh above the knee where surgery had been performed. The loss of the lower leg to gangrene was only a minor entry in his ledger of grudges and resentments. Greater damages had been inflicted in places nobody could ever see.

Donovan assisted him into a black BMW outside the terminal.

'Good to be out, I guess,' said Donovan as he turned the key in the ignition.

Pasco had resolved to play along with any charade going. 'Terrific,' he said.

'I'll bet,' Donovan remarked. He had a razor nick just under his jaw, a pinhead of hardened blood. 'You think you feel good now. But when we fly you back to the States . . .' With a suntanned hand he made an expansive gesture that suggested beaches, easy living.

Pasco stared from the window of the car. In the glass he observed a reflection of himself, his ruined face, eyes so sunken they might have belonged to a tubercular case. Back to the States, he thought. He was suddenly impatient, a feeling alien to him; the condition of his last ten years had been one of slow stubborn survival. He'd created a million pictures in his mind, of course. He'd imagined redressing the balance of things, sure. He'd fed upon the toxic nutrition of hatred, but even that had been a measured daily dose, like liquid dripped into his system intravenously.

He turned away from his reflection. The suit of rough blue serge they'd given him in Moscow was uncomfortable. The black shoe on his right foot pinched him.

'This is how it works,' said Donovan, whose voice was flat like that of a prairie preacher. 'You're booked into a downtown hotel for tonight. A five-star affair. You can relax. Watch a little TV. Order up some room service. Champagne, if it takes your fancy. Have a good long bath.'

'Sounds fine,' said Pasco. A bath, he thought. The simple luxury of a bath.

'Then tomorrow morning I'll call for you and we'll fly back to Washington. To the land of the living.'

Land of the Living, Pasco thought. And the Dead, blue eyes.

'You've had it pretty rough, I guess,' Donovan said.

Pasco said, 'I survived.' Fucking dumb kid. You don't know shit.

'I doubt I'd have your kind of fortitude,' Donovan said.

'Yeah, I got lucky,' Pasco said, and looked from the window again.

The BMW was heading through Hammersmith toward central London. Pasco thought it strange how freedom, for which he'd hungered so long, distilled itself in commonplace things – a flower vendor on a sunny pavement, a long-legged girl in a mini-skirt no larger than a handkerchief stepping out of a taxicab. Freedom was a series of quick sketches, cameos. But he knew there was a sense in which liberty was a trick of the mind. He shut his eyes, drifted a few seconds into a shallow sleep. When he resurfaced the BMW was parked outside a hotel.

'This is it, Mr Pasco.'

Donovan came around and opened the passenger door. Pasco had an urge to brush the kid's hand aside and walk into the hotel unaided, but then he thought: Let him help. Take advantage of all the help you can get. His stump ached, and his body felt like a construction of ill-fitted parts that might have been held together by rusted pins and rough-edged bolts.

Inside the foyer, a ludicrously sumptuous place with an infinity of chandeliers, Donovan said, 'I'll take you up to your room. Then I'll leave you in peace until the morning.'

Pasco expressed his gratitude. It was important to look pleased and perhaps even a little awed. God bless Freedom. God bless America.

The room was large and comfortable. A big rectangular tinted window overlooked Hyde Park. The afternoon sky was unbroken blue. Pasco stood at the window for a long time before he sat on the edge of the bed. He used the remote control to switch on the TV, stared at a tennis match, changed channels, changed them again

23

and again, flicking from commercials to news items to a quiz show and back again to tennis, as if he were in a hurry to assimilate the state of the world. Dizzied by the random assault of images, he clicked the off-button. He unlocked the mini-bar and surveyed the rack of miniature bottles. The variety unsettled him: he'd forgotten the simple concept of choice. He resisted the urge to drink. He wanted a clear head.

Donovan had told him that a complete change of wardrobe could be found inside the closet – a new suit, shoes, shirt, underwear, even a tie that matched the shirt. Pasco opened the closet, took out the jacket, tried it on. Ten years ago it might have fitted him perfectly. Now it hung loose on his body and the cuffs came to his fingertips. Whoever had purchased the wardrobe hadn't taken into account his years of deprivation. They hadn't thought about the fact he would have lost weight, they hadn't considered starvation diets and hard labour. They expected Richard Pasco to look as he had years before: but he'd been gone, and forgotten, and all the clocks of the life he'd lived in America had simply stopped.

He tossed the jacket aside, then lay down on the bed and shut his eyes.

Faces came before him. Landscapes flitted across his mind. He saw mountainous snowdrifts, barbed wire, makeshift huts with tar-paper windows behind which, on long black Siberian nights, kerosene lamps flickered. He heard the yapping of hounds, the distant howl of wolves. He saw a figure in a watch-tower. He felt the shaft of a hammer in his calloused hand, the motion of muscles as he raised the hammer above his head and then brought it down, minute after minute, hour after hour, on and on, an eternity of useless movement.

The world was either rocks to be smashed with

hammers, or snow cleared with shovels. The seasons dictated the form of labour, all of it meaningless: futility was the true punishment. Not the grindingly long hours, the thin soup and scraps of floating gristle, but the pointlessness of what you did every day, month in, month out. Without purpose you lost your way, you broke down and floated into the lower depths of yourself, dark abysses, places of hatred and rage so intense they caused you to lose whatever tiny foothold you still maintained on sanity. Hatred and rage, he'd come to realize, weren't abstract qualities. You could taste them. You could suck on them like cigarettes. They tainted your blood.

He stared at the ceiling. He raised his hands up. They were rough, hideous, inscribed by old scars that hadn't properly healed. He lowered them to his sides. Although sun shone through the window, he shivered. The cold had seeped into his bones so thoroughly he doubted he'd ever be warm again.

He shut his eyes and slept, dreaming of snow and dogs and the clank of chains and the motionless figure in the watch-tower. When he woke the sun had thinned in the room and his throat was dry and he knew that for the rest of his life the watch-tower would play a role in all his dreams.

Later, when the sky was dark, a visitor came, a tall man in an elegant double-breasted grey suit. His hair was neat and silvery. On the little finger of his left hand he wore a large black ring embossed with a gold eagle; it was the only hint of ostentation about the man. Pasco wondered if it were some kind of fraternity ring.

The man introduced himself as James. Was that his first name or last? He didn't say. He shook Pasco's hand briefly, pretended not to notice the scars. He smiled and flashed some expensive bridgework. He drew the curtains and sat down in an armchair at the window, crossing his legs.

'You've had a difficult time,' he said to Pasco.

Pasco wondered about the man's affiliation. Was he Langley? Did he work out of some anonymous branch of the Federal Government? Was he something else altogether? Pasco had been expecting a courtesy visit from somebody in an official capacity, maybe even the offer of a job back in Virginia. Something behind a desk, a few sedentary years paper-shuffling, followed by a pension. And then good night, chump, and thanks a lot. A consolation prize in return for his hardships.

'Injustice is always a hard pill to swallow. You chew on bitterness long enough, it leaves a lot of poison in your system,' James said.

Pasco nodded, said nothing. He was curious about this James, this talk of injustice and bitterness and poison. This wasn't quite what he'd anticipated. He'd fully expected the three-course American speech, you did your patriotic duty, self-sacrifice, we're all choked up with gratitude, we're thinking of naming a street in Le Mars, Iowa, in your honour, et cetera et cetera. This character James was heading off on quite another tack altogether and Pasco wasn't sure where he was going.

'The camp was unpleasant, of course,' said James, and touched his big pinky-ring.

'It was no Club Med,' Pasco said.

James smiled thinly. 'You have a lot of time to think in places like that. Think and remember.'

'Yeah, there's plenty time for that all right,' Pasco said.

'You think of the people that let you down. People that disappointed you. Then, maybe, you go beyond the people and start thinking about the country itself. It wasn't just so-and-so that left you stranded, it was the system, the company, America, the things you believed in. You think – the whole system is flawed. It's all a con. You were misled. You were bamboozled and brainwashed. All the colours have been bleached out of Old Glory.'

Pasco nodded. Where the fuck was this going? James was quiet a moment. Pasco studied him. He had a sudden flash that James wasn't Langley at all, he was coming from some other place. The question was where.

James got up, crossed the room, opened the mini-bar and took out a can of ginger ale, which he popped. Froth fizzed and surged across the back of his hand. This small spillage troubled him because he fussed with a paper napkin, dabbing the soda from his skin as though the liquid were caustic. He crumpled the napkin, discarded it carefully in the waste-basket. A fastidious guy, Pasco thought.

James said, 'You lost a leg. What for? The greater good of your country? Some patriotic reason you've never been able to understand?'

Pasco said, 'Tell me one thing. Who are you?'

James answered the question with several of his own. 'Do you intend to return to the fold, Richard? Is that how you see your future? They'll find you a meaningless little notch in a cubicle and you'll be thankful to them?'

'Maybe,' Pasco said.

'I don't think so, Richard,' James said. 'I don't think that's even remotely on your mind.'

'What are you? Clairvoyant? Suppose you tell me what's on my mind?'

'I think it's simple, Richard.'

'Yeah?'

'Desperately simple. Revenge.'

Pasco had a paranoid moment. Had this character been sent to test his loyalty, assess his state of mind? Langley was capable of shit like that, all kinds of underhand schemes. Everything was mirrors and distorted reflections and treachery.

'Revenge?' Pasco asked. He wasn't about to admit that. Not yet.

'Correct me if I'm wrong.'

Pasco coughed. His health was uncertain. The camp had caused severe deterioration in him. Shortness of breath, chronic chest pains, the pinched nerve in his shoulder, the ulcerated mouth. Revenge, he thought. It didn't give you back your health, and it didn't restore sanity. But it had other benefits. A great glow of satisfaction, for starters. The kind of jubilation that came from righting wrongs – as destructively as possible.

'Before we take this another step, I need to know who you are,' he said.

'Is that important?'

'I think so.'

'Why? You imagine I'm here to make out a report for some Langley shrink and have you certified as a basket-case and therefore utterly useless as a candidate for even the most menial janitorial position?'

'Yeah, I've considered it,' Pasco said. Guy was a goddam mindreader.

'You're wrong, Richard. I'm not here in that capacity. Nothing like that.'

'OK. So spell it out.'

'Some things you just can't spell out,' James said.

'Yeah? What are we talking about here? I'm to take you on trust?'

'Trust. Why not?'

'It's not my favourite word, friend.'

'I sympathize,' James said. He looked at Pasco in a pensive manner for a time. 'OK. I'll meet you halfway along the road, Richard. It's the best I can do. You have certain grudges. Understandable ones. You want to take action. You haven't quite thought it through yet. But there's a germ in your head and it's been festering there for ten long years. You've developed very deep resentments against certain people inside a certain institution. In a sense, you're still a prisoner. Not in some Russian gulag this time – no, you're a prisoner of your own hatreds and frustrations. Again, this is understandable . . .'

Pasco made as if to interrupt, but James stalled him with a motion of his hand. 'Please. Let me finish, Richard. I represent certain parties who bear resentments very much like your own. They have different reasons, but I'm not here to split hairs. Their goals are the same as yours.'

'My goals? What would you know about my goals?' Pasco asked.

'I didn't come here blind, Richard. I didn't come here on anything as slender as hope. I don't rely on fragile things. I have reports about you from the camp. I have records of statements you made to your fellow inmates about what you'd do to the people who betrayed you if you ever got the chance. And some of them make very dramatic reading.'

'Records? How did you get your hands on that kind of stuff?'

James said, 'In Russia you can buy anything if you're prepared to pay the price.'

Pasco was impressed, up to a point. 'OK. So I said some off-the-wall stuff to some guys. That still doesn't tell me anything about you, who you're working for. These certain parties, for example – what do they want?'

James shrugged very slightly. 'They're interested in disruption.'

'Disruption?' Pasco shook his head. 'Too vague.'

'Let me approach this in another way,' James said. 'My associates are interested in what we might call, for want of a better term, organized vandalism. They have reasons for wanting to cause some grief to the institution that wronged you, and the system that used you.'

'What reasons?'

'They're complicated. I can't go into them. Try and understand that.'

'You can't go into them.' Pasco forced out a little laugh. 'So we're back to trust again?'

'A little more than that, Richard,' said James. 'Something less abstract, more practical. For example – have you thought about the mechanics of revenge?'

'Mechanics?'

'Face it, sport. You're not in great health. Your financial situation isn't conducive to a campaign of vengeance. And even if you have some experience of the stealth needed for this kind of business, you're out of practice. You're rusty, Richard. Best-case scenario, you might somehow manage a cut-price airline ticket back to the States and get your hands on a Saturday Night Special somewhere, and if you're really on a roll you might just manage to blow out somebody's brains before you're caught – that's not what I'd call ambitious, Richard. It's a gesture, and it's pitiful, if you don't mind me saying so. Ten years just to pull a gun on one person who might or might not have set you up? I don't think so. Revenge is complex.

It has to be organized. The emotion itself isn't going to carry you very far.'

Pasco closed his eyes. He didn't want to admit it, but James was right, of course. He was dead-on. In the gulag, Pasco had seen vengeance as if it were some amorphous cloud. He'd never planned the particulars, never considered the details. He'd just lived inside this shapeless fog where he'd imagined all kinds of destruction and mayhem. This person would be taken out, that person would meet a horrible fate, he'd choke somebody with his bare hands if he had to – there was a whole goddam line of victims and targets. But he didn't have the stamina, and he didn't have the where-withal, and James knew it.

He stared into James's face. 'So what's the deal?'

'A question first. How badly do you want it?'

'Ten years' worth,' Pasco said.

James rose, went to the window, parted the curtain a second. Pasco wondered if this was some kind of signal to a person in the street; he was having too many of these paranoid flashes, he decided. James turned, smiling. The ginger-ale can in his hand glinted. He produced a brown envelope from the inside pocket of his jacket and passed it to Pasco.

'What's this?'

'Open it,' James said.

Pasco ripped the flap. Inside was an American passport made out in his own name; the photograph in the passport was one taken just before his enforced sojourn in Russia. The envelope also contained a savings-account passbook issued by Barclays Bank, also in the name of Richard Pasco. Pasco flicked the pages. The current balance in the account was $500,000.

'What's all this?' he asked.

'A token of our credibility, Richard,' James said. 'A demonstration of our seriousness. The passport's authentic. The money's real. First thing in the morning, you can go to any branch of Barclays and verify it.'

Pasco raised an eyebrow, glanced at the credit balance again, then looked at James.

'OK,' he said. 'Tell me more.'

They talked for almost four hours.

When the man called Ralph Donovan came to the room at five minutes before eleven the following morning, he found no sign of Richard Pasco. The new suit still hung in the closet, but the other clothing had gone. All that remained of Pasco's possessions were the ugly black shoes he'd been wearing on his arrival, a pair of off-white underpants, grey socks, and a soiled shirt.

Donovan thought: Every so often in goddam life things went off the way they were planned.

3

LONDON

A copy of every London daily lay on George Nimmo's desk. The headlines in the tabloids were predictably bold and drastic, and the so-called quality press was less than subdued when it came to reporting the previous night's events at The Hackenbridge Hotel. Nimmo, who had the face of a spoiled choirboy, a pendulous lower lip and plump cheeks, gestured at the newspapers in dismay.

'Death, death and more death,' he said. He was agitated and pale. He had three telephones on his desk that rang continually. Secretaries and assistants in an outer office picked up the calls. 'People from all over the world. Two from the States. Two from Saudi Arabia. Another from Mexico. Two from Canada. Three from Germany. On and on.'

Pagan, seated on the other side of Nimmo's desk, could read the headlines upside down. The number of reported fatalities varied from paper to paper. Fifty-three in the *Sun*. Fifty-four in the *Mirror*. Medical spokespersons, acting on the orders of Nimmo, who was the Commissioner of Scotland Yard, were being tight-lipped about the matter – but you couldn't keep the sharks of the press at bay for long. They clamoured for detailed information, and if you didn't accede to their demands, they indulged in speculation. Truth was a malleable commodity anyway.

Afternoon sunlight burned brilliantly on the window. Pagan shut his eyes against all this brightness, all this news of death. He'd been awake for more than thirty hours but felt no real fatigue. What he experienced instead was a fuse sizzling inside his skull. On one level, it was the spark of anger; on another, it was a fiery line leading to a dynamite-charge of self-reproach. He assaulted himself with ifs. If he hadn't left the hotel the way he'd done, if he hadn't jumped as soon as he'd received the phonecall, if he'd been more thorough in investigating the backgrounds of hotel personnel – conditionals were like hot sands in his brain.

On the other hand, even if he hadn't made that fruitless trip to The Swan, what could he have done to change the outcome of events in any case? The dinner would have gone on, the conference members would have picked up knives and forks, cut into the food, ferried it to their mouths. He couldn't have stopped that. This realization was no balm. The bottom line was that he'd been responsible for sixty-three people; and most of them were dead. And they'd died painfully.

'The medical chaps don't know what kind of poison was used,' Nimmo said. 'They're running tests. The trouble with tests is they don't bring back the dead, do they?'

'No, they don't,' Pagan said.

'So far, all we know is that the non-carnivores in the group didn't die. Conclusion, the poison was in the meat dish. I've got a copy of the menu right here. There was a choice of fish or beef. The fish-eaters survived. The others didn't. We'll have the substance identified soon enough, I daresay. Though it isn't going to do us a lot of good, is it?' Nimmo shoved his chair back from his desk and picked up a pen, tapped the surface of his desk, rap rap rap.

Pagan said, 'According to the head chef, the pastry-chef was responsible for preparing the meat dish—'

Nimmo looked at the menu and said, 'The *filet de boeuf en croute*.'

'Whatever. The task was hers. She was new to the staff. She'd been there three weeks. Came with good references. Hotels in Switzerland, Spain. They checked out. This chef's the manic type. He'd be very particular about who works in his kitchen. She didn't mix well, according to him. Kept to herself. Her passport identified her as Carmen Profumo, born Florence 1969. She put the *filet de boeuf* in the oven, the chef witnessed that much – after which she just disappeared from the kitchen. Later, when I went through her room at the hotel, I found no personal belongings of any significance. A hairbrush. Toothpaste. The usual. No books, papers, magazines, letters, diaries. A solitary woman.'

'And your people did their own preliminary check, correct?'

'Of course we did.'

'But you missed the woman?'

Pagan detected a small malice in the way the question was posed. 'The complex employs seventy-nine people, George. We were as thorough as we could be. We checked backgrounds, we ran names through the computers for criminal records, we did the passport routine—'

'But you missed the woman,' Nimmo said again.

'Her references were verified. The passport was genuine. What else is there to examine? When you've got seventy-nine people to run security checks on in

35

the hotel business – which is notorious for its turnover of personnel – there's always a chance you're going to miss something. It may be small, it may be utterly insignificant, but there's always that chance.'

Nimmo kept rapping the pen. 'So. Let us backtrack. She puts the dish in the oven, she leaves the kitchen. She telephones you. Asks you to meet her. You dash off. She doesn't show up. You return to the hotel, by which time—'

'By which time, people are dying,' Pagan said.

He remembers opening the doors to the dining-room. He remembers the eerie chaos of the scene. Diners coughing blood, some slumped back in their chairs, others rising from the table and wandering around in pain and confusion, still others lying on the floor, a few motionless, their bodies contorted and stiff, some crawling blindly in the throes of seizure. *He remembers the madness, the sounds of choking and coughing, the way plates and cutlery fall to the floor, people slithering from their chairs, the groaning, waiters fluttering around in confusion, a maid screaming, and he remembers thinking – this is a lopsided scene, everything off-centre, appallingly inverted, like something drawn in a lunatic's sketchbook.*

The memory froze him. He might have stepped inside a chamber of solid ice.

Nimmo said, 'She wants you out of the complex – why?'

'She doesn't want me to be one of the victims, George. I'm to be spared. She knows just about everyone else is going to be poisoned. She doesn't want me in that number.'

'Why?'

Pagan shrugged. There it was; that first little hint of fatigue, something solid as coal behind his eyes. 'Because she isn't ready to kill me. Because she wants

36

me to know how easily she can circumvent our security arrangements. Because she wants to humiliate me. Any of the above. All of the above.'

'She has, yo, a personal vendetta against you.'

Pagan pondered the meaningless *yo* which Nimmo had the habit of dropping, like a strange grammatical mark, into his sentences. A personal vendetta, he thought. It was one way of describing it.

'Something like that,' he said. His fatigue passed and his anger came rushing back. He heard it roar to his skull like a locomotive.

Nimmo appeared pensive, which involved a series of deep furrows in his forehead. 'Here's something that *really* bothers me. We've got more than fifty corpses on our hands, courtesy of this bloody woman. No ordinary corpses, mind you. Some of the best counter-terrorist minds in the world. Some of the very best. Visitors here. Invited guests. Distinguished people. A great loss to the world intelligence community, and a great victory for the woman – after all, she's just wiped out a whole slew of her potential captors, has she not? And we've spent – what? – thousands of man-hours searching for the bitch as a consequence of her deplorable terrorist activity last February, and God alone knows how many hundreds of thousands of pounds, and we haven't even caught a *whisper* of her. And yet somehow she manages to get herself a job in a hotel and commits this new atrocity. Is that what you'd call a failure, Frank?'

'I'd call it that,' Pagan said. A hard admission. He couldn't deny it. Thousands of man-hours, he thought. But this wasn't a realistic calculation, because it went beyond a mere matter of punching time-clocks. It was the kind of time you couldn't accurately measure. He'd dreamed of her in his sleep at night. He'd driven randomly around London during extended periods of insomnia in the chance that, by some major miracle, he might happen to see her on a street. A dozen occasions, he'd visited the underground station where she'd detonated the bomb last winter and he'd ridden pointlessly up and down the escalators as if he might somehow be given a sign, by the god who dictated such matters, of her whereabouts. Time like that, time of wishing and hoping and seeking revelations in futile car trips and escalator rides, couldn't be counted.

He got out of his chair, strolled round Nimmo's spartan office, beat his hands against his thighs. He struggled with his anger. He heard her voice in his head: *You're so very obedient, Frank. I like that. Babe,* she'd called him. An uninvited familiarity. He thought of people dying on the floor of the dining-room, and it depressed him. He thought of the widows and orphans of these people in countries he'd never visit. Blame. OK, up to a point, he'd shoulder it, even if it only served to further ignite his fury. Fury was useless, unless you channelled it into constructive areas. It was also unprofessional. You were supposed to be detached. You were meant to maintain a certain composure. He'd never quite achieved that state. Not where she was concerned.

'Why the failure, Frank?' Nimmo asked. 'Explain.'

The question was one that could only be stabbed at with the usual old complaints. 'Because we can't be everywhere at once, George. We can't cover every railway station, every airport, every square inch of the country. There's not enough manpower for that. You could give me ten thousand uniforms, twenty, more than twenty, and I still couldn't guarantee we'd find her.'

Nimmo said, 'We're powerless. Against one woman. She comes and goes as she pleases. Is that what I'm hearing?'

'George, there are a million places to hide in this green and pleasant land of ours. She could be almost anywhere. What do you expect? A door-to-door search of every house in the country?'

'I expect her to be caught, Frank,' Nimmo said. 'That's the only thing I've ever expected. I certainly didn't anticipate the fact that she'd somehow contrive to kill more than fifty important people at an English hotel crawling with your security personnel.'

'You blame me?'

'I'm not apportioning blame,' Nimmo said.

Lying bastard, Pagan thought. Nimmo shovelled blame wherever he could. He was in the business of remaining aloof from disasters, keeping his distance from them. If there was shit, he'd make sure none of it was going to stick to him. He had political ambitions beyond the confines of Scotland Yard. He saw himself in Whitehall, perhaps a future Cabinet position, God knows what. He needed knightly armour to protect his reputation.

Nimmo said, 'The public will have to be informed. I see no way around that. The press won't stand for any obfuscation on my part. Mass murder perpetrated by unknown maniac – I don't think that will wash, Frank, do you?'

'Probably not.'

'She'll have to be named. Not as Carmen Profumo. We'll have to use her real name. Even if I tried to withhold the information, one of our beloved tabloids would invariably ferret out the truth and print it. Which leaves me with egg on my face.'

Pagan was silent a moment. He tried to imagine the

goo of eggs slithering down Nimmo's face. It wasn't pretty.

'I'll catch her, George,' he said.

'Will you now?'

'Yeah, I'll catch her.' His hands, he realized, were clenched, locked tight. He was restricting his own circulation. He opened his hands, flexed his fingers.

'And how exactly do you propose to do that?' Nimmo asked.

Pagan looked Nimmo determinedly in the eye. He had no instant answer, he knew. He had no easy come-back to Nimmo's question. All he had were months of frustration behind him. Months of legwork. Months of false leads. 'Because she'll make a mistake, George. Because she's confident, and she's got the taste of blood in her mouth, and she'll take one step too far – and I'll be there when she does.'

Nimmo allowed himself a little smile. 'Let us hope you catch her before she commits yet another atrocity,' he said. For a moment George Nimmo looked as if he were enjoying himself at Pagan's expense. And why not? He was no great fan of Pagan. Never had been. In his book, Pagan was a relic of the regime of the former Commissioner, Martin Burr, now sent out to pasture. Pagan sometimes pulled things off, and when that happened Nimmo could bask in success and even take a large measure of responsibility for it. But when Pagan failed, Nimmo found it impossible to resist a small thrill of pleasure. More than fifty people were dead: it took a certain kind of man, one with brutalized sensibilities, to find a kernel of personal satisfaction in that statistic.

Pagan knew all this. He knew how Nimmo's clock ticked. The trick in remaining civil toward Nimmo lay in a refusal to descend to Nimmo's level of mean-spiritedness and spite. To ignore George as much as possible. To understand that he was back-stabbing, unscrupulous in pursuit of personal advancement. He'd kiss a slobbering baby with a rash of chickenpox if he thought it would help him an extra rung up the ladder.

Pagan wandered to the window, looked down into sunlit shafts between buildings. The world was too bright, he decided. And where you had brightness, you had shadows as well. Sunlight and shadow, and a woman who appeared to live in both dimensions with equal comfort. Another atrocity, he thought.

'Sands are running out,' Nimmo said.

'That's the nature of sand, George.'

'Indeed,' said Nimmo. '*Cherchez la femme*, Frank.'

Pagan understood he was being dismissed, sent back out into the heat of the late afternoon, where turbulence lay ahead of him, where he had questions to ask and no guarantees of answers. He opened the door and looked back at Nimmo, who was already speaking into one of his phones.

'I'll do a press conference tonight at nine,' Nimmo was saying to the minion on the other end of the line. 'Get that information out on the double.'

Pagan shut the door. Nimmo would appear on TV, his expression one of grave concern. But somewhere along the way he'd rally, change his manner, summon up the bulldog of self-righteousness and let it bark so loud and clear it could be heard all the way across the land. *Even as I stand before you,* he'd say, *even as my heart goes out to those who were murdered, I give you my solemn vow. Justice will prevail.*

What heart? Pagan wondered as he headed in the direction of the elevators.

4

BRIGHTON

Tommy Rafferty was not in demand for portrait work, which was why the woman's request surprised him. She'd turned up without an appointment, wanting a headshot of herself; it had to be black and white, six by four. She was very specific. Inside his studio, which was a bare leaky flat in one of the narrow streets below Brighton station, he had her sit in front of a crumpled cloth backdrop and tried to involve her in conversation while he fidgeted with his old battered Roliflex.

His hands had a constant tremble these days. The woman, who said very little, unsettled him even more than usual and consequently he dropped a lens-cap and had some trouble loading the camera with film. The amphetamine heebie-jeebies. Heart like a drumbeat.

He was a long-time speed-freak, a nervy emaciated man of about fifty. In the late 1960s he'd made a lot of money with his informal grainy shots of rising rock stars. These days he forged a marginal living from the occasional porn gig, and, infrequently, a bargain-basement wedding.

He tried to engage the woman in a story about the time he'd photographed Keith Moon in Soho one legendary drugged night. But she was all business, didn't have time for small talk. She told him the angle she was after, the look, the half-smile, soft light. He thought she seemed vaguely familiar, but in his concussed state a lot of people looked familiar.

'You want to tilt your head forward a little, love?' he asked. He peered through the lens at her, seeing her face in reverse image.

He couldn't decide if she was beautiful or not. The face was *structured*, he thought. It had a pleasing symmetry to it, and if she were in a more relaxed frame of mind it might have been . . . well, perhaps not *beautiful* as such, but certainly captivating. The mouth was a work of art, there was no denying that.

Rafferty looked at her through the lens. 'Hold that one.' Click. He stepped back from the camera, readjusted the lighting. That sense of familiarity came at him again, but it was lost in the general detritus of his brain. He stared at her green silk shirt, tailored black slacks, the way her hair, an intriguing blend of dark and light brown, fell just to her shoulders.

'I think if you bring the chin just a little more forward,' he said.

She did so, again without any indication of approval. She gazed into the lens, smiled – there was the tiniest of pouts to the expression, adorable – and Rafferty moved behind the camera and took the picture.

The woman stood up. 'That's enough,' she said. 'I'll wait.'

Rafferty was surprised. 'You want me to print them right away?'

The woman nodded. 'You'll be well paid,' she said. 'Don't worry.'

'Why don't you sit down and I'll do it as fast as I can.'

'What are you on, Rafferty?' she asked.

'What am I what?'

'I'd guess speed,' she said.

He shrugged. 'Old habits, you know what they say.'

'Speed kills,' she said.

'Everything kills, love. Booze, ciggies, sex,' Rafferty said, and moved toward the tiny chamber he used as a darkroom. 'I'll be as fast as I can.'

He went inside the darkroom, shut the door. Working in darkness, he listened to the rap of the woman's heels as she moved back and forth in the other room. He worked quickly. Stainless-steel spiral, developer, fixer. The air smelled vinegary, stuffy. He agitated the film in the developing tank, then thirty seconds in the stop-bath, four minutes in the fixer, followed by the wash in methylated spirits. This part of the process took about ten minutes and still the woman walked the other room impatiently.

She knocked on the door. 'How much longer?'

'I'm working as fast as I can, dear.' Why the great rush? Why only two shots when the roll carried twelve? What the hell, it was her money. He wondered how she'd found his name. He didn't even bother these days to advertise in the Yellow Pages. He had a sign outside, but it was weathered and almost illegible. Just passing by, sees the sign, wants her picture taken quickly? No, he didn't think so. There was more to it than that, but he wasn't inclined to ask. She was American, to judge from her accent. Not obviously American, just enough to notice.

Enlarge the prints, crop them to the size she wants, get paid and *auf Wiedersehen*. He took the prints from the dryer. As he was cutting them he studied her face, and just for the moment he thought he had it.

She was famous for something. He wasn't sure what.

He opened the door and went back inside the room.

'Let me see the prints,' she said.

He gave them to her. They'd turned out quite well. She examined them quickly in the direct light of his lamps. One she dismissed immediately. The other appeared to satisfy her.

'How much do I owe you?'

'A rush job like this. Let's say two hundred and fifty. All right with you, love?' He was suddenly more nervous than usual, not knowing quite why, probably the speed, the last dying rush.

She opened her purse, a big chubby leather job, stuck the prints inside. She removed a handgun with an ungainly silencer attached and shot the photographer once directly in the heart. He fell, bringing down tripod and camera as he dropped. Air escaped his lips, a hiss, like a note of irritation. She stepped over him, entered the darkroom, found the negatives, which she also placed in her purse. She struck a match, set fire to some old newspapers piled in the corner. When she was certain they'd caught and the place was filling with flame, she left the darkroom, closing the door behind her.

She glanced at Rafferty as she moved past him.

5

LONDON

Cherchez la femme. What else?

In the building in Golden Square, where his counter-terrorist section was housed, Frank Pagan looked at the photographs of the woman thumbtacked to the walls of his office. He'd collected a score of shots of her from various criminal archives around the world, mainly from the USA, where she was a fixture on the FBI's Most Wanted List.

The trouble with the photographs lay in their variety: she was never the same person twice. She had ways of rearranging herself – with make-up, hairstyles, wigs, expressions. She had a knack of shedding skins. This gallery of portraits underlined the difficulty in tracking her down; reported sightings of her were notoriously hard to check. And names – she used so many aliases that computer checks for such things as driver's licences and phone bills were pointless. Carmen Profumo, her latest, was new to him. Profumo, perfume, a phantom scent.

He surveyed the collection, as if he were seeking a constant. Her beauty was undeniable. Even in those shots where she contrived to look sullen or contemptuous, an element of that beauty always came through. Sometimes it had its source in the intelligence of her eyes, at times in the curve of mouth. In one or two shots, where her hair was cut boyishly short into her skull, there was a stark quality to her face, as if she were deliberately trying to negate her attractiveness. But she only succeeded in looking, Pagan thought, invitingly androgynous.

He glanced through the window down into Golden Square where people basked with what passed in England as abandon, men stripping to their waists and women wearing sleeveless blouses, their shoulders the colour of poached salmon.

He turned when he heard his office door open.

Foxie came into the room. 'The press wants you, Frank.'

'To lynch me?'

Foxie shrugged. 'You know how they are. They've been clogging the phone lines. You're in demand.'

'It's open season on Frank Pagan, is that it?'

'You're not at fault,' Foxie said.

'Nimmo thinks differently.'

'The idea of Nimmo thinking – isn't that an oxymoron?'

Pagan looked at his young associate with a certain fondness. In an often hostile world, Foxie could always be relied on.

'Tell them to fuck off. I have nothing to say, Foxie.'

'No comment is the phrase, I believe.'

Foxie leaned against the desk, arms crossed. He looked drained. He'd been up all night with Pagan, questioning the hotel staff, helping the medics when he could, supervising the movements of the security team. 'I keep thinking about the fact I *almost* chose the beef dish. At the last minute, I changed my mind. Don't ask me why. It was a toss-up, though. Beef or Dover sole, and the coin came down on the side of the

47

fish. Is there a patron saint of cops, do you think?'

'If there is, he's not always around when you need him,' Pagan remarked. He strolled the office, glancing at the photographs even as he tried not to. But the pictures drew him back time and again. A face – what could you really read from a face?

'The latest count is fifty-five,' Foxie said quietly. 'Five people chose the fish. Three who didn't managed somehow to survive and are presently in intensive care. The prognosis isn't good, because nobody's identified the poison. Without that knowledge, there's no chance of an antidote.'

Pagan thought about the woman, imagined her hands working dough, those long delicate fingers stretched across the uncooked pastry. The poison.

Foxie drew a hand wearily across his eyes. 'I keep seeing . . .'

'I know what you keep seeing,' Pagan remarked. He moved to his desk, scanned the computer printouts that lay scattered across the surface, then he raised his eyes to Foxworth. 'Did you run a check on this Carmen Profumo?'

Foxie nodded. 'With the usual results, I'm afraid. She's registered with the Inland Revenue. The address they have for her is the hotel, nothing else. She's never applied for a driver's licence, never been in trouble with the law. Her passport's the genuine article. And we double-checked her references. They're real. She worked at a hotel in Lucerne, and another in Seville.'

Pagan said, 'The question is – does she intend a follow-up? Is she here to do some further damage? What's her bloody agenda? Was last night just some kind of kick-off? I have this ongoing difficulty, Foxie. She can't be found and she can't be predicted. And when you can't predict, how are you supposed to act?

If she's going to do more terrorism, what the hell is her target?'

He wondered about the corridors of her mind, and he had an impression of dark, oddly-angled passageways leading to rooms, some with sloping floors, others with shuttered windows where no light penetrated. There were no straight grids, no intersections. He wanted to enter that head and walk those passageways; he wanted the intimacy of knowing her thoughts and dreams. Her plans.

Foxie said, 'We don't even know if she's still in the country. She might have gone. We've got the airports covered. The ferries. Bus and railway stations. God knows what else.'

Foxie walked in front of the photographs. Unlike Pagan, he didn't find the woman overwhelmingly attractive, unless you enjoyed a certain kind of facial architecture, angular and a little chilly. And when you took into account the monstrosities of which she was capable, her looks were irrelevant anyhow. Foxie was drawn a moment into an old New York PD mugshot of her, in which her appearance was particularly threatening.

He glanced at Pagan, and wondered, not for the first time, if Frank had developed a quirky attraction for this woman. In a manner of speaking, she was the only female in his life. She occupied his thoughts for long periods. He fretted over her whereabouts. These were symptoms of a kind, surely. And Foxworth wasn't convinced they were entirely healthy ones. *Obsession* – perhaps it wasn't that strong. But there were certainly the seeds of one. And they were firmly planted.

Pagan gazed at the sheets of paper, which were collations of reported sightings from around the world. He studied names and places and dates with a look of irritation on his face. He didn't doubt that some of these observers meant well. They believed they'd spotted the woman, but all too often the reports came from people who lived uneventful lives and needed the boost of thinking they'd seen a legendary terrorist.

He picked up the top sheet of the print-out and held it toward Foxie. 'Every time I look at these alleged reports, I feel like I'm hammering my head into a fucking brick wall. Example. Here's a guy by the name of Buddy Watts in a place called Sleepy Hollow, Oswego, New York. Sees a woman at a filling-station, thinks she's our wanted friend, so – good citizen that old Buddy is – he calls the Feds. The FBI send out two of their finest to interview Buddy. And what does it turn out to be? Nothing. In fact, Buddy, bless his heart, can't even describe the woman's car, can't remember the colour, the make, the place of registration. Buddy, in short, just wants some attention.'

Pagan flicked the sheet, as if it were something disgusting that had adhered to his fingertips. 'Example. On exactly the same day as Buddy is seeing our terrorist at a filling-station in upstate New York, a certain Mrs Wallace Drake of Torquay claims that the person who has come to live next door to her is the one we're looking for. I send a man all the way down there only to discover that Mrs Drake suffers from a mild paranoia induced by diet pills, and that her new neighbour is nothing more sinister than a dental hygienist.'

Pagan tossed the sheet down with a gesture of contempt. 'Nimmo's giving one of his press conferences tonight, which is going to mean, surprise surprise, a flood of fresh sightings. For Christ's sake, Foxie. We've already got thousands. Do we want thousands more to plough through? Do we want more and more of these pointless sheets to come spitting out of the computers? I don't need it, Foxie. I didn't become a cop because I have this hidden infatuation with paper-shuffling. The more paper, the less time I have to find the bloody woman. What am I? A fucking clerk?' Pagan crumpled a few sheets of paper quickly and dropped them on the floor, then kicked them furiously around the room. There was more than a touch of petulance in his manner.

Foxie, who'd been listening to the anger build in Pagan's voice, thought that Frank's moods were a planetary system with a gravitational pull all its own. He could be generous and kind, sympathetic and understanding; turn that around and you found stubbornness, impulsiveness. Foxie would never dream of questioning Pagan's humanity, his sense of justice, his perception of rights and wrongs – but sometimes the man yielded a little too quickly to anger, when calm was needed. Sometimes he went too close to the edge, when caution was required. Frank's history, the fact that his wife had been killed by a terrorist bomb one miserable Christmas Eve years ago in Knightsbridge, that he'd never remarried and his life was essentially a solitary one, could be invoked to explain the extremes of his character, to some extent; but Foxie, who was expert in making allowances for him, wished at times there was less of a headlong quality to his nature, and more cool contemplation. But when you worked for Pagan, you took him as he was or else you applied for a transfer.

Pagan said, 'I'm frayed. I'm bone-weary. And I'm frustrated.'

Foxie wondered if this was some mild form of apology for the sudden display of rage.

'And I'm going home. I suggest you do the same.

Get some rest. We've got some bloody hard work ahead of us.'

Foxie nodded, vanished with unusual haste out into the corridor. The room was hot and stuffy. Pagan rose, rolled up the sleeves of his linen shirt, and wandered in front of the photographs again. She'd just killed more than fifty people – so why couldn't you see the mark of the assassin in her features? Why wasn't there a sign of sorts – a craziness about the eyes, say, a murderous hint?

When you scrutinized a face long enough, it underwent changes in much the same way as the meaning of a word deteriorated the more you stared at it. Maybe something like that was happening to him now. He had a brief mental lapse, couldn't connect himself to the photographs, couldn't connect the pictures to reality – as if what he were looking at was some form of composite likeness you'd never find in the physical world.

He took his jacket from the back of his chair and draped it over his arm. Enough was enough. He'd go home, and if the mood took him, he'd listen to some music, turn the stereo up loud, banish the silences of his apartment with vintage rock and roll. He had a vast collection of old albums, many of them obscure. Thurston Harris and the Sharps. Freddie Bell and the Bellboys. Gary US Bonds. Frantic ghosts. Maybe he was in the mood for frantic ghosts because they filled the hollow places of his life. Because they erased on a momentary basis the fact of death, the memory of that dining-room, that killing banquet.

He left his office the back way. Phones were ringing throughout the building. He knew there would be reporters waiting for him out front by now.

*   *   *

Pagan's flat was located in Holland Park and over-looked a square, which at this time of year was a black-green riot of shrubbery and leaf and flower. He unlocked the front door, walked past the downstairs flat where the frail Miss Gabler lived with her colonial relics and dreams of a dead empire, and climbed the stairs. Inside his apartment he opened the curtains in the living-room and stared across the square, seeing an infestation of dogs and screaming children. An ice-cream vendor's van appeared, bells chiming. All the fun of the fair, Pagan thought, and wondered if his present mood of misanthropy warranted closing the curtains again.

He went inside the kitchen, opened the refrigerator, stared at the unappetizing contents. Two pork chops, and a clouded plastic bag of carrots. Who could eat anyway? Food was a turn-off. He opened a cabinet and took out a bottle of Auchentoshan and poured himself a generous amount, then carried the glass back inside the living-room where he sat down, kicking off his shoes. He listened to the sounds that infiltrated from the park: the malt whisky would mute these intrusions.

He sipped, closed his eyes, tried to make his mind a vacant place – a little chamber of Zen-like withdrawal which the woman couldn't enter, where she couldn't materialize in his head, where he wouldn't have to dwell on what she'd done at the resort – but external noises kept disturbing him.

The bedroom, at the rear of the flat away from the street, would be a better place to sit. He rose, carried his drink, wandered across the living-room – pausing a second to examine the bookshelves, thinking he might choose something in which to lose himself, but he'd developed a weird superstition about the books. They had belonged to Roxanne: the Penguin classics, the thin volumes of poetry – these were her books and he hadn't opened one since her death, and he had the feeling that if he were to do so it would be tantamount to unlocking a vault of memories he didn't need. So he passed the shelves by, and continued into the bedroom, on the threshold of which he stopped quite suddenly.

He was beset by a fluttering sense that something wasn't quite right. He looked round the room: whatever was different wasn't immediately obvious. There was Roxanne's photograph on the night-stand, the unmade bed, a couple of discarded shirts. A silly moment, he thought, the product of a mind that couldn't get out of overdrive. And yet he felt strangely unnerved as he moved toward the bed and lay down, carefully holding the glass of malt whisky.

He rearranged the pillows, raised the drink to his mouth, turned his face to the night-stand, froze. It was strange and terrible, he thought, how quickly the familiarity of things changed, how the commonplace bits and pieces of a life became charged with malign significance. A simple picture frame made of steel, a plate of glass, a signature across the bottom of the photograph: something he saw every morning of his life and didn't pause to think about it.

Now – now it was very different.

6

LONDON

Victoria Station was a huge noisy cathedral filled with people in too much of a hurry to worship. Locomotives shunted, pigeons flapped under the great glass roof, announcements warbled in a liquid way from loud-speakers. Pasco, as instructed by James, had taken a taxi from the hotel to the station. From Victoria, he was to hire a second cab to carry him to an address in Kilburn that James had given him. He understood he was travelling through the narrow arteries of a private network to which James belonged, one of cryptic connections and affiliations.

Cryptic – but there was nothing mysterious about the cash in the bank. Pasco had made certain of that as soon as he'd left the hotel. He'd even withdrawn some funds for carrying-around cash, fuck-you money – five thousand pounds. He'd purchased a small leather bag for his few new belongings, toothbrush, change of underwear, extra socks, a new shirt, and he'd bought an eelskin wallet he'd stuffed with crisp notes. Money boosted you: he had no doubt on that score.

The address he'd been given in Kilburn turned out to be a redbrick house in a dead-end street. He rang the bell and the door was opened by a slender woman in her late thirties whose plainness was exaggerated by a shapeless floral dress, thick-framed glasses, drab prematurely greying hair. Her expression was unwelcoming. Pasco was reminded of a woman who'd once worked in Statistics at Langley, a sweetheart really, but one of nature's spinsters. That's how she was known around the place. The Spinster.

He introduced himself as Richard Pasco. He told her she'd been recommended to him by somebody called Galkin, which was what James had told him to say. She hesitated only a second before she allowed him to enter the house, shifting her body slightly so that he could pass.

She showed him into a sitting-room, furnished with inexpensive pieces, worthless bric-à-brac. Grubby lace curtains hung at the windows. The room looked to him as if it had been assembled quickly with items purchased at Salvation Army shops. She didn't invite him to sit, which was what he really wanted to do, because his body ached.

'Where did you meet Galkin?' she asked.

Pasco foundered a moment. The woman made him nervous. Even though James had rehearsed him for several hours, and he'd concentrated hard on everything he'd been told, he had one of those moments of panic in which his memory fractured like a brittle cobweb.

'Where did you meet Galkin?' she asked again.

'I was in Russia,' Pasco said.

'And?'

The mechanics of revenge, Pasco thought. How goddam complicated they were. 'I met Galkin in prison.'

'How did he look?'

Pasco remembered the photograph James had shown him. 'He wasn't in terrific condition.'

The woman was quiet a moment. Her eyes had an interrogative intensity Pasco didn't like. He had the feeling she could see straight through him. *Don't look away from her*, James had said. *It's important you don't feel overpowered by her.*

'Tell me more about Galkin,' she said.

Pasco said, 'Mole on his left hand.'

'And?'

He scratches the mole a lot, James had said. *He can't keep from scratching it.* Pasco said, 'He never stops picking at the goddam thing. It bugs the hell out of him.'

'And?'

And what? Pasco wondered. He was filled with the urge to turn and walk out of here, forget the whole complicated situation, go back to the States and do the business himself, keep James's money and to hell with all this clandestine crap – but he had the feeling James and his people wouldn't be charitable in the matter of funds going astray. He had the distinct sensation that at the exact moment he'd withdrawn the five grand from Barclays Bank, he'd sealed an inexorable bargain, and there was no way out of it except in a rectangular box. What was more, he'd come to the conclusion that the people James represented were hard cases, gangsters, connected to that whole new breed of criminals Gorbachev had left behind in the turbulent wake of his reforms. They weren't the sort of people who took prisoners. They preferred death by Uzi to incarceration every time. Corpses you could dump; prisoners you had to feed. James had hinted at the nature of his associates' business quietly, nothing very specific, sure, but just enough for Pasco to get the general picture. What the hell, he was in now, he'd been dealt a hand of cards and all he could do was play them and swallow hard.

'And, Mr Pasco?'

'What else do you want to know?'

'Galkin. More about Galkin. First name.'

'Vladimir,' Pasco said.

'Besides the mole, what else?'

'Other blemishes, you mean?'

'You tell me.'

Pasco felt as if he were a ventriloquist's dummy sitting in James's lap. 'No other blemishes I could see. He was doing time for currency manipulation. Black market stuff. Five years.'

'Currency manipulation,' she said.

'Right.'

'And you were what – in the same prison?'

'Penal camp number six eight seven,' Pasco said. It was one number he'd never forget. Not until he drew his last breath.

The woman was quiet again. Her silences were like little hives buzzing with menace. Pasco wondered why he'd been sent to her, what was so important about this woman, what role she was supposed to play in the scheme of things.

'Show me your passport,' she said.

He produced the document, handed it to her. She flicked the pages and said, 'Old photo.' She returned the passport. 'What was your crime, Mr Pasco?'

Be honest when she asks, James had said. *Don't lie about that one.* He looked directly into her eyes and told her. 'I worked for the CIA and . . .' He faltered under her gaze. Despite his resolve, he felt a kind of withering.

The woman remained impassive. 'Go on.'

'They sent me into Moscow ten years ago. It was a simple deal, they said. My front was the usual kind of thing, American businessman interested in exploring new markets for textile manufacturing equipment. I had glossy leaflets, brochures, specs of machines, samples. Everything the Agency could provide in the way of an authentic identity. My real purpose, they told me, was to contact some former Politburo clown and bring out a few documents. Don't ask me what. I don't know. I was only a glorified errand boy.'

'And it all went wrong,' she said.

'Yeah, it went wrong.'

'How?'

'I was smuggling fucking drugs, that's what went wrong,' he said. 'I was set up and sent down the river without a paddle for ten years. Soon as I got off the plane in Moscow, they seized my luggage and ripped it open, and guess what? Fifteen kilograms of uncut cocaine. Fifteen, Christ. And I never even knew I was carrying the goddam stuff. But those Russian bastards did, because they'd been tipped off. They were waiting for me at the airport. Welcome to Russia, welcome to some real hard times.' He heard a whistling sound in his ears. The memory of this treachery always unhinged him. *Be controlled*, James had said. *Don't lose it in front of her.*

Easy for you to say, James. You didn't spend ten years in the tundra, did you? You didn't wake up every goddam day with acid burning in your gut and your bones aching and ulcers bleeding in your mouth, and you didn't catch your flesh on some rusted old piece of barbed-wire and it turned eventually to gangrene and you didn't undergo crude surgery and waken during the operation to hear the sound of the fucking saw grind through your bone, did you, James, whoever you are?

'Why were you betrayed, Mr Pasco?' she asked.

You were traded, James had told him. *Langley wanted*

a man out of Russia, and you were the currency of the exchange. Tit for tat. Pasco realized he was sweating. His hands had begun to tremble. He said, 'It was a swap. They had somebody Langley wanted. I was considered expendable. Fourteen years in the Agency, fourteen years I spent setting up complicated computer networks and satellite links, and I was suddenly expendable. Not incompetent, not dim-witted, not senile, and certainly not a security risk – none of that. Expendable. Big E.'

'Cruel,' she said, but without any judgement in her voice. 'Why tell me your story? Why come here and tell me?'

'Galkin,' he said. 'Galkin told me to contact you.'

'What exactly did Galkin say?'

Pasco heard James's words in his head. *Remember this, don't forget Galkin's exact words, they're very important. Get it wrong and you're going nowhere.* But his memory was fogged again, as if it were glass against which steam condensed. He was afraid of faltering. His lips were dry. The woman's spectacles caught sunlight and resembled two big slot-machine tokens.

'Galkin said, look for Carolyn. When you need her, look for Carolyn. She knows which way the ball rotates.'

'And that's all?'

The paper, James said. *Don't forget to show her the paper.* He put his hand in his pocket and from a compartment of the eelskin wallet drew out a weathered slip of cheap, rough-fibred paper. He passed it to the woman, who took it and regarded it slowly.

'He gave me that,' Pasco said.

She said nothing, just studied the paper. Then she handed it back to him.

'Follow me,' she said.

He felt he'd passed part of a test. The preliminary. There was more to come.

The woman showed him up to an attic room with sloping walls and a skylight, a narrow metal-framed bed, outdated copies of *Newsweek* on a bedside table. An old black-and-white TV set in the corner.

'You can stay here,' she said. 'We'll talk later.'

When the woman had gone, Pasco lay on the bed and stared at the skylight, a red rectangle of sunstruck glass. The space was stuffy but he didn't have energy to get up and open the skylight. For a long time he didn't move, conscious of how his breath came in gasps and a chill entered his bones.

He slept a half-hour, drifted, dreamed he was standing in the watch-tower looking down at a frozen white compound surrounded by an electric fence. When he woke he wondered what it meant, why he should be a guard and not a prisoner.

The chill had lifted from his body and he was breathing with some ease. He'd fallen asleep with the slip of paper still in his hand. He looked at it, read the words. *Caro. Provide the bearer with every assistance, for old time's sake, Vlad.* It was like some kind of currency, a promise to pay. He wondered what sort of world he'd fallen into – old messages on slips of paper, strange phrases about the rotation of a ball. A world of passwords, he thought. OK, he should have been used to that because that was the kind of world they taught him at Langley, but he'd been away for ten years, and you got out of old habits. You forgot stealth, you forgot the nature of secrecy, your nerve wasn't what it used to be, the iron inside you had turned to rust, and you weren't going to get a blue ribbon in the health department. Anyway, you'd had other things on your mind for ten years. You had good excuses for forgetting how that world of secrets operated. You had the best of excuses.

Caro, he thought. Was the plain bespectacled woman Caro, or some kind of intermediary? And Vlad, who the hell was Vlad? Too many questions. James had warned against asking himself too many questions. *Either you go all the way with this, or we back off now.* And so he'd trusted James, because that's what it came down to in the end, trust, a concept he never thought he'd use again in his life. But here he was, trusting a man he hardly knew – and on what basis? Half a million bucks and a new passport and the promise of assistance, that was the basis. Shit, you had to admit that was some kind of reassurance.

The woman made a phone call to a number in Biarritz. She was connected after an insufferable length of time to a man who announced himself as Galkin.

'Caro,' she said.

He spoke in Russian, his voice calm. 'It's been a long time.'

'Yes, it has.' She used English.

'This is so unexpected,' he said.

'I have an enquiry,' she said.

'Are we going to speak the same language or do you insist on using English?'

'I'll speak whatever I please, Vladimir.'

'Combative as ever,' he said. 'What do you want to know?'

'Somebody brought me an interesting piece of paper, Vlad.'

'And?'

'He calls himself Pasco. Richard Pasco.'

'Ah, yes, poor Pasco. A victim of injustice.'

'You gave him the note?'

'Of course, dear lady. I gave him the note.'

'Where did you meet him?'

'We were obliged to keep one another company in a certain penal institution. We became close. He confided in me.'

'Describe him.'

'Pale, not very interesting to look at. His hands are scarred. He's missing his left leg.'

'You trust him?'

'It's his hatred I trust. And since that's all there is of the man – well, yes, I trust him.'

'I don't approve, Vlad. I don't like anyone coming here. I don't like the idea of you sending this man to me. I happen to value my privacy.'

'Send him away then. It's up to you.'

'Goodbye,' she said, and hung up.

Later, the woman brought Pascoe tea on a tray, and digestive biscuits he washed down with the milky tea. She said, 'When you finish, come downstairs,' and then she left the room.

He sipped the tea, flicked the pages of the old magazines. The world had changed in the years of his imprisonment. People he'd never heard of had been elevated to fame. New politicians, as fucked-up as the old ones, ran the planet. New entertainers, sillier than before, had come to prominence. But beyond that, nothing seemed to have changed: people still killed each other in unholy numbers. Wars were abundant. The Cold War was a memory, and hot new wars had replaced it.

The world didn't interest him. His focus was narrow. He gave up on the magazines. What happened next? What was the next step? A coughing fit seized him, and the inside of his chest felt as if it were lined with corrosive fluids. He had to get up, couldn't lie flat on his back and cough up his lungs. He rose, walked the room, stifled the fit.

Out of nowhere he had a memory of his departure from Dulles Airport, July 1986. He remembered Sandy kissing him goodbye outside the departures gate. He remembered the smell of her lipstick, the breathless way she had of speaking. *I'll miss you, hon*, she'd said. *Still, it's only ten days.* (Ten days, right. Sandy had drifted out of his life, vanished into the shadows, probably married by now, and who could blame her after his prolonged absence?)

He remembered turning back as he passed through the gate, raising his arm in a farewell gesture. Sandy was waving in that frantic, motorized way she had. You'd think she'd wave her arm out of its socket.

And then he remembered how his eye had been drawn a moment past Sandy's face and beyond, to the crowd of people saying their goodbyes, and he'd seen Grimes standing a little way back from the throng, unsmiling in his lightweight seersucker suit, frowning like a man confronted by a sandwich of maggots. Grimes, a ten-year-old snapshot he'd never quite forgotten. Grimes had come to see him vanish through the departures gate. He'd come to preside over his disappearance.

He'd thought a lot about the seersucker during his time in the tundra. He'd thought about Grimes, and all the others, and the places where they trained agents, and how they recruited them – and all these thoughts and recollections formed a massive knot inside his brain. And that knot, so intricately tight, had to be undone.

It was time to go downstairs.

He opened the door. He stepped from the room, stood on a landing. The house was perfectly silent, a dead clock. He descended.

He entered the sitting-room where he'd been earlier. The woman sat in a large wine-coloured armchair. She held her hands rather primly in her lap. 'How much money do you have?' she asked.

'Enough,' he said.

'Be specific.'

'Half a million dollars, OK? Is that enough?'

Her eyes disappeared a second behind her glasses, which made exact interpretation of her expression difficult for Pasco. 'How did you get that much money?'

When she asks you that question, this is what you tell her, James had said. Pasco stepped further into the room and said, 'It's guilt money from Uncle Sam. They call it back earnings, plus interest, plus bonuses, plus hardship allowance, plus this, plus that. It's supposed to buy my silence.'

'Is that what you want, Mr Pasco? Silence?'

'Fuck, no. I want to make a hell of a noise.'

She removed her glasses and closed them with a tiny clicking sound.

7

LONDON

The day started in asphyxiating humidity. Pagan's shirt stuck to his skin, sweat glazed his forehead. No breeze moved the trees in Hyde Park. The surface of the Serpentine was still and glassy. When he came to an empty bench he sat down.

He turned his face to see Foxworth strolling along the path toward him. Foxie reached the bench, sat, fanned the dead air with one hand. Pagan opened a brown paper bag and removed a picture frame, which he passed to Foxie – who hadn't been puzzled by Frank's request to meet in the park; Pagan often suggested outdoor locations for a rendezvous, usually when he had something he didn't want to talk about in Golden Square, where George Nimmo had spies.

Foxie took the picture frame and stared at it. 'Where did this come from?'

'My bedroom,' Pagan said.

Foxworth placed the frame on his lap. He studied the woman's photograph a second, then the inscription: *For Frank, happy days.* 'How did it get there?'

Pagan took the frame back. 'Somehow she got into my flat, then proceeded to slip this photograph inside the frame, after removing the one already there – which was an old picture of Roxanne.' He wasn't sure what angered him more: the theft of Roxanne's picture, which had been precious to him, or the fact that the woman had invaded his privacy; or was it the idea that, despite the fact that her name was on every front page in the country this morning, she felt secure enough to break brazenly into his residence and leave behind an object she knew would taunt him, and remove another whose theft she believed would infuriate?

'She was never short of nerve,' Foxie said.

Pagan looked at the photograph. It was one he didn't have in his collection. It might even be recent. He imagined her going inside a studio, possibly right here in London, and posing for this. Her face was upturned just slightly, and her smile – which could dazzle and seduce – was insolent.

Something struck him then that hadn't registered before. The woman's pose was an exact replica of Roxanne's, the tilt of face, the way her hair touched the shoulders, the direct look into the lens. This realization appalled and jolted him. *She'd copied Roxanne's look.* Devastating, this impersonation of a dead woman's appearance. And depressing, because it reinvigorated a sense of old losses he didn't want to surface.

'Is there anything to suggest who the photographer is?' Foxie asked.

'Not a mark, nothing, nothing at all. I've been over it. Believe me.'

A bright red kite appeared briefly in the sky, then collapsed. Foxie watched it fall beyond the trees. 'She's thumbing her nose, Frank. She's telling us she can't be touched.'

'If she's thumbing her nose, it's a gesture aimed directly at *me*,' Pagan said. 'It's no big outrage this time, it isn't anything on her usual grand scale, it's nothing designed to cause public chaos – this is personal, this is for me alone. Definitely. Consider something else. The photograph she put in my bedroom fits the frame precisely. Which suggests she already *knew* I had a picture on the bedside table. In other words, this wasn't the first time she'd been in my flat. Christ, she probably even *measured* the bloody frame. Which means she wasn't in any particular hurry.'

'You might try a stakeout,' Foxie said. 'She might visit you again.'

'I'll arrange something,' Pagan said. He raised his face and gazed through the trees and wondered if, even now, she was nearby, concealed in the landscape like one of those kid's puzzles where you're supposed to find objects hidden in a drawing. She had to be watching him at least some of the time. She had to have known when he left his flat and went to the office, and how long he was likely to be gone.

He looked down into the woman's eyes. There was a seriously jarring disparity between her beauty and the brute ugliness of her actions. He placed the frame back inside the paper bag. He wondered where Roxanne's photograph had gone, and hated the idea it was in the woman's possession; something of himself had been plundered.

He got up from the bench and, followed by Foxworth, strolled in the general direction of Park Lane.

'Get some people onto the photographic studios,' he said. 'If the picture was taken here in London, I want to know who took it. I don't believe for a moment she left her address with the photographer, but we might learn something. There might be a detail, a trace.'

Foxworth wondered how many photographers there

were in London. It struck him as a grinding task, days of legwork and phone calls.

On Park Lane Pagan hailed a taxi. Traffic was dense, stop–start. He lowered the window, sought some trace of a breeze, but the air that whimpered into the vehicle was tepid and toxic. He was glad when they reached Golden Square and got out.

Before they entered the building, Foxie said, 'I assume you haven't mentioned the picture to George Nimmo.'

'I don't intend to. I can hear him snigger. Oh, she's breaking into your flat nowadays, is she? Well, well. She must feel pretty damn secure if she can pull a stunt like that. No, I don't want to mention this to Nimmo.'

'Did you see him on the box last night?'

'I gave it a miss,' Pagan said.

'He was in fine form. Full uniform, the whole thing. Almost sounded Churchillian at times. A bit of podium-thumping. He managed to come off as reassuring, if you wanted to be reassured. The British policeman is the best in the world, our Special Branch is second to none, the woman will be found. Manpower will be increased. Uniforms everywhere. Roadblocks. Door-to-door searches throughout the land. Quite a performance, really.'

They passed through the metal detector. The sergeant at the desk, Whittingham, looked attentive when Pagan came in sight.

'Stuffy old morning,' said Whittingham.

'A killer,' Foxie agreed.

'Rain'd be nice,' Whittingham added. He shook his head sadly. 'Terrible business, Mr Pagan.'

'Terrible,' Pagan said. The feebleness of words. Their inadequacy. They weren't equipped to carry anything but frail loads.

'And that woman's back,' Whittingham remarked.

'With a vengeance,' Foxie said quietly.

Pagan and Foxworth stepped into the elevator and rode to the second floor. Foxie said, 'I'll get started on this photography angle.'

Pagan nodded, entered his office, closed the door. He took the frame from the paper bag, then slipped the photograph out from under the glass and propped it up on his desk. He kept thinking of the women inside his flat, how she must have gone from room to room, perhaps looking through his clothes, reading his mail, then sitting on the edge of his bed and picking up the picture of Roxanne, studying it, staring at it, possibly thinking: *So you were Pagan's wife. You were the wife to whom he was faithful.*

Faithful. He'd come close to wrecking that fidelity eleven years ago when he'd captured the woman as she was passing through Heathrow airport. He thought about the hotel room where she'd been kept under guard awaiting the arrival in London of FBI agents intent on taking her back to the federal penitentiary in Danbury from which she'd escaped. He remembered the time he'd spent alone with her in that room, but the memory was awkward, and it still shamed him to recall the ease with which he'd been aroused by her gestures and words, how far he'd travelled along the road to betraying his wife; he'd understood then that there were unexplored flaws in himself, as if within Frank Pagan there existed another person altogether, one with unexpected needs and urges. The passage of eleven years might have blunted that appetite, if not the memory. Steadfast Pagan, the keen young cop, had glimpsed the edge of raw desire, and hadn't altogether enjoyed the sight.

The woman knew. *She'd known he wanted her.* And

now she'd stolen Roxanne's photograph and left one of her own as if to remind him that his marital fidelity had been constructed on a flimsy platform, that his moral sense was fragile. How could he keep law and order in the world if he couldn't keep it in himself?

He rose, looked out across Golden Square; it occurred to him that she must have been down there at times watching the building, perhaps looking up at the very window where he stood. He imagined himself as if viewed through the telescopic sight of a rifle, a target crisscrossed by lines.

What did she want from him? What was to be gained from infiltrating his life? From outrageous trespass? Tiny acts of mischief and malice might satisfy her for a short time, but sooner or later she always needed a bigger stage, a spotlight. That was her weakness; that was an area that might ultimately be exploited to his advantage. But when would she reappear? and where?

He made a phone call, arranged for an unmarked car to be situated in the vicinity of his flat; then he opened the bottom drawer of his desk and removed a file.

It contained a profile of the woman written by a prison psychiatrist in Danbury, Connecticut. She'd been born into a wealthy North Carolina family, father an unbearable autocrat given to strange mood swings, mother a drunk. She'd run away from one boarding-school after another, stabbed a classmate at the age of ten, then was institutionalized briefly at the request of her parents. At sixteen, she'd drifted into the radical underground. She'd participated in the bombing of a radio station in Denver, a bank robbery in Des Moines, the sabotage of a train carrying a shipment of arms to a naval base in San Diego. According to the shrink's report, she had a high IQ, and was fluent in

French, Russian and German. She was also sexually ambivalent: a nice catch-all phrase, Pagan thought. She used a variety of aliases, most of them drawn, for some reason, from the names of birds or animals. She'd called herself at various times Caroline Starling, Cara Raven, Carola Fox. She had, the psychiatrist had written, a penchant – such understatement – for violence. She needed no political motivation for violent acts. Politics, as such, appeared to be of no interest to her. A note appended to the end of the report had mentioned three applications of electro-therapy and an extended course of mood-altering drugs, neither of which treatments had made any apparent difference.

The bones of her life, Pagan thought. The unfleshed skeleton. It was the kind of material from which you couldn't fashion predictions about her future behaviour.

He had included his own report on her, written several months before, in the same file as the psychiatrist's, and he scanned it quickly. It mentioned her long convoluted relationship – love? hate? some combustible amalgam of the two? – with the late Tobias Barron, an international arms dealer who posed as global philanthropist, friend to the Third World, a man who supplied weapons to any country in need even as he funded health clinics in Angola and agricultural research stations in Cuba; Barron had never played favourites, never taken sides. And when business was slack, when the hotspots of the world threatened to lose their violent radiance, he'd used his complex chain of influential associates to exacerbate tensions in volatile countries – assassinations here, terrorism there, whatever it took to stimulate the need for arms. And the woman had gone along willingly in this partnership of destruction.

Pagan shut the folder. All this was history. It was the present that engaged his attention. He scanned the telephone messages that had accumulated through the night. Calls from various foreign embassies, ambassadors and consuls who wanted to know exactly what had happened in the placid Buckinghamshire countryside; demands from the press for statements; messages from an unhappy public. Is this what we're paying taxes for? Is nobody protecting us?

He set these aside. What could you say to console Jack Public? What could you tell the ambassadors and consuls of other countries when it came to the murder of their nationals? Sorry didn't take you very far.

He examined the reports that had come from Special Branch, which confirmed that airports were being monitored, railways, bus stations, points of egress kept under constant surveillance. Terrific, if you knew who you were looking for, if you knew the face she was wearing, the identity she'd assumed. Carmen Profumo, pastry-chef, would have been discarded by this time. Used, out of date, no further assistance. She'd already be somebody else, a different name, a different look.

His telephone rang and he was caught in two minds about answering it. One of the assistants on the top floor, that warren of cramped rooms, could pick it up.

The ringing stopped. Foxie appeared in the doorway and said, 'For you, Frank.'

'Who is it?'

'She wouldn't give her name. Said it was personal.'

Pagan picked up the receiver.

She said, 'Sorry you wasted your time in Stratton, Frank.'

He didn't speak. He looked at her photograph. The eyes had the effect of whirlpools on him. He covered

73

the mouthpiece with his hand and whispered to Foxie, '*Trace this. Quick.*'

Foxie left hurriedly, jacket flapping.

'What's wrong?' the woman asked. 'Am I getting the silent treatment? Fuck you, Frank. I save your life and you don't have a word of gratitude for me?'

'Thanks,' he said in a dry way. 'For saving my life.'

'That's better, Frank. I always appreciate gratitude.'

'I'll tell you what *I* don't appreciate. Somebody killing innocent people. Somebody going through my flat. What's the name of your fucking game? Planning some new atrocity? Poisoning fifty or more people wasn't enough for you? What I don't understand is why – why kill all those people?'

'Who knows? To get your attention?'

'My attention, Jesus Christ—'

'To remind you of me.'

'I hadn't forgotten—'

'It's been seven months and you haven't managed to find me,' she said. 'You needed to know I was still around. I was beginning to feel just a touch neglected.'

Neglected, he thought. She kills all these people because she wants attention? No, it was deeper than that, it went down through the corkscrewing layers of her being, this urge to kill, this need for a blood-fix; it went down into the core of herself, where there was chaos and madness and a desire to shape the world the way she wanted it to be, regardless of all the misery she created, a need to define herself in terms of violence because without it she had no fixed identity.

'I'd never used poison before,' she said. 'It's called Compound Zero-8. Neat name, huh? Sounds like a carpet-shampoo or something. It was developed originally by Hitler's scientists in 1940, but never used. I guess it was overlooked, or they couldn't find a way

74

to use it safely. It was refined by Saddam's specialists during the Gulf fiasco.'

A history lesson, he thought. He had a fierce desire to confront her physically, to be in the same space she occupied at that very moment. To put her hands around her slender neck and choke all the life out of her. That rage inside himself, he realized, was a murderous thing.

She said, 'What fascinates me about the compound is the fact that it acts like one of those spooky new viruses from Africa people are always talking about. It infiltrates the central nervous system within five minutes of ingestion. First symptoms are nothing much, a mild sense of disorientation, some nausea. Then tremors. Next, the poison attacks vital organs and glands. The liver comes under massive assault. There's renal failure. The lungs seize up. Intra-alveolar haemorrhaging. The gums bleed. The nose bleeds. This is followed by . . . are you still with me, Frank?'

'I'm listening,' he said. *But I don't want to hear this.*

'A whole gang of symptoms,' she said. 'Incontinence. Diarrhoea. Brain dysfunction. Hallucinations of a nasty kind. Then paralysis. Blindness. Pain, intense pain. Death comes as a blessing. And this entire process takes only thirty to thirty-five minutes. Three-quarters of an hour tops.'

The tone of her voice made Pagan think of a car salesman extolling the virtues of a certain vehicle. There was an infusion of enthusiasm, almost a pride, in the way she talked of the substance. It was ghoulish, more than ghoulish. He didn't know how to respond, what reactions were appropriate in the circumstances. But he had to keep her on the line. 'It's a tough act to follow, if you intend to follow it.'

'I haven't decided my next move,' she answered. 'I

might simply go away. You might never hear from me again. Then again, you never know. I think of what the compound might accomplish if, for the sake of discussion, I tossed a couple of ounces into London's water supply. Interesting notion.'

'Fascinating,' Pagan said. The water supply, he thought. Nothing was secure. Everything was vulnerable. Food, water.

'That could do some serious damage,' she said. 'Great for the funeral business.'

'Less great for the victims,' Pagan remarked.

She was quiet for a moment. 'You're tracing this call, I guess. I won't hang around much longer. Pity. I like talking to you.'

'Why did you spare me at the hotel anyway? Why do me a special favour?'

'You're like unfinished business. I have days when I can't get you out of my mind. Funny.'

'Very,' he said.

'I think back ten, eleven years when I first met you and I remember a time when anything seemed possible. Don't you find that getting older is a matter of diminishing possibilities?'

'I hadn't thought about it,' he said.

'You should, Frank. You should think about time passing. You also ought to give some thought to painting that flat of yours. Christ knows, it needs it. Know what your place really lacks?'

'You tell me.'

'A woman's touch.'

A cruelty, he thought. He said nothing.

'Maybe that's what you need too, Frank,' she said. 'A woman's touch. Soft, caressing, arousing. Nice and easy, a sweet, slow build-up, prolonged mutual exploration, then the big explosion.' Her voice was soft

76

now, liltingly seductive, almost a whisper. It was no longer that of some deranged woman enthusiastically praising the efficiency of a poison. The changes she continued to make in herself were seemingly endless. She spun cocoons around herself and each time emerged as a different entity.

'I'll catch you,' he said. 'You know that. Sooner or later, I'll catch you.'

'Ah, Frank, Frank. You just don't know when to quit, do you? Which is a perfectly desirable quality in a lover. Are you that kind of lover, Frank? Did Roxanne find you energetic? Did she find you indefatigable?'

'I'm not going to discuss Roxanne with you,' he said. 'I wouldn't waste my fucking breath.'

'I'm getting to you,' she said. 'I always do. Some things don't change.'

'Getting to me? You're not even close,' he replied.

'You're a bad liar, Pagan. You don't know the art of concealment, do you?'

Foxie came inside the office, holding a slip of paper. He set it down in front of Pagan. There was a telephone number written on it, and a location.

'I have to run,' she said.

'Wait—'

'Unfinished business,' she said. 'Oh, one last thing. I'm leaving something for you inside this phone booth, which no doubt you've traced by this time.' She hung up.

Pagan put down the receiver and looked at Foxie, then at the slip of paper. 'Kilburn High Road,' he said.

'That's where the call originated, Frank. A public phone.'

'What the hell is she doing in Kilburn?'

Foxie shrugged. 'What did she have to say for herself?'

Pagan told him about the toxic compound. The threat she'd made to the water supply. 'I want uniformed officers at every reservoir, Foxie. Starting now. I want a twenty-four hour guard wherever drinking-water is stored or treated. And I want them armed.'

'I'll get on it,' Foxie said, and frowned. He thought Frank looked pale, a man who'd encountered a ghost beyond the reaches of exorcism.

Pagan picked up the photograph of the woman and held it in a hand that was trembling just slightly. *I'm getting to you. I always do.* Yes, he thought, yes, you are. But he wasn't entirely sure in what ways.

8

FREDERICKSBURG, VIRGINIA

Mallory parked his car outside Max Skidelsky's country home ten miles from the town of Fredericksburg. It was an enormous Victorian house with a macabre look; the windows of the circular turrets might have scared an imaginative child into thinking the rooms contained mutant offspring fed raw meat through iron bars. Cameras slowly panned the vicinity from beneath the eaves. After dark, automatic sensor lights kicked in; at all times, a highly sophisticated security system was functioning. Max Skidelsky liked peace of mind.

Mallory got out of his rented Lincoln. His image was conveyed by the cameras to a series of indoor monitors. He rang the front doorbell and one of the cameras, alerted by a microchip, altered its trajectory and tilted downward. A zoom lens whirred.

The front door was opened by a young man in a three-piece black suit. His name was Larry Quinn, Skidelsky's number two in what Skidelsky, with a mischievous sense of humour, had called The Artichoke Club – a name derived from Project Artichoke, a crude mind-control programme which the Central Intelligence Agency had instigated in the early 1950s. Skidelsky was fond of little in-jokes.

Mallory followed Quinn across the parquet foyer and

was ushered into a games room where, instead of the predictable billiard table, there was a phalanx of video machines. Here, Max Skidelsky spent hours pursuing monsters, popping electronic bugs, zapping alien creatures from other galaxies.

Mallory sat down. Quinn, whose black hair was combed back flat, said, 'Max will be with you soon. He's running behind schedule this morning.'

'How's life, Larry?' Mallory asked.

'Buzzing right along,' Larry Quinn said. He smiled. He had bright white teeth, a square block of a jaw. 'Yourself?'

'Fine, just fine,' said Mallory.

'Trip went well?'

Mallory said, 'Yes.'

'You jet-lagged?'

'A touch.'

'You'll get over it.' Quinn left, still smiling.

Skidelsky's house had a disquieting effect on Mallory. You expected it to be filled with leather-bound volumes and old-fashioned wing-chairs. Instead you got an array of electronic games, canvas-backed director's chairs, a few minimalist prints on the walls, and piles of computer equipment scattered everywhere. The floor was covered with thick black cables running God knows where.

Max Skidelsky came into the room. He was dressed in an expensive beige linen suit, loosely cut, so that it created a kind of draped effect on his lean body. The pants were pleated. He wore canvas espadrilles imported from Lisbon. His movements were as loose as his clothing. His glasses had silver frames and lenses that changed according to the light. He had bright blue eyes. When he looked at you, he managed to convey an impression of intense interest in your life. He had the ability to make people think he was engrossed in them, and nothing else mattered.

'Jimmy,' said Skidelsky. He held out a rather chill hand for Mallory to shake. The handshake, though cold, was firm and confident. Skidelsky, a Yale graduate, a Rhodes scholar who knew a Soutard St Emilion from a Troplong-Mondot and was moved by Mahler's *Kindertotenlieder*, was bright, ambitious, and at the age of thirty-three knew, with all the certitude of people who haven't been on the planet long enough to be totally disenchanted, where he was going. More than that, he knew where the country was going.

'Good flight?' he asked.

Mallory nodded. 'Yes. Good flight.'

'Drink?'

'Soda, if you have it.'

'Perrier? Badoit?'

Mallory shrugged. One fizzy water was like any other to him. He hadn't bought into the imported water snobbery prevalent in the land.

'Try some San Pellegrino,' Skidelsky suggested. He poured two glasses, plopped cubes of ice in them, gave one glass to Mallory and said, 'Cheers.'

'Cheers,' Mallory said.

Skidelsky sipped his drink. 'Well, Jimmy. Are we in business?'

'I think so.'

'No, I don't want impressions, Jimmy. You know I have a hard time with them. Yes or no. Are we in business?'

Mallory hated the pressure of being backed into corners by Skidelsky's questions. 'I can only say it's looking good.'

'Looking good doesn't count,' Skidelsky said.

'Looking good is something you apply to clothes or shoes or a girl you see walking along the street.'

'I did what you told me, Max. I did everything you wanted. To the letter. On that basis, all I can safely say is that I think it's going to work out nicely.'

'The fish rose to the hook,' Skidelsky said. 'Is this what I'm hearing?'

'I'd say so.'

Max Skidelsky wandered off toward a video game. He pressed a button and the room was suddenly filled with weird noises, beeps and whistles and sounds suggestive of dolphins singing to their mates. With a look of concentration and aggression on his face, he punched away at buttons and directional controls, and whatever enemies confronted him on the screen were blasted into an electronic purgatory. He played for a couple of minutes, then stopped.

'This machine has infinite levels of difficulty,' he said. 'You kill the monsters, move up a level, other monsters take their place. You kill them, pop, you're on another level. The trick, Jimmy, is to stay alive through the levels. But what you're *really* looking for isn't mere survival. No, the object of the game is the quest for infinity. Which is something of a conundrum, because infinity, by definition, can never be reached. In that sense, the machine is always ahead of you. Unless . . .'

'Unless it's a con, and it doesn't have infinite levels at all,' Mallory said.

'You got it.' Max Skidelsky smiled. It was a beautiful smile, you had to give him that. And he knew how to use it. It was a thing of charm and wonder, a boy's smile. There was even innocence in it, which was the quality Mallory found most unsettling. It was about as innocent as a laser beam.

Skidelsky crossed the room and patted Mallory, sixteen years his senior, on the head. 'The nifty thing about *our* con, Jimmy, is that we *know* it doesn't have infinite levels. We programmed it ourselves, we know how it works, and we know how many levels it has.'

A parable, Mallory thought. An electronic parable. He sipped his San Pellegrino, which was already losing its effervescence.

Skidelsky sat down in one of the canvas-backed chairs and kicked off his espadrilles, revealing his bare feet. His big toes were spatulated. He took off his glasses and massaged his eyelids. He replaced the glasses and said, 'A good con's always basically simple. Rule number one. Never complicate. And whenever possible, don't fuck with the truth. The less you lie, the less you have to remember. Get caught in a lie, and the con's either threatened or dead in the water.'

Mallory nodded his head. Sometimes Skidelsky's energy level depleted him. He found he couldn't stay for long in the young man's company, as if he were afraid of being drained entirely. It was as if Skidelsky sucked the essence out of the people around him.

'So. The hook dangles, and the fish is rising, Jimmy.'

'Yes,' Mallory said.

'You can feel the tug, huh?'

'I can feel it, sure.'

Max Skidelsky frowned, something he rarely did. 'This poison business – is that going to affect us?'

'I doubt it, Max.'

'You know, she'd be terrific if she didn't have these psycho impulses. I mean, you don't just take out Christ knows how many people because you've got a bad case of PMS, right?'

'I don't think she needs PMS or anything like it to do what she does,' Mallory said. 'It comes naturally

83

to her. Like breathing. She needs the occasional fire-work display.'

'She ought to donate her brain to a research foundation, Jimmy. Let them check it out for structural irregularities, flaws, what have you. No matter what way you slice this lady's toast, she's not running on any battery known to mankind, that's certain. What about this cop?'

'Pagan?'

'The word is he's got something of a hard-on for her.'

'Maybe so. He's a determined man. He's had encounters with her in the past, and they've left him dented, which only makes him grit his teeth all the more. The way I understand it, she likes to provoke him.'

'Is he going to be a problem?'

Mallory considered this question before answering. 'He hasn't come within a mile of her in seven months. She's always just one step ahead of him. But if I was a betting man, I'd say he's the one most likely. She plays with him. And that's risky business.'

Skidelsky shrugged and said, 'If he becomes a genuine problem, there's always a quick solution. He's the least of my worries.'

Max Skidelsky emptied his glass and put it down on the floor. He ran a hand through his thick, shiny fair hair. Trapped in a rectangle of sunlight originating from a window, he looked impossibly young for a moment. He had the smooth unshaven appearance of a thirteen-year-old high-school kid.

Scary, Mallory thought. This kid, this hunger for power, this brain; and the kicker was always the smile, because you couldn't attribute anything shadowy to a face like that, you couldn't find duplicity in it with the aid of a microscope. You'd give this kid your last dime. And yet – he was Deviousness incarnate. He didn't lift a finger without thinking of the consequences thirty moves down the line. He was all careful planning and blueprints; his mind had to be a series of high mountain ranges from which he could see for ever. And that was scary too, Mallory thought. Satan in a Versace suit.

'When will we know if the fish is truly hooked, Jimmy?'

'In an hour or so, I'd say.'

Skidelsky tapped the face of his watch. 'What's an hour or so when you're dealing with the future of the United States?'

'I'll make the call from downtown,' Mallory said.

'Good idea. Any time you make an important call, use a pay phone.' Skidelsky, never still for long, bounded up out of his chair. 'I need some music. Anything you'd like to hear, Jimmy?'

Mallory shook his head. Skidelsky chose some jazz from the late 1950s, post be-bop. He stood beside the Bose stereo and tapped his foot in time to the music. Then he moved so that he stood directly behind Mallory. He laid both hands on Mallory's shoulders and gave them a light squeeze.

'We're going to win, Jimmy,' he said. 'You know why?'

'Why?'

'Because we can't fail.'

'If that was the only reason for winning at anything, everybody would win,' Mallory said.

Skidelsky rearranged himself in a squatting position and rocked very slightly on his bare heels. 'Sometimes I detect this tiny little chime of pessimism in your voice, Jimmy. Do you have doubts? Misgivings about The Artichoke Club?'

Mallory finished his Italian water. 'Things can go wrong, people can make mistakes, you know how it goes.'

'Mistakes? I don't have that word in my vocabulary.'

'Well, the world isn't perfect, Max. Other people make them.'

'Not when they work for me, they don't.' Skidelsky rose to a standing position. The great beam of his smile was focused on Mallory's face. It was like a magnifying glass through which sunlight was intensified. 'Perhaps you have doubts you don't want to express. Little matters of a moral nature, say?'

Mallory said, 'I know the country's in the shit, Max. I only have to look around. I'm not some god-damn ostrich. I see what's going on. Crime, disintegration, cops and Federal agents that have given up the ghost and turned to corruption. I see the Agency losing prestige. I see sleaze, the breakdown in the quality of our life in general – I'm not missing any of that, Max.'

'Let me guess,' Skidelsky said. 'You agree with the principles, you just don't like the means. Correct?'

'I have some reservations, OK.'

'Ethics,' Skidelsky said.

'If you like.'

'Odd word, ethics,' Skidelsky remarked. 'Derived from the Greek *ethos* – meaning, man's normal state.'

'I know where it's derived from, Max.'

'*Man's normal state*, Jimmy. What do you think that means?'

'We could debate that all day,' Mallory said.

'You think his normal state is anarchy? Crime? A capacity for evil deeds? Murder? Selfishness? Loathing? Or do you think the opposite – the normal state is one of aspirations, dreams of betterment, love, a secure and decent society? Which, Jimmy?'

Mallory felt he was back in his student days at Rutgers, trapped inside a lecture-hall by a highly irritating professor. 'You can't answer stuff like that off the top of your head.'

'Give me your hand,' Max Skidelsky said.

Mallory had been waiting for this. He stuck out his right hand and Skidelsky gripped it tightly. This was an odd form of bonding Skidelsky sometimes insisted on. The first time, it had made Mallory nervous. After the third or fourth time, you got used to it.

'Trust me,' Skidelsky said. He wasn't smiling. He was a study in the ferocity of concentration now.

'I trust you, Max.'

'No buts. No half measures. All the way, Jimmy.'

'All the way,' Mallory said.

Skidelsky's grip became tighter. Mallory felt great pressure on his bones. It was a strange thing, but he could swear he often felt a current run between himself and the younger man at these times. Maybe it was the same kind of electricity that flowed out of evangelists and made suckers and sinners rise up out of their chairs and give themselves openly to Christ. Skidelsky believed in himself, and what he was doing, he believed the angels were one and all aligned in his corner, and this business of gripping hands was a process of transfer, an invisible means of communication, even if, to a casual observer, it might appear slightly ludicrous. But it was Skidelsky's little ritual, his way of making affirmations, of passing on his strength – and as far as he was concerned it was all perfectly normal. There was nothing strange about it.

'Trust me, Jimmy,' he said. 'Are you trusting me?'

Mallory's hand was hurting. 'I'm trusting you,' he said.

'Are you trusting me?'

'Yes, yes. I'm trusting you,' Mallory said.

Skidelsky released him, and smiled. There was sweat on the young man's forehead. A muscular tic worked at the side of his neck. It was clear he put a great deal of mental effort into these bondings.

'Go downtown, Jimmy. Make the call. Then phone me and tell me you trust me, and I'll know the bait's been taken.'

Mallory rubbed his aching hand. 'Maybe I just don't like blood,' he said.

Skidelsky said, 'Blood? Or bloodletting?'

'Both.'

'In the old days, when somebody was sick, they used leeches. Think of the country as sick, Jimmy. Think of yourself as one of the physicians applying a few leeches.'

'I'll try,' Mallory said.

'I'll be waiting for your call,' Max Skidelsky said.

Mallory drove into the heart of Fredericksburg. The humidity was stultifying. He found a parking-space in a side street and walked to a pay phone and made a long-distance call with his credit card.

A man answered on the fifth ring. 'Yes?'

'This is Mallory.'

'Mallory. How are you?'

'I'm OK,' Mallory said. 'I'm more interested in what you have to tell me.'

'The call came.'

'And?'

'OK, everything is OK.'

'I have your word on that?'

'Sure, you have my word.'

'No suspicion?'

'Caution, of course. Not suspicion.'

'You're sure, absolutely sure?'

'Nothing is ever absolute, my friend. But, yes, I'm sure.'

'I want certainty.'

'I think you worry too much.'

'And I think you worry too little.'

'Life's short.'

'It's long enough,' Mallory said.

'My money . . .'

'It's been wired.'

'Try to relax, Mallory. If you remember how. But some men cannot change their nature. They can only camouflage it for a short time.'

'Sometimes you speak the most incredible bullshit, Galkin,' Mallory said. 'I think all that wine you guzzle has softened your brain. Go lie on the beach, or whatever it is you do.'

'I have every intention.'

James Mallory hung up. He rubbed the gold eagle on his black pinky-ring in the fashion of someone trying to summon a helpful genie.

9

LONDON

Pagan and Foxworth drove to Kilburn, a few miles north of Oxford Street. Kilburn High Road was busy, pedestrians strolling in the extraordinary September sun, the plate-glass windows of shops flashing reflected sunlight. It was a mixed neighbourhood. It had attracted enough Irish immigrants to earn the nickname County Kilburn, but immigration had also brought West Indians; for every Irish face you saw, you encountered an equal number from Jamaica or Trinidad. In more recent years, young professionals had bought and upgraded houses in the district, because they were relatively inexpensive and close to the West End. It was, Pagan thought, one of London's more atmospheric districts, and he might have enjoyed it in a better frame of mind.

The public phone from which the woman had called was located a hundred yards from the tube station. Foxie found a parking-spot and walked with Pagan to the call-box, a glass rectangle whose panes had been cracked and broken. Graffiti was spray-painted in every available place. Cheaply printed leaflets had been stuck to the glass. Cryptic messages, initials, call Josie at 756-4753 for a gum-job, John Major's a wanker, Free Ulster from the Brit fascist army pigs.

Across the street was a small supermarket packed with shoppers, windows plastered with announcements of bargains – bananas, half-price loaves, cheap liver. This was the view she would have had when she was phoning him. He imagined her looking at the supermarket, watching people come and go, shopping-trolleys, babies in pushchairs, the restless surge of humanity.

Pagan entered the call-box. The floor was littered with scraps of paper, pages ripped from directories, a few torn betting-slips. She said she'd left something here for him – but where? There were very few places inside a call-box where anything could be concealed.

He looked around. He sensed her presence inside the booth; he thought of her lips close to the receiver. *A woman's touch, soft, caressing, arousing.* There was a kind of clammy intimacy about standing where she'd stood not thirty minutes before. Why this call-box? he wondered. Why Kilburn High Road?

'See anything?' Foxie asked. He was holding the door open.

'Litter,' Pagan said. He scanned the floor, moved papers around with his foot.

Foxie squeezed inside, ran his fingers around the edge of the coin-box. He encountered something stuffed in the narrow space between box and wall, and he said, 'Ah,' and tugged out a thin brown envelope on which was written PAGAN in bold block capitals. The envelope measured roughly six inches by four. Foxie gave it to Pagan, who didn't open it at once.

Instead, he stepped out of the stuffy call-box, examined the envelope, held it up to the light, wondered if it contained perhaps a strip of explosive material that would detonate as soon as you tore the flap open. This was how she made you behave – as if everything commonplace concealed a hidden danger. But if she wanted to kill him, this wouldn't be the way she'd choose. He had the feeling she'd want to look him straight in the eyes at the moment of his death; she'd want that final intimacy, a last encounter. She wouldn't go for anything so ordinary and impersonal and easy as a letter-bomb. Where would she find any pleasure in that?

He thought, *I know what's in this envelope, what she left for me, I know.*

He ripped the flap, looked inside, slid out the photograph. It was, as he'd suspected, Roxanne's.

And yet it wasn't.

He stared at it, then turned his face away and tried to maintain control of himself. Foxie, who'd also glimpsed the picture, said nothing. Pagan slipped the photo back inside the envelope where he wouldn't have to look at it. His heartbeat felt wrong. The rhythm of his pulse was different, his mouth dry. He tapped the envelope against the back of his hand. *Some things were pointless in their cruelty.* He felt the sun on his face and smelled diesel fumes on the air and saw a double-decker bus reverberate past him – everything observed through a glaze.

'Are you OK?' Foxie asked.

Pagan said, 'I'm not at my best, no.'

'I just don't see . . .' Foxie left his sentence unfinished.

'What don't you see, Foxie?' Pagan asked, a sharp little note in his voice. 'The extent of her cruelty? How vicious she is? She leaves fifty-something people dead in a hotel dining-room, she kills more than a hundred in one mad moment in an underground carriage – what is it you don't understand, Foxie? Dear Christ, if she's capable of killing all these people without blinking her eyes, why shouldn't she be capable of something small and insignificant like this?' And he waved the envelope under Foxie's face. 'This is nothing, Foxie. This is chickenshit. This is only a fucking photograph of a dead woman. So what the hell is it you don't see?'

Foxie was unprepared for Pagan's tone of voice. He stepped back, as if the older man's rage were a virus you could catch from breathing the same air. 'It's what she's done to the photograph—'

'Oh, that really strikes horror into your heart, does it? Grow the fuck up. After mass murder, you should be astounded by what she can do with a few brush-strokes and some paint?' Pagan flapped the envelope against his thigh. 'What does it amount to anyway? A little desecration, eh? I mean, I can live with that, don't you think? I should be able to cope with that, shouldn't I? I shouldn't buckle under some minor act of vandalism, should I?'

Pagan's anger was a mixture of colours inside his head, a palette spilled. He was aware of the reductions in his life, things taken away from him, stolen. His dead wife, well, that was the big one, the major diminishment. That had changed the music of his world to a melancholic, minor key. But Roxanne lived for him still, even if it were only in little flutters of memory, or a collection of yellowed paperback books, or in the never-changing world of a simple photograph that sat on his bedside table.

But even the photograph had been taken away from him. And now, in a different form, a hideously un-acceptable form, it had been returned. He felt the curious clarity that sometimes accompanies an extreme emotion. Everything around him was suddenly sharp, well defined, bright, too bright.

He stared across the street at the supermarket. Bread

half-price. Calf liver reduced. Rice Krispies going for a song. The world was ordinary, if you made it so. It consisted of banalities, if you could numb the emotions in yourself. He continued to rattle the envelope against his thigh. It was only brown paper in which a photograph was enclosed, that was all. That's how you had to think of it. You couldn't let it unglue you. You couldn't come unravelled. She wanted to rattle him, and he'd allowed it.

'I'm sorry,' he said. He didn't look at Foxie. He'd revealed his rage and now he felt the need to withdraw to a quiet corner of himself where he might assess his wounds in private. He stuck the envelope in the pocket of his jacket.

'You have nothing to be sorry about, Frank.'

'Stop being so bloody forgiving,' Pagan said. 'You keep turning that other bloody cheek, don't you? I rant, I rave, I dump crap all over you – what are you made of, Robbie? Reinforced concrete? Or some saintly substance? How can you stand me?'

'Because I care, I suppose,' Foxie said.

'God,' Pagan said. 'You're too good for this world, Foxie. That's your problem. The world doesn't deserve you.'

'Why? Because I happen to have patience and a small amount of sympathy?'

Pagan watched the people come and go in the supermarket. 'If everybody was like you—'

He didn't have time to complete his sentence.

The blast was sudden, unexpected. The window of the supermarket disintegrated abruptly, the air was filled with glass shards that seemed to have been sucked rather than blown out of the window-frame. An empty baby carriage outside the store was thrown over and over, the red plastic globes of a child's toy jangled along the pavement, a shopping-trolley was turned upside-down, broken boxes of cereals and bags of sugar were dispersed by the force of the explosion, tomatoes and fruits turned in mid-air to pulp, and the shards of glass changed to hard, dangerous rain.

Pagan raised a hand defensively to his face, and for an instant following the violent crack of the blast there was profound silence, which he recognized as the lull before the outrage. And then it began – women screaming, rummaging with panicked cries among fallen shelves and ruined display cases for their lost children, men shouting, people struck by debris that had come down from the ceiling, chunks of cement, tangled wires, sparks that flickered from exposed connections. Black smoke was rising in thin palls from the back of the supermarket.

'Call emergency services, Foxie. Ambulances. Fire brigades. The local cops. *Now.*'

Foxie didn't hesitate. He went inside the call-box, and Pagan hurried to the other side of the street. I was meant to see this, he thought. This was intended to happen in front of my eyes. *This was designed.* He pushed his way inside the supermarket, shoving aside trolleys, cardboard boxes, broken shelving. Where to begin? The heat inside the market had the force of a blowtorch.

He smelled the scent of foodstuffs beginning to char. He saw shop assistants in bloodstained clothing try to free a woman stuck beneath an overturned refrigerated display case, he stumbled into a man whose face was covered in scores of tiny cuts from sharp flakes of broken glass, he moved over a floor littered with hundreds of battered oranges, he helped an elderly woman to her feet and tried to console her with a few quick whispered words, but she was shaken, brutalized, her expression one of shock. He moved on, drawn to the black smoke at the rear of the market, pausing here to free a tiny child from a soft-drink machine that had tilted and jammed the kid against the wall, stopping there to drag a man from under a concrete slab. The screaming was constant – and now there was not only panic in the sound, but disbelief: *this kind of thing didn't happen here, this was what happened elsewhere, this was stuff you read about in newspapers.*

He felt the smoke swirl about his face, clog his nostrils, darken his skin. He drew a small boy away from the area where electric cables released sparks and flickers of flame, and reunited the kid with his anxious mother who was wandering blindly a few yards away, and told them both to get the hell out of the store.

The smoke continued to thicken, and the flames, increasing in intensity, were made to change shape and leap dangerously forward by air forced through a ventilation system that was somehow still functioning. He wondered how long before the whole store blew, before naked flame reached the place where bottles of white spirit had been broken, and firelighters had been stored. Every now and then something popped like a gunshot – pressurized spray-containers of furniture polish, cylinders of shaving lotion, bottles of cooking-oil. When the flames made contact with volatile substances—

He coughed, smoke choked him, fire reared around him. The only course of action was to make sure the store was emptied before it finally exploded, but first he had to be certain nobody was injured and immobilized behind the smoke. He searched the area in a frantic way. His eyes smarted, and there was pain in his lungs. He found a half-conscious young woman and helped her to her feet and escorted her toward the door, and then he turned and went back again to the rear of the store, stopping every so often to shout commands that could barely be heard above the screams and cries – *Get out, everybody who can move, just get out into the fucking street and as far away from here as you can.* He plunged back into the fumes, but visibility had become a serious problem. He couldn't see more than a few inches in front of himself, and he was suffocating, coughing fiercely, and the flames were shimmying close to his body. The heat was insufferable, a thousand desert suns. He imagined his skin peeling away from bone. He clamped a hand across his mouth and moved through the blackness, as if he were pushing his way inside the airless territory of a bad dream. He saw, through a space in the smoke, a man in a white blood-soaked jacket, and he grabbed his shoulders and dragged him back in the direction of the front door, hauling him crudely across broken glass and smouldering rolls of toilet paper and the imploded relics of fruits, crushed plums, strawberries turned to purée. That was it, he couldn't go back, he didn't have the energy, the lung-power. If there was anyone else trapped at the back of the store, there was nothing more he could do. He found some last little reservoir of resolve and dashed around, herding people out toward the street, trying to impose his will on those too shocked to move, too traumatized to realize they were in danger. They passed through the door and into the street, not with the panic he might have expected, but in a zoned way, like people drugged. Shock was a narcotic. Fear paralysed. The survival instinct was numbed. He had to shout more, push harder, get them to move, get them all out of this place as quickly as he could – so he shoved, and bullied, and berated the stragglers, and cursed them for their slowness. And suddenly Foxworth materialized, helping, cajoling, his manner like that of a captain of a sinking ship steering people to the safety of lifeboats.

The sound of a fire-engine was audible, then the whine of ambulances. He helped Foxie bundle the people – fifty or sixty of them – down the pavement about thirty yards, where they came to a stop and gathered like mourners. The fire-engine appeared, bright red and comforting, and hoses were rolled out, hatchets unsheathed, sun burned on metal helmets. Pagan slumped against a wall, fighting for breath. Foxie looked at him with concern.

'You OK?' he asked.

'I wasn't . . . dressed for this kind of occasion,' Pagan said, and his voice was hoarse. His linen suit was scorched, his face blackened.

'Apart from the wardrobe, are you OK?'

Pagan nodded. 'I'll be all right.'

'Perhaps you need treatment,' Foxworth suggested. 'You must have inhaled a lot of smoke.'

'All I need is a drink,' he said.

'Alcoholic or otherwise?'

'What do you think?' Pagan asked.

'There's an off-licence down the street.'

'A cold beer, if possible.'

'I'll be back in a flash.'

Pagan rubbed his eyes. He looked at the faces around him of those who'd emerged from the ruined supermarket. They were stunned. They observed the firemen, but not with eager attention. They might have been watching a scene flashed by satellite from another continent. He wondered about the number of serious casualties, the possibility of fatalities. He listened to the forceful blast of water from hoses, the sound of more glass breaking. One of the firemen was making an announcement through a loudspeaker. *'Clear this area, please. Please get as far away as you can until the danger has passed. Please co-operate to the full extent.'*

Foxie came back with two bottles of chilled Heineken. Pagan gulped half of one immediately. It cooled his throat, created a pleasing icy sensation in his chest. A salve. He was quiet for a time, then he said, 'She puts on quite a display.'

'Yes, she does,' and Foxie's voice was low.

Pagan finished the bottle, reached for the second one. He sipped, coughed, his lungs hurt. 'I get the uncomfortable feeling this is just a side-show, Foxie. Something she wanted us to see because she knew we'd be in the neighbourhood.'

'For our benefit,' Foxie said.

Pagan clutched the beer bottle and turned his face back in the direction of the fire-engine. Our benefit, he thought. Or maybe just mine.

An elderly man, who stood a few feet away, his forehead covered in small cuts, said to nobody in particular, 'It's that bloody woman, I bet. The one in all the papers. I bet she's behind this . . .'

An overweight girl in blue jeans and sleeveless black top said, 'Yeah. Does what she bloody well likes, don't she? And nobody does a fucking thing about her.'

'Wouldn't have happened in my day, tell you,' the old man said. 'All this mindless violence. Not in my day.'

Pagan looked at the tattoo on the girl's arm. It was a pink heart pierced by an arrow. It was more suggestive of penetration and pain than it was of love.

10

LONDON

Pasco woke in the middle of the afternoon to find the woman standing over him. She handed him a cup of coffee. He sat upright, unsure of his surroundings. The woman was her usual unsmiling self – and yet there was something different about her now, a slight touch of colour in her face, a hint of lipstick. He sipped the coffee. She sat on the bed and looked at his scarred hands.

Pasco stared at her over the rim of his cup. His hands embarrassed him. Scar tissue that hadn't healed, creased pinkish areas that resembled skin-grafts badly done. He'd lost several fingernails that had never grown back.

'You had a rough time,' she said.

'Rough's one way of saying it.'

'You and Galkin,' she said. 'Both of you had it rough.'

'Galkin, yeah,' he said. He wondered if there were going to be more questions about this Galkin, and he dreaded the idea. What if she raised something James hadn't covered? Something out of the blue? What would he do then? You couldn't wing it when it came to this woman. He understood that. You couldn't spout half-truths and hope for the best. She was all concentration and attention.

She touched the hem of his blanket. He thought that if she did something with herself, changed her hairstyle, wore more attractive clothes, deep-sixed the terrible glasses – she might not be so bad to look at. But in her present garb she seemed to suck all light out of the room.

He gazed at her face. Where did she fit? he wondered. Where did she belong in this world James had created for him? Probably she was just some kind of bridge, a go-between, the person who'd shuffle him along the line of command.

He leaned on his elbow. 'So. What happens next?'

'It depends.'

'Depends on what?'

The woman said nothing for a time. That unnerving stare of hers. Chilly. 'On what you tell me.'

Pasco said, 'We already covered everything yesterday.'

'Let's cover it again, Richard,' she said.

'Is it really necessary?' he asked.

'Yes,' she said.

'Where do you want me to start?'

She thought a moment. 'The man who recruited you. Start with him.'

Pasco relaxed a little. He was on familiar territory. 'I attended Johns Hopkins. I intended going on to graduate school. Electronics. One day this guy Binns, an Eng Lit professor, stops me on campus. Says he wouldn't mind talking with me for a time.'

'And so you talked.'

'Yeah. We had three, four meetings.'

'And he persuaded you where your future lay?'

'Listen, I was gung-ho in those days,' Pasco said, and smiled at a lost memory of himself. 'It didn't take a whole lot of persuasion, you understand. My God, I was an impressionable kid. The Agency wanted me. They wanted *me*.'

'What happened next?'

'I spent three months at this training-camp place,' he said. Training-camp, he thought. Indoctrination house was more like it. You had it drummed into you again and again what the Agency stood for, how it protected a way of life that was the envy of the whole god-damn world, how proud you ought to be that you'd been singled out and blessed. Blessed, my ass. You were cursed.

'Where was the camp?'

'Near Roanoke. Ten miles, about.'

'Who was in charge?'

'Guy called Laird. But we didn't see much of him. He was a God, you know. Whenever he appeared, it was like he descended in a golden chariot from the clouds. He gave a couple of pep talks and off he went back to heaven.'

'So who were your regular instructors?'

Pasco thought a moment. He said, 'They kept changing. There was a guy named Backus. Electronic communications were his thing. Littlejohn was another. His function was to tell us the glorious history of the Agency. I guess he was there to beef up morale. There was a woman called Joan Dunne. Her field of expertise was how to conduct ourselves in overseas postings, if we happened to land one. How to deal with the natives, that kind of guff. How to stay out of romantic entanglements. Be careful of homosexual entrapment. But there were other instructors – I guess maybe eight, nine in all.'

'You remember the location of the camp?'

'How could I forget it?'

'Describe it for me,' she said.

As Pasco answered, he wondered why she wanted to hear all this again. Was she looking for inconsistencies in his history? He was on secure ground, though. His time with the Agency had been branded into his brain. And any little thing he might have forgotten, he'd remembered during his ten years in the penal colony, because there hadn't been much else to occupy his time other than to reconstruct the past.

'After this training, you went on to Langley.'

'Right. I was instrumental in planning the location of spy satellites. Don't misunderstand me – I was only part of a team. I didn't call the shots.'

'Who did?'

James had said *You must mention Naderson.* 'Guy by the name of Bob Naderson. Last I heard, he'd become Assistant Deputy Director for Science and Technology. Which means he had responsibility for a whole bunch of operations. National Photographic Interpretation Center. Office of Research and Development. Technical Services.'

'An important man,' she said.

'Yeah, well, he was one step below the Director for S&T.'

'And his name?'

James had told him: *Poole, you must include Poole.* 'Christopher Poole.'

'You met Poole?'

Pasco shook his head. 'He was high on the totem pole. I was only a regular Indian. I saw him maybe twice in my life.'

'Did you work for anyone else at Langley?'

'Kevin Grimes. He was my immediate superior for a couple of years. He was site director in charge of electronic radar stations.' Grimes. The seersucker suit.

Grimes with his distended mouth. Grimes, thoughtful, watchful, treacherous.

'Where?'

'He moved around. He was based in Delaware,' he said. 'Near Dover.'

Stroking her greying hair with one hand, she said, 'Some of these people are presumably retired. Maybe even dead by this time. Have you thought about that?'

'Yeah. But some of them are still running things.'

'You know in particular who set you up?' she asked.

'Does that matter?'

'It helps to focus, that's all.'

'Grimes, for starters.' Pasco shrugged. In the gulag, he'd never dwelt on particulars. His animosity and hostility had been fuelled by anything and everything connected to the Agency. He hadn't thought about focus. He hadn't wanted to narrow things down and restrict the boundaries of hatred. 'You could include Eddie Binns, Laird, or any of the instructors who trained me. Include Bob Naderson, Christopher Poole. But I don't think you're quite getting the picture. This doesn't have anything to do with *particular* people. This goes beyond individuals. Way beyond.'

She studied his face. Assessed him. He felt as if a flashlight had been turned on him. 'So you don't give a damn who actually put the drugs in your suitcase?'

'No, I don't. As far as I'm concerned, they were all responsible.' He remembered what James had told him. He recalled James, in that insidious voice of his, telling him what to say. *Impress on her the fact you want to hit the training-camp. That's important, don't forget that. You can forget other stuff, but you don't forget that. Make sure she understands that. That's your primary target.* Pasco pondered this instruction and wondered, as he'd done before, about James's personal agenda.

What the hell difference did it make? His locomotive and James's were running on parallel tracks, that was the only thing he needed to know.

He cleared his throat and said, 'If you asked me to single any one thing out, I'd have to say the camp near Roanoke would be my number one priority. That's the one I'd really like to get. Even if I couldn't lay a finger on anything else, I'd want that place destroyed.'

'Why?'

'Because that's where I first tasted the bullshit,' he said. 'That's where I swallowed the whole thing. I didn't stop to chew. I didn't stop to ask myself if I really liked the taste of what they were feeding me at that joint. I just gulped it down like a good little boy and they patted me on the head and told me I was doing terrific. I'd like to see that place demolished. I'd like to see it just blown sky fucking high.'

She was quiet a second. 'Tell me about your flight,' she said.

'Flight? What the hell has that got to do with anything?'

'Was it Washington direct to Moscow?'

'I changed at Heathrow.'

'So you carried the drugs through Heathrow.'

Pasco nodded. He wasn't sure where the woman was headed except into irrelevancies. 'What difference does it make? I wasn't stopped at Heathrow. My luggage wasn't examined. I sailed through smoothly. Why?'

'Curiosity,' she said.

'About what?'

'Maybe there was a deal,' she said. 'Maybe the Brits at customs had been tipped to let you pass through. Doing a small favour, say.'

'Does it matter?'

She rose from the edge of the bed. 'This business

is the most important thing in the world for you, isn't it?'

'You got it,' Pasco said.

She looked at him thoughtfully. 'I'll be back soon. We'll talk some more.'

'What more is there to talk about?' he asked.

'You've been gone ten years, Pasco. You should have learned something about patience in all that time.'

The woman stepped out of the room. A trace of her scent hung in the air. It reminded him of something growing, something suggestive of Fall and pale sunlight on fading landscapes, but he couldn't place it.

The woman left the house, locked it. She drove an old CV6 through a sequence of uninteresting suburban streets. Certain houses had striped canvas awnings that imparted the effect of a low-budget carnival. A man wearing rubber gloves clipped a bush in the shape of a stork. A woman in a wide-brimmed straw hat hosed her front lawn. The hot air was ripe with the smell of cut grass.

Traffic was dense. Stuck at traffic-lights, she found herself thinking about Pasco's hands, though she wasn't sure why. They looked unreal, theatrical, as if someone had applied stage scars to them. She wondered what it would be like to touch those hands, to place her fingertips upon the wrinkled discoloured tissue.

She thought he had a haunted look. He was running on loathing, which was a fuel that never took you as far as you wanted to believe it could. You needed additives for extra mileage – a sense of your own capabilities, an awareness of what made you vulnerable, a firm understanding that life was a transient business. She wondered if she entirely trusted him and his story. It was something she'd check.

At an intersection she encountered a police roadblock, four uniformed constables checking drivers. Four intense young men sweated in their pale blue shirts. She waited in line, edging forward slowly, and when one of the policemen tapped on her window she asked, 'Something wrong, Officer?'

The constable was very young, but trying to look hardened and embittered by a savage world. 'Routine check,' he said.

He hunched down, gazed at her face, then asked to see her licence, which she took from the glove compartment. The licence was made out in the name of Kristen Hawkins. The cop studied it for a moment, then returned it to her. Routine check, she thought. She knew better than that.

'Drive carefully,' the constable said.

'I always do.' She slipped the car past the knot of policemen and when she reached the next corner she made a right turn. She was conscious of more cops. They strolled around in pairs, muttered into their little hand-held communication devices on street corners. She was also aware of something else, dark tendrils of smoke that drifted over rooftops a few streets away and the smell, wondrously pungent, of charred wood.

She found a parking-space in a side-street. She picked up an overnight bag from the passenger seat, got out, locked the car, and began to walk. When she came to a pub she went inside and headed for the toilet.

11

LONDON

Pagan took a taxi back to his apartment in Holland Park. He didn't enter the place at once. He stared up at the windows of his living-room. He had no desire to go inside. The windows unnerved him. The rooms beyond were unwelcoming.

He looked in the direction of the small park. Twilight, and the place was virtually empty save for a few kids smoking reefer, passing a joint openly from hand to hand. Pagan sometimes had an urge to confront them, flash the ID – but he'd never considered marijuana anything other than a harmless indulgence. Let them smoke, he thought. Let them soar. God knows, there had to be escape routes from reality.

He looked along the street. The unmarked police car was a black Rover parked five or six houses away. He walked toward it. The cop behind the wheel was Detective-Sergeant Bennie Banforth, who rolled his window down. A pale cloud of stale tobacco smoke drifted out of the car. Banforth had the dull orange fingers of a chain-smoker.

'Nothing, Frank,' he said. 'No sign of her.'

'You been here long?'

'Just after you called me this morning. The only kind of activity I've seen is over there,' and he nodded in the direction of the square. 'At least half a dozen dope transactions in the past hour. Quite a little market-place, Frank.'

'And that's it?'

'That's it,' Banforth said. 'You look like you've been in the wars, old son.'

'You could say that.'

'You were at that explosion over in Kilburn, I hear.'

Pagan, conscious of the condition of his clothing and the smoke stains on his face, nodded.

Banforth said, 'The word is the woman planted the bomb.'

'The word is right,' Pagan said.

Banforth lit a cigarette. He wheezed a little as he inhaled. 'Good old George had a chat with you, did he?'

'I just spent two hours with him.'

'On his high horse, I expect,' said Banforth.

'He's not a happy man, Bennie.'

'He was born miserable, Frank.'

Pagan thought a moment about the uncomfortable scene in Nimmo's office. Nimmo's apoplexy was an odd thing to watch – the reddening of the plump cheeks, the agitated working of his eyebrows, how a jet of spit accompanied his every word like a form of damp punctuation. Pagan had been obliged to explain his reason for being in the neighbourhood of the bombing, which involved telling him about the business of the stolen photograph. Nimmo's anger had diffused itself in clumsy sarcasm. *Oh, she has a key to your flat, does she? Comes and goes as she likes, does she? Running an open house, are you, Frank? Tea and biscuits next, I expect. Why don't you hang up a bloody B & B sign?*

Pagan always countered Nimmo's sarcasm with anger. *You don't know what it's like out there, George.*

You haven't got a clue about police work. You're just too fucking busy sitting in this bloody office building your empire and giving meaningless statements to the press and yakking on TV. Pagan understood he'd gone too far, but he didn't regret that because it was like opening a clogged valve inside himself and releasing steam. This locking of horns had an element of satisfaction in the sense that it offended Nimmo, but George had at least one stinging comeback, which he was only too happy to fire. *Tell me one thing, Pagan. Tell me what you've achieved in the last seven months. Go on, I'm waiting. While she's busy murdering people in hotels with bloody lethal food and bombing bloody supermarkets, what have you actually accomplished apart from acting the bloody hero by pulling a few people out of a burning supermarket?*

It was a cutting question intended to wound Pagan, and one he had no answer for. It was pointless to tell George Nimmo about the difficulties of the search, the grinding hours spent assessing a relentless stream of misleading information, the accumulation of computer data, the assimilation of material from banks, motels, estate agents, government offices – in the hope you might come across one telling little item of information, that she'd opened a bank account, she'd rented an apartment, she'd stayed in a hotel, she'd applied for a credit card or had a telephone installed. It was useless to burden Nimmo with the menagerie of aliases Pagan had explored – the Lambs, the Starlings, the Foxes, the Birds, all the rest of it. Nimmo didn't want to hear any of this. He simply wanted a result. The rest was dross. And besides, if she'd given up using the names of creatures as pseudonyms, as she'd done when she'd found work as Carmen Profumo, then Pagan was chasing up and down blind alleys in pursuit of a phantom.

Bennie Banforth said, 'I heard there were no fatalities in the supermarket job.'

'A small mercy,' said Pagan.

'Something to be thankful for, old son.'

Pagan shrugged, then moved back in the direction of the house. He took his key out and opened the front door, stepped inside the hallway, looked toward the unlit stairs. He stopped outside Miss Gabler's door, knocked quietly. He heard her voice from inside. 'Who is it?'

'Your upstairs neighbour,' Pagan said.

He listened to the sound of a chain being slid back, a key turned. Miss Gabler lived in a state of apprehension. The neighbourhood had gone downhill and her world was one of potential robberies and rapes. Her face, weathered and creased, peered round the door at him.

'Mr Pagan,' she said. 'The hour is late. Is this a social call?'

'I was checking, that's all,' he said. The air from her apartment smelled of cumin.

'Checking on what?' she asked.

'Your well-being.'

'Why?'

'Common courtesy,' he remarked.

Miss Gabler, who complained habitually about the 'negro' music Pagan played, said, 'I've never associated you with courtesy in the past, Mr Pagan. However, it is quite refreshing to find this unexpected kindness, I must say.' She scrutinized his appearance. 'Have you been in an accident?'

'You might say.'

'Are you hurt?'

'No, I'm fine.' Pagan glanced in the direction of the stairs. 'I don't mean to alarm you, Miss Gabler. But

I'm curious to know if you've seen any . . .' How to phrase this without causing the old dear dread? '. . . any strangers lingering lately?'

'Lingering where?'

'Around the house . . .'

She shook her head. 'Only the usual louts who congregate at the entrance to our little park.'

Pagan hesitated a second. 'Have you heard anyone upstairs in my flat when I was out?' It was the wrong question. He saw at once he'd succeeded in upsetting her.

'Why? Have you been robbed? Have you been *burglarized*?'

He smiled and patted the back of her hand. 'No, nothing like that,' and he invented some yarn about a key he'd loaned to a fictitious friend, as if this fable might defuse Miss Gabler's state of alarm.

'I haven't heard a thing. But I really don't think one ought to be going around handing out keys willy-nilly. How do you imagine I would react were I to encounter a total stranger in the hallway, Mr Pagan? Or if I saw somebody I didn't know letting himself into the house?'

Pagan agreed it was thoughtless of him to give spare keys to other people without first informing her. He said good night to her in a reassuring way, then moved toward the stairs. He climbed slowly, reached the door of his flat, unlocked it. He stepped inside, groping for the lightswitch in the living-room. He flicked it: the overhead light came on. He moved to the centre of the room.

He heard the click of a safety-catch being slipped and the gun was pressed hard against his neck and he couldn't turn his face to look at the intruder. But he didn't have to. He knew.

12

LONDON

'Don't turn. Don't move,' she said.

'Believe me, I'm not about to,' he said.

He felt the barrel of the gun thrust against his neck muscle. He sought to give the impression of outward calm, as if having a gun held to his flesh were an everyday event.

'Your lock's not worth a shit,' she said. 'You ought to have it changed.'

'I'll see to it,' he said, and tried to twist his face round to look at her, but she thrust the gun harder into his skin, pushing at the soft flesh beneath his jaw. He flashed on the idea of raising his arm, swinging it swiftly round at her, or bringing up his elbow and digging it into her flesh, but the prospect of catching her off guard was thin. She'd simply pull the trigger. The End. Roll the credits. He smelled her perfume, an aroma softly suggestive of raspberries.

'And your friend sitting down there in the parked car – was he intended to be some kind of deterrent? You underestimate me, Frank.'

He wondered briefly how she'd managed to avoid Banforth's observation, but she had a mystifying way of gliding around obstacles. Her antenna was always active. Maybe Banforth had lost his concentration a moment. Maybe he'd been diverted by the dopers loitering at the edge of the park. Whatever. She'd gone past him unnoticed. He realized too late he should have posted more observers in the neighbourhood, but he hadn't wanted police presence to be obvious.

'Now you're here, what do you intend to steal this time?' he asked. 'I don't think I have any more photographs of my late wife for you to deface.'

'Gee, Frank. Did I make you angry?'

'What did you expect? Mirth and merriment?'

'I left a replacement,' she said.

'I wasn't happy with that either. Trespass and theft have a bad effect on me. And your kind of graffiti makes me sick.'

'Sometimes I don't like your voice,' she said. 'It grates on me. It's the self-righteous whine that bugs me.' She pushed the barrel harder into his flesh and he could feel steel bore into him and he thought of the fragility created by an undone safety-catch. A fraction of an inch: eternity.

'You need a shower and a change of clothes,' she said. 'You smell like burnt wood.'

'I have you to thank for my general appearance,' he remarked. 'Nice little number you did on the supermarket. What I don't understand is why you did it.'

'Because it was there. Because you'd see it.'

'One of your smaller spectaculars,' he said.

'A little light show, that's all.'

'And you arranged it just for me,' he said. 'What do you expect? Gratitude?'

'I enjoy a little appreciation at times.'

'The only thing I appreciate is that by some freaky miracle nobody was killed.'

'I wasn't trying too hard, Frank.'

He was silent, struggling with complex urges, most

of which came down in the end to the same problem: how to disarm her. But he didn't have a chance unless he was in the mood for dying, and he wasn't. He listened to the hush of the woman's breath, smelling her scent, feeling the gun bore into him.

He stood motionless, suddenly aware of a ludicrous intimacy, as if somehow the gun created a bizarre link between the woman and himself, a deadly little bridge of steel. And then he was conscious of the movement of her left hand, the free hand, moving against the small of his back even as she still held the gun under his jaw. Her touch startled him.

'You're lonely, Frank,' she said. 'I think of you and I think of a lonely man.'

'Don't let it get you down,' he remarked.

'Maybe you're still in love with your dead wife. Which would be pretty god-damn sick after all this time.'

He said nothing.

'And you're uptight. You're tense.'

She ran her hand under his shirt and laid her palm upon the base of his spine. He closed his eyes and tried to distance himself from this occurrence, tried to concentrate only on the weapon.

'You're tense,' she said. 'Stress kills. Don't you know that? When did you last get laid?'

Her fingertips were warm. She moved her hand around to the angle of his hip. 'When did you last fuck somebody?'

Pagan didn't answer.

'Been a while, right?' she asked. She was rubbing the base of his spine. 'What do you feel right now?'

'Revulsion,' he said.

'You're lying. I don't believe you feel revulsion. The opposite. Definitely the opposite.'

Her warm fingers caressed his skin. He remembered: those long fingers, how they'd impressed him when he'd first met her, how she gestured with them, the expressive way she used them. He had a sense of being stranded in a disturbing place, trapped between potential violence and this forced intimacy.

He had the shifting off-centre sensation of having stepped inside an erotic dream where his will-power was threatened and he could do nothing to prevent the erosion of himself. The impossible angles of a dream, the negation of geometry, the way desires blew up like unexpected storms out of landscapes you would never encounter in a waking state.

'We had an opportunity once,' she said. 'Long time ago.'

'I was younger then,' he said. 'I had less sense.'

'And less control? Is that what you're trying to tell me? That's bullshit, Pagan. You know what you want to do to me, don't you? You want to slip your cock inside me, don't you? You want me to spread my legs for you, don't you, babe? You want inside me, you want to know what I'm like, what it would feel like. I'll tell you this, it would be the most impressive experience of your whole fucking lifetime—'

He opened his eyes and tried to concentrate on anything other than her touch. Impressions of the room – his record collection, a couple of old rock concert posters. But even as he felt humiliated by her touch, by the weapon held to his jaw and his own power-lessness, he realized his body was responding to her. An undeniable warmth spread through him. He forced himself to remember the devastation she'd caused on the underground train. He brought to mind the scene in the hotel dining-room. The hand that touched him was the same one that had placed poison in the food, the same that only this afternoon had concealed an explosive device in a crowded supermarket. Don't forget those things, keep remembering them. The same hand. The same fingers. You feel nothing. Nothing. Any other response is impossible. Sick.

'You're firm, Pagan. You're in good shape,' she said. 'Well-preserved. I'm impressed. You want me to go on, don't you? You don't want me to stop. You want me to go further.'

He shook his head. 'Frankly, I'd prefer it if you pulled the fucking trigger.'

'I wonder why I don't believe that.'

She took her hand away from him suddenly. She stepped back. He turned and looked at her. She was smiling at him, but it wasn't the kind of smile you could easily read – coy, self-assured, triumphant: all these qualities. And loveliness. He could never quite get his head around that fact. She was blackness and light simultaneously, an angel fallen.

'I see through you,' she said. 'You're a window, Pagan. An open book. You're so easy to read it's laughable.'

He stared at the gun, her black cotton shirt, the way her hair had been combed back severely from her face and held tight by a clasp, the slight parting of lips. She wore a black beret, black jeans. She was dressed for darkness. He wondered about the nature of desire, the mechanics of arousal, the jarring distinction between the resolve of mind and the impulses of body.

'One day,' she said. 'One day I'll just close the pages.'

'What's stopping you?' he asked. He was breathless. He considered a lunge, a flying tackle; lethal thoughts.

'Because we're bonded, Pagan. Whether you like it or not, there's this weird link between us.'

'You're dreaming,' he said.

'I don't think so. Call it the magnetism of opposites. Everything you stand for, I couldn't give a shit about. Everything I do, you despise. You imagine law and order. I see chaos. You believe in the sanctity of human life, which I happen to think is pious crap. Reverse images, Pagan. But drawn to each other. Very much so. There's a deep attraction. Think about it.'

'I don't need to think about it.' He made a dismissive gesture.

'Of course you don't. It might upset the balance of your fragile little world. You like to believe things are either black or white, nothing between. You've got a job to do, and that defines your life for you. Nimmo tells you to drop everything, concentrate on catching me, nothing else is important. You had a better life when Martin Burr was running the show, didn't you? Times were good then. Burr gave you scope and freedom. Now you've got this idiot little bureaucrat in charge, and he's not your kind of man at all, is he? He doesn't trust you, Frank. Doesn't have faith in you. Doesn't believe in the old flash of insight, does he? He's a fucking pencil-pusher.'

He detected in her look a touch of malice: and why not? Her whole presence here was a form of incitement. *If you can't find me, I'll come to you.*

'When did Burr retire?' she asked.

'What difference does that make?'

'I'm curious.'

'Two years ago.'

'What's he doing with himself now?'

'Writing his memoirs.'

'Why not? He had an interesting career. He's got stories to tell. I hope I get a mention in these memoirs.'

'Count on it,' he said.

'I'd feel slighted if I didn't.'

Burr, he wondered. Why was she interested in old Martin? He said, 'You're running too many risks. You can't go on for ever. You'll slip somewhere along the way. You're bound to.'

'I can't imagine a life without risks,' she replied.

'You can't keep riding your luck,' he said.

'Is that what you call it? Luck? Luck doesn't enter into anything I do, babe.'

She raised the gun and pointed it directly at him. 'I don't expect you to come chasing downstairs after me.'

'You're armed. I'm not.'

'Smart thinking. I'll be around. I have this rule. I never quit while I'm having fun.'

'And this is fun,' he said.

'People's weaknesses are always fun. Especially yours.'

Weaknesses, he thought. That was a mild word. *Drawn to each other. This deep attraction.* He experienced a chill around his heart. Drawn, attracted. No.

'Don't forget. Change your lock.'

He watched her step from the living-room, saw her back to the door, then heard her footsteps on the stairs. He moved quickly to the bedroom, where in a shoebox located under the bed he kept his gun, a Bernardelli.

The box was empty. She'd found the gun and taken it.

He ran toward the stairs, hearing the slam of the street door. He hurried down, stepped outside. There was no sign of her. He walked toward Banforth's car and opened the door. Banforth was smoking a cigarette and staring at the street with the frozen look of concentration suggestive of a man baffled by a cross-word clue.

'Did you see her?' Pagan asked.

Banforth shook his head. 'See her? When?'

'A minute ago.'

'Where?'

'Coming out of my front door, Benny. *My front door*. About twenty-five yards from here.'

Banforth looked surprised. 'No bloody way,' he said. 'I haven't taken my eyes off your house.'

'Nice work,' he said. 'She came and she went and you didn't see a fucking thing.'

Banforth said, 'If she'd come out your front door, I'd have seen her, Frank.'

Pagan shook his head. 'So she just vanished into the ether, is that what you're telling me, Benny?'

'All I'm saying—'

Pagan went back inside the house and paused in the hallway. He thought: *I heard the front door slam when she left and I assumed* . . . He walked past the foot of the stairs to the back door which opened out onto a small patio that was the property of Miss Gabler. But the door was bolted from inside. *Therefore she couldn't have left by the rear exit unless she was bloody Houdini.* The question crossed his mind: was she still *inside* the house? He strolled quietly back down the hall and paused outside Miss Gabler's door. He knocked gently and Miss Gabler appeared in the slit of the doorway.

'Are you checking on me again, Mr Pagan?' she asked.

He said, 'I thought I heard the front door slam and I wondered . . .' He couldn't think of an explanation for having interrupted the old woman.

Miss Gabler shook her head. 'I was watching TV in my bedroom at the back. A very interesting documentary on lemmings, actually, and why they commit mass suicide. I heard nothing.'

'You're sure of that?'

'Mr Pagan, is something *troubling* you?'

He shook his head, mumbled something about duty and vigilance, then climbed the stairs to his flat. She comes, she goes, she defies physics. She appears, she dematerializes. He poured himself an Auchentoshan and felt as fragmented as a man who has stepped, not for the first time, on a buried claymore mine.

13

WASHINGTON

The Eastern Seaboard of the United States, like the rest of the country during the long dry summer, was suffering from a drought of biblical proportions. The view from the plane was dismal. Fields usually lush and green were brown and parched. Rivers had dwindled to streams, and streams had evaporated. Water sprinklers that otherwise would have been spraying crops were silent and motionless. Max Skidelsky, face pressed to the window of the aircraft, thought the condition of the landscape symbolic of the nation in general. Everything withered: grapes puckered on vines, turning prematurely to raisins, apples shrivelled and rotted, decaying from within.

He fastened his seat-belt in preparation for landing. He liked the tension of descent, the spooky moment when wheels touched tarmac, the great thrust of engines thrown into reverse. He was first off the plane, first inside the terminal, because he moved a step more briskly than anyone else. He always had. He crossed the arrivals lounge, then he went outside into the furnace of high noon.

The car was waiting for him. He didn't speak to the driver. He never spoke to drivers. They were of no significance to him, and their conversations invariably concerned basketball, which didn't interest him.

The car headed toward the city, over which a haze of heat and smog lay. He stepped from the black Cadillac outside a restaurant, hurried under the shade of a green canopy, ignored the doorman and went inside. He turned left, climbed a flight of stairs, entered a private dining-room with smoked-glass windows and maroon linen tablecloths and a basket of breadsticks. Bread was *verboten*; Skidelsky watched his diet like a man with an implanted calorie-counter.

The man who was already seated at the table acknowledged Skidelsky with a slight motion of his head. He was old and had undergone cosmetic surgery in recent years, but the result was farcical. When he spoke he could barely move his lips. The corners of his eyes were unnaturally smooth and the flesh across his cheeks had been stretched as tight as a drumskin. He reminded Skidelsky less of a human being and more of an artefact, an electronic creature – like the robotic Abe Lincoln displayed at Disneyland.

'Sit, Max,' the old man said.

Skidelsky smiled, sat down.

'How are you?' The question was uttered through almost motionless lips. Skidelsky was curious about the effects of cosmetic surgery, the pain of vanity.

'In good form.'

The old man patted Skidelsky's wrist. 'We'll have a wine, shall we? They have a pleasant Bordeaux here, a Lagrange. Are you familiar with it?'

'Whatever you prefer,' Skidelsky said. He knew the wine, but wouldn't presume to suggest an alternative. The old man liked to think he ran the show. And, for now, he did.

'I suggest the roast beef and Yorkshire pudding, if you have a taste for English cuisine.'

'Roast beef is fine.' He'd skip the Yorkshire pudding. Too heavy.

'Perhaps some green beans?'

'Certainly.'

'Asparagus for starters?'

'Why not,' Skidelsky said.

A waiter appeared, took the orders, retreated. The old man snapped a breadstick in two and placed one half in his mouth, and sipped from a glass of mineral water. He chewed for a time. He wore a navy and red striped tie and a crisp white shirt.

The waiter brought the asparagus and poured a thimbleful of wine for the old man's approval, which was duly given. Skidelsky looked down at the asparagus which lay in a puddle of a yellow substance. He forked one of the spears and raised it to his mouth. He choked it down with an air of determination.

'Mmmm,' said the old man. 'Exquisite.'

Skidelsky, already impatient with his lunch companion, finished his appetizer, laid down his fork and glanced round the room. Gloomy and clubby – a place where old geezers came to dine.

The old man edged his plate aside and drank a little wine. Then, somewhat stiffly, he turned his face to Skidelsky and said, 'The woman is active again, I see.'

Skidelsky had been waiting for this opening. He pounced at once. He was a leopard when it came to the prey of opportunity. 'What surprises me is that she hasn't been caught before now.'

'A pimpernel,' said the old man. 'They seek her here, et cetera. Who knows what fissures she inhabits, Max?'

'Just the same, you'd think that between the Brits and the FBI she would have been caught.'

'You'd think so, certainly.'

'I wonder . . .'

'Yes?'

'I wonder if the Feds are doing enough, that's all.'

'There is a spirit of co-operation between the FBI and Special Branch at Scotland Yard, Max. There is also a certain competitive edge to this co-operation, of course. I'm sure the Bureau is doing all it can. Keep this in mind. Her recent activities have been confined to the British Isles, which puts all the strain on the UK authorities, not ours. The Bureau supplies all the information it can, I'm sure.'

'What happens if she decides to grace our shores?' Skidelsky asked.

'Grace our shores? God help us.'

'Would the Bureau be any more capable than Special Branch?'

The old man shrugged. 'The answer would depend on who you asked, I suppose.'

Skidelsky said, 'I sometimes wonder about the Bureau's intelligence-gathering capabilities.'

The old man said, 'I make it a point not to criticize the Bureau.' The waiter was bringing the roast beef, the green beans, Yorkshire puddings, and a dish of gravy, all of which he set on the table. Then he left the room.

Skidelsky surveyed the food. The gravy looked suspect, thickened with cornstarch. He didn't eat cornstarch. He didn't eat potatoes. He picked at the green beans – overcooked, practically mush, all goodness boiled out of them – and then he sliced his knife through the surface of the beef, which oozed blood and God knows what else, antibiotics, hormones, steroids, anything breeders pumped these days into cattle to prepare them for the profit of slaughter. He tapped his fork on the rim of his wineglass. *Ping*.

He said, 'I don't mean to be critical of the Bureau

either, you understand. But the woman has been on their books for – what? More than ten years?'

'Indeed she has.'

'Without results.'

'Without results. Correct. They had her once, and she escaped. From Danbury, I recall.'

'It's not a record to brag about, is it?'

The old man said, 'It's not, I agree.'

Skidelsky said, 'I happen to believe we'd do a better job than the Bureau.'

'Possibly. Except for one fact, Max. It doesn't come within our province.'

'Then perhaps it's time for change.'

'Oh, this is radical talk, Max.'

Skidelsky wondered if he were being gently patronized. He knew the nickname the old man and his addle-headed cronies had for him: *Skid the Kid*. And he hated it. How he hated it. He put his knife down. 'If she comes here, do we stand to one side and let the Bureau handle it?'

'If she comes here, it's a domestic matter.'

'It's a *national* matter,' Max Skidelsky said.

'Let's not argue this point, Max. She comes here, it falls to the Bureau to handle it. That's the way it works. In any event, she probably has no intention of coming this way in the near future.'

'How can you be so sure? You think she's scared of the Bureau? You think the Bureau *terrifies* her? The Bureau couldn't catch her if she was wearing a luminous bathing-suit in a god-damn coal-cellar.' He'd overstepped a line here, and he knew it. He was becoming too intense. He had to rein his feelings in. The old man could only be pressed so far.

'The Bureau is mandated to handle internal terrorism,' the old man said, rather gently, as if he were dealing with an unruly boy and his enchanting impetuosity. 'Presidential Executive Order 12333 of 1981, which permits the Agency to operate domestically, doesn't have any teeth. It's window-dressing, that's all. It's of very little practical purpose.'

'I understand that. But what happens if, for the sake of argument, she has other targets in mind?'

'Such as?'

'The Agency, for example.'

The old man dabbed his weird lips with a napkin. He looked at Max with eyes that didn't quite belong in his altered, altogether unnatural face. 'Really, Max. I don't think that's likely. Langley is hardly a feasible terrorist target. The security there makes it impregnable. You know that. I know that.'

'People leave Langley at night. They go home to an assortment of suburbs. They have wives and children. Is their safety the responsibility of the Bureau?'

'I would have to say it is,' said the old man. 'But why cross bridges until we come to them, Max? One, the woman is unlikely to return to this country. Two, I can't imagine her singling out Agency personnel as targets. If she has destructive grudges, they're directed at the Bureau. After all, it's the Bureau that is engaged in the search for her, not the Agency.'

Skidelsky said, 'I'm thinking aloud, that's all.'

'A word of advice. Some thoughts are best kept to oneself. I've been at this since before you were born. Remember that. And experience is a crucible where ambitions are analysed and controlled. Remember that too.'

I'll remember it, Skidelsky thought. And so will you, you fucker. So will you. Experience is a crucible, sure – where smug old men catch fire and die.

'Dessert, Max?'

'I never touch it,' and Skidelsky patted his tight, lean stomach, as if to make a point.

The old man had another glass of wine. 'I think I might indulge myself in strawberries and cream. I'm not keeping you from something, am I?'

Max Skidelsky shook his head. 'I'll have coffee.'

The waiter brought dessert and coffee. Skidelsky drank his coffee quickly. It was Kenyan, and it had been stewing too long. Nobody knew how to make coffee these days. He set his cup down and stared at the old man, whose rigid features were fascinating in a grotesque way.

'What's the latest on this cuts business?' he asked in a casual manner. He knew the answer to his question in advance, but he asked it anyway, half in the hope that the situation might have changed, that the CIA lobbyists on the Hill had constructed a potent strategy.

'There's nothing new, Max. Our funding is still scheduled to be cut drastically, which will mean a general reduction of personnel all over the place. The President is keen to flash his knife and do some budgetary slashing. His argument is the same as always. The world has changed, the Cold War is over, the Agency must change with the world. We're no longer as useful as we once were. We must find a new purpose. As you're no doubt aware, we're *already* being used in the somewhat limited field of internal economic espionage, which is an awfully long way from our original function . . .' The old man shrugged. 'We're bringing pressure, of course. But our admirable Commander-in-Chief is not a man easily swayed. The cuts are one thing, but I find his other proposal somewhat less palatable. His idea of replacing the Director of Central Intelligence with somebody who has total control of *all* law-enforcement activities, internal and external, is misguided, at the very least.'

Misguided, Skidelsky thought. A king-sized understatement. A monstrous understatement. He said, 'I don't see the point of it. He shrivels the Agency, gives us demeaning little jobs like spying on Japanese or Korean corporations to keep us busy, and brings in some kind of super-cop to oversee the whole shooting-works—'

'It's called streamlining, I believe.'

'It's called cutting your own throat,' Skidelsky said.

The old man leaned across the table. 'I'll tell you this in confidence, Max. The man whose name has been suggested in connection with this mega-job – if the position is eventually created, which is a strong likelihood – is none other than Barclay Reeves.'

'*Reeves?*'

'Reeves. The former Director of the FBI.'

Skidelsky felt a series of balloons pop in his head. He heard little explosions, quick expulsions of trapped air released as if from some mineshaft of his feelings. 'Christ, if that happens, the Agency becomes just another branch of the Feds.'

'I think that's a little melodramatic, Max.'

'I don't. Reeves might be retired, but he's still got strings inside the Bureau. And he's FBI from the days of Hoover. He's never been a fan of the Agency. The idea of taking over everything must be causing him wet dreams. We get pushed to one side and squashed like a bug, and Reeves controls everything we do. It's totally unimaginable.'

'Sometimes the unimaginable happens,' said the old man.

'The Bureau is incompetent. Reeves is incompetent. Do we just lie down and roll over?' *Reeves*, Skidelsky thought: no, it couldn't be allowed to happen.

'We do whatever the President decides, that's what we do, Max.'

Skidelsky had hoped for more fire and spirit from the old man: a forlorn hope. What could you expect from deadwood anyway? The old man was brittle and dry and tired. He had about as much energy and enthusiasm as a haddock on a fishmonger's slab. *We do whatever the President decides.* There was enough deadwood inside the Agency to start a god-damn brushfire.

The old man poked a long spoon into the dish of strawberries. 'I understand how all this affects morale inside the Agency, Max. Believe me. That's why I planned the seminars. A mini think-tank, if you like. It's time to look at ways of boosting our people. Especially the younger ones. Our backs are to the walls and we have to come out fighting. We have to show the President that the Agency still has a vital function.'

Seminars, Skidelsky thought. Think-tanks. What the fuck did the old man think he was running here – a state campus? A hick college? Seminars! Ponderous chat, droning voices, old men locked inside flashbacks of The Great Days. Pass the sherry, let's talk about how it used to be when we had a role to play, when we showed the world what democracy was all about. Christ, yeah, seminars were the answer.

The old man changed the subject. 'I don't remember a summer this dry and hot in years. Do you know, I read in a newspaper only the other day that some tribe in Oklahoma – Navajos? – had actually performed a rain ceremony? That's how bad it is.'

The weather. The drought. Indian rituals. Seminars. Skidelsky wasn't interested in chitchat. His mind was already racing elsewhere. Out of this restaurant, an ocean away from here. The old man finished his strawberries and smacked his lips and tossed his napkin down.

When they left the restaurant, they stood beneath the canopy while the old man waited for his car to arrive. He asked, 'Can I give you a ride to Langley, Max?'

'I have an appointment in town this afternoon,' Max said. He looked across the sun-white street, smelled gasoline and the dryness of the city in the air.

A well-dressed middle-aged man, walking a tiny dog on a leash, emerged from an apartment building. From nowhere, conjured out of sunlight it seemed, two kids in hooded jackets attacked the man, shoving him to the ground and booting the dog unconscious. The kids rifled the guy's pockets and sprinted away with his wallet. It was a swift business, accomplished in a matter of a few seconds. A well-tuned little operation.

'My God,' said the old man, shaken. 'Did you see that?'

'Yes,' Skidelsky said.

'In a neighbourhood like this . . . you'd think . . .' The old man faltered.

'Happens all the time,' Max Skidelsky said.

'A mugging, broad daylight.'

'Nobody's safe, Christopher,' Max said. 'It's a condition of the times.'

The restaurant doorman was crossing the street to check on the victim. Blood leaked from the dog's open jaws.

The old man shook his head just as his chauffeur-driven black Continental appeared. 'It's a tragedy, Max. I can't believe we just saw that . . .'

The old man's chauffeur opened the back door of the car. 'Ready, Mr Poole?'

'I believe so,' said Christopher Poole. 'I enjoyed our

lunch, Max. In spite of . . . well, that awfully unfortunate scene.' And he stepped inside the car and the door was closed and he was whisked away back to his big air-conditioned office in Langley.

Max Skidelsky thought: *That awfully unfortunate scene.* Mild, everyday stuff, Christopher Poole, Mr Executive Director, sir. Just your common mugging. Nothing in the bigger scheme of things.

He touched the wire he wore under his shirt. It was uncomfortable and hot and it made him want to scratch himself.

He stared at the uniformed doorman stooped over the victim on the opposite sidewalk. But his head was once again elsewhere, his hyperactive mind was flying in the direction of another continent. *She's coming, Mr Poole. You may be sure of that. And if a simple mugging mortifies you, you don't know what mortification is.*

14

LONDON

Surrounded by cardboard cartons that contained his old case-files, Martin Burr spent most of each morning labouring over his memoirs in his flat in Knightsbridge. Sometimes he'd rise and pace his narrow study and, in search of the impish muse, gaze absent-mindedly out into the garden. He was new to this writing game, but he'd already come to terms with the idea that the muse was a fickle sort of slut, sometimes teasing you with a hint of wings stirring behind your back. He read what he'd written, deleted a few sentences, then closed the word processor down and wandered inside the kitchen to make a cup of tea.

His *Times* lay unread on the kitchen table. Earlier, he'd glanced at the headlines, noticed a photograph of George Nimmo. *NOTORIOUS TERRORIST CARLOTTA ACTIVE AGAIN IN ENGLAND. Scotland Yard Chief Announces Most Intensive Manhunt in History*. He adjusted his eyepatch. The whole front page was dominated by the fall-out from Nimmo's press conference. Burr looked for a mention of Pagan, but couldn't find one. Nimmo hogging the limelight. It was a sign of an undernourished ego, Burr thought.

He sank a tea bag in his cup, then plucked it out by the little string. He added a dash of milk, a packet of saccharine, and stirred. He blew across the surface of the tea. Nimmo, he thought, was going about this business in a wrong-headed way. Nothing was ever gained by instilling panic into the public. In his day, Burr would have done it quietly, no fuss, no press conferences, no TV chin-wagging.

He finished his tea and tried to stall the moment of going back inside his study. He thought of Pagan, wondered how Frank was coping. The deaths at the hotel, the supermarket bombing in Kilburn yesterday that had been reported in all its destructive glory by TV crews. *The woman.*

He went back inside his study and stared at the screen of his machine. He typed: *After my career in the Navy, I was offered the chance to . . .* Boring. Why not begin with high drama? Wasn't that the way to hook the reader? Begin with a homicide. Or a major drug confiscation from the few years he'd spent with the Drug Squad. Begin with action and blood. Yes. People liked a little blood, and the young editor who'd commissioned the book had been at pains to point out the importance of 'snagging' the reader from the very start. He began to type again in his two-fingered way, suddenly absorbed in work and unconscious of passing time.

He was disturbed after half an hour by the sound of his doorbell ringing. He found Frank Pagan on his doorstep.

'Am I interrupting anything?' Pagan asked.

'Good lord, no,' Burr said. 'In fact, I was thinking about you only an hour ago. Come in, come inside, Frank.'

Burr was glad to see Pagan. He missed his former associate more than he'd anticipated. Retirement deprived you not only of your lifetime's work, your sense of purpose, it also took your friends and colleagues away from you. Retirement was a leper colony.

Burr ushered Pagan into the drawing-room. He sensed that Pagan's mood was unsettled; Frank sometimes couldn't conceal his feelings.

'Tea? Sherry?' Burr asked.

'Not for me,' Pagan said.

'I'll just help myself then,' Burr said. Moving with the help of his walnut cane, he poured himself a small glass of sherry. 'I'm here on my own, which explains the clutter. Marcia's down at the cottage in Sussex, Doing Things. I'm not sure what. It's all very vague. Something to do with painters and local builders.'

Pagan sat on a sofa. Burr settled himself in an armchair and sipped his sherry.

'Well. Pleasant surprise to see you, Frank. What brings you here?'

Pagan, whose genuine fondness for the old man had grown all the more strong since the ascendancy of George Nimmo, took from his jacket pocket the brown envelope that had been left for him yesterday in the call-box. 'Have a look at this,' he said.

He passed the envelope to Burr, who opened it and gazed at the photograph with an expression of distaste.

'Your late wife,' he said.

Pagan nodded.

'Defaced,' said Burr. He continued to examine the photograph. It had been black and white originally, but a malicious hand had changed it. It was no simple mischief; care had been taken over the colours, great care. 'I don't have to ask who did this, do I?'

'No.' Pagan mentioned the replacement that had been left on the bedside table and the manner in which the original had been returned.

Martin Burr got up and walked back to the decanter and replenished his glass. 'So she steals a picture which is of considerable sentimental value to you and leaves one of her own in its place. And then she returns this . . .' Burr picked up the photograph and scanned it, frowning. 'It's an ugly piece of work, Frank. Profane.'

Yes, Pagan thought. Profane was a good word.

'She's made Roxanne look like a tart,' Burr said.

Tart, Pagan thought. It was a quaint term and belonged in another time. Burr had set the photograph down alongside him in such a position that Pagan couldn't help but see it.

Roxanne's mouth had been painted a deep provocative scarlet; a paler red had been used, like rouge, to adorn her cheeks; dark, finer strokes had been applied to her eyes to lengthen the lashes. The eyes were changed too, blue in a way they'd never been in her lifetime. As much as the defilement of her face appalled him, the extraordinary care that had gone into the recreation disturbed him on a deeper level. The whole thing was done with loving attention to detail. How many hours had been spent remaking Roxanne?

Burr tasted his sherry and pondered the altered photograph and his mind drifted back years to that bloody hotel room where Pagan had the woman under lock and key for a few hours, the way she'd been sitting on the bed, the suggestive brevity of her skirt, the length of luscious thigh. She was surrounded by random particles of sexuality. She gave out stunning electric signals, maps to the paradises in all the secret places of her body. She'd caused blood to rush to Pagan's head; and elsewhere, no doubt.

He hesitated a second before he said, 'When you were alone with the woman . . . I had the distinct feeling as soon as I walked through the door that I was interrupting something rather delicate. The atmosphere, shall we say, was *charged*. Decidedly so.'

You notice everything, Pagan thought. 'She attracted me.'

'Attracted, Frank? *Attracted?*'

Pagan looked away from Burr's rather bright good eye, which just then reminded him of a hawk. He'd never confided any of this to Burr before, but he felt the need now. The confessional urge: bless me, Martin, for I have sinned in my heart. 'All right. More than that. It was the only time in my life when I could literally *taste* lust. I know that sounds vague but I can't think of any other way to describe it. I admit I enjoyed the feeling. At the same time it horrified me.'

Burr smiled softly. 'Why are we so often astonished by unwanted feelings, I wonder. The older I get, the less I find surprising in the human condition. We're all cocktails of this and that, Frank. A bit of envy, something of love and charity, a dash of dark desire.'

Dark desire, Pagan thought. That described it well enough. He stood at the window. The garden at the back of the house was an extravaganza of flowers, bright colours. The way sunlight moved in shrubbery suggested presences, hidden shapes. All you need now, he thought, are delusions. Seeing her in the shaded cavities of hedgerows and rose-bushes.

Burr said, 'There's been a strong personal element involved ever since that first encounter. Something private between you and her. Not a vendetta, exactly. That isn't the word I'm searching for. Look, I may be way off the mark, and you can object if you wish, but I've often thought it was like some bizarre and violent form of extended foreplay on her part.'

Extended foreplay. Pagan turned the phrase around

in his mind. He remembered her touch on his skin the night before. The rebellious reactions of his body. He said, 'That may be the way she sees it, Martin, but along the way a lot of people are being hurt and killed. There's too much pain and too much grief. If it was just confined to her and me, I could find a way to deal with it, but it's not . . .' He was silent a while. 'She came back to my flat last night. She was waiting for me when I got home. Armed.'

'And?'

'She was only there to prove she could come and go as she pleased.'

'You might have been killed, Frank.'

'I have the impression she's not quite ready for the last act. She's turning a screw and she's tightening it a little bit each time she comes into my life. One day it can't be turned any further. We're playing this by her rules, Martin. I've done almost everything I can think of, followed all the usual procedures, ploughed through tons of material, logged thousands of miles and more. What else can I do? Hang around? Wait for her next step? I'm not built for that. I don't like being forced into that position.'

'I suppose it does no good to remind you that patience is a virtue.'

'I never saw any virtue in it.'

'No, you never did, did you?' Burr poked the rug with the tip of his walnut cane.

Pagan said, 'One unusual thing. She asked about you.'

'About me?'

'She wanted to know what you were doing in your retirement.'

'Odd,' Burr said. 'Why would she express any interest in me?'

'I get to a point where I can't explain her actions. She fades out into mystery.'

Burr was about to respond when the doorbell rang. He muttered something to himself about the nuisance of unexpected callers and got up from the sofa. 'Excuse me, Frank. I expect it's somebody collecting. It's always somebody collecting. We have more charities in this country than you can shake a stick at. Sometimes I wonder where all these contributions go . . .' He wandered toward the hallway. The doorbell rang a second time. 'Coming, coming,' he said.

He moved down the corridor, opened the door.

The woman stepped inside at once. The gun in her hand caused Burr to flinch and lurch backward and he almost lost his balance. His cane slid from his fingers and rolled along the floor and blood raced to his head. The important thing, he told himself, was calm – but he'd already shown surprise, which put him at a disadvantage. The only possible weapon had been the cane, and he could hardly grovel along the floor for it. He looked at the woman's face.

'It's been a long time,' he said.

15

LONDON

She didn't speak. She kicked the door shut behind her. For support, Burr found himself leaning against a small table. He was conscious of a porcelain vase filled with fading flowers. Wrinkled petals lay on polished mahogany and created dull reflections in the wood. He thought about Pagan inside the drawing-room, wondered if the noise of the door slamming and the cane dropping would attract him into the hallway.

'Years,' he said.

She still said nothing. She was dressed in a business-like black trouser suit with a double-breasted jacket. She wore a necktie loosely knotted. She looked, he thought, like an effeminate man, delicate, attractive if you went in for that sort of thing.

'That time . . . that time in the hotel,' he said. He wanted to play this situation with more aplomb, a little dignity, but his balance was off, he needed the cane. 'I do believe that was the last time I saw you. With Pagan.'

'Yes,' she said. 'I remember.'

'Why the gun?' he asked. He tried a little smile, but he couldn't get it right.

'Guess,' she said.

'I'm past the age of guessing games. You'll have to enlighten me,' he said.

'The sins of the past, Burr.'

'I don't follow. Sins? What sins? I seem to have committed so many along the way.' Burr, who was still labouring at a forced flippancy, turned his face briefly, looked along the hallway, saw a rectangle of sunlight on the floor where the drawing-room door lay open.

The woman had obviously followed his line of vision. She missed nothing. She gave the impression of being attuned, like a predatory animal, to any slight movement her victim might make.

'You're not alone,' she said. 'You have company, right?'

Burr gestured vaguely with his hand just as Pagan appeared in the doorway. The woman looked along the hallway and smiled. Pagan didn't move. The triangulated nature of the situation was off-centre, distorted.

'Surprise,' she said.

Pagan took a hesitant step forward. 'You keep turning up,' he said.

'It's one of my talents.'

She moved the gun, directing it at Pagan a second, then turned it back on Burr, who was thinking all kinds of desperate thoughts – how to reach for his cane and use it against her, which involved a complex sequence of movements, and he was slow with age. He stared at Pagan and frowned, hoping Pagan would have the presence of mind to retreat inside the drawing-room and lock the door and perhaps – perhaps what? Call the police? Jump from the window? Burr was beset by hopelessness. Even if Pagan made a sudden move, what good would it do? He was fifteen feet away, he couldn't reach the woman and disarm her.

'What brings you here?' Pagan asked.

'Martin Burr,' she said. 'Good old Martin.'

Burr turned to look at the woman. He managed to get an imperious note into his voice. 'Is it your intention to use that weapon?'

The woman flicked a strand of hair from her brow. The smile was absent from her face now. She had an unsettling ability to go from a bright smile to deadly seriousness in a flash. She could change right before you. Her eyes were lethal.

Pagan took another small step forward and Burr said, 'For God's sake, go back, go back, man.'

'He won't go back,' she said. 'You don't know how to go back, do you, Frank? Retreat wouldn't enter your mind, would it?'

Pagan understood he was being taunted. He watched her. 'You say you came to see Martin. Why?'

'A business transaction, Frank.'

'I know your line of business,' he said. 'I just don't see how it relates to Martin, that's all.' His voice, he knew, was calm. That was superficial. The weapon emphasized the acute uncertainty of things. The air was still and unbreathable and dangerous. He looked at the woman's black suit, the necktie, the gun in her hand. He recognized the pistol. It was the one she'd stolen from his flat. It was his own gun that was turned on Martin Burr.

She said, 'He did something wrong, Frank. Now it's time to make good again.'

'What exactly did he do?' Pagan asked.

'Martin knows,' she said. 'Don't you, Martin?'

'Afraid I haven't a clue what you're talking about,' Burr said.

'No? Let's refresh your memory. What does the name Pasco mean to you?'

'Pasco?' Burr asked.

'Richard Pasco,' she said. 'Is it coming back to you?'

Burr made a gesture with his hand that might have suggested puzzlement. Pagan couldn't be sure what the movement meant.

The woman smiled and shot Martin Burr in the leg. The abruptness of the action was startling. Burr shouted and dropped in an ungainly way to the floor and Pagan, without thinking, took a couple of steps toward the old man. He went down on his knees beside Burr. Blood flowed from the old man's shattered thigh, but he was conscious despite his obvious pain.

'Dear God,' he kept saying. 'Dear *God.*'

Pagan, trying to assess the extent of Burr's wound, placed a hand on the old man's shoulder. A gesture of comfort, the kind of touch that meant *you'll be OK, we'll get an ambulance, don't worry.* Turning, Pagan looked up at the woman.

'Why? For Christ's sake why?' he asked. 'What's the point of this—'

The woman held her arm out stiff and straight. She fired a second shot. It creased the air around Pagan's head and struck Burr in the centre of his chest. The old man's body buckled and he slumped against the wall. His blood flecked Pagan's arms. Pagan leaned to one side, lost his balance. He sat with his back to the wall and gazed at Burr, who lay motionless.

Slowly, Pagan began to rise. He was aware of a numbness in his legs, an arterial sluggishness such as you might experience in a nightmare when you can't get your limbs to respond and the horror just behind is gaining on you.

But this was no dream. You couldn't just open your eyes and the world would be all right again. You couldn't do that. He stared at Burr, then gazed at the woman. Questions crowded him, but he found speech impossible. His brain was impeded, his tongue useless. He was novocained, but the dosage wasn't enough to kill all his senses.

She said, 'You've got something to think about, haven't you?'

He watched her open the door, heard it close behind her, and when his shock had diminished to the point where he could operate, he hurried to the stairs. His sense of time was stripped down. She might have left three minutes ago, or thirty seconds. The staircase was empty and deep in shadow, and far below the glass of the street door glowed in acid sunlight. He moved to the steps and rushed downward, raced to the front door and pulled it open and went out into the burning white street. Left, right, it didn't matter. There was no sign of her. She'd disappeared in the brilliant sunshine like a night star.

16

BIARRITZ

At three p.m. she caught a flight from London to Paris.
At Heathrow there was massive armed police presence,
not just uniforms but Special Branch officers she could
spot in an instant because they had the hard-eyed look
of men who had been trained, or so they like to believe,
to detect anything out of the ordinary, evidence of
suspicious behaviour, give-away tics of menace. There
was nothing exceptional about Kristen Hawkins. If she
emitted uneasiness at all it was the standard behaviour
of a timid woman apprehensive of air flight.

Passports were scrunitized with more than usual
diligence. Officials were tense and cranky. Kristen
Hawkins carried a European Community passport
issued in London and the photograph inside bore no
resemblance to any police poster, so the examination
of her passport didn't worry her. Her document wasn't
a forgery, which might easily have been spotted, but it
was more than the validity of paper that gave her
confidence – it was a matter of self-conviction, of
believing you were the person your passport said you
were. You projected around yourself a force field of
authenticity.

She passed through the baggage examination. The
official rummaged grimly in her possessions. What was

there to see in her small suitcase anyway? Some changes of clothing, modest underwear, cleaning fluid for her glasses, simple toiletries, everything you would expect of Kristen Hawkins. She was anonymous, another guileless traveller among thousands.

From Paris she flew to Bordeaux where she rented a car, using an American Express card. She drove south through hazy sunlight. She arrived in Biarritz where the hotels along the seafront shimmered. She travelled a network of quiet backstreets where the accommodation was far less ostentatious than anything along the Grand Plage. The downside of Biarritz, decrepit little houses, stucco peeling, sun-cracked window frames.

She parked the car and got out. She took her suitcase from the back seat and followed a short path that led under a faded canopy to an open door.

She stepped inside the shadowy interior. A fan was turning. Paper streamers attached to the rim of the fan were blown backward by the blades. The room smelled of fried garlic and onions.

The man who appeared in front of her wore only a pair of outsized shorts. In one hand he held a wine bottle, in the other a glass. His lips were stained with wine.

'Galkin,' she said.

He came closer, narrowing his eyes. When he was only a few feet away from her he smiled. 'You amaze me. As always, you amaze me.' He reached for the woman's hands and held them between his sticky fingers. She allowed herself to be touched by Galkin for only a moment because there was a demonstrative side to him she didn't like to encourage, hugs, kisses, hair-stroking.

'You look spectacularly unappealing,' he said.

146

'I'm supposed to.'

'Of course you are. Of course. The grey hair. The terrible glasses. And that pallor, my God. Utterly downtrodden. Please, sit down. This is a pleasure. I cannot describe. Wine, you must have wine.'

'No. No wine.'

'I remember a time when you would not have refused,' he said. He poured a generous quantity for himself. 'To your health. So; what brings you here?'

'I wanted to see you,' she said. She sat down in a cane chair that creaked. She took off her glasses and felt warm air, propelled by blades, rush against her face. Galkin gulped his wine. Alcohol was a greased slipway to indiscretion, which was the reason she rarely drank these days.

'You've put on weight,' she said. 'You need to lose twenty pounds.'

'Age and inactivity,' he said. 'French food and wine. Time has not been kind to me. You, on the other hand, appear to have struck a bargain with the years. I look below the disguise, I see no blemishes, none of time's nasty little scars. You must have a secret, eh? A pact with the devil?'

'Yeah, a pact with the devil,' she answered. 'You must have made a few pacts of your own in recent years, Galkin.'

'I live quietly,' he said, and smiled his wary smile. 'I keep in touch with certain parties. You know how it is.'

'I know how it is,' she said. Galkin's world would be populated with redundant intelligence agents, broken-down men stripped of purpose; dreamers. Their hard currency was usually information, but more often they dealt in the counterfeits of gossip and rumour. And there would be grand plans, of course, schemes to sustain them – the rumoured possibility of freelance intelligence work in Iraq or vague promises of even more vague assignments in Central America for agencies too mysterious to name. Galkin's world was one of capsized souls.

'Talk to me about Pasco,' she said.

'Ah, Pasco. A victim of American treachery. Poor fellow. Have you decided to assist him?'

She didn't answer. She detected in Galkin a certain uneasiness. Her sudden appearance must have been the last thing he expected. Speaking to her on a telephone was one thing: he had the safety of distance. Seeing her in the flesh was altogether different. He was troubled, and trying to hide it. But she knew.

'Did he pay you for the introduction?' she asked.

'Dear lady. You do me an injustice. It was a favour – gratis – for a man who'd spent ten years of his life suffering for no reason.'

'You acted from the kindness of your heart,' she said.

'Of course.'

He was lying, of course. He wasn't adept at it. Money had changed hands somewhere along the way. There had to be profit in helping Pasco. She remembered how Galkin used to look, slim and handsome and self-assured, trim in his KGB uniform, hair always neatly combed. The downhill slide had been fast. The weather in Siberia had begun the rot; the warmth of South-West France had done the rest.

'It's wonderful to see you after all this time,' he was saying. 'And so unexpected. Out of the blue.'

'I always arrive out of the blue, Galkin. You should know that.'

'Yes, yes.'

She'd first met Galkin eight or nine years ago when

she'd gone to Moscow at the request of the Third Directorate. Would she be interested in short-term employment? Would she undertake – for a generous fee, of course – the task of bringing together what remained of the radical German underground, by then splintered and spiritless, and create a unified force out of these remnants for the purpose of certain terrorist acts in West Germany that would disrupt the prospect of German reunification? A silly scheme. The senile German underground had fallen apart in internecine bickering, for one thing. Besides, the process of reunification was inevitable, it had an emotional momentum of its own, and no number of assassinations or terrorist activities could ultimately interfere with the general public will. She'd said so at the time, and Galkin had concurred with her judgement. The scheme had been abandoned.

She'd lingered in Moscow for weeks after as Galkin's guest. On one blizzardy night they'd become lovers in her hotel room, an accidental business provoked by tedium and Crimean brandy. For her it was meaningless, a diversion, like filing your nails. Galkin, though, had taken it all with enormous gravity, wooed her with flowers and bad poems. Within days she was bored by him. He was easily demolished – a curt word, a change in her mood, these things plunged him into despair. He drank more, dabbled in the illegal currency markets, and became an easy target for his rivals inside the KGB. Welcome to Siberia, comrade.

She said, 'I resent the fact you gave my London address to a stranger, Galkin.'

'He's no stranger, dear lady, an old friend—'

'He's not *my* old friend, that's the point. I don't give a shit if he's your *soul* mate, Galkin. I don't appreciate you sending him. I like the anonymity of that house. I also get a kick out of coming and going in London without certain people knowing.'

'By certain people, you mean Frank Pagan,' he said. He smiled in a sly way. 'How apt. He hunts for you, while all the time you are on his own doorstep. You play with flame. He's become a fixation.'

She said nothing. She walked round the room, conscious of the way he watched her. She remembered Pagan's apartment, and thought how the memory of his dead wife must still vibrate inside him. Invading his life, swapping the photograph and altering the original, these small acts of desecration had been designed to undermine Pagan, to remind him he was vulnerable, to make him understand she had his number, she knew his heart.

'You are back in the newspapers in England, I see. An impressive manhunt.'

'A waste of time.'

'And Frank Pagan? What is written in the stars for him?'

'I don't believe in the stars, Galkin.'

'This fascination of yours with Pagan . . .' Galkin let the sentence drift unfinished.

Fascination. 'I want to kill him,' she said. 'It's no great mystery.'

'Ah, but we both know it's far more complicated than that. You want to kill Pagan, yes. But first, there is other business. You want also to corrupt him.'

'Corrupt him? God, you have some quaint expressions. Exactly how am I meant to *corrupt* him?'

'You demoralize him. You weaken him. And then, only then, you kill him.'

'Is that what you think?'

'You have seen the light of corruptibility in him, and this pleases you, but where is the pleasure in killing him until he has tasted degradation for himself? There is a deep cruelty in you, dear lady, and that is what keeps this business with Pagan alive. You do not enjoy the idea he might somehow manage in the end to elude you. He might contrive to emerge victorious. And so you weave your sticky little strands around him. You draw him in, a little at a time . . .'

'You make me sound like a fucking spider,' she said.

He reached for his wine and said, 'Let me go one tiny step further. This is what I see. You want to make love with him because in that act you will have dragged him into the last submission. Sex before death. Passion before murder. Orgasm and annihilation. Intimacy and destruction.'

'Orgasm and annihilation. Intimacy and destruction. If you mean I want to kill him on my own terms, you're perfectly right. I want him to see himself for what he really is.'

'And what exactly is that?'

'Somebody who likes to think he's straight as they come. Who doesn't want to acknowledge his own . . . longings, because they don't fit conveniently into his ideal of himself. He lives a lie and he won't admit it.'

'Do you desire him?'

'Desire doesn't come into it.'

'But you will take him to bed, *if* you can, and you will murder him there.'

'Maybe.' Pagan as lover. How had Galkin phrased it? *The light of corruptibility.* She'd seen that in Pagan a long time ago. She'd smelled it on him, the musk of a longing he didn't like to acknowledge. But it was there, and Pagan still carried it around inside himself like a tiny stunted bloom. She remembered the way she'd pressed the gun into his face and how hard he'd worked at remaining calm. She'd wanted to pull the trigger there and then in his apartment, to send a solitary bullet through his skull – but she'd drawn back from it, because that kind of death was easy, too easy.

Galkin said, 'So you leave a trail for Pagan to follow. He chases you. You may even give him the satisfaction of catching you. At which point . . .' He shrugged. 'Perhaps you even feel some distorted form of affection for him. Who knows?'

'Affection? I don't think so.'

'It's only theory, dear lady. Only theory.'

'Wild theory, Galkin.' *Distorted affection.* 'I need to shower,' she said. 'Journeys make me feel grubby.'

'Be my guest.' He pointed to a door on the other side of the room. 'You'll find a towel in there. And soap. Shampoo.'

She stepped inside the bathroom, a rectangle of cracked ceramic tile and peeling lime-green paint. She locked the door then turned on the water in the shower. She listened to its drumming sound briefly but she didn't undress, didn't get in. She could hear Galkin moving on the other side of the door. She regretted the old weakness in herself that had prompted her to tell Galkin about the house in London which she rented under the name of Kristen Hawkins, Kristen Hawkins who never spoke to a soul, never encouraged banter with neighbours. Why had she ever mentioned it to him? Perhaps in a moment of intoxicated intimacy before she'd wearied of him, but more likely to boast, a little arrogantly, of her ability to come and go in London as she pleased without Special Branch knowing. And with a lover's keen eye for detail he'd stashed it in the back of his mind. She'd given away something she should have kept to herself.

She stepped up onto the rim of the bidet and pushed open the window, then she lowered herself into the alley behind the house. She walked quickly. She reached the end of the lane, turned, found herself back in the street where she'd parked her car. She went toward the house, passed under the canopy, entered. She moved without sound. She had a dancer's affinity with grace and silence.

Galkin stood outside the bathroom door, his back to her. In his right hand he held an old-fashioned revolver. His body was tensed, his head inclined toward the bathroom. He was listening to the shower running, waiting for her to emerge.

Don't look round, Galkin. Don't turn your face.

She reached carefully for the wine bottle on the table and she stepped forward and raised her arm upward, which was the moment Galkin must have been alerted by something, a whisper of air, the intuition of a presence. He swung round, his mouth open in surprise, and lifted an arm across his face for protection; but the bottle was already coming down, a full dark green solid arc. It struck his forehead, glass upon bone, and he staggered back against the bathroom door.

She hit him a second time, cracking the bottle against his ribs, and he gasped. Blood ran from his forehead into his eyes. Blinded, he raised the hand that held the gun, but she slammed the bottle hard into his knuckles and the gun jumped out of his hand and clattered across the floor. He slipped to his knees, a palm pressed against the serious gash on his brow. She thought he looked like a pale pig bleeding. She picked up the gun and held it against the side of his skull.

He gazed up at her, blinking through the stream of blood. He wheezed. His hands were covered with blood. It coursed down his face and neck, created wayward little rivers on his hairless chest.

'You were going to shoot me,' she said.

He shook his head, protested. 'I intended only to protect myself, no more than that. I imagined you had come here to kill me. To silence me. Because I sent Pasco to you.'

'Get up,' she said. 'Get up on your feet.'

He rose slowly, groaning. She prodded him with the gun. The barrel sank into his belly. She forced him back against the wall.

'Dear lady,' he said. 'I swear. I had no intention of shooting you.'

'Bullshit.'

He clapped a hand to the wound on his forehead. 'You have it wrong, all wrong.'

'I don't think so, Galkin.'

He blinked, rubbed his eyes, looked at the smears of blood across his hands. 'You came here, I was scared, I admit it, I needed to take precautions. I said to myself as soon as you appeared, Galkin, she wants you dead, you know too much about her, all kinds of thoughts were swarming through my head. But believe me, I had no intention of harming you or betraying you.'

His slack lips hung open. Blood ran over his eyelids. The whites of his eyes were pink, discoloured.

'Here's the way I see it, Galkin. One day you wake up, you're running real low on the cash front, you don't know where your next bottle of *vin ordinaire* is coming from, so you make a long-distance phone call. Maybe you speak to Special Branch. Maybe you ask for Pagan—'

'No, no—'

'Maybe you think – hey, I know how I can raise some bread. I have information on a fugitive, I know she has a house in London.'

'You're wrong, oh very wrong—'

'I don't think so, Galkin.'

He looked at her imploringly. 'I would not betray you. There are no circumstances in which treachery would enter my mind—'

'Bullshit, Galkin. How much did Pasco pay you?'

'Nothing, absolutely nothing, I swear.'

She prodded him again with the gun, which vanished in the soft depths of his flesh. 'How fucking much did you get, Galkin?'

'Dear lady,' he said, and his voice was subdued. 'If you must know the truth, and I see I have no other option, I received a certain consideration from a man called James Mallory.'

'And who is James Mallory?'

'I don't know his precise affiliations—'

'Don't fucking lie to me!' She struck him then. She brought up the gun and rapped it against his mouth and his lip split and he moaned. The terror of other people fascinated her, the way they shrank from violence, the way they diminished. She liked seeing the rawness of fear, the nakedness. She watched him cower and raise a hand to his lip.

'Who the hell is Mallory, Galkin?'

Galkin tried to speak. His lip was already swelling. When he spoke he mumbled. 'Mallory asked me to send Pasco to you. It's all I know. He gave me money, I contacted you because I thought you'd be interested . . .'

'Why did Mallory come to you in the first place?'

'He knew Pasco would seek out my help. Pasco had nowhere else to turn. He and I struck up a friendship in Siberia—'

'This is pure crap, Galkin. You never met Pasco in Russia. I don't believe you and Pasco have *ever* met. Whenever he talks about you it's like he's quoting lines out of some textbook he's memorized. This is some kind of fucking set-up and I'm supposed to walk straight into it, yeah?'

'No, no, nothing like that—'

She struck him again across the mouth. There was a certain feverish pleasure in hurting him. An electricity. He'd ceased to be human. He was pulp, broken flesh. He raised a hand feebly in an attempt to deflect the blow, but he couldn't. His head jerked back. His eyes were opaque, impenetrable items of costume jewellery. He was coming apart.

'Tell me the god-damn truth, Galkin. Who is Mallory?'

'OK. The truth. He's CIA,' he said in a broken little whisper.

'He's CIA. And he comes to you, he pays you to send Pasco to me, he lays a little background on Pasco, just enough for me to believe that Pasco knew you in Russia. Why, Galkin? What's the agenda here?'

'Pasco wants revenge. And Mallory needs that revenge much as a carpenter needs a saw. But Pasco's an amateur and Mallory needs a professional, and so he links Pasco up with you. Because he knows you can do the job.'

'So I'm supposed to be working for the CIA,' she said.

'For or against,' Galkin said.

'Explain.'

'There's only ever one explanation, dear lady. Power.'

'Mallory wants some serious damage done to the Agency, and Pasco's just a convenient moron, right? Pasco happens to have a long list of grievances and Mallory would like to see these grievances avenged – why?'

Galkin blinked blood from his eyelids. 'I told you.

Power. It's always about power. The CIA plays games with itself. One faction wants the power that another faction has, and so there's friction, and friction turns to fire, and fire consumes.'

'And after I've performed my professional duties, what then? What's supposed to happen then?'

Galkin shrugged. 'I don't know.'

She took a step back from him. 'It's an easy guess. They grab me. Is that it? I'm their trophy. They can accomplish what Special Branch can't. What the Feds can't. Big triumph. Is that it? Oh, I like it, I like it, Galkin.'

Galkin quivered. He didn't speak.

'Galkin, Galkin,' she said. 'You're a treacherous little piece of shit. Give me your hand.'

'Why?'

'*Give me your hand.*'

He stretched out one trembling bloodstained hand. She wrapped her fingers around it. Then she acted so swiftly he had no time to resist, no chance to see what she was doing. She plunged his hand into the blades of the fan. Screeching, they slashed the tips of his fingers. Blood and flesh flew from the blades, spraying the air, staining the streamers of flapping paper. He pulled his hand away and, groaning, went down on his knees. The useless hand, fingers sliced and broken, hung at his side. He rolled over on his back, his eyes shut in pain, his mouth opening and closing as if far inside him were a scream he couldn't release.

She pushed the gun against the side of his head and pulled the trigger: jammed. Nothing happened. She pulled it again. Again it jammed. Galkin was crawling away from her, heading blindly for the doorway. *God help me*, he was saying. *God help me*. He left in his movement a scarlet trail of his own blood. She blocked his passage to the door and pressed the gun into his scalp, but the revolver was useless, the stiff trigger wouldn't move. She struck him with the butt of the weapon, bringing it down into his skull, and he slumped, still saying *God help me* even as she battered him a second time, a third time, with the dysfunctional gun.

He kept moving, kept trying to crawl around her, his eyes shut, his face turned toward the doorway like the snout of some blind grovelling animal. She hit him on the back of the neck and still he crawled, drawing from Christ knows what source the energy to propel himself laboriously across the floor. She reached for the fan, jerked it out of the wall and, straddling him, wrapped the electric cord around his neck, drawing it as tight as she could. He struggled, bucked, then collapsed under her as she yanked the flex harder round his fleshy neck. She snapped his face back, saw his open eyes fill first with panic and then, inevitably, with despair. Breathing hard, she held the cord tight for as long as it took.

He was a long time dying. He kicked now and then, but with decreasing strength each time. Once, he tried to get his fingers under the electric cord, but the effort was feeble. He slumped forward on his face and she stepped away from him. There was the stench in the air of his urine.

She walked inside the bathroom and peeled off her stained clothes, which she dumped in the bath-tub. She looked through the open door at Galkin, to whose neck the cord of the fan was attached. She washed her face and hands and arms. She cleaned under her fingernails. She looked at her face in the mirror. She felt very calm, very controlled, as if she'd somehow stepped out of her own body and was observing herself from the corner of the room. It was the calm of sheer indifference she felt, and indifference was just another form of liberty. She was free; and nobody could catch her unless she wanted to be caught.

She looked at her watch. She had to hurry back to Bordeaux: she had a plane to catch.

17

LONDON

George Nimmo wanted The Matter, as he called it, kept quiet. It would do no good to splash all over the newspapers the fact that Martin Burr had been shot to death by the woman. One had to think, yo, how it would reflect on the police that the former Commissioner of Scotland Yard had been murdered in his own home by the very person who was the object of an ongoing manhunt. The information was to be kept strictly in-house. The phrase to be used when it came to Martin Burr was that old standby, that reliable chestnut: *murdered by a person or persons unknown*.

It was, Pagan knew, a whitewash job, a miserable cover-up. Well, he had his own version of a cover-up under way. He'd informed Nimmo how the killing had occurred – but he'd kept back one significant detail: the name the woman had mentioned just before she'd shot Martin Burr.

Richard Pasco.

He'd never heard it before. She'd left it deliberately hanging in the air, a tease, a come-on: it was a lock she'd given him to open, if only he could figure out the appropriate combination. He'd confided this information to Foxworth. Now, as he walked with Foxworth toward Golden Square in twilight, passing under streetlamps that glowed faintly, Pagan was struck by a delayed sorrow. He'd worked hard at suppressing the graphic memory of the scene in Burr's flat, but it was impossible to keep the images in abeyance for long. In the hours that had passed since the slaying, he'd floated through events – the interview with detectives from Special Branch, the prolonged meeting with Nimmo: he'd barricaded himself from the reality. But you couldn't keep doing that.

He sat down on a bench in the square, hunched, hands on his knees. Foxworth sat alongside him. There wasn't any great need to talk. Pagan's affection for Burr had always been a given.

'I keep thinking I could have done something,' Pagan said. 'I could have intervened. I could have made some kind of effort to wrestle the gun away from her. Something. Anything.'

'She was armed. You weren't. What were you supposed to do?'

Pagan seemed not to hear this. 'All right, I could say I was shocked, everything happened so damn fast, I could say Martin's murder short-circuited me – but I'm trained to react, for Christ's sake. I'm trained to respond to situations like that.'

'You can't blame yourself.'

Pagan turned his face toward the front door of the office on the other side of the square. The building was dark, save for a light in the entranceway. He didn't want to go inside. Not yet. He was thinking of the woman. The effortless way she'd fired the gun. Not once, but twice. The first shot had been ruthless. The second had finished the old man. Pagan had lost an old friend, and he'd reached a stage of life where old friendships are precious and new ones difficult to cultivate.

He looked at Foxworth. 'She said Burr had done something wrong. She said it was time to make good again. I don't see how killing Martin could make anything good again.' Pagan gazed in the direction of his office again, thinking how the move to Golden Square had been initiated by Burr years ago, creating a place where Pagan's anti-terrorist office could be located. Burr's careful fingerprints were all over his career. 'And then she comes out with this name. Pasco. Richard Pasco. Which means nothing to me. Presumably it meant something to Martin . . . God knows what.'

Pagan slammed his hands together in a gesture of frustration. 'But she wants me to find out because she wants me to go after her. Come on, let's see what you're made of. And just to make *bloody* sure she has my full attention – as if she doesn't already know that – she comes up with some reason to kill Martin Burr.'

Foxie, who detected a note of mild hysteria in Pagan's voice, knew that the woman had eluded Frank last February in Venice, but he also understood there had been another escape many years before, when Pagan had been holding her in a London hotel room. Somehow she'd managed to get away. Dressed as a maid, a bribe to a porter – nobody had discovered how she'd done it.

Pagan got up from the bench. He moved slowly across the square. Foxworth followed. Inside the building Sergeant Whittingham was behind the desk, pretending to be busy. His big ruddy Devonshire face was sombre. He looked like a farmer at a funeral.

'Shocking business, Mr Pagan,' he said. 'Shocking. I always liked Mr Burr. There was nothing high and mighty about him.'

Pagan moved toward the elevator. It was a fair

assessment. Martin had never lost the common touch. He'd always taken an enormous interest in the welfare of his people. Unlike Nimmo, he hadn't courted favours from the powerful. He'd avoided politics and all the donkeylike braying involved. He believed, as Pagan did, in an uncomplicated notion of justice. He might have approached it in a different manner – quietly, with less of a headstrong impulse – but the goal was the same.

Pagan listened to the elevator creak in the shaft, the straining of pulleys. When he yanked the iron door open and stepped out, he headed along the darkened corridor to his office, where he turned on the light. The room was bright and unappealing. The photographs on the walls seemed to reproach him for his failure to protect Burr.

'Do me a favour, Foxie,' Pagan said. 'Take them down.'

Foxie unpinned the pictures and stacked them on the corner of Pagan's desk. Bare walls. A kind of exorcism.

Pagan didn't hear Marcia Burr enter the office.

'Frank.'

He stood up. 'Mrs Burr,' he said. He moved around his desk and reached out to take her hands, which were cold and glassy.

Marcia Burr was in her early fifties, fourteen or fifteen years Martin's junior. Normally she carried herself in a sprightly straight-backed manner. But tonight she wore no make-up, her cardigan was wrongly buttoned – the carelessness of grief, Pagan thought – and she slouched. Pagan held her hands and said nothing. Words didn't present themselves. He resented the inadequacies of language.

'You were there,' she said. 'You were with him.'

Pagan nodded. Marcia Burr stepped away from him. Foxworth helped her into a chair, holding her elbows gently and easing her down.

'I don't want details,' she said. 'I couldn't live with details. Don't tell me what it was like.'

Pagan said nothing.

'It hasn't hit me yet, you know. It hasn't quite sunk in. They say it takes time before you actually realize . . .' She looked at Pagan. She had the pinched appearance of the newly-bereaved. 'Martin was very fond of you, Frank. Sometimes he called you his best student. Sometimes he cursed you, too, but always with affection. Pagan is the bane of my life, he'd say. Never listens. In one ear and out the other. He'd thunder at you, but he didn't ever mean it in a harsh way. I think you understand.'

Pagan said he did.

'He was very proud of some of the things you achieved,' she said. 'He would never have told you to your face. But I know. We talked about his work frequently. I was rather like a sounding board for him.' She smiled softly, then inclined her head and covered her face with her hands. She didn't cry. She was the kind of woman who would yield to grief only in private. Public sorrow was without dignity. Pagan had the stranded sensation of being a witness to someone else's heartache. He watched her take a Kleenex from the sleeve of her cardigan and press it against her lips.

'He was so busy trying to organize his memoirs. He hated retirement, you know. He once said it made him feel utterly useless. I suppose the memoirs filled a space. Between ourselves, I doubt if he'd ever have finished writing them . . .' She stared at the Kleenex in her hand, as if it puzzled her. She was, Pagan realized, miles away, lost perhaps in a recollection. She crumpled the tissue into a wad and let it fall from her fingers. 'You'll find her, Frank.'

'Yes,' Pagan said.

'I know you'll find her.'

Pagan had a longing to destroy something, to perform an act of mindless vandalism, like kicking a hole in the wall, or throwing a telephone through the window. Something energetic yet ultimately useless. A sign of life, a vicious little pulse.

Pagan moved toward her. He lowered his body so that his face was level with hers. He laid his fingertips on her wrist. Her skin was suntanned. 'I have one question for you, if you're up to it,' he said. 'Did he ever mention anyone by the name of Pasco to you? Richard Pasco.'

'Pasco? Why? Is it important?'

Pagan said it was. Marcia Burr looked around the office. She said, 'I don't believe he ever did. No. I can't remember the name. Perhaps . . .' There was a very faint trace of her origins in her accent. Pagan remembered she'd been born and raised in the United States – Ohio, Iowa, he wasn't sure. But she'd been in England so long the accent had almost entirely vanished inside the consonants and vowels of the Home Counties.

The unshaded light in the room created little pockets of darkness under her eyes. 'Perhaps it's in his files. He's got boxes of them. Tons of papers. I always complained about the clutter he made. You're welcome to look, Frank. If it helps.' She opened her purse and removed a key, which she handed to him. 'That's the key to the flat in Knightsbridge. If you need to go through his files, please, feel free. I'll spend the night in London, but I'll go down to Sussex first thing in the morning. Do you have the phone number in case you need to get in touch with me?'

'I can find it,' Pagan said.

Marcia Burr stood up. She was a little unsteady. She leaned toward Pagan, who caught her, holding her against his body. Small comfort. He walked with her to the door and along the corridor to the elevator. She kissed him on the side of his face. Her mouth was chilly.

'Don't bother to come down,' she said. 'I'll manage. I'll ask your desk sergeant to find me a taxi.'

'You sure?'

'I have to get accustomed to being on my own, Frank. I have to get accustomed to a great many changes.' Pagan opened the elevator door for her. She stepped inside. He drew the door shut and looked at her through the iron grating.

'Do it, Frank,' she said. 'Find her.'

'I promise you.'

The elevator shuddered, and began its whining descent. Pagan lingered a moment, listening to the mechanism of the lift, then went back to his office.

'Sad,' Foxie said.

Pagan thought of the woman wandering out into the night. He considered the sudden emptiness in her life. Sad. More than sad. But her appearance had the effect of stirring him out of the vapours of sorrow; she'd animated him, and now he had to shake off the unhappiness he felt, because Burr wouldn't have wanted him to dwell on anything so self-indulgent. The work at hand, Martin would have said. Nothing else matters. Only the work.

'Let's go upstairs, Foxie,' he said. 'Let's see if we have anything on Pasco.'

★ ★ ★

They left the office and went toward the staircase that led to the top floor where the computers were located. Pagan had little affinity for these machines, but Foxworth knew his way around them.

Foxie switched on a light and sat down in front of a machine and pressed the power button. He rubbed his hands together briskly and lowered them over the keyboard and punched in the code-word that gave him access to the mainframe, which not only contained internal data, but was linked to other sources of law-enforcement information in Europe, the United States, the Far East. There was a whirring sound and the word READY blinked, with manic electronic urgency, on the screen.

Foxworth located the program he needed, and typed in a second password, followed by the name: *Pasco, Richard*. The machine whirred, then responded after a prolonged searching period. *No record*.

'Zero, Frank,' Foxie said. 'No criminal record here or anywhere else.'

Zero. Pagan walked toward the shadows in the corner of the room. Windows overlooked the square, which was empty. Two thirty a.m., and nothing moved down there. Zero. He tried to think his way inside her mind. She killed, and she enjoyed killing. She destroyed, and was in love with destruction. He forced himself to imagine how it would feel if you were enchanted by murder, if you loved the sensation of snuffing out somebody's life – but it was too far away for him to grasp. Another zero.

What motivated her? The pleasure of cruelty, yes. The gamble of risky killings, sure. The idea of eluding her pursuers, certainly. Did she consider herself immune to capture? Flip the coin: did she want to be captured? Did it all come down to something as simple as the elemental thrill of the chase in the end, the adrenalin of the hunt?

He brought back to mind the way she'd looked when she'd fired the pistol at Martin Burr. It was the expression of somebody on a target range, concentrated, focused; and yet there was more – an indifference, as if the target were not human but an inanimate thing, a clay pigeon. There had been a certain . . . *serenity*, in her look. He couldn't think of another word. Another thing struck him: even in the act of killing, she'd shed none of her beauty, no ugly frown, no determined distortion of the lips, as if she were utterly detached from what she was doing. She was in another realm, a world she'd created for herself.

He turned to Foxworth and asked, 'Could Pasco be listed under some other heading? Another file, say?'

'It's possible, Frank.'

'Try Martin's name. See if you can find any mention of Pasco under Burr.'

Foxworth did so. The machine was silent for a time. Then it responded with *Burr, Martin*, followed by a list of dates – the year he joined the Yard, the years he spent in charge of the Drug Squad, his various promotions up to the rank of Commissioner. *Retired 1993*. There was a series of messages directing the computer operator to sub-files where more detailed information on the old man's career could be found. Pagan was about to instruct Foxworth to start searching these secondary files when he noticed, at the bottom of the screen, a brief message. *THIS FILE LAST ACCESSED 3 SEPTEMBER 1995, 0930*.

'This morning,' he said, and pointed his finger at the message. 'Somebody looked at this bloody file only today. A few hours before Martin was murdered. Who?'

Foxie was gazing at the screen. 'It had to be somebody who knew the codes, Frank.'

'How many people are we talking about, Foxie?'

'God, dozens, I suppose.'

'Is there any way of narrowing it down?'

Foxie was quiet for a moment. 'I'm not sure—'

'Think, Foxie. There's got to be some way of finding out who broke into Martin's file. It's too much of a coincidence that somebody accessed the material on the morning of his death. I'm not happy with coincidences at the best of times – and this, God only knows, isn't the best of times.'

Foxie pushed his chair back from the computer. He was aware of Pagan's sudden energy as if it were a force field. 'There's a code for backtracking through logs,' he said. 'I've never used it before, but I can try.'

'Try then.'

Foxie hunched over the keyboard. 'I might screw it up, of course. Lose some data.'

'I'll take the chance,' Pagan said. He stared at the screen, drawn into its light.

Foxie pondered the keyboard. He pressed a couple of keys in unison. The computer didn't respond.

'What's happening?' Pagan asked.

'So far, nothing. Let me think.' Foxie placed his fingertips against his lips and contemplated the screen. There were certain key combinations, he knew that much, but it depended on getting them correct. An operational manual was kept at the Yard, but you had to sign in triplicate to get it, and at this time of night that involved awakening a senior officer who wouldn't be overjoyed by a disturbance.

'Are you thinking?' Pagan asked.

'Damn, yes, I'm thinking—'

'Think deeper,' Pagan said, impatiently. 'I want to know who looked at Martin's files.'

Foxie raised his hands over the keyboard again. Pagan's hovering made him nervous. Another combination of strokes – OK. He punched two keys simultaneously. The screen blackened a moment, then was filled with a slightly startling amber light.

'Abracadabra,' he said.

Pagan leaned even closer to the screen. A series of black letters fluttered across the amber background. *Inquiry Log. Enter request.* Foxie tapped out a series of letters and the screen flashed a couple of times and Pagan, more tense than he realized, was transfixed by the video console.

'Here we are,' Foxworth said. 'The source of the inquiry isn't named. The only thing recorded here is the telephone number used to gain access to the computer line. Zero one seven one six two five eight eight five six.'

'London,' Pagan said. 'So all we need is an address.'

Foxie located a reverse directory and began to search through its pages. Pagan, restless, moved away from the glare of the screen. Somebody hacks into the computer, opens Martin's file. For what?

Foxie found what he was looking for. 'Kilburn again. Number 36 Brondesbury Terrace. Somebody called Kristen Hawkins.'

Kilburn, Pagan thought.

And he heard the woman's voice zone in from nowhere, uttering the words he'd last heard her say in wintry Venice when she'd escaped from him. He remembered the canal, the black waters parting with the force of her body, the damp scent of the night.

Catch me.

18

LONDON

In her room at The Dorchester, Marcia Burr thought grief the most devastating emotion of all: numbing, numbingly final. Recovery was never complete. A part of you simply failed to come back from the trenches of loss.

She'd taken two sleeping-pills but they'd managed only to make her groggy. Such defences as she had against the fact of Martin's murder were fragile. What was strange was her inability to shed tears; she supposed they'd come later, perhaps at the funeral, perhaps when she met her son Kenneth who was flying in from Hong Kong, or when she was obliged to go through Martin's belongings, the shirts and shoes and suits, all the relics of his life. What did you do with a dead husband's possessions? What did you do with your *own* life?

She picked up the telephone and called room service. She asked for hot chocolate to be sent up. Then she took the bottle of sleeping-pills out of her purse; she'd swallow another one as soon as the hot chocolate arrived.

She rose, walked the room, glanced at her face in the mirror and thought how small and lonely, how bedraggled, she looked. Self-pity: she wouldn't give in to that. She'd always been sensible, practical, far more down-to-earth than Martin. God knows, for a man in his position he'd been uncommonly vague, absent-minded. Half the time he seemed elsewhere. Had he been the one to survive her, he would never have managed the rudiments of basic living, the little intricacies that constituted a life.

The room service waiter came. She tipped him generously. When he'd gone she popped the sleeping-pill in her mouth and sipped some hot chocolate. She sat on the edge of the bed and wondered at the silence in the room; it was vast, immeasurable, as if all sound had been drained out of the world.

It was a chilling revelation to understand that for as long as you lived you would never see your husband again. She shut her eyes and said his name aloud.

'Martin. Dear Martin.'

She wondered about the notion of the recent dead lingering invisibly nearby, their souls still bound in a mysterious way to the trappings of life. Was Martin close? Was he listening? She liked to think so.

She turned her wedding ring round, twisting it, seeing how the flesh around it swelled because it was too tight ever to remove. She wouldn't dream of taking it off anyway. She tilted her head slightly to one side in the fashion of someone who has detected an unexpected presence nearby.

'Martin,' she said. 'If you're listening, forgive me.'

He's listening, she thought. *He is listening.*

She gazed around the room as if for some small sign of him, a quiet movement perhaps, the shiver of curtains, a cloud crossing the mirror. Nothing. Of course there was nothing. She was sick, deluded by grief. But she sensed her husband anyway, his nearness, the tap of his cane, the awkward way he moved.

'Forgive me for lying to Pagan,' she said. 'I was trying to protect you, Martin.'

19

LONDON

Richard Pasco heard footsteps on the stairs. They were light and unhurried. He didn't know how long the woman had been gone. He'd slept, wandered the house, looked inside rooms – most of which were unfurnished. At one point he'd wondered if she'd simply gone away, abandoned him. Maybe she'd come back when he was sleeping, then left again, he didn't know. The skylight was dark. He sat on the edge of the bed. His chest ached. The ulcers in his mouth stung.

The door opened. The woman on the threshold of the room wasn't the one he expected. She moved toward the bed, stood looking down at him. Her hair was reddish-brown and hung to her shoulders. She was, Pasco thought, a looker, the kind who might take your breath away, the sort you'd turn your head to appreciate on the street. It was a long time since Pasco had felt anything of a sexual nature; that part of his life had been eclipsed. He looked up into her face, saw how light reflected against pink lipstick and glowed in the soft contours of her hair. It was hard to estimate her age. Middle thirties at least, possibly zoning in on forty; she carried time beautifully. Her neck was smooth, and such faint lines as she had on her face seemed to enhance her.

He concealed his hands in his pockets. The woman smiled at him. It was a sympathetic expression, as if she understood that the disfigurement of his hands embarrassed him. She moved closer to him. He lay very still, waiting for her to speak, but she appeared perfectly content just to watch him. It was strange how comfortable he felt. Her scrutiny of him was a gentle business.

'Don't get up,' she said.

Pasco, who had started to rise, obeyed. He wasn't sure why he was feeling this contented. With the other woman, he'd moaned and bitched about the urgency of his business, but with this one he felt no such inclination. She emanated a confidence of manner. She appeared to be at peace with herself. She had elegance, not the kind that overwhelmed and intimidated you, the remote kind you saw in fashion magazines, but something understated.

She sat on the edge of the bed. She was still smiling at him. She raised a hand and pushed a lock of hair back from her face. Then she let the hand fall upon his leg and left it there and Pasco felt a flush of intimacy. He wouldn't go so far as to pretend she might be interested in him physically, but the touch was nice.

'How are you feeling?' she asked.

Pasco's lips were dry, 'I guess I've been sleeping most of the time. Where's the other woman?'

She placed her fingertips on his mouth for silence. 'She's gone. It's my business now.'

Pasco closed his eyes. Her touch, her proximity, he could lose himself in all this, he could forget his wasted years, he could perhaps even forget the fanatical need for retribution that had so possessed him. He'd settle for this brief illusion of belonging somewhere.

'I'll take care of it all for you,' she said. She brought

her face very close to his. Her breath was clean and warm.

'I need to go away for a few days,' she said.

'Why?'

'There are certain preparations, Richard.'

'Yeah, of course,' Pasco said.

'I can't take care of all your business by staying here. And I can't take you with me this time.'

'But you'll come back.'

'Of course I will. Then we'll travel to America together. You didn't think I'd just go away and not come back, did you? There's plenty of food in the kitchen. I brought you some books. I also stopped at a pharmacy, got you some painkillers and cough medication.'

Pasco shook his head. Something ghosted through his mind just then, a quiet shiver of recognition, as if somewhere he'd met this woman before, only he didn't know where or when. A familiarity, and yet not.

Pasco felt the woman's mouth touch his lips lightly a moment. He shut his eyes again. Old longings burned inside him. The darkness was sweet. Her fingertips moved to his lips, parting them slightly. Then he felt her hand go to his groin and he was instantly hard, too many years had passed without love, without sex, without affection. He imagined that if she were to slip her hand inside his fly he'd explode. He was burning.

He smelled her perfume and it reminded him of something, something in his recent experience – Yes. He had it. The scent was suggestive of crushed raspberries, the death of autumn, the tang in the air of winter. He opened his eyes in surprise.

'*You*,' he said.

⋆   ⋆   ⋆

She knew she didn't have much time, that she was already pushing her good fortune, and yet this knowledge charged her with excitement. The need to move, to move rapidly, to get out of this house that was no longer safe. She'd only dressed and changed her appearance for Pasco because she wanted to bring him a moment of quiet arousal, a little flash in the gloom of his life. Call it a gift. She changed her clothes and her make-up quickly, rearranged her hair, then hurried from the house and drove until she came to an all-night cafeteria on the outskirts of London.

She went inside, bought a cup of coffee, carried it to a table. The big fluorescent room was deserted. On the wall before her was a poster with a photograph and the question *Have You Seen This Woman*? The photograph depicted a face too harshly lit, creating a misleading impression of gauntness.

Her attention was distracted by two uniformed cops entering the room. They went to the counter, ordered cups of tea, carried them to a table a few yards from her. They lit cigarettes and sat hunched over their teacups like a couple of tired conspirators.

She was conscious of one of the cops gazing at her, a beefy man with a trim black beard. She met his eyes briefly, then looked away. She was aware, on the periphery of her vision, that he was rising from his chair and moving in her direction. What was there to see? A plain woman dressed in a cheap dun-coloured lightweight coat, no stockings, a pair of flimsy sandals. Nothing special. She gazed into her coffee just as the policeman's shadow fell across her table.

'Excuse me, miss.'

She looked up at him. She ran a hand through her hair, which was pulled back tightly. She knew she had the complexion of a pumice-stone. She adjusted her glasses, which pinched the bridge of her nose.

'You don't mind me asking if you have any form of identification on you, do you?' He had a deep pleasant voice. He seemed slightly embarrassed by his question.

'I don't mind, Sergeant.'

'Constable,' he said. 'Constable Graham.'

'Am I suspected of some illegal deed?' she asked.

The cop smiled. 'Nothing like that. We're looking for somebody.'

'Of course.' She opened her purse. 'The woman in the poster,' and she gestured toward the wall. 'I follow the news.'

The constable reached out to take the driver's licence she offered him. He studied it a few seconds, checking the picture against her face. She wondered if he sensed anything about her, if she emitted some kind of strange vibration – like a tuning-fork – a barely audible buzz that might alert him. But he had no affinity for hidden nuances. He intuited nothing, none of the dangerous fire inside her. He was a policeman ploughing through his daily grind, devoid of insight, and no challenge to her.

'You don't think I look like *her*, do you?' she asked. 'She's so . . . I don't know, well, glamorous.'

'She's glamorous all right, Miss Hawkins.' He handed the licence back. 'Sorry to have troubled you. We have to check.'

'No trouble,' she said. She put the licence back in her purse and shut the clasp. She watched the constable go back to the table where his colleague sat. They finished their tea and went outside.

A manhunt, she thought. Exhaustive. No stone left unturned. She finished her coffee, set the cup down, gazed through the window across the parking-lot. The police car was driving away.

She looked round the empty room, watched the cook in his grubby white uniform wipe down a stainless steel grill. Much of her life was spent in places such as this. All-night cafeterias, airless waiting-rooms in railway stations, ferry ports. There was always a sense of time suspended in these places. Lonely travellers, salesmen, hikers with backpacks, odd types who clutched books about Etruscan ruins or bird-guides to the Algarve.

The anonymity of transient places appealed to her. She could be anyone she liked. Withdrawn and moody, unapproachable, brooding over something too deep to explain. If the whim moved her, she could be mildly gregarious, indulging in the kind of idle gossip people in transit usually shared. Weather, timetables, this hotel or that, a restaurant recommended. It sometimes happened a man would indulge in a slight flirtation with her, and she'd despise the empty chatter and the fake smiles and the way a hand would linger a second too long on her arm. At these times she was conscious of abrupt changes inside herself; it was as if she suddenly lost altitude and something in her head popped and she wasn't the person she'd been only minutes before. A shifting took place, and she was somebody else. Kristen Hawkins, for example. A dowdy woman in heavy-framed glasses, she projected dullness. She wasn't the kind who'd attract strangers. The slight downturned set of her lips suggested a lifetime of emotional parsimony. Kristen Hawkins might have given her heart only once, and then to somebody who'd crudely mishandled it, and now she preferred her own company. She wore her disappointment like a brooch.

Identity was all loose surfaces anyhow. You could slip and stumble on the uncertain shale of identity. Besides, where was it written that you had to be the same person all the time? The tedium, the predictability, the maintenance of a constant self was a chore. She was in a state of permanent flux. Nothing was real. Nothing bolted down. It wasn't that she acted out roles: she became other people. It was a form of possession. Even her memories, those roots of self, were uncertain things, images seen through clouded glass.

She found herself thinking for some reason of her parents: how long was it since she'd seen them? Years and years. Were they dead or alive? She didn't know. She pictured her father, that mad blind ranting bigot; and her mother, a gauzy drunken belle whose face she couldn't bring to mind, but she could hear the light tinkling voice going on about how things had been better in the old days when servants were never a problem and the blacks knew where their bread was buttered, and how that Luther King fellow had just about wrecked everything, and on, and on.

She remembered the house, the creepy old mansion where they'd locked her in the basement when she'd misbehaved, and how one time they'd sent her away to some clinic where she'd stayed for three months, *for your own good, sweetheart, you understand, don't you . . .* ? The guy in the clinic, Dr Lannigan, had asked her questions, stupid questions, what do you think of your parents, do you love your mother, does your father communicate with you, dumb-ass questions. When he wasn't asking questions Lannigan was giving her downers and she'd pretend to let him hypnotize her and he'd put his hand under her skirt and play with her clitoris, which she'd enjoyed, even though she had to pretend she wasn't feeling anything.

She thought of poor, sad, broken Pasco: yes, yes, she'd be his angel of vengeance, not because she felt any sense of duty or obligation to him – these were moral imperatives, ridiculous concepts – but because the presumptions of the man known as Mallory amused her. The arrogance of the CIA amused her. They thought they could use her and that when they'd done that they'd *capture* her – like a minor piece in a board-game? Just like that? She smiled at the notion, at the conceit of it. The idea of anyone capturing her – the FBI, Special Branch – it was inconceivable. She felt immune to the dangers around her, the pack that pursued her. She was above them. She soared in other realms. She wasn't earthbound.

But it was more—

There was a delicious symmetry the past sometimes threw into the present, old accidents of fate that turned out years later to have a design that could never have been predicted at the time of their occurrence. Martin Burr and Richard Pasco. That was a perfect example of how these streams of events, simmering quietly away for years in subterranean places, surfaced and conjoined. And then there was Pagan, who wouldn't let the killer of Martin Burr stray too far away from him. No, Pagan would hunt her, Pagan would chase her to the ends of the world, because he knew no other way. Because, like herself, he couldn't walk away from unfinished business.

The CIA and Frank Pagan: two birds, one slingshot.

She shifted the angle of her face, her attention drawn to a calendar on the wall. It depicted a bright primrose. The colour induced a sudden sharp headache. She shut her eyes, tried to quieten the pain. But there was an erosion inside her, something giving way. She thought of mine shafts collapsing. The yellow of the primrose was burning into her. Even with her eyes shut she retained a vivid impression of the colour.

She sensed slippage in herself, as if she were tumbling through cracks of identity. Kristen Hawkins. The girl Carlotta who'd been born in a decrepit old plantation house in North Carolina. Other incarnations down the years. Alyssia Baranova, Russian security agent in Venice. Caroline Starling, who'd once dynamited a train ferrying weapons to San Diego. Karen Lamb, the London underground bomber. Carmen Profumo, pastry-chef. An uneasy splintering was going on. She had the strange feeling of racing toward a void where she'd cease to exist entirely.

The yellow – it reminded her of something unpleasant and painful. She opened her eyes, *yes, she had it* – the shrink they'd sent her to when she'd been incarcerated briefly in Danbury, the guy with the putty-coloured face and an air of professional sympathy, the way she'd been strapped to a table as if to be made ready for execution, the wires that ran from a box to the sides of her head, the cold feel of petroleum jelly, the plastic disc inserted between tongue and palate – and then, then the hideously stunning jolt of electricity, the rip of current through her skull, the scrambling of images and perceptions, and the pain, the God-awful yellow pain, that cutting serrated yellow pain.

She rose and went outside. She needed the night air. She walked to her car. The headache passed, the outbreak of panic was over. She stood directly under the big sign that said OPEN 24 HOURS and she thought about Pagan and the trail she'd left for him.

20

LONDON

Number 36 Brondesbury Terrace was a Victorian redbrick house in a cul-de-sac. Foxie parked the car across the street from the front door. Pagan was already climbing out and heading in the direction of the house, which was in darkness. He walked up the path and Foxworth, wondering at Pagan's lack of stealth, the way he allowed himself to yield to urgency, followed.

Pagan rang the doorbell. Nobody answered. The house was silent, a dead house, black windows.

Pagan tried the door handle. Locked. He rang the bell again. Again there was no answer.

'You want to do the honours?' he asked Foxworth.

'Why not,' Foxie said. He went back to the car and returned with a tyre-lever and an old oil-stained sheet. He wrapped the tyre-lever inside the sheet and tapped the window a couple of times in a gentle manner and the glass broke. Pagan carefully picked out a few remaining slivers and climbed through the space, and Foxie clambered in behind him.

'Find a light switch,' Pagan said, stumbling into an item of furniture.

Foxie fumbled around the room, reached a doorway, flicked a switch. 'Lo and behold. And there was light.'

The room they'd entered was airless, stuffy, plainly furnished. No sense of permanence. A place to stay a night or two, nothing more. A convenience. The walls were unadorned, the wallpaper faded. The kitchen, which they entered next, contained a few items of cheap Formica furniture, an old gas stove, an antique refrigerator. If houses could be said to reflect the souls of those who inhabited them, this one couldn't have told you much about its tenant's personality.

They left the kitchen, entered what was clearly a sitting-room. Couch, a couple of shabby armchairs, a table, thin curtains hanging at the window.

On the table lay a paintbox and a tiny sable brush. The paintbox was labelled *Photo Technology*. Pagan studied the brush, which had been meticulously cleaned, and imagined her sitting in this room, labouring diligently over her warped reworking of Roxanne's portrait, stroke after fastidious stroke.

'This is the place,' he said. 'This is Carlotta's lair.'

Carlotta's lair, the centre of her web. He wondered how long she'd been in this house, how long she'd lived in this part of London – leading, at least superficially, an ordinary life, surrounded by ordinary neighbours, walking the streets, going inside stores, being to all intents and purposes normal, unremarkable – and yet knowing all the time she was running the risk of discovery. He imagined it delighted her. He thought it thrilled her, this domicile in a city where she was sought after by law officers, and her photographs appeared in newspapers. Living on an edge, and loving it.

They explored the downstairs rooms, ransacked the drawers of a bureau and found nothing of interest. A few bills addressed to Kristen Hawkins, no personal mail. Kristen Hawkins, Pagan thought. Another new alias. Hawkins was close to hawk, but far enough removed that the name wouldn't jump up at him out of a computer as one of her likely aliases.

They went upstairs where there were a number of small rooms, most of them unfurnished. In what had obviously been Kristen Hawkins's bedroom, there was a big double bed with a red velvet quilt, a wardrobe, a dressing-table with an oval mirror.

The drawers of the dressing-table contained a large arsenal of make-up, lipsticks, powders, dozens of cylinders and small jars of cream and powders. Hair-brushes, eyebrow pencils, several pairs of glasses, bottles of hair colouring preparations, rinses. Inside a small plastic box were contact lenses of different colours: blues, greys, greens. The bottom drawer was stuffed with an assortment of wigs: short, long, black, blond, grey.

Seated in front of this very mirror, Pagan thought, she must have studied her own reflection hundreds of times from hundreds of angles, applying a touch of make-up here, there, experimenting with lipsticks, changing the colour of her eyes, brushing her hair in different styles, trying on wigs. Her life was a kind of spillage in which identities ran one into another.

Inside the wardrobe was an array of clothing, most of it unappealing, mass-produced beige slacks, pleated skirts in autumnal colours with chain-store labels, matching blouses, cardigans, sandals, unfashionable shoes. Kristen Hawkins had been carefully thought out, an innocuous woman you wouldn't look at twice. A little shy, lacking self-confidence, tiptoeing through life as if she expected at any moment to be startled by a sudden movement: he could imagine Kristen Hawkins.

At the back of the wardrobe, half-hidden, hung the sharply-tailored black business suit she'd worn when she'd killed Martin Burr; Pagan reached in, touching the material of the garment as if he were somehow compelled to do so. Alongside the black suit were several cocktail dresses with designer labels. One was bright and spangled and glistened faintly; another was red and bold with a low-cut neckline. Underwear was scattered on the floor of the wardrobe – flimsy silken things crumpled together, some transparent, some exotic. An entanglement of erotic garments. Pagan looked, felt the rush of an intimacy he didn't want, then closed the door.

Foxie said, 'The lady in the magician's cabinet. Now you see her, now you don't.'

Pagan wandered out of the bedroom and along the landing, and Foxie followed. A flight of steps led up to an attic room. He climbed, thinking how the atmosphere of this house settled on him like a weight. He paused outside a door, pushed it open, entered a bedroom with a skylight. Foxie came just behind him.

'Christ,' Foxie said.

The man who lay on the bed had been shot directly through the mouth. His face was gone. Pagan noticed the bloodstains on the pillows and the wall. He stared at the dead man's hands, which were covered with ugly scar tissue. Several fingernails were missing. Death, of which he'd seen so much, still sickened Pagan. He'd never developed an immunity toward it. He forced himself to look at the bloodstains. They hadn't had time to darken.

'He hasn't been dead long,' he said. 'An hour, maybe two.' He turned and walked away from the bed and stood at the other side of the small room, where there was a fireplace in which something had recently been burned. He poked among the ashes, retrieving a couple of scorched documents, both of which he held rather delicately between thumb and forefinger, as if they might disintegrate under his touch. He gazed at a smoke-stained photograph stuck to a page whose edges had been blackened by flame.

'What is it?' Foxie asked.

'An American passport made out in the name of Richard Pasco.' Pagan studied the photograph a moment, trying to make connections. Then he looked at the remains of the other document; a bank-book, issued by Barclays, Pasco's name on the first page. The other pages, which recorded deposits and withdrawals, were illegible. 'Pasco comes here – why? Does he need Carlotta?'

'She only provides one kind of service, Frank,' Foxworth said. 'Destruction.'

'And Pasco needed her for that – why? what kind of destruction? Just to kill Burr? What for? Where does Martin come into the picture?'

Foxie shrugged. He glanced at the dead man, then looked back at Pagan. 'Until we know a little more about Pasco, all we can do is make wild surmises.'

Pagan was still examining the passport as if it might contain further information. It had been issued in Washington DC, but the date of issue was scorched. He moved back toward the bed and looked down at Pasco and drew a sheet across the man's shattered face.

Foxie said, 'She didn't do a very thorough job of burning the passport, did she?'

'No, she didn't.' Deliberately so, Pagan thought. A sign. Something she'd left behind for him. An arrow he was intended to follow. 'Let's get out of this room.'

They went out together to the landing. Foxie shut the door behind him. They descended, entered the sitting-room.

Pagan stood at the table where the brush and paintbox lay. Suddenly it seemed to him that the house was filled with echoes of her movements, her hands working the brush in whispered strokes, the slither of clothing sliding from her flesh as she undressed, the creak of the mattress as she climbed into bed: she was everywhere and nowhere, indistinct, lingering in impenetrable shadows. The house, a place of death, unsettled him.

Pagan sat down at the table and idly picked up the paintbrush and was overcome by an unnerving feeling. He didn't believe in psychic vibrations, but he experienced something inexplicable for a fraction of time – the sense that Carlotta's hand was covering his own as he held the brush, a ghostly touch. Puzzled, troubled, he dropped the brush on the table and the feeling dissolved as quickly as it had arrived. A little shaken, he stood up. Call it an off-centre moment, he thought. Call it the imagination working on over-load, circuits temporarily rearranged, sleight of mind. However you named it, it spooked him.

He rose, wandered the sitting-room, tried to slow the rhythms of his thoughts. On the far side of the room a curtain had been drawn across a closet, and he drew it aside out of curiosity. A computer and a modem sat on a small desk that occupied the tiny cubicle. It was from here that she'd hacked her way inside the Yard computer system. He imagined her punching keys, plundering data: anything stored in the system would be available to her with a few keystrokes, as long as she had the passwords. How had she discovered the entry codes? he wondered – but the question wasn't one that occupied him for long. *She can do almost anything*, he thought. Obstructions were meaningless to her. Obstacles didn't exist, or if they did she found some way around them.

His attention was drawn to a slip of paper stuck to

the keyboard. He removed it, stared at the message. He handed the paper to Foxie. It read: *TURN ON, SEE PAGAN*.

Foxie switched the machine on, typed the letters of Frank's last name. The screen was immediately filled with a grainy photograph of Pagan's flat – the bedroom, the unmade bed, the indented pillows; and Carlotta, legs spread apart, sat on the edge of the mattress. Her blouse was undone, her breasts visible. Her hands were cupped just under her breasts, elevating them slightly. On the bottom of the screen was the caption: *SELF-PORTRAIT, PAGAN'S BEDROOM*. Pagan stared at this a moment, drawn into the provocative pose, which seemed to him to have been staged in a deliberately tacky manner, like a cheap porn-shot in a low-budget skin magazine. Her face was tilted backward so that she looked toward the camera lens at an angle. She was smiling; a glossy-lipped come-on. How many hours had she spent in my flat? he wondered. How many times had she intruded?

Pagan switched off the machine and said, 'Let's get out of here,' and he put the passport and the bank-book in the pocket of his jacket. He moved into the hallway and Foxie, pondering the personal significance of the computer image he'd just seen, came after him.

21

VIRGINIA

James Mallory hated guns, the feel of them, the noises they made, the savage uses to which they were put throughout the nation. Skidelsky, on the other hand, was something of a gun-freak and liked target-shooting. Presently, on a hot floodlit field some miles from Fairfax, Max was testing a modified Ram-Line Ram-Tech Auto Pistol, holding it in the standard two-handed manner and blasting away at pumpkins that had been arranged on a fence. He missed a couple of times, exchanged the Ram-Tech for a Sig P-225DA, and fired off a couple of shots. Mallory, who wore soundproof ear-muffs, observed one of the pumpkins explode under the bright arc-lights, and inevitably thought of a human head blitzed. Skidelsky fired again, struck another of the gourds, and it blew apart.

'Like it,' Max said. 'I prefer the walnut stock to the rubber, I have to say.' He turned to Larry Quinn, who was standing alongside a Cherokee, the interior of which contained a variety of handguns. 'What else have we got there, Larry?'

Quinn ran off a bunch of names. 'A Hammerli 212. A Glock 21. An H & K P7M8.'

'That the one with the squeeze-cocker?' Max asked.

'Yeah,' said Quinn.

'What else is there?'

'Let's see, let's see.' Quinn rummaged inside the Cherokee. 'A Desert Eagle Magnum. A Colt Combat. There's a Bryco 59 auto. Also a Calico M-950 with the retarded blowback action.'

'Toss me that one,' Max said.

'You got it.'

Skidelsky took the Calico – which Mallory thought an odd shape, like something out of an old sci-fi movie – and took aim. More pumpkins were blown up under the glare of the lights. The air was splattered with flesh-coloured pulp and broken fibre. Mallory noticed how fond Max Skidelsky was of this destruction, the concentration in his face, the mouth tensed. Quinn, hovering in the background, looked on approvingly. Larry was another gun-buff. Max and Larry spoke with great enthusiasm about things Mallory didn't even try to understand – flash suppressors, combat-type trigger guards, ambidextrous cocking knobs. There was a whole weird terminology about weapons, a terse technical language constructed around guns, as if it were designed by PR agents to disguise the fact that basically guns were for one thing only: killing people.

Killing people. Mallory edged some yards away from Skidelsky, who'd traded the Calico for an AMT Hardballer Long Slide, which had to be about nine inches in length. Max said something unintelligible about the bevelled magazine well – whatever that was – and then fired the gun at the collection of gourds, missing with two of his four efforts. Gunshots echoed all around the big field, like nearby thunder.

All the barren heat of the day was trapped in darkness; nightfall hadn't alleviated it. Mallory's cotton shirt stuck to his flesh. His armpits were soaked. The lights hurt his eyes, so he turned away and looked in the other direction, back across the field where the electricity didn't penetrate. These Wednesday night gun-shows were a regular fixture in the calendar of the Club. The usual attendance was six or seven, and sometimes as many as a dozen, but sometimes other members were overseas, or doing business, like Ralph Donovan, in other cities, and so tonight there was only himself and Larry and Max. It occurred to Mallory that he didn't know the exact membership. Max never talked numbers. There might have been twelve. There might have been fifty. Mallory had never asked.

Skidelsky said, 'Your turn, Jimmy.'

Mallory always dreaded this bit.

'What takes your fancy?' Max asked.

'Any old thing, doesn't matter.'

Skidelsky slung an arm around Mallory's shoulder and squeezed tightly. 'Give us more *enthusiasm*, Jimmy. Let me hear desire.'

Mallory laughed uneasily. 'I'll try the Glock.'

'Give the man the Glock, Larry.'

A gun was pressed into Mallory's hand. Its weight was oppressive. How could twenty-five ounces of steel feel so heavy?

'Concentrate, Jimmy. Believe in yourself. Believe you can't miss,' Max was saying.

James Mallory raised the Glock, took aim, fired. His shot went winging off harmlessly into the night.

'Again,' Skidelsky said. 'Make believe the pumpkin is the head of somebody you don't like or somebody who's a threat to you. Barclay Reeves, for instance. Or old Christopher Poole.'

Barclay Reeves, former Director of the FBI. Mallory tried to imagine the pallid, pinchpenny face of the man who was rumoured to be in the running for The Big

Job, if such a thing ever came to pass. Mallory, who always thought Barclay Reeves resembled an ascetic monseigneur, narrowed his eyes, fired, missed.

'Again,' said Max.

Again. This time Mallory's shot grazed the edge of a pumpkin, shifting the gourd just a little.

'Mmm, not bad, Jimmy.' Skidelsky took the Glock out of Mallory's hand. 'You just need more practice. More faith.' He gripped Mallory's arm and grinned. 'What the hell. You've got talents more important to us than hitting pumpkins.'

Mallory wondered about his talents. He was good when it came to arranging matters, overseeing details that might have escaped others, such as Skidelsky, whose vision was generally directed at the totality of things. Mallory was wonderful with the cogs and tiny wheels and making them fit so that the machinery ran smoothly. He supposed it was for this reason that Skidelsky – who held, at a relatively early age, the important position of Assistant to the Executive Director, Christopher Poole, who in turn was just below the Deputy Director – had first approached him some six months ago and befriended him. Max had that way of making you feel special, you weren't just some nobody in Research at Langley, just some guy whose function it was to evaluate the voluminous material that came out of the espionage archives of the former Soviet Union, usually offered for sale by pale Slavic men in ill-fitting suits, men you met in cheap hotels in shabby Balkan countries, men you interviewed in isolated pavement cafés and small bars in sidestreets in Rome or Athens or Marseilles. Max drew him out of this drudgery with flattery, generosity, the bright smile of friendship – and before he'd realized it he was sucked in, brought under Skidelsky's starry wing, he was part of the clique, the group, he belonged, and by Christ, didn't that make him feel privileged? Hanging out with the smart kids on the block, the movers and shakers in their fancy suits and expensive restaurants and the good-looking bimbos that drifted in and out of their orbit.

The point was: you belonged. You were a member of a new élite. And this élite sometimes drank late into the night and talked about the state of the nation and what was wrong and how it could be put right – and even if Mallory felt uneasy at times, a conspirator against the organization that employed him, he realized he sympathized with much that Skidelsky and his friends had to say. The cops were thugs with holstered guns, the Feds were top-heavy and incompetent, the politicians were bullshit artists looking after *numero uno*, the Agency was menaced by a skinflint Administration, the system was going to hell in a handbasket – *we're on a sleigh-ride down the glacier of mediocrity and the huskies are gathering speed and we don't have any fucking seat-belts*, as Max had phrased it – and it was high time to change things before the bell of doomsday was the only sound you could hear.

Heady stuff. Exciting. Mallory liked the buzz of being around Max. He liked doing things for him. He liked being entrusted with tasks, some of them no more than tiny chores – copying certain documents that crossed Mallory's desk, sometimes providing him with data from files. And the recent task, the trip to London, the meeting with Pasco, the arrangement with Galkin, all that – well, that had been the single most important function he'd had to perform. And Max had persuaded him he could do it. *You have a certain gravitas, Jimmy. You'll have Pasco eating out of the palm of your hand. You wear the right clothes, you got that slightly Ivy League look about you, you're the right age. You think Pasco's going to listen to some kid?*

And Mallory had pulled it off. So why didn't he truly feel a great sense of achievement? Why did something niggle and wriggle on a hook at the back of his head all the time? He remembered the conversation he'd had with Max about ethics: that was where the problem lay. If he was entirely honest with himself, he liked the entirety of the scheme more than he liked the parts. There was no point in saying so to Max, because he had that way of convincing you your thinking was wrong; you were still a prisoner of old loyalties that had disintegrated long ago; all the past bargains were off; fresh approaches were needed to the Problem of America. And then there would be a bout of hand-bonding. *Trust me, Jimmy. Trust me. Trust is the basic article of The Artichoke Club. What we're doing, we're doing for the common good.*

But people will die, Max.

Yes, and that's unfortunate, and I feel for them, but you can't build up the new unless you do away with the old. Law of nature, Jimmy. Like gravity.

Larry Quinn was opening a styrofoam cooler packed with bottles of Czech beer. He passed one to Skidelsky, another to Mallory, who wanted to think of this gathering in the field as something innocent, a boy's night out, shoot off a few rounds, slug a few brewskies.

'Cheers,' said Quinn.

The three men stood at the back of the Cherokee and drank for a time in silence.

Max Skidelsky said, 'Something I want you to hear,' and he fished around inside the vehicle until he found what he was looking for. A small cassette-player. He stuck a tape inside it, pressed the play button. There was a second of hissing before the recorded voice of

Christopher Poole could be heard saying, *One, the woman is unlikely to return to this country. Two, I can't imagine her singling out Agency personnel as targets. If she has destructive grudges, they're directed at the Bureau.*'

Max clicked the recorder off. 'From the horse's mouth,' he said, and laughed, shaking his head as he did so.

Quinn laughed too. Mallory managed a small smile. The heat in the field was devouring him. Mosquitoes and assorted night pests fluttered around his face and he flapped them aside. Max, who did a devastating impersonation of old Poole, stiffened his lips and said, '*One, the woman is unlikely to return to this country* . . . What planet does Poole live on? Is he actually alive at all? I hear him breath, and words come out of his mouth, but I can't find the point where anything about him interfaces with reality as we know it.'

Quinn slugged his beer and laughed again. 'You think Poole's the only one that's funny, Max? Yesterday I'm talking with Naderson and he suddenly segues into some tired adventure yarn about what the Agency did down in South America in the Fifties, when America really stood for something, and the peasants were glad to see people in their jungle fatigues bring democracy *all de way down* to Bananapulca, or wherever. It isn't only Poole that's out of it.'

Mallory listened in silence. The enthusiasm of these young men engaged him. They had the critical energy of stars, especially Skidelsky. Sometimes, though, Mallory felt a barrier between himself and the others. He often wondered if it was an age thing. And sometimes, when they came out with parodies, a few admittedly amusing, of the Pledge of Allegiance, he had to still a small resentment in himself. But it was too late for resentments, too late for regrets. He was in; he belonged. He was part of it all. Like a marriage – for better or worse.

Skidelsky looked up at the night sky. 'I wonder where she is at this precise moment,' he said.

'She's on her way,' Mallory said quietly.

Skidelsky, who only ever allowed himself one beer, raised an arm and tossed his empty bottle off into the darkness. 'And where, I wonder, will she begin?'

'Good question,' said Mallory, and raised his face to the sky too, thinking of airplanes, the multitudes of passengers crossing the heavens, most of them ordinary travellers, businessmen and women, tourists. But one of them was different; one of them was carrying death.

22

LONDON

They returned to Golden Square through the dark empty streets of the city. It took Foxie a couple of hours to explore those electronic networks whose dispassionate function it is to record human movement and business transactions, and to learn that a woman by the name of Kristen Hawkins possessed an EEC passport issued in London, an American Express Gold card, and an Access Card obtained from the National Westminster Bank in Kilburn, where she kept an account into which deposits were made twice a year by wire-transfer from a bank in Venice. And there was more: she'd leased the house in Kilburn for almost twelve years, and rent had been paid annually, via draft from a financial institution in Liechtenstein, to the company, Greater Southern Properties Ltd, that owned the house.

Twelve years, Pagan thought. *For twelve years she'd had that house in Kilburn.* He wondered how often she'd gone there, slipping in and out of the city unseen. He shouldn't have been surprised, but he was; frontiers meant nothing to her. There were no borders in Carlotta's world, neither geographical nor moral.

Foxie kept tapping keys, tracking the person known as Kristen Hawkins. He stopped abruptly and looked at Pagan with a curious smile. 'God. You're going to love this one, Frank. Our dark lady of the sonnets actually worked as a temporary secretary, from 3 July until 5 July this year, at Scotland Yard.'

'She did *what*?'

Foxie read from the screen. 'She was sent to the Yard by an employment agency called The Quik-Help Bureau, and she spent three days in the accounts department. If she used her initiative, she found out how to break into the computer system.'

'I don't doubt it for a moment.' Pagan tried to imagine her strolling the corridors of Scotland Yard. Unassuming Kristen Hawkins, temporary secretary. Nobody would notice her, nobody would remember her. Moving quietly, she would pass unobserved in and out of offices, perhaps clutching files under her arm – a drab little nobody who'd wander around unquestioned. So much for internal security, he thought. So much for screening procedures. For three short days, he and Carlotta had been colleagues in a sense, both employed by the same organization. *We're bonded, Pagan. Whether you like it or not.* The most wanted person in the country – and she'd been secure under the umbrella of the Yard.

'What else can we get on her?' he asked.

'I think I've dug out just about everything I can dig,' Foxie answered, and he leaned back from the screen, clasping his hands together, cracking his knuckles. 'I don't know where else to search.'

Pagan looked from the window, saw the city coming to life, cars in the square, pedestrians moving to their places of employment. He thought: Pasco goes to her for help. What kind of help? He remembered the burnt bank-book. Had Pasco offered her money for this unspecified assistance? Money didn't interest her.

Besides, she obviously had enough of it stashed away in Venice and Liechtenstein, and God knows where else – no, she wouldn't want Richard Pasco's cash. And if Pasco had offered her any, he'd clearly misjudged her. She wasn't for sale. She couldn't be bought. Question: who the hell was Pasco? This was what it kept coming back to.

He wandered away from the window and stood behind Foxie. 'Bring up Martin's files,' he said.

Foxie tapped the keys. The screen changed. The outline of Burr's career appeared together with a list of sub-directories. Foxie, beset by a sense that he might go blind if he kept staring at the console, said, 'Now what?'

'Look for Pasco.'

Foxworth punched the keyboard. The word SEARCHING flickered on and off hypnotically. Then it stopped. The name *Pasco, Richard*, appeared, followed by a command to open a file called MB/DRGS/86/35H.

Foxie typed in the appropriate letters. The file appeared. Pagan leaned over Foxworth's shoulder to read it. It simply said: *Deleted and transferred to private papers, August 1986. Authorized Martin Burr.*

Pagan studied the message a second, then he felt inside the pocket of his jacket and produced the key he'd been given by Marcia Burr.

'Let's go,' he said.

A lifetime of work, big cardboard boxes of old files, manila folders stuffed with official papers, some of them yellow and faded with the passage of time, notebooks filled with Burr's precise handwriting: in Martin's Knightsbridge apartment Pagan felt like an archivist dismayed by an abundance of uncollated material. He and Foxworth sorted through the cardboard boxes, which had been marked by years in thick black felt pen. 1976, 1977, 1978 and so on. Pagan found the one they were looking for – 1986 – after a few minutes. He dragged it into the middle of the floor and opened it.

In 1986 Burr had been in charge of the Drug Squad. The box contained details of busts, cargoes seized from ships, cocaine, hashish. There were also monthly notebooks, which Burr had kept conscientiously; these consisted of private reflections, comments. *The only way to beat the smugglers*, Burr had written in March 1986, *is to legalize the bloody stuff and have it available by prescription*. Martin the heretic. Who would have suspected that Martin, so correct, would have been an advocate for the decriminalization of drugs?

Pagan kept turning the pages. It was disconcerting to be sifting through the private observations of a dead man. Martin had written: *If a man wants to use dope, it's his own business, provided he doesn't hurt anyone in the process. Legalization would also provide a means of taxation*.

Pagan raised his face, looked round the room, found himself gazing out into the hallway through the open door. It was half in shadow, the way it had been when Martin was murdered. He got up from his chair and looked along the corridor almost as if he expected to see the woman standing by the door. In the place where Martin had been slain, there were bloodstains on the rug and a few dried petals from a flower vase.

He returned to the notebook. Pressed between the pages was a photograph of Martin taken in the hold of a cargo vessel surrounded by tarpaulined bales of reefer. Burr looked vaguely forlorn.

Pagan found the notebook for August 1986. He had

the makings of a dull headache behind his eyes. His mind drifted to the woman. He pictured her out there somewhere, perhaps even in London still, and he imagined he could hear her laughter. *Pasco, Pagan. Look for Richard Pasco.* A voice from nowhere, a maddening whisper from space. It instilled him with a sense of urgency.

He kept flicking, flicking. Sometimes a personal note was added in a margin. *Seventeenth wedding anniversary. Must buy flowers, book a table at The Connaught. Important* – underlined three times.

Seventeen years of marriage, Pagan thought. Which meant that Martin and his wife had only last month celebrated their twenty-seventh year of marriage. And now it was all blown away, it was sand. He pondered Marcia Burr, wondered if she'd gone down to the cottage in Sussex to see if it were possible to pick up the slack of her life—

It came off the page at him suddenly. One short ungrammatical string of words that didn't immediately yield meaning, almost as if Burr had jotted them down without really thinking, as if he were disturbed to the point where he wasn't able to formulate the sentence properly.

Pagan said, 'Look at this.'

Foxie peered at the notebook. 'Pasco,' he said. 'But what does it tell us? It's garbled.'

With the notebook open in his hand, Pagan stood up, wandered the room, then sat on the edge of Martin Burr's desk. What Martin had written wasn't clear at all. The other entries in the notebooks had reflected calm detachment, but this one had been written without any apparent attention to structure, simply something Burr wanted to skip over because—

Because what?

Poor Pasco, Marcia says forget, hands grubby.

And that was it, that was all. 'Poor Pasco,' Pagan said. 'Why poor Pasco? And hands grubby? What is that supposed to mean? And this – Marcia says forget?'

'Ask her,' Foxie said.

'I asked her last night. You were there. I asked her if Pasco meant anything to her, and she said it didn't.'

'Perhaps she's lying.'

'She might have forgotten. This notebook is ten years old.'

'Then we jog her memory, Frank.'

Pagan stared at the entry. Even the handwriting seemed different, hurried. 'It's not the best of times to ask questions of Marcia,' he said. He remembered her drawn features, the sorrow in her eyes, the tentative gestures. He recalled the misbuttoned cardigan: bereavement created imbalances. Everything was awry because there were no longer any foundations. Ask her gently, he thought. And if she didn't remember? Or if she chose not to remember? If she'd been deliberately lying? What then? How could he pressure her into telling the truth?

'So?' Foxie asked. 'What do we do?'

'There's only one thing we can do,' Pagan said. 'It means going all the way down to Sussex.'

Pagan wondered about the times of trains to Lewes. He turned from the window, walked to Martin's desk, gazed at the word-processor. Scraps of paper, on which Martin had scribbled words and phrases, lay alongside the keyboard. *Rule number one – Begin at the beginning*, Martin had written on the back of an envelope. Everywhere you looked there was a reminder of Burr, traces of a life violently interrupted.

But life goes on, Pagan thought. Killers have to be

caught. Especially this one. Especially. He had a flash of the hotel, the dining-room, the chaos.

'Phone the station, Foxie. Check the times of the trains.'

Foxworth found a phone directory and leafed through the pages. Pagan looked again at the notebook. *Hands grubby*: it suggested that whatever Martin had been involved in with regard to Pasco had left him feeling unhappy, even ashamed. *Poor Pasco*.

Foxie had dialled a number. 'Bloody recorded time-table,' he said after a moment. 'They're always scratchy and inaudible. Why can't they pay somebody to answer inquiries?'

Pagan heard the sound of a key turning in the lock. He went into the hallway, saw the front door opening.

Marcia Burr, dressed in the black of mourning, stepped inside the apartment. She moved a couple of feet forward and seemed to sway gently, as if her balance had been undermined by the shock of realizing that the place where she stood was the precise spot her husband had been killed. Pagan hurried toward her, caught her by the elbow.

'Are you all right?' he asked.

'Yes, yes, fine.' Her voice was thin. A black veil hung across her face. 'I hate this, this *thing*,' she said, and shoved the veil away, as if in doing so she might diminish her grief, deny the condition of widowhood. 'I hate black. Why can't we wear red or something bright? Where is it written that one has to wear black? It's so cheerless. So *final*.'

Pagan escorted her along the hallway. He tried to divert her attention from the bloodstains, but it was too late. She'd already seen them. He wondered what was going through her head. She'd perceive this apartment differently now. It would be alien to her, and horrifying.

She looked round the drawing-room. She might have been seeing it for the first time; she seemed to recognize nothing. How can I ask her questions when she's in this state of mind? he wondered. Last night in Golden Square she'd given the impression of marginal self-control – but a form of collapse had taken place in the hours of darkness.

'Is there anything I can get you?' he asked.

She shook her head. She stared away from him, her attention drawn to a glass case inside which sat a stuffed partridge. There were several taxidermized game birds in the room, each entombed in a case. 'Those damned birds. I always loathed them,' she said. Her voice was flat and hollow.

What was he supposed to say? Pagan wondered. Could he come right out with it? *What role did Pasco play in Martin's life?* Foxie appeared in the doorway, then stepped quietly into the room.

Marcia Burr removed her black gloves and laid them in her lap. 'I only dropped in to see how you are doing, Frank.'

No, he thought. It was more than that. He caught a wary edge in her voice, something she was trying to guard. She turned her face to him. Her lipstick was badly done, raggedly drawn with a hand that must have been shaking. Pagan felt useless. What comfort could he possibly bring her? He sat down on the sofa facing her. Foxie, hushed, lingered near the window.

'Our son arrives today,' she said. 'From Hong Kong.'

'I'm glad you won't be alone,' Pagan said.

'Yes. Yes. Of course.' She fidgeted with the gloves, stared at Pagan, then at Foxworth. 'I'll sell this place.

205

I'll put it on the market as soon as the funeral is over. It's no use to me now.'

She was talking round the edges of things. Pagan realized that. The unspoken name of Pasco lay between them like a third party in the room. She must have known he'd come across the name somewhere in Martin's papers. She tossed her gloves aside and pressed her fingertips to her eyelids.

'Are you sure I can't get you a drink?' he asked.

She shook her head. 'I miss him, Frank. I miss him terribly.'

'I understand,' he said.

'I know you do. You've been going through the boxes, I assume.'

He nodded.

'So much paper,' she said. 'Martin was like a jack-daw.'

'Yes.'

She was quiet a second. 'Have you found anything interesting?'

You know we have, he thought. 'There's so much material to get through,' he answered quietly.

'Frank. Why don't you just say it? I'm a bad liar.'

Pagan mumbled some mild protest, made a gesture with his hand.

'Oh, Frank, I don't like it when somebody demurs,' she said. 'I'm just not very good when it comes to fibbing. You saw the name, didn't you?'

'Yes.'

'And you're too tactful to ask about it.'

'Respectful more than tactful,' Pagan said.

'Respect won't help you find this wretched woman.'

Pagan stood up. He wandered to one of the glass cases and peered inside. Lustrous feathers, glazed glass eyes.

'Richard Pasco,' Marcia said. 'Martin worried himself sick about the man. You know how bloody high-minded he could be at times, Frank. Anything that offended his sense of ethics caused him sleepless nights.'

'Tell me about Pasco, Marcia.'

She slumped back in the chair, tilting her face, gazing up at the ceiling. 'Pasco, yes. I'll tell you about him. But I believe I'll have that drink first, Frank. If you'd be so kind as to do the honours. Gin if there's any. A dash of tonic.'

Pagan went to the cocktail cabinet and poured a glass of Beefeaters. He added a touch of flat tonic water and took the drink to her.

'Thanks,' she said. 'Martin always felt guilty about Pasco. I tried to tell him he was judging himself far too harshly. But you know what he was like. He was his own most severe critic.'

Pagan leaned back on the sofa. What had Martin written on the back of the envelope? *Rule number one – begin at the beginning.* He said, 'Why don't we go through it slowly, Marcia. From the very start.'

'Yes,' she said. She tasted her drink and stared at Pagan over the rim of her glass. 'Why don't we?'

23

BALTIMORE, MARYLAND

Professor Edward Jay Binns sat in his bed and browsed the pages of a skin magazine called Studs, which depicted perfect specimens of suntanned young manhood. He was in his early sixties and rarely lectured these days, perhaps once a year if he was feeling up to it, or if he had some fresh insight to add to his life's work: a study of the relationship between the philosophy of Immanuel Kant and the Romantic poets. He was one year short of statutory retirement, although the Dean had promised him office space after that – nothing commodious, you understand, Ed, a small token of our esteem.

Binns passed much of his time reading and making notes and conducting the occasional seminar or tutorial. What he really enjoyed was a one-to-one situation with a student, preferably a good-looking boy, and preferably in the comfort of his own house on the leafy outskirts of Baltimore. Between reading and scribbling notes, he haunted sex shops and purchased magazines.

He was presently examining a study of two naked young men, one black, the other white. They were a wondrously muscled pair, and each had an erection. The black boy's hand was curled around the white penis, which was large and swollen. The black penis was slightly shadowed by the white boy's body, but it was discernible, and bold, a flamboyantly proud mauve-headed thing. The professor, who didn't believe in the current fad of 'outing', as it was called, stared at the photograph.

His absorption in it was such that when he heard his front doorbell ring he was frankly irritated. He had half a mind to let it go unanswered, but it kept ringing. He got out of bed and wrapped a robe around his spindly white nakedness and made his way downstairs, passing portraits of Coleridge, Wordsworth, Shelley and Keats – all his heroes. He opened the front door. His first impression was of a good-looking young man in a black leather jacket and blue jeans, short black hair slicked back, an earring attached to one lobe and sparkling in the morning sunlight.

'Professor Binns?'

The professor realized at once that his first impression was mistaken. It was no young man who stood on his doorstep – *au contraire*, it was a woman, an attractive woman who might have passed as an effeminate good-looking man.

The professor peered at her. 'Yes?'

'I don't mean to trouble you,' she said. 'You were recommended to me by the English department.'

'Recommended?'

'Yeah,' she said, and swept a hand across her glistening hair. 'I'm an exchange student. From Cornell?'

'Cornell,' said Binns. 'And?'

'I'm doing a thesis on the Lake Poets.'

'And so you were sent to me,' he said.

'They said you were the man to see.'

'It's my field, certainly.'

'Look. Can I come inside? It's pretty hot out here.'

Binns looked past her the length of the street. The morning sun was like light from a steel foundry. It burned in the dry trees; you could almost imagine it crackling against leaf and twigs. The sky was cloudless. Binns longed for rain, good rich Lake District rain, shrouds of damp mist. He stepped aside, let the woman come in. She carried a small leather briefcase. He led her inside the sitting-room where he kept souvenirs of his trips to the Lake District, as well as a few items he'd picked up in Königsberg, Kant's home town.

'Wow,' the woman said, looking round the collection. Old books and prints, clay pipes, old glass jars alleged to have contained Coleridge's narcotics, a willow-pattern plate that had belonged to Wordsworth, a teacup and saucer said to have been Dorothy Wordsworth's. Binns had labelled each of these precious items.

'Pretty impressive,' she said.

'I'm proud of them,' said Binns. He surveyed his collection, then turned back to the woman. 'Did you give me your name?'

'No. It's Phoenix. Carly Phoenix.'

'Unusual name,' Binns said. 'What's your specialty?'

'Coleridge. *The Ancient Mariner* is the subject of my thesis.'

'Ah, indeed, indeed.'

'I'm interested in the theme of punishment,' she said, and she smiled at the professor in such a way that even his old pederast's heart managed a slight flutter. 'You kill a harmless living thing, and you get punished. I like the equation. The balance.'

'Well, of course, it goes beyond punishment,' Binns said. He looked at the woman and thought how hard it was to estimate her age. Thirtyish, perhaps older. As one began one's trek toward the seventies, it was difficult to guess the ages of younger people.

She said, 'It's the idea of retribution I like.' She picked up one of the professor's souvenirs, a framed sketch of Lake Windermere drawn in 1870 by an unknown artist, and gazed at it. 'The fact you can't get away from your own actions and their consequences.'

'There's also the possibility of redemption, of course,' he remarked.

'Maybe. Of a kind.'

Binns quoted, '*He prayeth well who loveth well, Both man and bird and beast.*'

She countered with another quotation. '*I pass, like night, from land to land; I have strange power of speech . . .*'

Binns pondered this familiar couplet a second, then asked, 'Who was your adviser at Cornell?'

She seemed not to have heard the question. She stared at the framed sketch. A certain slight glaze crossed her vision, as if she were under some mild kind of trance.

'Was it Professor Robinson, by any chance?' he asked.

'Robinson, no,' she said. She stirred herself from her odd lethargy and replaced the print on the shelf.

'Parrish?'

She shook her head: no, not Parrish.

'If it was neither Robinson nor Parrish, who was it?' he asked.

She moved around the room, reflected sunlight glowing in black leather. The professor felt a weird little flash of uneasiness. Somebody turns up on your doorstep and you invite them inside without asking to see any credentials – this was folly in the modern world. Of course, she'd used the magic password, the open sesame of the Lake Poets, because this was the professor's obsession, but just the same there was a quality to this person he couldn't quite define. A sense, perhaps, of energy only loosely held in check? some wayward little glimmer in her eyes? She had undeniable presence, and beauty of an idiosyncratic sort – and something else, a toughness, perhaps, a hard edge, although this quality may have been associated with the black leather jacket and tight blue jeans. The professor liked to examine his own impressions; analysis was the habit of a lifetime.

'I know most of the people in my field,' he said.

She balanced herself on the arm of a chair. Her briefcase lay in her lap. Her stare was unblinking and in its own way harsh, like a flashlight shining on the professor's face. 'Pasco,' she said. 'Richard Pasco.'

'Mmm. Doesn't ring a bell, I'm afraid. Is he new at Cornell?'

'No, not really.'

Binns was puzzled. 'Odd I haven't heard of him. Has he published?'

She shook her head. 'I don't think so.'

'That might explain it,' said Binns. Pasco, he thought. He made a mental note to check on Pasco and his teaching creds. He liked to keep abreast of new people in the field. He liked to be informed when he went to conferences.

'I think you've heard of him, Professor,' she said.

'No, I can't say I have.'

'You've just forgotten, that's all. You may have shot down the albatross of memory,' and she smiled. 'Or simply clipped a wing.'

The professor said, 'I doubt if I'd be so careless, Miss Phoenix.'

'We're all careless at times,' she remarked.

'I may be edging closer daily to what Browning called "The Arch Fear in visible form", but I assure you my memory's still in fine condition.' The professor took off his glasses and cleaned the lenses in the folds of his robe.

'The Arch Fear,' she said. '*The press of the storm, The post of the foe . . . For the journey is done and the summit attained.*'

Binns replaced his glasses, looked at the woman. He wanted to get back upstairs to his magazine, to the splendid picture of the two young men. 'My journey isn't *quite* done, Miss Phoenix. Perhaps you might be good enough to tell me how I can be of assistance to you regarding your thesis?'

'How long have you been recruiting people?' she asked.

'*Recruiting* people?'

'Don't be coy, Professor. There's no need for reticence.'

'I'm not following you, I'm afraid.'

'I think you are, Professor.'

Binns fanned the stuffy air of the room with his hand. 'Who are you exactly?'

'A friend of Richard Pasco.'

'There's no thesis, is there?' Binns's throat was suddenly dry, like a small pond drained in a matter of seconds.

'No thesis. No exchange student crap. There's just you and me and the spectre of Richard Pasco.'

The professor sat down. He saw very little future in denying his involvement in the recruitment process, even if he hadn't done that kind of thing on a grand scale. Thirty, forty young people over a period of thirty years. That wasn't exactly a huge trawl, compared to other academics he knew.

'You recruited Richard Pasco,' she said.

He was flustered, his forehead hot. 'I don't remember him.'

'Take my word for it. You recruited him. You passed him on to Langley. He was good Agency material, I guess. Young, halfway bright, not overwhelmingly ambitious, patriotic, easily swayed. Just the type.'

The professor had the feeling his larynx was coated with chalk. 'Miss Phoenix, if that's your real name, I carried out a few favours for certain people. That's all I did. I happen to believe, and I still do, that a well-informed intelligence service is essential to a nation's security. Consequently, I passed a few likely students down the line for interviews. They weren't forced, you understand. Nobody twisted their arm.'

'Who did you pass them to?' she asked.

'Really, I'm not at liberty to divulge names—'

'Don't bullshit me, Eddie. You sent them down to a place near Roanoke for training under a guy called Laird. Correct?'

'Well, Laird was one, yes—'

'There was somebody called Backus. Littlejohn. A woman by the name of Joan Dunne.'

'You're well-informed.'

'Up to a point,' she said. 'Inform me further, Eddie.'

'In what way?'

'Are these people still around?'

The professor got up from his chair. He plunged his hands in the pockets of his robe and strolled about the room. He'd never had any misgivings about the recruiting business. He'd simply seen it as a way of bringing promising young people to Langley's attention. He was part of a network of academics who did exactly the same thing. Besides, it hadn't been illegal. In fact, he'd been pleased to do it—

'Are they still around?' she asked again.

He said, 'I don't have to answer your questions.'

'You're not getting the picture, Eddie.' She undid the clasp of her briefcase and stuck her hand inside, and although she didn't produce a weapon she left Binns with the definite impression that she carried a gun in the case.

He said, 'Laird's dead. Cancer, a few years back. Backus, Littlejohn – I believe they still work at the training facility. Dunne – I think she was promoted to Director of Training five years ago. I don't keep in touch with these people . . . I hear a few things now and again, that's all.'

'James Mallory – does that name ring a bell?'

'No,' he answered.

'You're sure?'

'Of course, I'm sure.'

She was quiet a moment. 'Nice system,' she said. 'Pick out a few students, pass them down the conveyor belt, give them a little flag to wave.'

'Companies recruit from universities,' he said, defensively. 'They do it all the time.'

'With a little more publicity than the Agency,' she said.

'The nature of the beast requires discretion, that's all.'

'Tell me about a man called Naderson.'

'Bob Naderson's about to retire in a couple of months. He has something to do with Science and Tech, I believe.'

'What about Grimes?'

'Kevin Grimes?' She hadn't taken her hand out of the briefcase, he noticed. 'Electronic radar stations management.'

'And Christopher Poole?'

'Poole was made Executive Director two years ago.'

'A hotshot.'

The professor asked, 'Are you through with me?'

She shook her head. 'I asked a few questions about you on campus this morning,' she said.

'And?'

'Your nickname is Queenie Binns, did you know that?'

'Don't be absurd,' he said.

'Queenie. I like it.'

The professor felt flushed, knew his face had changed colour. He made a dismissive gesture. 'I don't believe a word of it.'

'Believe, don't believe. That's what they call you. It doesn't leave a whole lot to the imagination, I guess.'

'This is preposterous—'

'Queenie Binns,' she said. 'Hey, why deny your nature anyway? Why hide your preferences? Ashamed of them, that it?'

'I think I'd like you to leave—'

'I'm not finished, Professor.'

'Please,' he said.

She said, 'Let me see your bedroom.'

'My bedroom? Why would you want to see my bedroom, for heaven's sake?'

'Oh, because I'm curious.'

The professor's heart quivered, jumped a beat. He had a flash of insight. 'This is blackmail, isn't it? You've come here to blackmail me. I'm not a rich man, you're wasting your time, really—'

'Just show me your bedroom, Prof. Then I'll leave you in peace.'

The professor turned his face toward the staircase. 'You'll leave. I have your word on that?'

'Sure,' she said.

'Up here,' and he began, with a weary movement, to climb the stairs. Uncovered, he thought. Exposed. The notion was humiliating. He couldn't go near the campus again. Queenie Binns – the nickname was mortifying. He stopped halfway up, turned. The woman was one step behind him. He supposed he could try something, maybe give her a quick push, but the look in her eye was one of determination; she wasn't the kind you could catch off balance. She was too aware. She had a feline quality. Her instinct would be razor-blade sharp. Besides, he was too old for any kind of heroic gesture.

He opened the door of his bedroom. The magazine he'd been pawing through lay open on the bed. The room was flowery, a little overdone: he saw it through the woman's eyes. She glanced at the magazine, picked it up, studied the photograph of the naked young men.

'Nice,' she said. 'Well-endowed.'

Binns said nothing. He was embarrassed. He was aware of the stack of magazines on his bedside table, the box of Kleenex, the hardened yellowy tissues that lay around like so many crumpled, misshapen flower-heads.

'Never be ashamed of your proclivities, Prof,' she said, and finally she took her hand out of her briefcase. She held a length of rope that dangled from her fingers as far as the floor.

'Remember,' she said. 'We are what we are.'

When she returned to the motel she undressed and sat on the edge of the bed, curtains closed, air-conditioning unit rattling under the window. She lay down on her side and closed her eyes and she was at once overwhelmed by remembered fragments of recent experience – the quick flight from London to

Washington, the hop from DC to Baltimore, the kid in the next seat who threw up his in-flight dinner into a sick bag, the loudmouthed guy in the seat behind who got blitzed on miniatures of brandy and rattled out stats about airplane safety. Her head was a chamber filled with voices. She heard the professor say *I'm not a rich man* . . .

She picked up a pencil and scribbled on a scratch pad. She wrote down the name *James Mallory*. Beneath this, she wrote a second name: *Pagan*. Around *Pagan* she doodled an abstract series of shapes that suggested scimitars and cubes.

She slowly spread her legs and imagined Pagan coming into the room, the lover in shadow. She imagined him touching her. She stroked her breasts, then lowered her fingers between her legs; her hand lay motionless. Nothing. The subsidence of imagination. She didn't want to masturbate thinking of Pagan; a counterfeit experience. She got up, opened the tiny refrigerator, hacked out some ice-cubes and rubbed them in circles against her hard flat stomach and stood very close to the air-conditioner with her legs apart – almost as if the combination of ice and icy air were some private form of self-flagellation.

24

LONDON

Inside the pub on Beak Street, it occurred to Pagan that he wasn't sure when he'd last slept. It was strange how fatigue seemed just to fade away at times, and you were blessed with that quality known as a second wind. He wondered if there were winds beyond the second one, a third, a fourth, an infinite number of them – each with diminishing returns.

He finished his Scotch and thought about the information he'd been given by Marcia Burr – if given was the word; *dragged from* might have been more appropriate. She'd begun confidently, relieved to unburden herself, but after two gin and tonics she'd become increasingly reluctant, wondering aloud if she were damaging Martin's reputation. He's dead, she'd kept saying. He isn't here to explain himself. The dead have a right to be left in peace, don't they?

Pagan had found himself in the unenviable position of having to apply a little pressure, an occasional gentle prod. Slowly, then, she'd doled out her narrative, but even when she'd finished, Pagan had the distinct feeling she'd left something out, she'd edited the story, sanitized it.

Foxie, facing him across the table, had asked him a

question he hadn't heard. He raised his face and said, 'Run that past me again.'

'Do you want another drink?'

'Please.'

Foxie picked up the empty glasses and headed toward the bar. Pagan idly struck a match, allowing it to burn down between his fingers. The air smelled, appropriately, of sulphur. Complicity, he thought. Treachery. Qualities he wouldn't have associated with Martin Burr. Qualities he *still* couldn't associate with him. He'd always considered Burr a figure of rectitude. He'd played by the rules, he'd never been underhand, he'd guarded his integrity jealously. But ten years ago, for some reason, he'd slipped.

Foxworth came back from the bar with two double Scotches and said, 'What do you make of Marcia's story?'

Pagan raised his glass. 'Martin got himself involved in a business that left a bad taste in his mouth, and he regretted ever having participated in it. He looked the other way, Foxie. He stepped aside when perhaps he shouldn't have done. That's how I see it. God knows, I'm not going to sit here and criticize the man for a decision he made more than ten years ago. He was involved in the set-up of Pasco – a disagreeable fact, but you can't go back and change it.' Pagan wondered what had gone through Burr's head all those years ago. Perhaps there were pressures Pagan knew nothing about. Perhaps promises of reciprocity had been made to Burr. *We owe you one, Martin.* Whatever, Burr had gone along with a plan that hadn't made him happy in the least.

He said, 'According to Marcia, in whom Martin apparently had the rather endearing habit of confiding everything, Richard Pasco arrived from Los Angeles at

Heathrow in July 1986 *en route* for Moscow. Burr had been informed that Pasco was carrying a good amount of cocaine. The old false compartment in the suitcase routine, which is bloody corny and obvious as hell. And that's the way it was meant to be. Easy to find. The first place any trainee officer would look. But here's the thing: Pasco was *not to be searched*. He was to sail straight through. No baggage exam, nothing. In short, it was intended that he deliver the goods to Moscow.'

He ran a fingertip round the rim of the glass. 'The request for Pasco's free passage came to Burr from a man whose name Marcia doesn't know, but she believes he was an agent of the Central Intelligence Agency. It sounds to me that what really troubled Martin was the fact he *knew* Pasco was a fall guy. The drugs were in Pasco's possession without Pasco's knowledge. But Martin – and this is totally out of character – swallowed his misgivings and kept his head down. Pasco cleared Heathrow and was pinched in Moscow and shipped off, again according to Marcia, to the icy wastes for years.'

Foxie, hunched in an attitude of concentration, said, 'And Martin deleted all this from the computer because it wasn't something he wanted on his record.'

'If you're ashamed of something, your natural inclination is to expunge it,' Pagan said. He thought of the woman: if he'd been in the habit of keeping a diary, would he have mentioned the business with her? Would he have set down on paper his complex physical responses? He seriously doubted it. The idea of some hypothetical future reader was a deterrent.

Pagan said, 'Marcia's understanding is that the CIA wanted to get one of their own out of Russia.'

'She was muddy on that point,' Foxie said.

'Sure, but it has the ring of truth. The CIA gives the

Russians a drug smuggler, a quote unquote capitalist degenerate. In return they get back their own man. Cold War business as usual. People were for barter. Question: where does Carlotta come into this? How did she get involved with Pasco? And who the hell was Pasco anyway? If he was a regular drug smuggler, Martin wouldn't have bothered his arse about him. He certainly wouldn't have let the matter haunt him. And he wouldn't have deleted the record. So was Pasco just some innocent businessman set up for the fall?'

Foxie drew a hand across his face in a weary manner. Entanglements of the past, he was thinking. The mysteries of history. You could never reconstruct anything precisely as it had happened. 'Let's say Pasco wanted revenge, a justifiable desire in the circumstances. He knows how to locate Carlotta. I can't get a grasp on the mechanics of how he knows that, but he decides to enlist her help. She discovers Burr was involved in the set-up . . .' Foxie shrugged. He was circling the delicate notion that what lay between Pagan and the woman was a personal matter. He thought of the computer image, the way she sat on Frank's bed. 'And by killing Martin, she pulls you a little deeper into her jetstream, in a manner of speaking.'

Jetstream, Pagan thought. Turbulence, great disturbances of air. *I've been in her jetstream too long, Robbie.*

Foxie continued, 'But Martin wouldn't be the only one involved. The CIA officer who set up the exchange was another. Perhaps there are others involved in Pasco's downfall. Are they on her hit list as well?'

'If a hit list exists, they're on it,' Pagan said.

'So . . . what we're saying is that Carlotta is Pasco's agent of vengeance.'

Agent of vengeance. Pagan again struck a match, set

fire to a strip of cellophane in the ashtray and watched it burn. Ten years ago a man passes through Heathrow on his way to Moscow unwittingly carrying a generous amount of cocaine. Ten years later, Martin Burr is murdered. All because he'd been involved in the entrapment of an innocent man; because he'd given a helping hand to some devious plan originating within the CIA.

Ten years. Pasco harbours a grudge year after year. He plots his revenge. The weather in his heart turns ever more bitter by the day – and who could blame him for that? Yet it was revenge at one remove, carried out not by himself, but by the woman – who'd certainly leap at the opportunity to shoot somebody as close to Pagan as Martin Burr.

Her terrorism was a complex business because it operated on different levels. At the lower end of the spectrum it was designed in a narrow way specifically to hurt him – the theft of the photograph, the intrusion into his apartment, the slaying of Burr; at the far end, her scope was broader, ranging from the bombing of the supermarket to the deaths at the hotel. And yet it wasn't really complex, not when you analysed it, it was all personal, because the things she did, large or small, touched his life adversely – and now he was being pulled into another of her worlds, one that involved a man called Richard Pasco. *Jetstream*, he thought. A good choice of word. He was imprisoned by her movements, sucked inside her activities, which was exactly the way she wanted it.

And maybe, God help him, that was the way he wanted it too.

He clasped his hands round his drink, squeezed the glass tightly. He raised his face to look at Foxie, and he said, 'Martin's assistant in the Drug Squad was a man called Anthony Trotter. It's possible he might be able to shed a little light on what happened ten years ago.'

'Is he still active?' Foxie asked.

'It's easy to check.' Pagan released his glass and pushed it aside. He rose, stepped out of the pub and into the sunlit street. Late afternoon, and the world was all too bright. Starlings screeched over the rooftops of Soho, reflecting sunlight in black oily flashes that were suggestive of polluted water rippling.

They went inside Pagan's office where Pagan made a phone-call to personnel and asked about Trotter. He was informed that Trotter had retired and lived in a nursing-home in Colindale. Pagan scribbled the address and phone number down. As he slid the sheet of paper across the desk toward Foxworth, the phone rang.

He picked up the receiver and spoke his name. He immediately flicked the switch for the loudspeaker and glanced at Foxworth; the woman's voice came out of the small beige amplification box.

'Frank,' she said. She sounded distant. She dragged out the vowel in the middle of his name. *Fraaank*. Pagan placed a hand to his mouth and bit on the corner of a fingernail.

'Not in a communicative mood, Frank? Don't want to talk to me?'

She spoke with an exaggerated Southern accent, Georgia, Alabama. Pagan still didn't say anything. He wondered who she thought she was today, what role she was enacting, what character she'd become.

'I do believe you're playing the silence game,' she said. 'Are you unhappy with me, Frank? Am I making you miserable? Doncha wanna talk to lil ole me?'

Pagan stared at the sunlit window. The call was long-distance. He was certain of that much. There was fuzz on the line; the connection had a slight echo. He wondered where she was phoning from. Stick a pin in a map of the world. She could be anywhere.

'Jeez-us, it's hot here,' she said. 'It's so god-damn hot you wouldn't believe what I had to do. I had to take off all my clothes and rub my body with ice. Everywhere. Every little corner. Breasts. Stomach. Between my legs. I'm doing it right now, Frank. Even as we speak. God, it feels good. It feels really good . . .'

Pagan looked at Foxie, who was sitting with the palms of his hands pressed to the sides of his expressionless face. What was Foxie making of this? What was he thinking?

She said, 'It just feels so cold, slippery, wet . . . Can you imagine it, Frank? Can you see it? Can you feel it?'

Yes, he thought. I can imagine it. He could see icy water sparkle on skin, rivulets running formlessly the length of her body.

'You know what I wish, Frank? I wish it was you holding the ice. I wish it was your hand. Wouldn't that be something?'

He said nothing, wasn't sure how to respond.

'Say. Are you alone? Is somebody with you? Is that why you can't speak? Am I embarrassing you, Frank?' She laughed softly.

'I'm not embarrassed,' he said. 'I don't give a shit what you're doing to yourself. Ice. Whipped cream. Chocolate sauce. Smear yourself with anything you like. I don't give a damn.'

'Oooh. Mister Cool. You can't imagine what a fucking turn-on it is when you talk like that. It gets me off. You wouldn't believe. Frank Frank *Frank*. I ever tell you how much I enjoy your name? I just love that name. And Pagan. There's a name that has all kinds of dark little echoes to it. It has this wonderful rough secretive feel about it. Pay-gan. It feels good in my mouth. It feels good just saying it.'

'Great. You like my name. That's terrific.'

'Oh shit. I just dropped the god-damn ice. What the hell. I'll get some more from the freezer. Gotta go. Gotta keep the fantasy running. Can't lose the momentum.'

'Wait,' he said.

'Wait for what, Frank?'

'Talk to me about Pasco. Talk to me about Pasco's list.'

'Pasco's list? Very good, Frank. Very good indeed. If you were here right now, I'd give you a special bonus for all your hard investigative labours. I'd fuck your brains out for you. I'd fuck you so you'd never forget it. It wouldn't be like anything you ever experienced before. Not with anyone. Not even with your wife.'

He ignored the reference to Roxanne. What was the point in rising to her bait? He needed control, not the dissipation of his energies into anger. 'There's just one small problem regarding your generous offer,' he said.

'Yeah, I know. A long-distance phone-fuck's not exactly the real thing, is it?'

'Exactly.'

'So if you want to claim your bonus, you'll just have to find me, won't you?'

'Right. And since you're not about to give me your address, why don't we pass a little time by discussing Pasco's list?'

There was a long silence. Pagan thought she'd

226

severed the connection, but he hadn't heard the click of the receiver going down. The palms of his hands were damp.

'You still there?' he asked.

'Sure I am.'

'Do we talk or what?'

'Talking's a bore. I prefer action every time. Don't you, Frank?'

'Pasco,' he said. 'Why don't we—'

She interrupted him. 'This ice is just running all over me, Frank. Running down my tits. Making my nipples hard. Running over my stomach. Down and down – oh, yes – into my cunt. I'd like you to be here, I'd like you to lick me dry. You'd enjoy that, wouldn't you? Your head between my legs. Your lips. Your tongue. I can imagine it. I can just imagine you down there. And I'd take your cock in my mouth the way I'm doing with this ice right now. I'd suck your brains out of your head. You have no idea what I'm capable of. This is turning you on, Frank. This is really making you sweat. Don't deny it.'

An indeterminate longing rushed to his head and he thought: a phone-job, electronic foreplay, masturbation with a satin glove on. It was tawdry and cheap, and there were numbers you could call twenty-four hours a day right here in London and get the same kind of service, and it would never have crossed his mind in a hundred years to dial any one of them – so why was he getting a buzz out of this? Because it was Carlotta and not an anonymous stranger, because she knew which buttons to push, because she was right when she'd said she could read him like a book. Because she had a way of imbuing her sleaze-speak with a certain authenticity, even a strange erotic elegance. Because he had this bloody disease, this fever, this wretched fault line in his character. *I'd fuck you so you'd never forget it.* Because because because.

'Pasco,' he said again.

'I don't want to talk about Pasco,' she said.

'Listen—'

'You ever visit Washington, Frank?'

'Why?'

'There's a very nice hotel I'd recommend. The Madison. You heard of it?'

'No.'

'Twenty-four-hour room service. I like room service.'

'Is The Madison where you're calling from?' he asked.

'You don't really expect me to answer that, do you? I'm hanging up now, Frank.'

'No, wait, just wait—'

'The ice is melting, Frank.'

He sat forward in his chair. 'Let's talk about Pasco,' he said again.

Again she was silent for a long time. There were background noises he couldn't identify. A door opening, a hinge creaking, he wasn't certain. 'Carlotta,' he said. 'Are you still there?'

'There's no Carlotta here,' she answered. And now her accent had completely changed; it was crisp, perfect Home Counties English, almost officious, as if she were a receptionist determined to let nobody pass her desk. She'd slipped from one persona to another seamlessly in that disconcerting way she had; an exchange of souls. 'You're speaking to Kristen Hawkins, and Kristen Hawkins isn't the kind of person who talks to strangers on phones. Kristen Hawkins is a very private individual. A very private individual altogether.'

The line was dead. Pagan hung on a few more seconds before he replaced the receiver. He swung round in his chair and looked at Foxworth. He wondered what Foxie saw in his expression, if there were any detectable signs of agitation on his face, any indication, however small, that the woman's words had had an effect on him. Suddenly angry with himself, with the fact that he'd participated for a fraction of time in the fantasy Carlotta had created, he got up and walked to the window and laid his forehead upon the glass and was struck by the urge to break the pane with a quick gesture of his skull, as if this might allow fresh cleansing air to circulate around and through him.

Foxie said quietly, 'It's none of my business.'

Pagan didn't turn round. 'You're right. It's none of your business.'

Pagan watched the sunbathers in the square, patches of reddish human flesh exposed to the sky. He said, 'I just don't want you to get the wrong impression, that's all.'

'I don't know what impression you think I have, Frank.'

'It must have sounded to you . . . I don't know . . . as if there was something between her and me. It's not like that. We've never . . .'

'She was the one doing all the talking,' Foxie said.

'And I was doing all the listening.'

'Did you have a choice?'

Pagan wondered about choice, the sloping alleys of motivation and need, those inclines that led you down into darkness and the recognition of a dreadful appetite inside yourself. He turned to look at Foxie, and said, 'You're too sympathetic, you know. I ought to be more thankful.'

Foxie shrugged. He gazed at the blank walls where

only lately Carlotta's photographs had hung. What the hell did it matter to him if Pagan had a weird *thing* for this woman? Chemistry happened. Contrary feelings rose like sap. It wasn't something you went looking for. So Pagan had a hard-on for the woman. This wasn't exactly a revelation. The way he'd studied her photographs, the manic determination of his search for her, his recurring bouts of crankiness and frustration – you didn't have to be the world's greatest detective to catch on. But the whole thing was worrying Pagan, it was something he was carrying around inside himself, and he couldn't shake it free. Foxie wondered: *Did he want to? Or was he getting a charge out of it?*

'I wish I could explain . . .' Pagan said. 'But I don't think I'd know where to begin.'

Foxie shook his head. 'There's really no need. Basic biology, Frank.'

Basic biology, Pagan thought. Foxie had a way with charitable expressions.

Pagan said, 'She's a monster. She kills the way other people blink. *I know all that* . . .' He looked remote all at once. 'What do you suggest? Therapy? Exile on Elba?'

Foxie understood that in all the years of their relationship this was probably the closest he'd ever come to Pagan. He'd been ushered into Pagan's private world and introduced to his devils, and he didn't know how to behave. 'Frank. So far as I can see, there's only one cure. We find her and we lock her away.'

Pagan thought: lock her away for the rest of her sorry life in black solitary confinement. Deprive her of all human contact. But would that liberate him? He placed a hand on Foxie's shoulder in a friendly manner.

'Do one small thing for me,' he said. 'Get somebody to run a check on the airlines. I don't know where the hell she was calling from, but it sounded a long way off.'

'Consider it done,' Foxie said, and he left the room slowly, as if he were reluctant to leave Pagan alone with his demons. But you could do nothing about another person's private demonology; you couldn't free other people from their own hells.

Pagan sat motionless at his desk, thinking of the woman's voice. *I'd fuck you so you'd never forget it.* Sergeant Whittingham appeared in the doorway, coughed politely to catch Pagan's attention.

'Don't mean to disturb, Mr Pagan,' he said. 'But this just came for you.' He was carrying a cardboard box, which he held tentatively. 'Messenger service.'

He approached the desk with the box. Pagan saw the label: *Alpha Express Delivery*.

'You think we should open it or send for the bomb experts?' the Sergeant asked.

Pagan said, 'We'll open it.'

'Is that wise, Mr Pagan?'

'Wisdom's overrated,' Pagan said.

'Just the same—'

'Give me the box, Sergeant.'

Whittingham did so. Pagan unravelled the tape and stripped off the brown wrapping paper, then looked at the sergeant. 'If this worries you, Whittingham, you don't have to stay.'

'No, I'll stay, Mr Pagan,' Whittingham said.

'You're sure?'

Whittingham nodded, although he was frowning, a man on the edge of a flinch. Under the wrapping paper was a shoebox. Pagan slowly raised the lid and saw his gun wrapped in pods of plastic packing-material. There was a small handwritten card: *You might need this. Happy hunting.*

'You see, Sergeant. Nothing to worry about after all.'

Whittingham said, 'Will there be anything else, Mr Pagan?'

'No, that's all.'

Whittingham stepped out of the office and Pagan looked at the pistol. This was the gun that had killed Martin Burr. He was plummeted back into the hallway of the apartment, hearing again the sound of the gun exploding. Seeing Martin die. He drew the pistol out from the mounds of packing-material and was holding it just as Foxworth came back inside the office.

Pagan said, 'It's not a suicide attempt, Foxie. Don't look so damnably worried.'

'Did I look worried?' Foxie asked. 'You're too interested in survival to think about suicide. You're much too self-centred, Frank, to think of eliminating yourself.'

'We'll postpone the character analysis for another time, Foxie. What have you got for me?'

'Stroke of luck, actually. The first airline we checked – she popped right out at us. Kristen Hawkins flew from Heathrow to Washington on American Airlines last night. At roughly the same time we discovered the body of Richard Pasco.'

'Timing,' Pagan said and weighed the gun in his hand. Washington from Heathrow. A quick hop.

'We only just missed her,' Foxie said.

Pagan smiled in an off-centre way. He had in his eye a deliberate light, one Foxworth had seen many times before, a grey determination, an inward focus, as if – having weighed the future – he'd come to the only possible conclusion.

25

CAPSICUM, NORTH CAROLINA

In a Chrysler rented under a false name, Ralph Donovan drove through the town of Capsicum at five o'clock in the afternoon. It wasn't much of a place. The fastest moving thing in the small town was the lengthening of shadow as the sun descended. Main Street was moribund, a dead-dog thoroughfare where a few stores were open for business, and the others had been vacated and boarded-up.

A diner called Molly's, a general store, a barber's, a filling-station – everything else had gone, although you could still read the signs. Jenn's Bridal Wear. Frank Saxx, Men's Clothing. Cutesy's, Everything Your Pet Could Want. Donovan wondered what kind of lives people led in these doomed places.

He switched off his air-conditioning, because he worried about the engine overheating – which would mean getting stuck in this butthole burg for hours – and he rolled down his window, allowing his arm to hang outside. The heat was palpable, the air dry as kindling. It was the kind of heat that constituted a personal assault, an insult to your body. People who lived here would surely shrivel. Eyes would dry in sockets, skin peel from bone.

Donovan left Capsicum and drove three miles on a

233

narrow blacktop whose surface had begun to melt. It was a straight road and it shimmered in front of him, and the sun, glinting with outright malevolence, blinded him. He slipped on his dark glasses.

When the house came in view he turned into the long driveway. The house, surrounded by thick willows, was an old plantation number that had been allowed to run into a state of fatal disrepair. The stone steps crumbled, the columns were larded with birdshit and smothered in deep red ivy, and a couple of upstairs windows were broken. Not at all a cheerful place. He caught a glimpse of dilapidated shacks out back, old slave quarters surrounded by a forest of weeds. He parked his car at the foot of the steps and got out.

He wiped sweat from his eyes as he reached the columns. He'd hoped the shadow beyond the columns would provide some respite, but they didn't. If anything, it was hotter in shade than in direct sun. Maybe heat just got trapped here in the unstirred, heavyweight air. He rang a doorbell and waited.

Skidelsky had said that only two people lived in the joint – an elderly man in a wheelchair, and his mildly deranged wife. As he waited, Donovan had the feeling he'd stumbled inside the attic of America, the place where everything useless was stored – houses like this, slave shacks, faded newspapers, sepia photographs, maybe even broken-necked banjos. Hey-ho, he thought. The business wasn't going to take long, provided somebody came to answer the god-damn door. He rang the bell again. Nobody came.

He decided he'd step inside anyway. Maybe they had ceiling fans, cool air. He found himself in a big gloomy entranceway with open doors on either side. A great staircase swept in a curve to the upper part of the house. He shouted for attention, but still nobody came.

He hadn't expected the place to be empty – it would be a drag to have to come back again.

'Yo-ho,' he called out. He walked to the foot of the stairs, called again, heard nothing. He moved back across the foyer. The air smelled dusty and clammy. 'Yo-ho! Anybody home?'

Finally something could be heard, an odd squeaking sound coming from the depths of a room. Donovan took off his dark glasses, stuck them in the breast-pocket of his shirt. The squeaking came closer. Out of the gloom a shape emerged, an old guy in a hand-propelled wheelchair, fluff of white hair uncombed, strange pink eyes, head tilted stiffly to one side. Skidelsky had said the old guy was blind – or half-blind anyway. But where was the wife? Donovan wondered. He wanted them both in the same room, because it was more convenient that way.

The wheelchair rattled and came to a stop a few feet in front of Donovan.

'Sorry to bother you, sir,' Donovan said. 'I rang the bell, nobody answered.'

Saliva dribbled from the old guy's mouth. The head remained at the same bizarre angle. 'Who the fuck are you?'

'You wouldn't know me, I'm just passing,' Donovan said. 'Tell you the truth, I got lost. I need directions.'

'Yeah, we all need directions, sonny. Whole god-damn country's lost.' The old man's voice was decidedly strange, a muted sort of trumpeting, sometimes close to a honk. 'If it ain't politicians, it's priests. You a Papist, boy?'

'No, sir. Methodist.'

'Methodist, huh? Can't say much about the Methodists, except they ain't Papists. Counts for something, I guess. Where you headed anyway?'

'Raleigh,' Donovan said. He was surprised by the spleen in the old guy's tone.

'They got priests in Raleigh, boy. They got RC churches there. Place is damned. This is supposed to be America, right? So what the fuck is Rome doing interfering with us?'

'Rome?' Donovan asked.

'Papal bull comes from Rome,' the old guy said. 'Papal bullshit, you ask me. Hell, priests are everywhere. Black suits, collars, god-damn crucifixes, fucking saints and stigmata. What the hell they doing in America, boy?'

'I don't—'

'Converting us. Or trying to. Catholic creed equals Catholic breed. No condoms. Oh, no, no condoms. Keep your peckers bare and breed like horse-flies. Ask yourself this. You think the Pope don't jerk off into a lace hankie?'

'Maybe he does,' Donovan said. Where was the wife, for Christ's sake? The air in this place stifled him, and there was a faint whiff of urine rising from the old guy's grey flannel pants.

'Sure he does, jerks off, gets one of his fucking bishops to dispose of the evidence. Don't tell me otherwise, boy. I got evidence.' The old guy tapped the side of his nose, a gesture of secrecy. 'Man can't get along without a little ejaculation now and then.'

A woman appeared out of the dimness of things. She was tall and skinny, emaciated even, and she wore a 1940ish satin dress, the kind you saw singers wear in nightclubs in old movies. Her gloves reached her elbows.

'A visitor?' she asked, and glided toward Donovan.

'I was just asking directions, ma'am.'

She tipped her face to one side, the gesture of a

236

ruined coquette. 'And Harry has been ranting at you, has he?'

'Ranting, bullshit,' said the old guy.

'He was expressing his opinions,' Donovan said. He wanted to get this over with and be on his way back to Capsicum.

'That's all he ever does,' the woman said. She must have been breathtakingly beautiful at one time, Donovan thought. The bone structure of her face was amazing still; but her skin was raddled, stricken and dried by too many Southern summers.

'Boy's a Methodist,' said the old guy.

'Well, isn't that a nice thing to be,' the woman said.

'Beats the holy shit out of Rome.'

Donovan smiled, shuffled his feet. The woman had a hand on his arm. 'It's so hot, so terribly hot. Can I get you a glass of lemonade? Orange juice? Perhaps something stronger?'

'I'm fine, ma'am, I just want directions to Raleigh,' Donovan said.

'But you've only just arrived.'

'I'm pressed for time,' Donovan said.

'Rush rush rush,' said the old guy. 'The whole goddam world's heading for cardiac arrest.'

'Which will keep the priests busy administering last rites, I daresay,' the woman remarked.

'Talk to me about fucking priests!' the old man said.

'Priests,' the woman hissed.

'I warn you.' The old guy turned from his wife and peered unseeingly in Donovan's direction. 'My wife has Roman blood in her, boy.'

'I do not,' she said.

'Your goddam father gave a mountainload of money to that fucking bishop in Raleigh.'

'So what if he did?'

'Treacherous Papist bastard, he was.'

Donovan had an insight into what it was that bound this weird couple together. It was mutual contempt and madness, assisted by lavish amounts of goading. She goaded him, he goaded her, and they'd goaded each other over the brink of sanity. It was one way of keeping a relationship going, he guessed. He stepped back, shrugged aside the woman's hand.

'I'm sorry,' he said. 'I have to be on my way.'

'Oh, dear, do you really?'

'Sorry,' he said again. He heard a trickling sound and realized the old guy was pissing himself. He reached down and took from the inside of his right boot an Accu-Tek 9mm pistol. He fired it directly into the old guy's heart and then turned the weapon on the woman – who'd taken an involuntary step back – and he shot her in the chest. Accuracy was everything. He surveyed the old guy slumped in the wheelchair, looked at the woman where she'd fallen – knees upraised, old-fashioned suspender-belt visible – and then he left the house and walked down the steps to his car.

He drove back into Capsicum. He parked outside the filling-station and took a small brown-paper bag from the glove-compartment. A kid in dungarees came out of a boxlike wooden structure. He had big hands slick with oil.

'Twenty bucks unleaded,' Donovan said.

'Passing through?' the kid asked.

'Sure am.'

'Can't say as I blame you. Capsicum ain't much.' The kid shrugged. You might read a lifetime of nothing in that simple gesture, Donovan thought.

'Where's the john?' Donovan asked.

'Out back behind the building. You gotta jiggle the handle a bit, you want it to flush.'

238

'I'll jiggle,' said Donovan. He made his way to the back of the wooden shed and found the washroom – thick with flies, thousands of them. They beat against his face and neck. He flapped them aside as best he could, then he took the lid from the cistern and placed the paper bag just above the waterline, taping it securely against porcelain. He flushed the toilet, watched the cistern fill. The water didn't come within two inches of the paper bag. Satisfied, Donovan replaced the cistern lid, then walked back out to his car.

'Awright?' the kid asked.

'Yeah, I jiggled it.'

'Keep saying I'll get it fixed one of these days,' said the kid, and took the twenty-dollar bill from Donovan's hand.

Donovan got inside the car. He had exactly ten minutes to clear Capsicum. Time enough.

'Go careful,' said the kid, and smiled.

'You bet.'

Donovan was beyond the Capsicum town limits within thirty seconds. Ten minutes later he was eight miles away, but he could hear the blast even from that distance.

26

LONDON

It was early evening when Foxworth arrived at the hospice in Colindale on the edge of London. It was a pleasant building, ivy and gentle sandstone – if any kind of place where the terminally ill came to die could be called pleasant. He parked beneath a laurel tree and entered the building, where he was met by a nurse.

'We'd appreciate it if you restricted your visit to fifteen minutes,' the nurse said. Her complexion was wondrously unblemished, and Foxie – given to romantic rushes – was immediately attracted to her. Her name was Sally, according to her badge. 'Mr Trotter's on very strong medication, you understand.'

'I won't take up too much of his time. I promise.'

'Good. If you'll follow me . . .'

Anywhere, he thought. Just name it. Admiring Sally's legs, he trailed after her along a corridor. He thought about Pagan, and wondered why Frank hadn't come with him to this place. He suspected he knew the answer. He'd suspected it from the moment Pagan had ordered him to visit Anthony Trotter, because Frank had said in a misleadingly vague way that he had certain other business to attend to . . . Yes, Foxworth thought. You have. The jetstream.

Sally said, 'You'll find him alert enough. We spike

the morphine with an effective stimulant, you see. The idea here is to die with dignity. To be alert, but not to be in pain.'

Foxie made a sympathetic sound as Sally opened a door and showed him inside a small room where Anthony Trotter was sitting up in bed and gazing at a TV, which he at once switched off with a remote control. He was frail and practically transparent. His hands were almost fleshless, appendages of bone. He turned his face as Foxie entered. Sally withdrew from the room.

'Ah-hah,' Trotter said. 'Fellow from Special Branch. Told me you were coming.'

Foxie pulled a chair up to the bed.

Anthony Trotter nodded at the window where a rose-bush pressed against the pane. 'Couldn't ask for a better place to kick the bucket. All sweethearts around here. None of that business of waking you up at some ungodly hour for a pill. Civilized, you see.'

Foxie watched the head of a pink rose, disturbed by a quiet breeze, knock almost cheerfully upon the window. 'Very civilized,' he said.

'Do me a favour, would you? Pour me some of that orange juice there. Good fellow.'

Foxie obliged.

Trotter sipped through an angular straw. 'So, laddie. How is Special Branch? Still the same old cesspit of ambition and backbiting, eh? Same old slurry-tank of bad feelings?'

'There are some rivalries,' Foxie said.

'More than rivalries, I'd say. Fellows there would cut one another's throats.' Trotter gazed out at the rose-bush.

Foxie was quiet a second. Death and rose-bushes. Sunlight coloured the old man's sparse hair. He'd obviously made an effort to comb the few remaining strands across his bald spots. A little attention to appearance at death's door: Foxie was touched.

'Expect you're here about Martin.'

'It's connected with Martin, yes,' Foxworth said.

'Bad business,' Trotter said. 'Very bad. You couldn't ask for a finer fellow to work under.' He shook his head, frowned. He finished his orange juice and looked at Foxworth a moment. His blue eyes were lively. 'Well. You have questions, fire away. Memory's still functioning, you know. I may be standing on the edge of eternity –' and here he tapped his skull – '*compos mentis* just the same.'

Foxie felt like an intruder. This was wrong, this interruption of a dying man's fragile little world. He hesitated.

'No need to hold your fire, laddie. Ignore my condition and blast away. Ask me anything you like. You'll get a straight answer.'

'You worked with Martin as his assistant in the Drug Squad, right?'

'Before he was kicked up the ladder, yes.'

'Do you remember ever having heard the name of a man called Richard Pasco?'

'Pasco Pasco. Give me a moment.' Trotter squeezed his eyes shut. 'American fellow, yes?'

'Right.'

'Arrested in Moscow?'

'That's the one.'

'For cocaine smuggling.' Trotter emitted a ragged laugh. 'I spent years fighting the people who traffic in cocaine and here I am imbibing it myself on a regular basis. It's in the cocktail they give you, you see. Morphine and a dash of liquid cocaine. Ironic rather.'

'Yes, I suppose it is.'

'Keeps the head clear. I gather some people consider it a highly controversial treatment. Godsend, if you ask me. Recommend it to anyone in this condition.'

Foxie leaned a little closer to the bed. 'Pasco travelled through Heathrow with the cocaine in a suitcase. You remember that?'

'Most certainly do. Martin was very unhappy. But we had instructions to let Pasco slip out of London unmolested by customs officials.'

'These instructions. What do you remember about them?'

Trotter said, 'Martin was fuming. I remember that very well. It wasn't so much an anger directed at the instructions. It seemed to me at the time that it was more of an inner business, as if he were raging at himself. I couldn't for the life of me think why he would have reason to be angry with himself.'

'Do you recall where these instructions originated?' Foxie asked.

'Oh. CIA. Definitely. CIA fellow came to us.'

'Do you remember his name?'

Trotter bent his straw and crammed it inside the empty orange juice glass. 'Do let me ponder that a moment, laddie. Every now and then there's a hiatus in the old memory cells. I always think of them as vacant rooms in the Replay Hotel.'

'Please. Take your time.'

Trotter tilted his head back against his pillows. Foxie wondered if he'd need to prod the old fellow along more vigorously. No, be patient. He'd wait for Trotter to remember. Earlier, when Marcia Burr had shown a certain reluctance to talk about her late husband, Foxie had been surprised by the aggression in Pagan's questions. It was restrained, and Marcia may not have noticed it, but it was evident to Foxie, and it had annoyed him just slightly. Pagan's impatience often took him in the general direction of discourtesy.

Trotter snapped his brittle fingers and said, 'Poole. That was the name. Christopher Poole.'

Foxie scribbled this in his notebook. 'Do you think he's still active?'

'I haven't kept in touch with that world in recent years. He'd be rather close to retirement, I'd say. I only met him once. Martin wasn't entirely expansive in his introduction. It was all rather hurried, I remember. He wanted Poole in and out quickly. He acted as if he were embarrassed by the fellow.'

'Do you know why Martin agreed to go along with Poole?'

Trotter looked beatific, as if impending death had bestowed an enviable serenity on him. 'As I understood it, Poole needed a lamb for sacrificial purposes. And Pasco was just such an animal, poor chap. A squalid little bargain had been struck with the Russians. They had a man Poole wanted out. Pasco was the coin of exchange. Why Martin agreed – well, I wouldn't even hazard a guess at his reasons. He could be mysterious at times.'

Like somebody else I know, Foxworth thought. 'Do you recall the name of the man Poole wanted out?'

'Certainly do. Bob Naderson. He'd apparently been arrested by the Soviets during a routine visit to Moscow. I'm not absolutely sure what "routine" means in this context. I remember it was the word they used at the time.'

Foxworth wrote this down in his notebook. 'Was Naderson released?'

'Oh, most certainly. He was an important man in the Agency. They couldn't let him languish inside a Russian jail, could they?'

Foxie asked, 'Was there any special reason they chose Pasco as the lamb?'

Trotter shook his head. 'Funny lot, the CIA. Never really understood them. The way they use their own people.'

'Their own people?' Foxie asked.

'You didn't know Pasco was CIA?'

'No, I didn't,' Foxie said.

'I remember being appalled by the fact that they could rid themselves of their own so callously.'

Foxie closed his notebook. *Pasco had been CIA.*

'Any help to you, laddie?' Trotter asked.

'I believe so,' Foxie said.

'Good. Nice to be on one's deathbed and still be of some use.'

Foxie couldn't think of a response to this. A life goes out slowly; an old man lies dying, dying and remembering. He stood up.

'Off and running,' Trotter said.

'You know how it is.'

'Indeed. Only too well,' said the old man.

Foxie thanked him and moved toward the door, where he turned to look back. He was affected by a curious trick of the eye for a second: Trotter seemed to float on a cushion of sunlight a few inches above the bed. Foxie raised a hand in a gesture of farewell, and stepped into the corridor where Sally was waiting.

'Lovely old man,' she said.

'Yes.'

She escorted Foxie along the corridor to the front door. 'He's such a sweetie to deal with.'

He left the building and walked back to his car. As he drove away, he observed Sally in the doorway waving one hand in a friendly manner and he entertained the notion that he might one day find himself back in this neighbourhood. *To dally with Sally*.

He travelled by underground back to Piccadilly Circus, then walked to Golden Square. Pagan's office was empty, as he'd known it would be. On the surface of his desk lay an envelope addressed to Foxworth and marked PERSONAL. Foxie opened it. Inside was a slip of paper on which Pagan had scribbled: *Mind the store for me, and if George comes looking, tell him anything you like – I've checked into an asylum, I've gone on a binge, I've been beamed up by an inquisitive UFO for a medical probe. You can reach me at The Madison Hotel, Washington, telephone 202 862 1000. If it's any consolation, I'm flying coach.*

Headstrong Pagan, Foxie thought. Gone. Mind the store for me. He stuffed the paper in his jacket pocket and surveyed the stack of photographs of Carlotta that still lay on Pagan's desk.

Idly, he sifted through them. She gazed back at him from a number of poses. He saw in each a common element, and it wasn't danger, it wasn't menace, it was something else: the bloom of death. It was in her eyes. It was in the set of her mouth. It was a quality that, as soon as he'd pinned it down, slithered evasively away from him, and left him to wonder if he'd imagined it in the first place. He put the pictures back in place and saw that the charred remains of Pasco's bank-book lay on the edge of Pagan's desk, and he raised it carefully, smelling the scent of burned paper and remembering the way Pasco had been shot.

I hope you catch her, Frank. Catch her before she catches you.

27

WASHINGTON

Max Skidelsky always used the same high-priced call-girl agency when he wanted sex without commitment. The girls were invariably tall and fair-haired, because that was the way he liked them. Generally, they were hard-up students working their way on their backs through expensive colleges. They used names that were patently not their own – they called themselves Ophelia, or Candice, or Leticia, which was a step up from the more vulgar *noms d'amour* such as Brandy, Cinnamon or Honeydrop. Skidelsky expected a certain level of conversational skill as well as sexual, because he considered communication an important aspect of foreplay.

The girl who presently lay on the sofa in his Washington apartment called herself Amaryllis, one of his regular visitors. She was a third-year history student at Penn State, a fact Skidelsky had managed to coax out of her during their last encounter. Her real name was Mary Margaret Kennedy, which she didn't think sufficiently exotic for business purposes. It wasn't exactly a come-on to have a name like a Mother Superior.

Skidelsky poured two glasses of white wine and sat alongside the naked girl. 'Cheers,' he said.

She stretched out one arm to take the glass from him. 'Cheers.'

Skidelsky sipped his wine. He surveyed the lines of her body, impressed by the perfection of the nipples, the light hair that grew under her navel and darkened as it spread down her flat belly. She had light green eyes and a good jaw and a wide mouth. Max Skidelsky enjoyed the geography of women, the way they were sculpted. He sometimes thought of them in terms of terrain, contoured maps.

'You were a little . . . quick tonight,' she said.

'Is that a criticism?' he asked.

She shook her head. 'No. You just seemed very tense. Anxious. Are you anxious, Max?'

He smiled. 'Not especially.'

She changed her position, sat upright, drew her long legs under herself. 'Every time I come here I think the same thing – why does a guy that looks like you want to pay for sex? You must have women throwing themselves at you. Maybe you just like the idea of paying for it. Some guys do. They find it a turn-on.'

Skidelsky said, 'I don't respect women who throw themselves.'

'But you respect a woman who charges money?' she asked.

'It's open, it's honest, it's a straight transaction without complications. I like some things in life to be simple.'

'I can see that,' she said, and looked round his apartment – which was spacious but seriously under-furnished, no more than a sofa and two chairs, a TV and a coffee-table. No prints hung on the walls. 'This is all a bit monastic, Max.'

'Why encumber yourself with stuff you don't need?'

'Why indeed.' She peered at him over her glass. 'You're a mystery, Max.'

'Me? A mystery? I'm an open book,' he replied.

'If you're an open book, I'm a virgin cheer-leader.'

'Why do you find me mysterious?' he asked.

'I don't know anything about you, what you do, where you work, what you think about stuff—'

'What kind of stuff?'

'Stuff stuff. You know, politics, current issues, books, movies.' She gave a languid little shrug. 'I mean, you give the impression of this highly focused kind of guy, except I don't know what you're focused on. Does that make sense?'

Skidelsky held her hand. He inclined his head and brushed his lips across her knuckles. Then he raised his face to her. 'I don't read books except histories, I don't have time for movies—'

'OK. That leaves politics.'

'All politicians are scum. Without exception. They couldn't run a dog-pound, never mind a nation.'

'A serious charge,' she said, wide-eyed.

'You wanted to know. What else was on your agenda? Current affairs? I can cover that in a sentence or two. The country is bent out of shape. People can't even walk their own neighbourhoods at night. They're terrified about taking their kids to the local friendly fast-food joint just in case some disaffected psycho decides to let off a few rounds of ammunition, and they don't feel secure going to work in their high-rise hives because they don't know if they're terrorist-proof. Americans look ahead and the crystal ball's gone cloudy and we're scared because we don't know what's coming next. The comfort of prediction is gone. The eiderdown of assurance and self-confidence is moth-eaten, sweetheart. We used to be able to project, and what we saw on the horizon was always rosy and nice. But now we're well on the way to becoming a Third World country. There are areas in some of our cities as bad as anything you'd see in Manila or Rio.'

'You see a cure for all this?' she asked.

'A quick solution, no.'

'So we sit round and drink and maybe try to fuck our way out of all this gloom?'

Skidelsky set his wineglass aside. He'd reached his alcohol limit for the day. 'Maybe that's the best response,' he said, and smiled at her, and drew her face toward his. The kiss was all electricity, charges rushing through his head and body. He placed his hands on her breasts. There was a sudden renewed intensity about him, which the girl felt, a force almost frightening. She reached for him, held him in the palm of her hand, felt the tension in him as if it were hot iron. She rolled a condom over him, parted her legs. As he entered her he knew it was going to be quick again, because his blood was racing. His orgasm was like a flower violently opening. He laid his face against her shoulder and his body shook.

She was silent for a while, then she said, 'You know what you really need, Max?'

'Tell me.'

'A massage.'

'A massage?'

'Seriously. Lie face down on the floor.'

The telephone was ringing. Max reached out to pick it up.

Larry Quinn said, 'Eddie Binns is dead. They found him in his house in Baltimore. There's going to be a scandalous fall-out in academic circles.'

'Scandalous how?'

'He was hanging from a rope in his bedroom. He

was dressed in what you might call revealing underwear of the female variety. There were also magazines of an explicit homosexual nature. The cops think he was trying to achieve one of those mind-blowing mid-flight orgasms, and it went wrong because the chair fell over and he choked on the god-damn rope.'

'Inventive,' Skidelsky said.

'Yeah. Somebody less refined could just have gone in with a gun. You have to give her points for creativity, Max.'

'I don't think her creativity was ever in doubt, Larry. Her stability, sure. But never her inventiveness.'

Larry Quinn laughed. 'Turn on your TV in a few minutes, Max. CNN channel. I understand there's something coming on that might interest you.'

Skidelsky hung up. He looked at the girl. She was studiously staring at a copy of a newspaper she'd found because she didn't want him to think there was even the smallest possibility she was an eavesdropper. He was a good customer, and usually a surprisingly pleasant lay, and gentle to her – and in her line of work discretion was paramount. Max was the first client she'd ever really grown to like. He had a boyish quality that appealed to her, and sometimes she experienced little protective urges toward him. A maternal thing, she supposed. He looked at times so god-damn young.

He turned on the TV and lay on the floor.

She climbed on his back. 'That's the idea,' she said. 'Watch a little TV while I work those tensed muscles of yours. Just relax. Breathe deep and easy.'

He gazed at the CNN logo and thought about Eddie Binns hanging from the end of a rope, dressed in frilly panties. *She knows her stuff*, he thought. *The woman knows her stuff all right.* An announcer appeared on the screen, a black guy in an open-necked shirt. Directly behind him a row of buildings smouldered; fire-trucks could be seen, cop cars, ambulances. The girl ploughed her fingers into Max's shoulder muscles while he listened to what the black guy was saying in his breathless heart-of-the-action manner.

'Terrorism came to this small sleepy North Carolina community today. The town of Capsicum, population two hundred and sixty, has almost totally been destroyed. You can see the devastation,' and he made a sweeping gesture with his arm. 'Federal agents are busy at the scene . . . and I'm reliably informed by sources at the heart of the investigation an explosive device placed in the vicinity of a local gas-station was the cause of this mayhem. It's going to take experts days to put the pieces of this tragic jigsaw puzzle together, but the question on everybody's lips is Why? Why Capsicum, of all places?'

Max Skidelsky watched as the black guy was joined in front of the camera by a chubby man in a sheriff's uniform.

'This is County Sheriff Jay Blades.'

The county sheriff, unaccustomed to TV appearances, nodded in an embarrassed way. His eyes were rimmed with smoke stains.

'Sheriff Blades, are there any theories why this happened?'

Blades said, 'Right at this moment, Dave, we don't have a whole lot to go on. We're looking at several angles.'

'You want to expand on that a little for us?' Dave asked, poking his microphone forward. He was obviously a graduate of the Persistent School of TV Journalism.

'Nope, because right now the investigation's at

a delicate stage, and I don't want to play guessing-games.'

The sheriff was drifting away from the camera. The reporter, Dave, caught hold of the lawman's sleeve and said, 'One last question, Sheriff. There's a rumour that Capsicum was the birthplace of the notorious terrorist known to the world as Carlotta—'

'I don't discuss rumours,' said Blades, and moved away. 'I got work to do.'

Dave turned back to the camera and looked grim. 'We'll have updates throughout the night. This is Dave Witherspoon, Capsicum, North Carolina.'

Max punched the off button on the remote. He felt the girl's fingertips work into his flesh in deep, satisfying strokes. So, the Carlotta angle was being played down – clearly an FBI decision. The Feds didn't want the great US public to think the woman was back in business in America. They liked to create an illusion of calm. *Carlotta? No, she's got nothing to do with this. She's out of the country. There's no way she could come back here and try this kind of thing. Life goes on.*

'That's pretty scary,' the girl said. 'A quiet town like that . . . and you were just talking about terrorism.'

'The world is full of coincidences,' Max Skidelsky said.

28

WASHINGTON

Pagan felt the gears in his brain slip. The five-hour flight from London, most of which he'd managed to sleep through, had dehydrated him, and now the fluorescent enormity of Washington International Airport dazzled and diminished him. Because he carried a firearm, he was whisked off to a small interview room where he was asked by an Immigration official to show his Special Branch ID and complete certain forms. Name. Occupation. Affiliation. Purpose of visit. Make and number of gun. Passport number. A pen was stuck into his hand. The world was being asphyxiated by red tape. He scribbled quickly, handed the forms back to the official who studied them.

'You're a tad vague when it comes to purpose,' the man said eventually.

'You know how it is,' Pagan remarked. 'Sometimes it's hard to be specific in this game.'

The official examined Pagan's official ID, holding it under a desk-lamp as if he suspected that direct light might reveal some flaw in the laminated card. 'I guess it's all in order. Just don't forget you're legally obligated to advise the local police department of your presence here. That's the rule.'

'I'll do it at once.' Pagan took back his card, picked

up his bag, a leather valise he'd packed hurriedly in London, and moved toward the door. He crossed the massive terminal, following signs and arrows that indicated the location of car-rental companies. He hired a two-door Ford compact, basic wheels. He filled in more forms – Land of the Free, provided you signed in triplicate – took the keys from the clerk and when he stepped from the air-conditioned building the night heat smacked him with the concentrated ferocity of a karate blow. He felt himself buckle as he went in search of the car-hire lot.

He drove into the city, checked into The Madison Hotel on 15th Street Northwest. He made inquiries at the desk about the woman, using only her most recent alias of Kristen Hawkins. He talked to the assistant manager who, anxious to help a law officer, allowed him to look through records of guests in the last day or so – but there were none who might have been Carlotta. *I'm here because she wants me to be here*, he thought. *Because she knows where to find me. Because she needs control.* His room was small but, in the language of hoteliers, 'elegantly-appointed'. He showered, changed clothes, called Foxworth's number in London. He found Foxie in a sullen frame of mind.

'Nice one, Frank. You waited until my back was turned and you sneaked off, leaving me with the cheerless prospect of explaining your disappearance to Nimmo.'

'Has he asked yet?'

'No, but he will. He's bound to. Christ, Frank. The least you could have done was to discuss this overseas jaunt with me—'

'You're whining,' Pagan said.

'If I'm whining it's because I feel bloody excluded.

I'd like to believe, after all this time, that I've earned your confidence.'

Pagan said, 'I need you to be there, Foxie. In Golden Square.'

'For what? To make excuses on your behalf?'

Pagan sat on the edge of the bed. He wondered briefly about the nature of long-term working relationships, whether they transmuted into a kind of asexual marriage over the years. What Foxie sounded like was a wounded spouse.

'You just jump on a bloody plane, Frank. Have you got a plan of action worked out? Or are you following some kind of musk, like a dog in heat?'

'That's a fucking low blow, Foxie,' Pagan said.

'I'm sorry, I know it is,' and Foxie lapsed into a regretful silence before he added, 'I take that back.'

'What did you learn from Trotter?'

Foxie's voice brightened. He couldn't maintain the whining mode for very long because he was not by nature a grudging man. 'Trotter gave me some interesting stuff. Got a pen?'

'Fire away.'

'First, the agent who approached Burr is somebody called Christopher Poole. Second, the exchange of Pasco was designed to engineer the release of a man called Bob Naderson. I ran a little background on both men. Naderson is currently Deputy Director for Science and Technology. Poole's a different fish altogether – Executive Director of the CIA, which places him just below the Deputy Director of Intelligence, who in turn is just one tiny rung beneath God himself, the Director.'

Pagan wrote this down on hotel notepaper. 'What about Pasco?' he asked.

'Ah, I was saving that. Pasco turns out to have been CIA too.'

'One of their own,' said Pagan.

'Indeed. One of their very own.'

'A discard,' Pagan said. He thought of the dead man in the house in Kilburn, the charred passport – the remains of Richard Pasco. 'He must have known the Agency betrayed him, Foxie. He had years to think about it. One dreary day after another – what else does he do to pass the time except chew on reconstructions of betrayal? And when he's released, he's carrying a whole lot of poisonous baggage, and he's got to dump it somehow.'

'And in the process, alas, he got dumped himself,' Foxie said.

Pagan capped the ballpoint pen. 'You get too close to Carlotta, that's the risk you run.'

'I assume you'll remember that, Frank.'

'Count on it.'

'One last thing, Frank. Just keep in touch.'

Pagan said he would, then put the receiver back in place. He looked at his watch, set it to Washington time, then he went downstairs to a place called The Hideaway Bar and drank three cups of coffee. He was moderately refreshed. How long the condition would last he didn't know.

He finished his third cup, looked round, felt the slightly skewed sense of displacement that happens when you've transferred yourself through time zones and across an ocean. He examined the names on his slip of paper – Bob Naderson, Christopher Poole. These would be on Carlotta's list – these and how many others? His thoughts drifted off to Martin Burr and again he wondered about the reasons behind Martin's decision ten years ago. Had Martin known

Pasco was an Agency employee? He tapped his fingers on the surface of the table, feeling the nervy little zing of caffeine in his system.

'Pagan,' the man said.

Pagan looked up to see Artie Zuboric standing beside the table. Pagan held out his hand; Zuboric's grip was slack and moist and quick, barely a contact at all. It had been a long time since Pagan had last seen him – eight years ago, back in the days when together they'd formed a tetchy alliance, Special Branch and the FBI, in pursuit of the Irish assassin known as Jig.

'You've put on weight,' Pagan said.

'Thanks for pointing that out, Pagan. Happens to some of us. You look a little different yourself. More gaunt, maybe. Hollow, kind of.'

'So we've both changed,' Pagan said.

'Don't be fooled by superficial things,' Zuboric said. 'Some stuff doesn't change.'

Zuboric had shaved off the Zapata moustache he'd worn years ago, and the bushy sideburns had been clipped back, but his thick mat of hair was much the same as it had been – crow-black, although Pagan suspected the colour these days came out of a bottle. Zuboric clicked his fingers for the attention of a waiter and asked for a bottle of Bud in a voice as loud as the baggy short-sleeved summery shirt he wore, a linen menagerie of tropical parrots. Zuboric wasn't big on buttoned-down FBI chic.

Pagan said, 'Thanks for meeting me.'

'You think I'd let you wander at will around my turf? I like the notion of having you where I can see you, Pagan. When I heard you were coming, alarms started going off inside my head.' Zuboric drank his beer straight from the bottle.

'I didn't come to Washington to look for a nanny, Artie,' Pagan said.

'Yeah. I know what you're here for. But she's on my territory now, and you ought to keep that in mind, Pagan. We got first dibs on her. Plain and simple.'

'I've never been petty when it comes to matters of jurisdiction,' Pagan said. 'I just want her caught and put away. Here, there, anywhere, it doesn't matter.'

Zuboric scratched his hairy arms. 'Boy. She did a number on your so-called security conference. Jesus Christ. How the hell did you let that happen?'

'I didn't *let* it happen, Artie,' Pagan said. He tried to retain some measure of self-control. An old animosity existed between himself and Zuboric, and it hadn't mellowed. Zuboric's nature was gruff at the best of times, but the presence in the United States of an Englishman from Special Branch exacerbated this streak. Besides, he'd never cared for this particular Englishman. Push Artie, and he might let slip a tiny phrase of grudging approval for some of Frank's past successes, but that was about as far as he would go – and only then under pressure.

'You were in charge, from what I hear. So how did she slip right on past you?'

'Another identity. Different papers.'

'Same old story.'

'Same old story,' Pagan agreed. He was about to remind Zuboric that the woman had escaped in the first place from the US Federal penitentiary at Danbury, but what was the point of resuscitating ancient history? It could only lead to further hostilities. And he didn't need a hardening of Zuboric's attitude.

Zuboric said, 'I heard about Martin Burr.'

Pagan said nothing, merely moved his head in a quiet form of acknowledgement.

'You were there when it happened,' Zuboric said.

'Yes.'

'And you . . .'

'Couldn't do anything to stop her? Is that what you were going to ask?'

'Crossed my mind.'

And it keeps crossing mine, Pagan thought. 'I didn't get the chance, Artie.'

Zuboric scratched his arms again and changed the subject. 'Fucking mosquito bites,' he said. 'I have this allergic reaction to the damn things.' He took out a cigar and ripped off the cellophane. He struck a match and peered at Pagan through the yellowing flame. 'So. You've come all this way in the hope of catching her.'

'Yes,' Pagan said.

'You expect the Bureau to assist you?'

'I don't expect anything, Artie.'

'You're sure she's in the States?'

'I'm sure.'

'How come?'

Pagan smiled. 'Sources, Artie.'

'Yeah, we all got sources.' Zuboric blew smoke in a huge pale cloud then picked a fragment of tobacco from his lip. 'She's here, Pagan. She's come home. You got that right. In fact, she's already active. You can read this in tomorrow's papers, so I'm not giving away any trade secrets. She exploded a device in a small town called Capsicum in North Carolina, which blitzed the whole place. Her home town, in fact. Just to round things off real neat and tidy, she shot her parents.'

'You're sure it was her?'

'Let me put it this way, Pagan. We're not altogether overloaded with alternative candidates. Who the hell else would do something like that? We're talking your basic one-street town, population next to nothing. And her parents – well, that's the frosting on the cake. That's like leaving your fingerprints behind.' Zuboric slugged his beer. 'You seem underwhelmed.'

Pagan asked, 'Why would she go to the trouble of killing her parents and blowing up her birth-place?'

'You're supposed to be the big expert on Carlotta's head,' Zuboric said. 'You figure it out.'

Pagan was puzzled. He thought he'd grasped her agenda, the focus of her business in America, but this new information threw him. Either she'd widened the range of her targets, or Capsicum was somehow connected to the Agency or to Pasco; maybe it was something else, something simple by Carlotta's own corkscrewing standards – she'd decided to attend to a personal matter, in her own lethal fashion, because she happened to be in the general vicinity.

'Is there anything special about Capsicum?' he asked.

'Special? It was just another half-dead community in the middle of nowhere. We got a million of them. What could be special about it? It didn't have any local industry. It's po-boy country, Pagan, bone-dry and rotting away from the inside. It's the kinda place where pulses quicken when people see a car with out-of-state plates. Maybe she just had this insane grudge against the whole place, including her parents. I read her case-file, and the way it looks she didn't have a whole lotta love for Mom and Dad anyway. Seems she harbours some real deep resentment about the fact they kept sending her away – boarding-schools, a clinic. So she shoots them, then zaps Capsicum out of existence to the tune of about seventy fatalities and serious injuries. You got a problem with that notion?'

Pagan shook his head. 'No, not really.'

'You don't sound convinced. You know something I don't know, Pagan?'

'Nothing, Artie.'

'Don't hold out on me.'

'Would I do that?'

Zuboric puffed furiously a few times on his cigar and then crushed it. 'Yeah. I believe you would, because you always were a secretive sonofabitch.'

'Me? Secretive?'

'Don't fuck with me, Pagan. You know something, you show me your cards.'

Pagan showed Zuboric his empty palms. 'See. Nothing hidden. Nothing up my sleeve.'

'It ain't your hands I'm interested in. It's what's inside your head, Pagan. For instance, what's your next move? What's your strategy? What fragments are you trying to glue together?'

Fragments, Pagan thought. Fragments of self, perhaps, but that wasn't an answer he could offer Zuboric. Artie Zuboric wasn't the kind of man comfortable with riddles and paradoxes. *I'm hunting the woman, and she's hunting me.* Why would she go to Capsicum and set off an explosive device and kill her parents? Why that wayward activity, that murderous side-trip? To conceal her real purpose? To confuse? But why do something that was certain to create huge publicity and bring her name back into the public eye and activate the Bureau? OK, so she liked headlines, she liked spotlights and all the attention of her notoriety, and maybe she just wanted America to know she'd finally come home . . . Pagan's thoughts fizzled out once again in the maze of trying to understand the woman. He felt a little slippage, a dull reverberation of fatigue. The caffeine was dying in his system.

Zuboric said, 'I'm waiting.'

'I don't have a strategy, Artie.'

'You come all this way on something as vague as what you refer to as "sources"?'

'Pretty much.'

Zuboric shook his head. 'That's your story.'

Pagan said, 'That's my story.'

'Here's the Bureau's official position on you, Pagan. You don't interfere with our investigation at any level. You stumble across any information relevant to our inquiries, it comes to me immediately. You get lucky and find out where the woman is, you don't go in solo for the kill, you pick up the nearest phone and you contact me. The Bureau takes the view that you're a tourist who just happens to be a cop. You're way out of your jurisdiction, and you don't have the privileges of an accredited law-enforcement officer.'

'The spirit of co-operation,' Pagan said. 'I like it, Artie.' *You give me nothing, Zuboric, and you get nothing in return*, he thought.

Zuboric stood up. 'I don't give a shit what you like, Pagan. I'm telling you the way things are from the Bureau's point of view.'

'You want my gun? My badge?'

Zuboric said, 'You get to keep those.'

'An act of kindness.'

Zuboric said, 'Call it charity, Pagan. Because that's what you are. A charity case.' He took something out of the back pocket of his pants and tossed it down on the table. It was a small diary.

'What's this?' Pagan asked.

'What's it look like to you?' Zuboric tried an English accent, which he didn't do with any conviction. 'It's a gift from the Bureau, old boy. It's all you're going to get in the way of handouts.'

'Is this an early Christmas present? Or am I expected to keep a bloody log?' Pagan asked.

'Religiously. Who you phone. Where you go. Who you see.'

Pagan said, 'This is embarrassing, Artie.'

'Aintit just,' Zuboric said and smiled. 'Every now and again I'll check in on you, and I'll ask to see the log, and it better be accurate. And remember what I said. We'll be keeping an eye on you. You just won't know when. *Ciao*.'

'Big Brother,' Pagan remarked, but Zuboric had already wandered away from the table and didn't hear the comment.

Pagan fingered the pages of the diary. Zuboric wanted him to keep a record of his activity: the Bureau wanted him to feel like somebody on probation. He supposed he ought to be grateful they hadn't attached an electronic beeper to his ankle. OK, he'd keep a log, but he'd do it his own way.

He went back upstairs to his room. He checked the telephone directory for the names of Naderson and Poole, and found neither. He wasn't surprised. Both men were unlisted, which meant that if he wanted to talk to either of them he'd have to contact them through Langley. Naderson, he assumed, would be more accessible than Poole, because he didn't have Poole's status. First thing in the morning, he'd contact Naderson and try to arrange an appointment.

He undressed and lay face-down across the bed. He was asleep within a matter of minutes. He dreamed.

He dreamed the woman came to him. She stood at the foot of the bed. She removed her clothes and tossed them aside. As they fell they seemed to hang, with the contrary gravity of dreams, in the air; clouds of silk, transparencies of lace. She climbed onto the bed and slid toward him. She drew the bed sheets aside. She caressed him with a tenderness he hadn't expected. *This is what you want*, she said. *This is what you really want.* Her voice was a whisper. *I excite you, Frank. Admit it. I excite you.* He kissed her, touched her breasts, felt her hip against his, the delightful stretches of her thighs against his skin. *Admit it. You're burning. You can't hold back. Come inside me. Fuck me.*

Yes, he said.

He was lost in her, a ferocious entanglement. He disintegrated. His heart was dynamited.

He tried to speak, couldn't.

I control you, Frank, and you like it, you love it—

—he sat upright, sweating, the dream fresh and stunning in his head, so realistic, so convincing, so *solid*, he was astonished to find himself alone in the room. He pushed the sheets aside. His face and hands were damp. He might have been stricken by a fever.

The rich language of dreams. The secret voices. The seductions. All the static that lay just under the surface of consciousness refined itself in images of startling clarity.

Dreams. They weren't supposd to be interpreted literally. They were symbols, graphic puns, the mind at play. So why did he still feel the woman's touch?

His mouth was sleep-dry. He walked to the window and tugged the cord that opened the curtains. Dawn was lightening the sky across the city; he could sense the heat of the day begin to gather in the crevices of shadows where sun barely penetrated.

29

WASHINGTON

At six a.m. she was sitting inside a rented Honda Civic in the parking-lot of a truckstop when she saw him. He still had a small billygoat beard and wore a maroon beret and a long lightweight coat to his sneakers. His angular face had the texture of creased leather. He entered the restaurant.

She waited, watched, wondered if he had backup in the vicinity, if he had thought to bring along with him any of his friends. No: he wouldn't take the chance of trying to deceive her. She knew too much about him. For all he knew, she might have records stashed away, revelatory documents to be opened in the event of her death.

She waited a few minutes then stepped out of the car. She made her way between parked trucks and entered the restaurant, scanned the room, saw him at a booth in the back. She moved toward him, conscious of the weary faces of truckers turning to assess her.

They looked at Carly Phoenix and they were instantly revitalized. She made things happen for them. She stirred them. The long monotonous white lines of the highways were burned out of their memories. They liked the look of her, the provocative glossy mouth, the eyes hidden by shades, the tight blue jeans and the black leather jacket, the boots, the whole style. They wanted her to fuck them. They wanted her to dominate and humiliate them. She was made out of dark dreams and longings.

She thought Carly Phoenix a stripper's working name, one you might see on a sleazy marquee; or a porn queen, somebody who bared everything in a hardcore fast-fuck film. Carly Phoenix would glisten on a stage under lights, she'd savour the feel of her own perspiration, she'd look out across the rows of darkness and enjoy the shadows of men who watched her with palpable desire. A pelvic shimmy, a breast teasingly revealed, a hard spangled nipple, a nice tight ass turned to the audience. She'd think of erections, men sitting in the dark and growing stiff, perhaps surreptitiously fingering themselves or going to the john to jerk off.

One of the truckers looked up from his breakfast and said, 'Hey, sweetie, need a ride?'

She smiled. Her lips were like glass recently drizzled by rain. 'I already got wheels,' she said. She smiled and it dazzled him.

'Not like the wheels I got, honey. I can go any way you like. North, south. Up, down, sideways. Round the world. You only gotta name it.'

'Some other time,' she said.

'Zat a promise?' The guy was drooling yolk down his chin.

She kept moving to the booth at the back of the room. She slid into the seat facing the man with the maroon beret. She laid her purse on the table.

'Chico,' she said.

'Hey, like the style,' he said. His voice was unusually deep, a frog's croak. He had small bad yellow teeth. 'I always had this thing about leather.' He lit a cigarette and fingered his beard.

She picked up a salt-shaker and rattled it in her hand. She observed Chico for a time. He was uneasy in her presence. He was anxious to get the business over and be gone, back to his beloved Appalachian hollows where in isolated places he grew reefer and sometimes ran guns to Brownsville, Texas. She enjoyed his discomfiture; it was as if she had a hook in his flesh and liked to see the barb bring blood. She liked the way she could bring pressures to bear on other people without really trying.

The waitress came to the table. She ordered coffee. Chico dropped his cigarette on the floor, ground it underfoot, lit another.

'You're crazy to come here,' he said. 'And I'm crazy to be with you.'

She laid a hand over his knuckles. 'So we're both a little crazy.'

'Yeah. Well, you always did like taking chances. But not me, not me.' He ran a hand across his forehead, smoked fiendishly.

'Relax,' she said.

'I don't have relax in my vocabulary. I am deeply concerned by the Feds, who take a very dim view of my kinda private enterprise. Right, so I sell a few guns to some rebellious individualists in a land directly to the south of these United States and I grow a little weed – big fucking deal. Relax, you say?'

'It was your choice to meet me, Chico.'

'My ass my choice. You got me by the goolies.'

She leaned her head back against the wall. 'I'm not forcing you into anything, Chico.'

'Right. Tell me I'm here of my own free will. Make me a believer.'

'You could have refused. You could have hung up the phone any time you liked.'

He looked directly into her eyes. 'Bullshit. All I had to say was I wasn't gonna show and you drop a dime and I got Feds going down my windpipe and, zip, before I know it they're coming outta my anus.'

'You really think I'd turn you in, Chico?'

'You'd smile when you was doing it.'

'Maybe. Maybe not.'

'Yeah well, I ain't taking the chance. I don't trust you. I never trusted you. You're one dangerous bitch, and I ain't gambling with you.'

'Then don't.'

'The worst thing I ever did was business with you,' he said.

'It was profitable, Chico.'

'Sometimes money turns out to be irrelevant. Sometimes peace of mind is the preferred choice.'

'Certain Iranian parties needed your assistance. I don't remember you refusing them.'

'I was naïve back then.'

'You've grown up in four years.'

'I like to think so.' He turned to the door and frowned. 'For instance, I'd never use a go-between again. And if I did, I'd make god-damn sure he or she knew sweet fuck all about my operations.'

'A go-between,' she said. 'I always considered myself more like a temporary partner.'

'Partnership with you's a damn one-way street. You learned everything about the way I worked. My customers. My bases. Every god-damn thing. And what did I learn about you in return? One thing. One useless thing.'

'And what was that?'

'You're a fucking chameleon, that's what.' He lit yet another cigarette.

She brushed smoke aside. She wondered if Pagan still smoked. Ten years ago he had, and she'd teasingly criticized him for it. She thought about him at The Madison. She remembered how he'd looked as he'd approached the registration desk. His face was somewhat hollowed by weariness, but he had an air about him of concentration, perhaps even determination. He didn't slump; straight-backed, a man ready for the fray, ready for destiny. She'd watched him talk to a hotel official – a manager, somebody like that; he'd probably been asking questions about her. You'll have your answers soon, Pagan, she thought. A time is coming when there will be no more questions.

Chico pointed the burning cigarette at her. 'OK. This is the score. I'm gonna do you the favour you asked. And that's it. End of the line. You don't call me. You don't visit. No more favours. Deal.'

'Deal,' she said.

He shook his head in a bewildered manner. 'I can't believe I'm sitting here going through the motions of making a deal with you, for Chrissakes. You wouldn't know a deal from a kazoo.'

'You could always turn things around, Chico. You could always drop a dime on me. That's an option.'

He laughed, coughing out uninhaled smoke. 'An option? Hey, you come and you go like the fucking wind, you turn up here, you turn up there, you vanish inside cracks. How could I drop a dime on you? By the time anyone showed up, you'd be gone.'

'I take precautions,' she said.

'Precautions. You give a whole new meaning to the word.'

'So,' she said. 'I'm listening.'

'First off, I got the piece you asked for. It's in the trunk of my car. Second, this guy you mentioned.'

She was all attention. She brought her face close to Chico's.

'This guy's a Company man,' he said. 'Research, what I hear. Connections with all the old networks that have broken down in Europe.'

The old networks, she thought. That explained how Mallory had entered Vladimir Galkin's orbit. Galkin had KGB scraps to sell, information as useful as wood-shavings. 'What else do you know, Chico?'

Chico adjusted the brim of his beret. 'You know I had to work my balls off to get that much.'

'I need more, Chico. Like, if you were looking for him, where would you look?'

'Try his place of employment. Try Langley.'

'Langley. Sure. That's a great help.'

He smiled at her for the first time since she'd arrived. There was a slight hint of admiration in the smile; despite the fact he didn't trust her, he liked her in a contrary manner. Maybe it was the dangerous way she lived. Maybe it was her sheer balls. The Feds would have coughed up a fortune for information about her and here she was in the US, right under their noses. She lived beyond all reasonable margins. She was wild. An American original.

'Get serious, Chico. If you were planning to visit his home, where would you start?'

'I need a little more time on that one.'

'How much more time?'

'A day, maybe less. I got a guy working on it. I'll call you.'

'No, Chico. You know better than that. I don't go round giving out my phone number. I'll call you.'

'Trust nobody. Trust nothing.'

'Exactly.'

'It's a sorry old world,' Chico said, and stood up. 'You wanna walk with me to my car? I need to get the hell outta this city before I totally crack up. You can't breathe the fucking air here. And there's too many cops. Too many Federal offices.' Chico shuddered. His little beard shivered.

She left some coins on the table and followed Chico out of the restaurant. His car was an old Ford Fairlane parked at the side of the truckstop. He unlocked the trunk. Concealed beneath a spare tyre and a tool-box was a grease-stained towel.

'Open your purse,' he said. 'What you're getting is an FEG GKK-45. Hungarian. I added three extra clips. You never know. I put in a silencer. What you also got there are two miniaturized high-tech doodahs of Czech origin. They don't come with instructions, but I figure you've seen them before.'

She opened her purse and he dumped the towel inside it, then shut the lid of the trunk.

'I'll hear from you,' he said and got inside the Fairlane.

'You'll hear.'

She returned to her car, drove away from the truckstop. When she reached her motel, which was close to Washington International Airport, she parked and entered the building, pausing in the lobby because her attention was drawn to the newspaper display, and in particular to a headline in the *Washington Post*. She pushed coins in the slot, opened the glass lid, removed a copy of the paper and walked slowly toward the stairs as she read the front page.

30

VIRGINIA

James Mallory thought: THIS IS WRONG.

The white-hot early morning sun spread light across the country-side, rendering meadows and trees strange and hallucinatory. Mallory wore only light-weight cotton pants and a short-sleeved white shirt and yet his clothing might have been welded to his flesh. Sweat accumulated on the ridges of his eyebrows and slid down across the lids and slithered in broken lines the length of his nose to his lips. He tasted the salt of himself. When he emerged from the car and touched the door handle it burned his skin. The air was purgatorial, the kind of heat you might imagine in the antechamber to hell. He longed for rain. He *ached* for rain. But the sky was cloudless to infinity, an infuriating blue.

Donovan stepped out of the passenger seat. Blond Ralph, looking like a lifeguard, a Boy Scout. But there was a darkness at the heart of Donovan's sunny appearance, a quality Mallory had glimpsed from the first day he'd met him. Skidelsky had once described Donovan as a surfer from hell. And Mallory was uneasy just being around the guy; but he was a member of the Club, and he operated directly under Skidelsky's command – so Mallory was obliged to set his discomfort aside. It wasn't easy. What Mallory couldn't get his mind around was Donovan's capacity for violence. Capsicum, North Carolina, too much blood, too many killings – why did Skidelsky's master-plan involve such bloodletting? Max had once said *It's the one thing people really react to, Jimmy. The sight of blood.* Think of yourself as a leech, OK, but there was a point where even a leech became gorged and bloated. Metaphors didn't erase moral considerations, not for Mallory. You couldn't find a hiding-place behind figures of speech.

He moved toward the shade of some dried-out fir trees. Donovan followed him. Wasps buzzed in the dusty air. A butterfly, a bright red beauty, flapped kamikaze fashion against Mallory's face.

Donovan said, 'I could have done this on my own.'

'You keep reminding me.'

'Why did Max saddle me with you?'

'I'm sorry if I'm a burden, Donovan. But it's the way Max wanted it. And Max always gets what he wants.'

'I didn't say you were a burden, Jimmy.' Donovan stared across the meadow. The farmhouse was white and still. The barn behind the house was painted deep red and glowing in the sunshine.

Mallory said, 'Maybe he thinks it's time for me to get some real experience. The nitty-gritty.'

'This is a stroll,' Donovan said. 'This isn't your line of work.'

A stroll, Mallory thought. No, it wasn't that exactly. He felt nervy. The heat zapped energy out of him. He looked in the direction of the farmhouse, the shadowed porch, blinds drawn down on windows. Picturesque rural Virginia, white fences enclosing meadows, a herd of horses grazing a field in somnambulist fashion. The essence of tranquillity. Mallory took his eyes away from the house.

He asked, 'You ever feel anything, Ralph?'

'Feel? Like what? Remorse? Guilt? That kind of thing?'

'Yeah. That kind of thing.'

'It's business, Jimmy. It isn't personal. It's as if I'm not really involved. I can't explain . . . I see somebody else going through the motions.' Donovan licked his lips, across which he'd smeared some kind of sun-protection cream that tasted of apricot. 'If I have a bad moment, I just shake it off. Maybe I jog. Or go down to the gym.'

'And that does it?' Pumping iron as a prophylactic against ethical qualms. Against guilt attacks. How simple Donovan's world had to be.

Donovan shrugged. 'Usually. And if that fails, I try to see my actions from a different perspective. Long-term, if you like. The general interests of the country.'

Mallory heard an echo of Max in Donovan's words. *Long-term. The general interests of the country.* You could take that view, he supposed, if you were formed like Skidelsky. You could stand at that questionable junction where ends and means intersected and feel perfectly comfortable. He was queasy. He wondered if Max's insistence that he accompany Donovan was a test, an initiation ritual. Skidelsky the Examiner. The Controller of Rites. The High Mason of the Lodge. Let's see if you've got the stuff, Jimmy. Let's see what you're made of. This is the real version of bonding.

Donovan opened a small black leather bag he'd brought with him. The clasp made a clicking sound like that of a cricket. Inside was a gun and a clip of ammunition and a small plastic cylinder which Mallory figured was similar to the device Donovan must have used in Capsicum. He tried to distance himself from these objects but it was difficult. They had a lethal potential you couldn't just step back from. On the barrel of the gun were the words *Accu-Tek, Chino, Ca.* Donovan slipped the clip in place with a deft movement.

'Let's go,' he said.

Mallory wanted to linger for ever in the fragile scented shade of the firs. He followed Donovan into a meadow filled with long dehydrated flowers that crackled against his arms. Moths flew out of the rustling stalks. A couple of distressed bluejays screamed. The house was a mere fifty yards away, the only dwelling-place in sight. The horizon was lost in trees and thickets and long grass.

Outside the house a Range-Rover was parked, silver and shimmering.

'I hope this Lannigan doesn't have a guard dog,' Mallory said quietly.

'No dog. No burglar alarm. We do our homework.' Donovan brushed a sprinkle of small purple petals from his shirt. 'Lives alone. Retired.'

Mallory wondered about the isolation of this place. Maybe if you'd spent your life as a shrink you'd want to retreat from the sad babble of the human race at the end of the day. You'd want the loveliness of silence away from an ocean of troubled voices.

Donovan quietly opened the gate in the white wood fence. Mallory went after him. On the porch was a motionless rocking-chair. The path was paved, the lawn on either side sparse and brown. A hose lay in a tidy black coil, like an inert mamba. Donovan moved toward the porch and Mallory, glancing quickly at the daffodil-coloured blinds on the windows, followed him.

'See,' said Donovan. 'Trusting kind of guy. Doesn't even lock his front door.'

Mallory watched Ralph Donovan turn the handle and push open the door. Inside a ceiling-fan turned lazily. The rooms were shadowy, almost cool. The blinds imparted a lemon tint to the interior. Apart from the slight whirring of the fan's motor, the house was silent. Donovan walked to the foot of the stairs with the gun in his hand. Mallory felt a troublesome lump of tension in his chest. This is wrong, he thought. This isn't what I want to be doing. He had an urge to turn, to go back outside into the merciless sunlight, which would be immeasurably preferable to this.

Donovan was already moving up the stairs. For a big man, he moved gracefully and quietly. Mallory took a deep breath and put his foot on the first step. Donovan had turned and was looking down at him and making a gesture of impatience. *Come on, let's get this done.* The step creaked under Mallory's foot and he cursed his own clumsiness, his lack of stealth. He was an organizer, a detail man – not an accessory to murder. Above him, Donovan continued to climb. Mallory grasped the handrail and went up after him. Donovan was at the top now, on the landing, where sunshine came fractured and discoloured through a window of stained glass. Mallory made it to the landing.

What now? Did Donovan know which room to enter? Had he done all his homework?

There was the sound of a toilet flushing, the sudden whish of water being sucked out of a bowl, the gurgle of a cistern refilling. A man appeared in a doorway. He was tall and tanned and lean, and his short hair was white. He was sixty, maybe more, maybe just less. Mallory couldn't tell. He was dressed only in a green robe that was unbelted and hung open. Mallory had a flash of the man's pubic hair, his long penis, the circumcised head. Surprised, the man opened his mouth and stepped back and Donovan shot him once in the centre of the chest and he fell against the bathroom door and continued to stagger back, losing his balance with each tiny retreating step until his body struck the glass surround of the shower and he crashed through it, creating an ugly cacophony of shattered glass. And then he dropped back, bleeding, into the porcelain shower-stall, and Mallory looked away, even as Donovan walked inside the bathroom and fired a second shot.

Donovan came back from the bathroom and said, 'Done.'

But it wasn't done, because another door along the landing opened and a girl stood there; she had to be twelve, thirteen, a narrow-hipped nymph, naked, pubescent little breasts, long stalk of neck.

She said, 'Hey—'

And Mallory looked at her, seeing her stunned expression, and in her eyes a look of fear he'd never seen before, something he never wanted to see again. Beyond her, he was vaguely conscious of a double bed, a tangle of bed sheets, pants and a discarded shirt lying on the floor, flimsy underwear on the carpet, pillows heaped at the top of the bed. And other details, the child's make-up, the streaked mascara surrounding her eyes, faded lipstick. And this, the one he'd remember most later, the one that would keep coming back to him: in her right hand she held a used condom, a ridiculous length of limp, wrinkled latex.

Donovan raised the gun and levelled it at the child.

'*No,*' Mallory said.

Donovan fired. He fired directly into her young heart. Mallory turned away. He half-stumbled down the stairs, clutching the handrail. His stomach was a see-saw. His mouth flooded with acidic saliva. He had the sense of teetering on the edge of collapse. Donovan came down after him and grabbed his shoulder and pushed him against the wall.

'Can't take it?'

Mallory said nothing.

'Can't take it, Jimmy?' Donovan slapped Mallory across the cheek.

'I,' Mallory said. Words coagulated in his head.

'Guy was a scumbag,' Donovan said. 'You saw it, Jimmy.'

Mallory wasn't sure what he'd seen. He was fighting to regroup, but bits and pieces of himself went zooming off in odd directions.

'He'd been screwing that kid. I mean, it was goddamn obvious. A pervert, Jimmy. A sexual pervert. A child-molester.'

Mallory put his hand to the place where Donovan had slapped him. He could feel a tingling sensation.

Donovan said, 'Think of it as doing society a favour, if that helps.'

If that helps, Mallory thought. What if I don't want to do society any favours?

'He was trash,' Donovan said.

Mallory nodded. He heard the fan stir air. He thought of the condom in the girl's hand. She must have been going to dispose of it, he thought. On her way to the bathroom to flush it. Never got there. Never made it.

'An old guy like that. The kid was young enough to be his granddaughter.'

'You didn't need to,' Mallory said.

'Didn't need to what, Jimmy?'

Mallory glanced back up the stairs at the stained-glass window.

'Do the kid, is that what you mean?' Donovan asked.

Mallory didn't answer. He moved to the foot of the stairs as if he were walking through molasses. He walked out onto the porch and he leaned over the rail and stuck a finger down his throat, but nothing came up. Donovan was standing directly behind him, patting him on the back.

'First time's tough,' Donovan said. 'If Max asks, I'll tell him you were a trouper, Jimmy.'

Mallory felt intense pressure inside his ears, a whining. A trouper, sure, you tell him that, Ralph. Dear God, a trouper.

Donovan had the plastic cylinder in his hand. He said, 'OK. This is all set and running. We got ten minutes to get back to the car and get the hell out of here, Jimmy. So I suggest we move.'

Mallory's eyes ached now. He followed Donovan across the meadow and back to where they'd parked.

'You want me to drive?' Donovan asked.

'I'll do it,' Mallory said.

Donovan shrugged and opened the passenger door. 'A retired shrink,' he said. 'And he's screwing some young kid. Makes you think.'

Of what? Mallory wondered. Of dead children? Of blood? He rammed the car into gear with a violent gesture and drove it along the dry rutted dirt road that would take them back to the highway.

31

WASHINGTON

Pagan slept only in a shallow way after his dream, as if his consciousness were resisting the notion of further sleep and the possibility of deeper revelations from the macabre videotape library of the mind. When he woke it was nine a.m. and the images of the dream still lingered in a way he found uncomfortable. He rose, showered, then dressed in blue jeans and a white cotton shirt.

He had room service deliver coffee and, as he drank it, he looked up the number of the Central Intelligence Agency in the phone book. He pondered the apparent anomaly that not only was the Agency's number listed in a phone directory, the legend *Central Intelligence Agency* was also posted on freeway signs as you approached Langley: public access to a place of secrets, he thought. The contradictions at the heart of a society that considered itself open.

He dialled, asked for Bob Naderson and was put on hold.

A man came on the line. 'Can I help?'

'I want to talk to Bob Naderson.'

'Mr Naderson isn't in his office at the moment.'

'When do you expect him?'

'Possibly this afternoon.'

'Are you an associate of his?'

'I'm his assistant,' the man said.

'I need to contact him urgently,' Pagan said.

'Can I help?'

'I don't think so. It's personal.'

'May I ask who I'm speaking with?'

'Frank Pagan.'

There was a pause, a tiny skip of silence. 'I wish I could be more helpful, Mr Pagan. Can't you give me some indication of what this urgent matter's about?'

Pagan said, 'No. It's for Mr Naderson's personal attention. I can't go any further than that.'

'Then you'll have to phone back—'

'Why don't you give me a number where I can reach him?'

'I can't do that, Mr Pagan.'

'Because you don't know where he is? Or because it's policy?'

'Policy, Mr Pagan.'

'But you *could* contact him in an emergency if you had to,' Pagan said.

'Well, I guess so.'

'Fine. Then let me clarify the situation for you. This happens to be an emergency.'

'Mr Pagan, I hope you don't misunderstand me, but unless I know the nature of the alleged emergency, I can't possibly interrupt Mr Naderson.'

Officialdom, Pagan thought. Worse than that: CIA officialdom. The hooded voices, the masks, cloaks and bloody daggers. These guys were caught in a time warp. He felt a serious darkening of his mood. 'Let me have your name,' he said.

'Why?'

'Because I can tell Bob Naderson when I see him – and I *will* see him sooner or later, have no doubts on that score – what an obstructive little bastard he has for an assistant.'

'I don't think you're approaching this too constructively, Mr Pagan—'

'Put your ear close to the phone and listen carefully. I'll say this once. Either you tell me where I can contact him or I go direct to Christopher Poole.' A rabbit from the old hat, the bluff disguised as a threat. Pagan put a hard spin in his voice. If he resented anything, it was trumped-up assistants who tried to give you the no-go treatment, men and women whose desk drawers contained all the rubber-stamps of authority and yet had no genuine authority themselves. Nickel-and-dimers, the parasitic goblins of bureaucracy.

'Christopher Poole?'

'You heard me. I talk to Chris Poole.'

'Mr Pagan—'

'I didn't mention I'm from Special Branch, did I?' Pagan asked, wondering what substance that might add to his general approach: very little, he suspected. 'I've come from London specifically to talk to Bob Naderson and I don't have time to fuck around. Do you understand that?'

'Look, I sympathize—'

'I don't want sympathy,' Pagan said. 'Let me see if I can phrase this in such a way you can get your head around it. It's an emergency, and your Mr Naderson's life may depend on me.'

There was a prolonged silence. Pagan wondered if he'd made any advance, even a tiny one.

'I'll tell you what I can do, Mr Pagan. I can contact Mr Naderson and tell him you want to talk to him. If he's agreeable, he'll call you back himself.'

'That's the best you can do?'

'That's the best. Give me your phone number.'

Pagan read the number to him, then said, 'If I don't hear from him within the next ten minutes, I'll call you back. And if you refuse to take my call, I go direct to Chris Poole. Is that position plain enough for you?'

'Plain as the nose on my face,' the man said.

'What is your name anyway?'

'Quinn,' the man said. 'Larry Quinn.'

'I'll be waiting.' Pagan hung up.

The conversation had irritated him more than he needed. He wandered the room, stood by the window and tapped his fingertips against the pane, then – remembering his conversation with Zuboric about Carlotta from the previous evening – he turned on the TV, punched the remote until he had a twenty-four-hour news channel. A keen-eyed woman with perfect hair was standing in front of a weather-map of the United States. Sunshine everywhere. Drought in the Southwest, the Midwest, water rationing in many of the other states. A storm front was forming in the Atlantic, but its movements were unpredictable. *We may be in for some rain, folks. That's going to be welcome news for most of us. Especially our farmers.* Why were these TV meteorologists always so cheerful? They could announce approaching tornadoes as if they were impending marriages.

He sat down with the telephone in his lap and watched the picture change. He found himself looking at a smouldering group of houses and stores, fire-trucks, ambulances. A TV reporter, a black man in an open-necked shirt, was getting quite worked up about the destruction. Pagan leaned closer to the TV.

'Official sources are saying nothing about the possibility of a connection between the destruction here in Capsicum and the terrorist known as Carlotta. On the other hand, there appears to be a general consensus of opinion among the people of this small rural community that nobody else could have been responsible for this attack. I'm talking to Eugene Boyd, whose son Dick, who ran the gas-station, was a victim of the blast.'

A red-eyed man appeared in front of the camera. Pagan didn't like the crass manner in which the media intruded on the grief of people, and he liked even less the concomitant notion that stricken people were somehow *expected* these days to go on TV and bare all their emotions. Private feelings became public spectacles. The vampire that lurked in everybody had to be satisfied.

'Course it was her, had to be her,' Eugene Boyd was saying, and drew the back of his hand across his face. 'Nobody else gonna come to a quiet place like this and do this . . . atrocity. Don't know why they don't just come right out and say it.'

The TV reporter asked, 'You knew the family?'

'I knew the mother and father, yeah.'

'What impressions did you have of them?'

'Impressions?' Eugene Boyd asked. 'They kept pretty much to themselves. Private folks. They didn't take part in this community.'

'Did you ever meet the daughter?'

'I see her once or twice when she was a kid, that's all.'

The reporter wanted more. 'You ever talk to her?'

Boyd said, 'Once maybe twice. It was a while ago.'

'But you didn't really know her?'

Boyd shook his head, raised a hand to cover his face, and Pagan thought: *Nobody really knows her*. He sympathized with the unfortunate Eugene Boyd, who'd drifted away from the camera just as the reporter's image abruptly disappeared and the location changed to that of the studio where a blow-dried, pancake-faced anchorman sat behind a desk. 'Sorry to break in on you, Dave, but news is just coming in from Caroline County, Virginia, where the home of the well-known psychiatrist Patrick Lannigan has been the subject of a vicious fire-bomb assault early this morning . . . Dr Lannigan is thought to have been inside the house at the time. Firemen at the scene say they've recovered two bodies, but identification is going to take some time. Patrick Lannigan is well known for his bestselling book on the psychology of terrorism and his most famous case study was that of Carlotta in her teenage years, so there may well be some connection with events in Capsicum and the apparent slaying of Dr Lannigan, although this remains speculation for the moment—'

Dave's face reappeared. 'It's all speculation at the moment, Don.'

Lannigan, Pagan thought. One of Carlotta's past analysts. What the fuck was she doing? Erasing everything connected to her past? Destroying everybody and everything that had anything to do with her history? For what reason? Yes, Dave, it's all speculation; you're dead right about that. It's all sheer speculation.

His phone rang and he picked up the receiver at once. The voice on the other end of the line said, 'Bob Naderson here. I understand you want to see me, Mr Pagan.'

Pagan followed the directions he'd been given by Naderson. He drove with his air-conditioning unit on maximum as he headed west out of the city. He checked his rear-view mirror regularly, but he saw no consistency in the vehicles immediately behind him, no one car dogging him with persistence: Zuboric or his hounds could be back in traffic somewhere, of course, but Pagan had no way of knowing because traffic was dense, slow-moving; pollution created a haze around the sun. His thoughts drifted to Capsicum, North Carolina, and then to the news flash concerning Dr Lannigan. *Carlotta*, he thought. *What exactly are you doing?*

He drove on Highway 66 beyond Arlington and Fairfax. Naderson had instructed him to head for Manassas Park and beyond that to look for a sign directing him to a place called Maryville. He found the sign, turned off the main highway, drove for several miles until he reached Maryville, an uninteresting place, the bones of an old community around the central spine of which had been constructed a series of big redbrick houses in post-Colonial style, each occupying a two-acre site. There was the quiet hum of wealth here, tucked behind redbrick walls and wrought-iron gates and dense trees.

Pagan found Mulberry, and looked for number 324. He uttered his name into an intercom located on the wall and the gates swung open to admit him. A paved driveway led to the house. He parked his car and got out. A man was standing in the open doorway of the house.

'You gave Larry Quinn a hard time, I hear,' the man said, and smiled. 'You have some ID, Mr Pagan?'

Pagan handed his ID to the man, who studied it a moment before returning it. 'We called London, of course. We had you authenticated.'

'Naturally,' Pagan said.

'Your name's not exactly unknown to us, of course.' The man held out his hand to be shaken. 'Bob Naderson. Come inside. It's damnably hot out here.'

Pagan followed Naderson inside the house and was led to a room that was a kind of atrium stuffed with fresh herbs in a multitude of ceramic pots. Under a large skylight plants lavishly perfumed the air. Thyme, basil, rosemary, mint; the place smelled like an overwhelming pot-pourri. Naderson suggested he sit in one of the two dark green cane chairs that were camouflaged by plants. Pagan did so.

Naderson, crossing his legs, sat facing him. He had candid brown eyes and an earnest look. His bearing suggested that of a retired banker, a kindly man whose business life has been characterized by discretion and old-fashioned honesty. Clandestine wasn't an attribute that would come immediately to the casual observer's mind.

Pagan said, 'Nice room.' He surveyed it quickly, noticing on a small circular wicker table a number of old silver-framed photographs. Family groups taken thirty or forty years ago. He thought he could pick out Bob Naderson in a couple of them, young and fair-haired and athletic, a fine honest smile. There was one picture in which a man who was apparently Bob in his forties was depicted alongside a young woman; the shot had been taken on the steps of a gazebo in bright sunlight. Bob and the girl were smiling, arms around each other's waists. A fiancée? a friend? Pagan looked at the young woman's face; something about it troubled him, although he couldn't say what.

'Organic herbs,' said Naderson, gesturing round the place. 'Out back, free-range eggs. A sizeable vegetable patch. Sweet corn. Runner beans. No great crop this year, of course . . . I'm very careful what I put in my body. I sometimes think half the trouble with the world is nutritional. Too many chemicals and pesticides, small wonder the race is in a state of such decline . . . So. Special Branch indeed. What is this emergency that has you jumping across the ocean and terrifying young Larry Quinn?'

Pagan sat back in his chair and contemplated the older man. Naderson's manner was disarmingly gentle.

'It's an old matter,' he said finally.

'Ah. My past has come back to haunt me,' Naderson said, and smiled as if at some private joke.

'A man called Martin Burr was murdered in London a few days ago.'

'Burr,' Naderson said, and looked like someone skirting the edges of a faint memory. 'I think I read something about that in the newspapers here.'

'Did you ever meet him?'

Naderson shook his head in a puzzled way. 'No. Why would you think that?'

Pagan paused a second before he said, 'Because he was instrumental in helping Christopher Poole get you out of Russia.'

Naderson frowned, reaching for a plant and stiffly grasping a leaf between thumb and index finger and raising it to his nostrils. 'Mind if I call you Frank?'

'Feel free.' Pagan glanced again at the photograph of Naderson and the girl. Whatever had troubled him about it a moment ago seemed to have dissolved. His eye shifted to the telephone that sat amidst the photographs. He read Naderson's number on the dial and made the effort of committing it to memory.

Naderson said, 'Russia. Now that was a bad business all round, Frank. Tell you the truth, I never understood the mechanics of my release. Certain arrangements were made, but I was never privy to them. God knows, I was glad to get out. I was there for six weeks. Constant interrogations. It was downright unpleasant. But nobody ever told me how my release was worked.'

Six weeks in exchange for Pasco's ten years. It wasn't

much of a trade, if you'd been Pasco. Pagan leaned forward in his chair. 'You were traded for somebody by the name of Richard Pasco. Does that ring a bell?'

'Pasco? No.'

'Pasco, it seems, was a fall guy. An innocent. He did ten years in highly unpleasant circumstances so that you could be returned to the fold. And you've never heard of him?'

'Never,' Naderson said. 'You say he did ten years despite the fact he was *innocent*?'

'Right. Burr came to an arrangement with Poole.' He studied Naderson's face a moment. What he was looking for was some kind of tic, a flicker, an ocular shading – any little sign that Naderson was lying when he said he'd never heard of Pasco. But Naderson emitted only a certain blandness. Pagan wasn't inclined to buy his way into this impression; maybe Naderson was just a bloody good liar. If he and Poole had worked together for years, if he'd been a spook important enough for Poole to engineer his release, then he'd surely know about the arrangement carved out with Martin Burr, and the betrayal of Pasco. Naderson would have asked questions about the way the exchange had worked, and Poole must have answered at least some of them. If they were old comrades in the cloak and dagger trade, they were certain to have shared all kinds of confidences.

Naderson said, 'What I don't see is where you're going, Frank. What are you after? You told young Quinn you had an emergency on your hands – so what has that got to do with my time in Russia and this Richard Pasco?'

'A couple of things. I want the person who murdered Burr. And I want to know why Burr went along with Poole's scheme in the first place.'

'How the devil can I help? I never knew Burr. I never heard of Pasco—'

'Then I should talk to Poole.'

'He's a hard man to see unless you give him a specific reason,' said Naderson. 'But, gosh, I just don't understand how there can be any useful connection between myself or Chris Poole and the death of Martin Burr.'

Gosh, Pagan thought. It was a nice old man's expletive. It resonated with lifelong membership of a white-framed Methodist church in the wheaten heart of Kansas, old geezers whittling sticks on the porches of lonesome houses in the middle of nowhere.

Pagan said, 'Carlotta.'

'Carlotta?' Naderson asked, and frowned.

'She's the connection.'

Naderson said, 'You're losing me, Frank.'

'She killed Martin Burr. She also killed Pasco. And I want her.'

'The same Carlotta . . .'

'The same Carlotta in today's headlines. The very same Carlotta you can catch on your TV round the clock. There's only one Carlotta, which is something we ought to be thankful for.'

Naderson seemed slightly flustered by this information. 'Put this in some perspective for me, Frank. I'm not absolutely sure what I'm hearing right now.'

'I'll put it bluntly, Bob. She means to kill you.'

Naderson smiled and shook his head. 'Kill *me*? Whatever for? I've never had any association with her.'

'It doesn't work like that,' Pagan said. 'You don't need to have had any *kind* of association with Carlotta for her to want to kill you.'

Naderson plucked at another leaf, rolled it between the palms of his hands. 'I'm still in the dark, I'm afraid.'

'Let me throw a little light, if I can. Pasco came out of Russia with a major grudge against the Agency. Imagine ten years in the permafrost, ten years of vitamin deficiency and God-awful food, ten years of pure bloody hell. Obviously you're not quite the full shilling at the end of all these miserable years. Certain things may have been rearranged in your head after all that time. Whatever, Pasco somehow made contact with Carlotta on his release. Carlotta, who's been known in the past to have devious schemes of her own, enters into a contract with him – I use "contract" loosely, Bob, and not in its legal sense – to settle his grudges for him. These grudges included Martin Burr. They probably also include your good self and Christopher Poole and God knows who else was involved in the wretched betrayal of Pasco. Is that clear enough for you, Bob?'

Naderson sat back in his chair. He looked like a man perusing a loan application made by a deadbeat. 'You think I'm in danger. You think she may well come here to my home and . . .'

'Oh, I think it's more than a possibility, Bob,' Pagan said. 'If not to your home, then somewhere else. Your golf club. Country club. You name it, she may just turn up there. And you won't know until it's too damn late.'

Naderson's expression changed slightly. He looked a few years older all at once; a muscular collapse had taken place in the jaws and cheeks. 'I should take steps to protect myself, that's what you're saying.'

'I'm not sure what steps you can take when it comes to Carlotta. She's like rising damp – you seal her off in one place, she comes out another. You can get yourself some heavies to keep watch over you, but she works on the principle that the more difficult the target, the more of a challenge she finds it. Her life is all challenges and derangements, Bob. She isn't like anyone you ever met before.' Pagan observed Naderson and detected in his otherwise mild appearance something of the school sneak caught in an act of blackmail. He wanted to say, *There's always consequences, Bob. For every act we commit, there's always a reaction. Something has been tracking you for ten years, old fellow. And now you can hear it rustle in the sunlight outside your window.*

Naderson said, 'The FBI will be taking exhaustive steps to find her . . .'

'They're taking steps all right, Bob. And I don't doubt they're turning over every stone. But whether they're turning over the right stones is another matter. She plays with her pursuers. She toys with her assailants. She's got gifts that very few of us are given in quite the same combination. She has cunning. She has absolutely no sense of remorse. She thinks like a predatory animal. She puts no value on human life. Add to that the fact she's very bright, she's a natural mimic, she can conceal herself with all the skill of a praying-mantis on a leaf – you're talking about a special individual, Bob. And don't forget: she's acting alone, she's a solo performer, which gives her agility and freedom. The FBI, by comparison, is a bloody herd of elephants. She can hear them coming for miles.'

Naderson tipped back his head and looked up at the hanging plants, fuzzy green suspensions in sunlight. He asked, 'What do you suggest?'

'Suggest? I can't suggest anything,' Pagan said. 'You work for the Agency, they've got security experts, they can advise you. Ask them.'

Naderson stood up. A bone creaked in his leg. 'A question occurs to me,' he said, frowning. 'How did Pasco discover . . . how did he find out the names of the people involved in what you call his "wretched betrayal"? How did he know that?'

'Good question,' Pagan said. 'I don't have an answer for it. Maybe he just worked it out for himself. Maybe he spent years creating a list of candidates. By a process of elimination, he came up with certain names. Here's another possibility. Maybe somebody gave him the names. Somebody with an interest in Pasco's grudge. Somebody who knew where to dig up the bones.'

Somebody, Pagan thought: who was this enigmatic somebody who might have given the names to Pasco? It was an angle Pagan had never explored before, for the simple reason that he'd been focused, as usual, on only one individual, and she had a way of eclipsing broader considerations, she had a knack of seriously limiting his horizons.

Naderson looked perplexed. 'It would have to be a person inside the Agency. A person with access to certain material inside the Executive Director's personal files.'

Pagan shrugged. 'I don't know how your labyrinth works, Bob. That's something for you to find out.'

'I don't see what anyone would stand to gain by releasing that kind of material,' Naderson said, and sounded all at once like a fussy old man upset by his own advancing years and their toll on his body.

'What do people normally stand to gain from giving away secrets? Money. Power. Erasing an old resentment. Take your pick, Bob. Motive is a bottomless pit.'

Naderson withdrew into himself; his face was blank for a moment, his eyes focused elsewhere. 'I have to speak with Christopher Poole.'

'I wouldn't mind speaking to Poole myself,' Pagan remarked.

'That's up to him, of course. I'll call him. I'll get back to you. In the meantime, thanks for the warning.'

'You keep a gun,' Pagan said.

'A few.'

'You know how to use them?'

'If I have to.'

Pagan walked to the door. He thought: You'd never get a chance to use them, Bob. Not if Carlotta comes your way. You're too easy for her. Too soft.

He went outside and Naderson drifted after him into the distracting heat. The sky was vast and cloudless. Pagan wondered about the woman and where in this huge continent she might be. He had a sense of an inevitable collision, her comet impacting with his, a crash of fates. *Bonded*.

Naderson said, 'Thanks again.'

Pagan climbed inside his car. Thanks for what? he wondered. For bringing you news that somebody is stalking you with lethal intent? That your own devious history has just exploded in your face?

He drove back to the city, back to his hotel.

Inside his room he sat on the edge of the bed and opened the little logbook Zuboric had given him and he thought for a moment before he inscribed the words: *Watched TV, read the newspaper*. Then he shut the book.

A slight sound made him raise his face in the direction of the bathroom door. Instantly alert, he stretched his hand toward the bedside table, thinking of the drawer in which he'd placed his gun, but before he could reach it the bathroom door opened and he saw her standing there, dark and lustrous, in half-shadow.

'Don't even think about it,' she said.

32

LONDON

Robbie Foxworth had a way with bank managers. It had to do with the authority inherent in his upper-class accent. At times his pronunciation and cadences of speech rang a residual little bell of class inferiority in certain people, and they were reminded of their own less elevated backgrounds. John Black, the manager of Barclays Bank on the Strand, was one such person.

He could tell Foxworth was very well-bred, his origins had been privileged, and that even if he were only some kind of policeman, just the same he came from old moneyed stock. Black imagined him to be the eccentric offspring of landed gentry, and that his affiliation with Special Branch was simply a kind of hobby, something his blue-blooded family had grudgingly accepted without true enthusiasm. He caught the whiff of hunting and fishing and country estates about Foxworth – a world of hunt balls and aristocratic shenanigans, a place of wealth and mystery beyond the reach of a bank manager with a degree in Business Studies from the University of Leeds.

As a consequence of the bank manager's sense of social inadequacy, the charred bank-book Foxworth had placed on his desk was no mere object of curiosity, but a document demanding his immediate attention.

Foxworth said, 'Clearly, I'm in no position to divulge how I came into possession of the thing. You understand that.'

The bank manager nodded. 'The delicacy of an investigation, Mr Foxworth?'

'As you say,' remarked Foxie, who was dressed this morning in a sharp three-piece pinstripe suit from his Jermyn Street tailor.

'I understand,' said the bank manager. 'Perhaps if you'll explain the nature of your needs . . .'

'One, who opened the account. Two, how much was deposited. Three, have there been withdrawals.' Foxie thought the bank manager was really a wonderful specimen of a groveller. It was a strange thing about the English, the way they were often cowed by authoritative accents.

'The account number is barely legible, Mr Foxworth.'

'Yes, but not the account holder's name.'

'Pasco. Richard Pasco.' The bank manager prodded the burned document with the tip of a fountain-pen. 'Strictly the bank is under no obligation to provide information without appropriate supporting documents – warrants and such.'

'Quite,' Foxworth remarked. 'But I think we have a gentleman's agreement, yes?'

Black nodded. 'Of course, of course.' He was a dapper little man whose small snout of a nose had recently been exposed to sunlight, and the skin peeled. He peered in a sniffy manner at the wreck of the bank-book. 'I remember this particular transaction.'

'Do you remember the name of the person who opened the account?'

'An American gentleman who was acting on behalf of a company called Mongoose Enterprises.'

'Mongoose Enterprises?'

'Yes. He provided me with a specimen of Richard Pasco's signature and Pasco's passport, as well as a cheque drawn on a bank in Zurich for half a million American dollars.'

'A considerable sum,' said Foxie.

'Considerable,' Black said.

'The man gave you his name, I suppose?'

'Yes. But I'll have to check on it to refresh my memory. If you'll excuse me . . .'

The bank manager left the office. Alone, Foxie looked through the window. Below, traffic passed along the Strand in bright morning sunlight. He was feeling reasonably self-assured this morning. For one thing, Nimmo had not appeared demanding an explanation of Pagan's absence, which meant he hadn't yet learned of Frank's departure – although sooner or later it was inevitable. For another, he felt an unexpected liberty with Pagan gone, and he was exercising it profitably, using his own initiative, answering only to himself. Pagan, he felt, had dismissed the bank-book all too quickly, failing to see that it might open rooms of useful information. But that was Frank for you yet again, that was a flaw in the man – scurrying to the heart of the action without taking into account the rich seams that might be quarried around the peripheries. Scurrying, almost breathless, in an unseemly way, toward Carlotta.

Foxworth hummed the tune of a popular song that had lodged in his head. Five minutes elapsed. He watched buses and taxi-cabs plough through smoky sunlight in the direction of Trafalgar Square.

The door opened and the bank manager stepped

back inside the office, bearing a document. He sat down behind his desk. 'The account was opened on 15 August this year by a man named Jason Mannering. A withdrawal of five thousand pounds was made by the account-holder, Richard Pasco, on 2 September at a branch in Oxford Street.'

'And that was the only withdrawal?'

The bank manager said it was.

'Tell me about this Mannering,' Foxie said.

'Quiet, mid-forties, well-groomed. He provided me with identification of his own, a prerequisite in any banking transaction. We have to be careful, naturally, all the more so when large sums of money are involved. He showed me his passport, which was American. He was, as I recall, an executive director of Mongoose Enterprises.'

'Is there an address for this company?'

Black studied the sheet. 'Mongoose Enterprises has an office in Richmond, Virginia. But its head office is in Zurich.'

'Can I have a copy of that sheet?'

'I don't see any problem with that, Mr Foxworth.'

'Isn't it unusual for somebody to open a bank account on someone else's behalf?'

'Nothing is unusual in my business,' said Black.

'Sounds a lot like mine,' Foxie remarked.

'I imagine so.' The bank manager smiled with Masonic secrecy. 'I'll have a copy of this made for you, Mr Foxworth. Come this way.'

Foxie followed the bank manager into an adjacent office where a pretty young woman sat behind a typewriter. She had short dark hair and a luminescent complexion and eyes the colour of unsweetened chocolate.

'Sheila,' said the bank manager. 'Run off a copy of this for me, please.'

Sheila rose and said, 'Of course,' and smiled in a sweet way at Foxworth whose first thought was to transfer his bank account and his trust fund to this particular branch at the earliest opportunity.

33

WASHINGTON

In a downtown fast-food restaurant that smelled of deep-fried putrescence, Max Skidelsky fidgeted with a waxen cup that contained the dregs of a Diet Dr Pepper. The clientele of the place was mainly young and pimpled, an assortment of adolescent geeks from an electronics college located nearby. Skidelsky drained his drink. He was anxious to be out of here and on his way.

He watched Larry Quinn pick french-fries out of a cardboard carton and said, 'Let's assess the situation, Larry, before I die of grease inhalation. Pagan meets with Naderson.'

'Right,' said Quinn. 'Then Naderson comes into the office an hour ago in a state of some agitation.'

'And confers with Poole.'

'Right. Then Naderson asks me to find him some specialized home help. People who know their way around a gun. A couple of live-ins.'

Skidelsky rattled ice-cubes. 'Because he's scared shitless of the woman.'

'Shitless, right.'

'Did you find him help?'

'I pulled a couple of names out of the graveyard files. Old freelancers. These guys couldn't hit a barn door point-blank. They've been in the graveyard files so long they're practically embalmed by this time.'

'Fine.' Skidelsky's eyes gleamed behind his glasses. He took off the glasses and wiped the lenses with a special anti-static cloth. 'Let me tell you what Poole is up to. He wants a complete record of all activity relating to his personal files during the past twelve months. Who had access. Who looked at what. Who signed the register. The whole thing. All because Pagan came to Naderson with questions concerning our friend Richard Pasco. So you got two old guys desperately trying to find out who leaked the names to Pasco. Two old guys with troubled consciences.'

'Is this a problem?' Quinn asked.

'How do you define problem?' Skidelsky stared at a chinless girl munching into a half-pound cheeseburger that oozed mayo. 'You don't imagine I left my fingerprints on the files when I ransacked them, do you? You don't imagine I made an entry in the god-damn log after I'd copied the information, do you?'

'Who else has access to Poole's personal files?'

'Apart from Poole and myself, Poole's personal secretary, Wanda. And Poole's assistant personal secretary, Gilda. Wanda and Gilda – it sounds like some kind of shabby high-wire act in a poky one-ring circus.'

Quinn smiled, chewed on a fry.

Skidelsky continued. 'The thing is, Poole thinks the sun rises and sets on my halo. I'm like the kid he never had. A little unruly at times, maybe, sometimes a bit on the rebellious side, and just maybe I need a dressing-down once in a while to remind me to cool the jets of my youthful eagerness – but *untrustworthy*? *Moi*? Not in a thousand fucking years, Larry. That would never cross Poole's mind. So Gilda and Wanda are the ones walking the tightrope, so to speak. They're the potential leaks. They'll be questioned until they've got steam coming out their ears.'

'So you're out of the frame,' Quinn said.

'The frame doesn't even *exist* when it comes to me.'

Quinn wiped his greasy salty fingers on a napkin. 'What about this Pagan?' he said.

'Ah, well, Pagan. I'm not sure. Persistent bastard. I figured he'd come after the woman, so it's no surprise he's here. What I didn't take into my calculations was that he'd get to Naderson—'

'I could hardly stall him,' Quinn said. 'He said he'd go to Poole if I didn't help.'

'Pure bluff, Larry. But it's piss down the sewage-pipe anyway. It happened and we live with it. The way I had it figured, he'd flap around in dark waters, maybe consult with his associates in the FBI – who won't give him the time of day because he's a limey and *ipso facto* a competitor in the Carlotta stakes – probably make a few dead-end inquiries here and there. And, just like the FBI, he'd get nowhere. But I didn't foresee him getting the skinny on Bob Naderson, at least not this quickly. If the god-damn woman hadn't taken it into her mind to shoot Burr . . . that's where the trail began for Pagan.' Skidelsky shook his head. 'That's the problem with her, Larry. We need her. She's the star of the show. She's a top box-office draw. But you have to take her the way she comes, and that includes weird, that includes volatile. She comes as she is. No way round that one.'

'Where's Pasco?' Quinn asked.

'Does it matter?'

'I'm curious, that's all. Is he travelling with her or what?'

'I don't see that somehow. When she goes, she goes alone. No excess baggage.'

'You think Pasco's . . .'

Skidelsky waved a hand. 'You might look into that one, Larry.'

Quinn said he would.

Skidelsky said, 'There's always the other solution to Pagan.' He caught the stench of melting lard, blown directly at him by the blades of a high-speed fan. He needed to get out of this dump. He slid off his stool and walked outside, and Quinn followed him into the ravenous heat.

Skidelsky walked quickly, seemingly immune to the climate. Quinn had to hurry to keep up with him.

'We could make it look like the woman, of course,' Skidelsky said. 'She's already blown up half a town in North Carolina, and only this morning at dawn she killed her old shrink Lannigan . . .'

'She's on a roll,' Quinn said.

'She's on a roll all right,' Skidelsky said. He paused at a Don't Walk sign and grinned that special grin in whose confident light all problems, no matter how tricky, simply withered away. 'So why stop her?'

34

WASHINGTON

Pagan watched her, smelled her scent in the air, saw the glossy dark hair brushed back, the little thrust of hip as she moved. Her black leather jacket hung open. She wore a black T-shirt, sunglasses. He was conscious of the shape of her breasts, the gun in her hand, the way she dominated the room by her presence, as if space were a mere extension of her body. He thought again of his gun in the drawer and considered going for it, but he'd given the intention away in his expression because she opened the drawer of the bedside table and found the Bernardelli and removed the clip, emptying cartridges on the floor, click click click. She tossed the gun down and kicked it underneath the bed. Then she turned the chair around at the dressing-table and sat in a straddling position.

'Welcome to Washington,' she said.

The triadic arrangement of mirrors behind her created views of her from different angles. Pagan realized that if you looked at the mirrors from a certain perspective you might see her multiplied and reflected to infinity. An endless number of Carlottas.

She drummed the barrel of her gun upon her thigh. 'It's been a long time since you and I were alone in a hotel room,' she said.

'A long time.'

'Takes me back,' she said. She removed the sunglasses, stuck them in a pocket of the leather jacket.

He watched the way the gun tapped against her thigh. He moved his body, propped his back against the headboard of the bed.

'Does it take you back, Frank? Or don't you like time travel?'

'Some things seem to have faded in my memory,' he said.

'Bullshit.'

He shrugged. 'You know you're running a serious risk coming here. The FBI are watching over me.'

'Guardian angels,' she said.

'Or demons.'

'They don't impress me,' she said. 'Nothing bothers me right at this moment.'

She smiled. It was a marvel, luscious and dangerous. She allowed the hand that held her silenced gun to fall against her thigh and she moved the barrel back and forth across her jeans, creating a gentle whispering friction. Pagan listened to the sound of metal on denim and tried to think himself into a safe room of the mind where he wouldn't have to look at her.

She released the smile, but none of her beauty went with it. Pagan detected in her some indefinable shift of mood and he wondered if she was going to turn on him suddenly and use the gun in her hand – and yet he had the feeling that the time hadn't come, it wasn't the moment.

'We might be the only two people in the world right now, Pagan. This room could be a capsule in space. Just you and me and a great expanse of stars. Think about it. It's a romantic thought.'

'Romantic? I don't really think so.'

'One day you'll crucify yourself on your own denials, Pagan. Look at me and tell me you don't like what you see. Look at me and tell me you don't want me.'

'I don't want you,' he said.

'No?' She stretched her legs.

'No,' he said.

'I don't believe you.'

'What you believe doesn't concern me.'

'*What you believe doesn't concern me.*' She mimicked him accurately. It was an acid little response, designed to ridicule. 'You've always wanted me, Pagan. Maybe I've slipped your mind from time to time over the years, but I keep coming back to the surface. Why pretend? What is it with you anyhow? This wall you've built around yourself.'

This wall, he thought. He wondered how solid it was. He remembered when she'd come to his apartment, how he'd responded when she'd touched him, the disgust he'd felt at himself, except it wasn't disgust in the end, it was something else he didn't like to consider, an attraction driven by lust. But certain attractions, in Pagan's book, were perversities – priests buggering small choirboys, men who yearned to be dominated and made to bleed: did he fall into that category? The stigma of unacceptable needs. He remembered dreaming of her, the pulsating thrill of the dream. *I keep coming back to the surface* . . .

'The wall, as you call it, protects me,' he said.

'From me.'

'Among other things.'

'Your problem is you try to filter the world, Pagan. You don't let it come at you in a great rush. You try to keep out what you believe you don't need. I like the rush. I don't stop to sift through details. I don't analyse everything to death like you.'

'You're an expert on the subject of Frank Pagan, are you?' he asked.

'I told you before. I can read you. You want to hide from me because you want to be the fine upstanding cop. Trustworthy, reliable, Mr Terrific. You like to believe you don't want me, because the opposite is more than you can bear. But it's inside you, and you can't get rid of it. You want me, Pagan. You want to fuck me.'

She said *fuck* in the most provocative way Pagan had ever heard. She might have coined the word; it might have belonged only in her private vocabulary. She gave it a potent intimacy, a freshness.

She smiled and undid the buckle of her belt and slowly opened the buttons of her jeans. He saw a flash of white underwear, a lacy waistband, a soft down of pubic hair fading in the smooth stretch of skin between the band and her navel. 'Tell me again, Pagan. Say it nice and clear. Let me hear it. You don't want me. Let me hear you say it.'

He didn't speak, didn't know what to say, didn't know how to acknowledge the power she had to make him feel the way he did. He watched her slide her hand inside her underwear, saw her part her legs a little, the motion of the hand beneath lace. She didn't take her eyes away from his face.

'What is this doing for you, Pagan? What are you feeling? Tell me. Speak to me.'

He said nothing.

Her hand went deeper. She slid the underwear down a little way, creating lacy disarray. He saw the soft inviting crop of pubic hair, imagined the descent into the cleft, imagined getting up from the bed and going toward her and, on his knees, burying his face in her flesh and losing himself there in sweetness and humiliation. After forty-six years on the planet, what do you really know about Frank Pagan? he wondered.

'Tell me you don't want me, Pagan.' She opened her mouth, stretched her legs wider, tilted her head back just a little. He was bewitched by the angle of her face, the slope of cheek, the way her eyes narrowed as if she were directing her vision deep into herself.

'You want to fuck me,' she said. 'We're not separated by thousands of miles now. We're not talking on a telephone. You want to fuck me.' She slid her hand deeper still, reaching between her thighs, tugging the lace down to reveal the pubic cluster in its entirety, the private geography of herself, one long finger sliding gently in the slit where the hair parted. Pagan had the illusion that the room was pounding against him, perceptions roared at him, the woman touching the core of herself, her reflections multiplied in the mirror.

She said, 'For once in your life, Pagan, tell the truth about what you're feeling.'

He observed the motion of a dark red nail against her hair, saw the gun hang from her other hand. Tell the truth, he thought. What was the truth anyway? That he was capable of ignoring the cruelties of the woman for a few minutes of pleasure? That he could set aside her violent history for the sake of fucking her? What was he supposed to do? Pretend she was a stranger from an outcall agency, the kind of woman who went to men in motel rooms and brought them quick satisfaction? No, he couldn't make-believe she was somebody else. She wasn't a stranger. She'd lived inside his head for too long. He gazed at her stomach, the mysterious concavity of navel, followed the line of her arm upward, looked at her face. He was thinking of the hours he'd spent studying her photographs in

Golden Square, that whole obsession he'd tried to rationalize away as duty.

'Do you want me to order you to perform, Pagan? You get some kick out of fucking under duress, is that it? You need a gun pressed to the side of your skull?'

He said nothing. He turned his face from her. He didn't have to look at her. He didn't have to sit through this performance. He could stare at the walls, the window, anything. *I'm not compelled to watch*, he thought.

But you are. You are. All the signs of an orderly moral universe are awry.

She shrugged off the leather jacket. Her unbuckled belt lay against her thighs. The blue jeans had slid from her hips. She used the barrel of the gun to push the black T-shirt up. Her breasts were firm, finely marbled with pale sky-blue veins. He shut his eyes as if he might distance himself from the sight of her, but darkness reinforced the effect she had. He heard the sound of her breathing, the way it quickened as she stroked herself. He fought against the rush of blood, the lava raging along veins. He was hard. *She doesn't even have to touch me*, he thought. *She doesn't even have to come near me.*

He gazed at her hand working back and forth, the motion of her fingers. He raised his face and her eyes held his in challenging complicity.

'You've got a hard-on, Pagan,' she said. 'You're hard as a rock. I can see it. You're big and swollen and I'm driving you up a fucking wall because you don't know what to do, do you? You don't know how you're supposed to behave, do you? You want me. You want to get your cock inside me, don't you? You want to go down and kiss my cunt, Pagan. You want it all, you want everything, but you don't know how you can do it, because you don't know how you can live with yourself if you do because you've got this prim bullshit thing . . . But I've got you going, Pagan. All this is getting to you. *It's getting to you.*' And she arched her back suddenly, violently, and halfway shut her eyes and pushed her hips forward and moaned as she shuddered, and her hand with its glistening fingertips rose from between her legs to her thigh and lay there, palm upturned lazily. Then she subsided into silence for a time, the private aftermath of pleasure.

She looked at him. Looked between his legs. 'You've still got a hard-on. And I gave it to you. I made it happen. I didn't even have to come within six feet of you. I didn't have to breathe on you.'

Pagan felt no release from his own tension. Only a sense of disturbance, a massive shadow in his head.

'And that gives you power over me?' he asked.

'It gives me a kick you wouldn't believe. I had you going like some schoolkid. You were about to come in your pants.'

You had me going, he thought. Yes. He watched her buckle her belt, tuck her T-shirt inside her jeans. For a long time he didn't move, wasn't sure what he felt, frustration, shame. She was able to take the map of his emotions and redraw it at will. He was still aroused.

'I've cut off your avenues of retreat, Pagan. You don't have any denials left. I get to you. And it's so easy. It's just so god-damn easy. I could have made you fuck me. I could have made you do anything. Anything.'

Yes, he'd wanted her. Yes. If she'd insisted, if she'd forced him, held a gun to his head . . . He thought of her hand between her thighs, and how she'd explored herself with all the delicacy of a careful lover. He thought of the way she'd caressed herself in growing excitement, the intensity of her breathing, the final landslide of herself.

She said, 'Let's call this foreplay, Pagan. The real thing lies ahead.'

'I don't think so.'

'No?' She picked up her leather jacket.

'It doesn't end like this,' he said.

'You still have this idea of capturing me. Bringing me to justice.'

'It's more than an idea.'

'Justice. That's funny, that's deeply ironic,' she said. 'Two Pagans. One that gets a hard-on watching me jerk off in front of him. The other that wants me jailed. You've got a problem you need to fix before you can even think about justice.'

'I'll find a way to deal with it.' Two Pagans, he thought. Dark set against light, warring twins. A way to deal with it – it sounded good, but he had no idea how the mechanics of it might be made to work. Right and wrong, two tributaries of the same roaring river. And you were clinging to a raft of balsa-wood.

'Maybe you will. Maybe you won't.' She stepped toward him and raised her hand and touched the corner of his mouth with the fingertips that only minutes before had been between her legs. He moved his head away from her touch, from the taste of her skin and sex. She forced his face back toward her, inserted a finger between his lips.

'Taste me,' she said.

He felt her finger on the surface of his tongue. The intimacy was overwhelming, the way she moved the finger slightly back and forth, the way his lips closed around it. He felt as if he were ensnared in a perfumed web. He drifted a second, down into that place where all his sedimentary passions were stirred – and then he caught himself and pulled his face away. She laughed, throwing her head back a little.

'A man of iron,' she said.

Iron. He didn't think so. OK, so he hadn't risen from the bed and gone to her, he'd disobeyed the dictates of his own body, he'd fought against his impulses. But he hadn't been able to obscure them – and he was a long way from exorcizing them. Iron wasn't quite the word. Something far more malleable than iron.

She took a step away from him. He considered the possibility of making a lunge at her, but it wasn't a prospect he took seriously. She had the weapon, he didn't. As soon as he made the wrong move, she'd shoot him. It was a certainty.

He said, 'I know about Naderson. I know about Poole. I know they're your targets.'

'You're a bright boy,' she said. 'What else do you know?'

'This much. You're cutting your own throat,' he said. 'Naderson and Poole will have round-the-clock protection. You can't get near either of them.'

'But you know better than that, don't you?'

'It's still a risk. You're not infallible.'

'Risks are for other people,' she said. 'Anyhow, do you really believe I'd let anyone but you get within an inch of me? Dream on. It's between you and me. That's what it comes down to. You and me. All the rest is background noise.'

Background noise, he thought. The deaths in the hotel, the supermarket bomb, the killing of Burr. Of Pasco. 'Capsicum – was that background noise as well? And your parents? And Lannigan?'

'I had nothing to do with any of that,' she said. 'Somebody else is doing all that stuff, Pagan.'

He believed her. He wasn't sure why; but he believed her. 'And blaming you,' he said.

'Blaming me. Strange, huh.'

'I'd say more than strange. What's the point of it all?'

She shrugged. 'Maybe I've got a secret admirer out there. A copycat.'

'I don't think so. The way I see it, somebody wants the world to believe *you're* responsible for those acts.'

'Maybe so.'

'Why is somebody going to all the trouble of all this destruction just so you can be blamed? What is there to gain from that?'

'You tell me.'

Pagan stared at her. Just for a moment he imagined something gave way in her face, a yielding took place, and she seemed like a lost child, distressed, out of place in an adult world – like a kid who has wandered away from her parents at a crowded ballgame in a huge stadium. He saw softness in her, and uncertainty. But the moment passed, the illusion vanished. She was destruction incarnate. She was blood and death. She was infatuated with violence. It had been a folly on his part to imagine otherwise, even for a second. A weakness in himself, perhaps even a doomed attempt to locate something human in her, something that might justify this attraction she held for him. An excuse for his desires.

He looked away from her, drawn to the bright window. 'Somebody wants to panic the public. Somebody wants to make sure your name is firmly back in the headlines.'

'I don't need anybody to grab headlines on my behalf,' she said, and there was petulance in her voice.

'No, you don't. But somebody is making bloody

315

sure the headlines keep coming, even if you're not responsible for them. In your position, that would worry me. Maybe somebody's setting you up.'

'Nobody gets up that early in the day, Pagan.' She raised the gun suddenly and levelled it at him, squinting the length of the barrel. 'Boom,' she whispered.

'What's stopping you?'

'Because I haven't got what I want yet.'

'And what's that?'

She didn't reply. She gave him an enigmatic little smile that was almost one of shyness – but he wasn't going to be sucked into that. He watched her as she moved toward the door.

'So you go to Naderson or you go to Poole,' he said.

'Maybe. Maybe not. Maybe you don't have the complete list, Pagan. You ever think about that?'

'I've thought about it.'

She reached the door, turned to look at him. 'Did Roxanne ever masturbate for you, Pagan? Did you ever watch her get herself off in front of your face? Did you ever suck her fingers after?'

Roxanne. Sex with Roxanne had been gentle, an act of mutual consideration, tenderness.

'You're not answering me, Pagan. Why? Too personal for you? Maybe she wasn't into that kind of thing. Was she coy, Pagan? Was there some sweet shy retiring thing about her that turned you on? Maybe you've never been properly fucked.'

She smiled and went out, leaving Pagan alone with the taste of her in his mouth and the dying echo of Roxanne's name in his head.

35

DELAWARE

She drove the freeway, windows down, warm air streaming against her face and hair. She was thinking of Pagan, the concentration on his features, the way he'd closed his eyes when she'd placed a finger between his lips. I had him, she thought. I had him where I wanted him.

She drove for miles and miles. Suburbs faded out in scattered tract houses, then mobile-home parks where laundry hung motionless on lines and barebacked kids played a makeshift game of basketball in the fretful heat.

She saw a bar alongside the freeway and she turned the car toward it. She parked and went inside, passing a collection of motorcycles and pickup trucks. It was a redneck joint, sawdust on the floors, half a dozen or so bikers, a few good old boys on bar stools. Heads turned in her direction, she was assessed and appreciated.

She went up to the bar and asked for a Bacardi and Coke – Carly Phoenix would drink something like that, but never to excess because she liked to keep a clear head. She saw herself in the mirror on the wall – Carly Phoenix, a walking temptation, her whole being a come-on. She sipped her drink, set the glass down, thought about the hotel room, about Pagan. His world was eggshell thin. And cracked, badly cracked. And that was the way she wanted it. Power was the buzz, the mainline high that made you feel nothing could ever touch you, nothing could ever harm you: as close to immortality as you were going to get in this lifetime.

One of the bikers came toward her with a pool cue in his hand. He was sweaty in his sleeveless T-shirt. Tattoos covered his arms. 'You play?' he asked.

'Depends on the game.'

'Eight-ball,' he said. He was about thirty and his hair was greasy. In his right ear lobe was a small silver crucifix.

'Eight-ball,' she said. 'Not my game.'

'Yeah? Name your game, lady,' he said.

'You guess.'

'Guess?' The biker had yellow teeth. 'Maybe something more lively?'

She was thinking of Pagan again. She'd excited him and then she'd let him go because she thought it was enough, but now – now she wasn't so sure. She pictured his grey eyes, the small lines etched at the corners of the mouth, the lean face that was at times almost haunted. *Intimacy and destruction.* She wondered if Galkin had been right, if what she felt toward Pagan was a form of affection so badly bent out of shape it couldn't be categorized. No. No. *I want him dead. There's no affection. Nothing like that. Not even remotely.* And yet – there had been something contagious in Pagan's physical agitation, something that had moved her.

The biker set the pool cue on the bar and said, 'Folks call me Ronnie Bear.'

'Bear, huh.'

'That's what they call me. Real close friends call me something else.'

'Yeah?' She stared at him through her shades. He bored her. He was trespassing on her privacy.

'My real close friends, and I'm talking *real* intimate now, they call me Kingsize.'

'I wonder why.'

'Three guesses.'

'I wouldn't need three,' she said.

He winked at her. 'Yeah. You sure as hell wouldn't need three, lady.'

I let Pagan off the hook, she thought. She was disturbed by a sense of unfulfilled desire, of discontent. Her thoughts drifted to the attack on Capsicum, the murder of her parents, the explosion at Lannigan's house; she circled these happenings, as if they were flames she didn't want to approach. *Maybe somebody's setting you up*, Pagan had said. She remembered her final encounter with Galkin, the idea of a set-up that had crossed her mind then. The game Mallory was playing, one faction of the Agency at war with another, the idea that she could somehow be drawn into this game and used and finally *captured* . . . Was Mallory the one behind the acts of violence for which she was being blamed? She wasn't sure how to react, whether to be outraged by the way her name had been used, or amused by the arrogance of the perpetrator. Games – she was beyond all that.

She thought of her parents dead inside the plantation house – but she felt nothing, they weren't her parents, they had nothing to do with Carly Phoenix. Carly Phoenix didn't have parents, Carly would have been orphaned at an early age and forced to make her own way in the world. She would never have been sent to a clinic and fondled by the seriously sick Patrick Lannigan.

'Whadda you do?' Bear asked. 'For work, I mean.'

She turned her face slowly to the man. 'I take off my clothes.'

'A stripper, you mean?'

She covered a pretend yawn.

One old toothless geezer in a black leather vest said, 'Take em off, lady. Shows yer knockers. Shows all you got.'

She said, 'I don't want to be responsible for bringing on a heart attack, pops.'

The bikers laughed and banged their Bud bottles on the table. Bear edged a little closer to her. 'I never met no stripper before.'

She faced the mirror, looked at her reflection, saw the smoothed black hair, the leather jacket, the dark lipstick, the shades – a catalogue of impressions, a list of the components that constituted Carly Phoenix, stripper. All the others that had existed inside her were dead. She didn't have room for memories and resurrections.

Bear was watching her. He licked his sun-cracked lips. 'Say. Any chance of a private performance, lady? Like you and me go someplace, and you show me your routine? Hows about it.'

'Why don't you just evaporate,' she said.

Bear laughed in a broken way. 'You're funny.'

'I'm funny all right,' she said.

'Seriously now,' he said.

She sipped her drink. She had a sense of danger emanating from this character Bear, the feeling that violence lay very close to the surface of the man. The notion didn't trouble her remotely. She could handle anything he started.

'You refusing me?' he asked.

'You got it in one.'

He turned his head and looked at his biker associates. 'You all hear that? I been turned down, guys! I been rejected by a stripper! Well, roll me on my hip and fuck me sideways.'

The bikers, like apes taught to behave by a mal-adjusted trainer, banged their beer bottles on the tables and screeched. Bear looked back at her and said, 'They don't approve, see. They think I should get a private show. They think I deserve one. So – you gonna oblige?'

She looked directly into his eyes. He was nothing, scum blown in on a Harley-Davison. She set her glass down on the bar. He met her eyes without flinching and she thought: He doesn't understand what Carly Phoenix can do to him. She'd been raised on rough streets, she'd graduated the school of hard knocks with a first-class diploma. Carly Phoenix knew her way around morons like Bear. She had them for breakfast and didn't even notice.

She said, 'You're not man enough, Bear. Come back when you're all grown up.'

The bikers hooted. Bear reached out and caught her right wrist. He was strong. His fingers closed around her like metal hinges. She removed her sunglasses with her free hand and stared at him because it was important to maintain eye contact. She wanted him to see into her, she wanted him to sense her potential if he could, if his antenna was receptive, but she had the feeling he was too stupid to have any fine instincts. He grunted and drank and belched his way through the world.

'Let go,' she said.

'Ooo, let go, she says. You hear her, guys?'

The bikers were working up quite a rhythm now with their beer bottles, like a drum section on strong reefer.

'I only ask once,' she said.

'Wow, I'm all shivery, lady,' he said. He tightened the grip, a muscle strained in his arm, a blue tattoo of a naked girl was stretched out of shape on his skin.

'You've been warned,' she said.

Bear threw back his head and howled like a wolf under a mad moon on an empty prairie.

This is nothing, she thought. This is too easy. He wasn't worthy of her. She moved deftly, pushing herself away from the bar, reaching with her left hand under her jacket to the belt of her jeans, and she took out the gun and shoved it into his throat – everything was too quick for him to follow.

'The safety's off, hotshot,' she said.

'Hey, hold on,' he said.

'Get the fucking hand off my wrist,' she said.

'Easy now,' and he took his hand away.

She raised her arm and pointed the gun at his head, forcing the barrel into his skullbone. She caught the silver crucifix and ripped it out of his ear lobe. He groaned with pain and immediately raised a hand to his wounded ear, which was bleeding.

She said, 'Say after me. My name's Bear and I'm a total asshole.'

'You didn't have to yank my fucking ear halfway off—'

'You've got another one,' she said.

'Holy shit, it hurts—'

'Now say it. Say what I told you to say.'

'My name's Bear and I'm a total asshole. Jesus Christ . . .'

'Good. Now unzip your pants.'

'Unzip my pants . . .'

'Do it!'

'Wait a minute, lady—'

'The safety's off and I've got a nervous tic in my finger, Kingsize. The zipper.'

He undid the buckle of his belt, pulled down the zip of his jeans. They slithered to his ankles. He had thin white legs and orange boxer shorts.

'Good,' she said. 'Now show me.'

'Show what?'

'Show me how you got your nickname,' she said.

'Listen, lady—'

'Come on, Kingsize. Show me.'

The other bikers were silent now.

'Come on,' she said. 'The world's waiting, Bear.'

'This is . . . this is . . .' He lowered his hand to his groin, reaching for the flap in his shorts.

'I'm holding my breath,' she said.

'Lady,' he said.

'Let's see the pecker, let's all see this whopper,' she said.

He opened the boxer shorts and fumbled inside and produced his limp white penis, clutched between thumb and forefinger like a slug shrivelling in salt.

'Kingsize?' she asked. 'I guess it deflates when it's scared, huh? Wrinkled little thing. Turn around. Show your friends what you got there, Kingsize.'

She prodded him with the gun, forced him to turn to the gallery of bikers. He did so quickly, then swung back round to stare at her and she said, 'I guess your new nickname's Peanut, or Walnut Dick, or something like that.'

He reached down and drew up his jeans and, flushed with anger, buckled his belt. 'You fucking bitch,' he said.

She picked up her drink and emptied the glass. 'Which bike is yours?'

'Go fuck yourself.'

'Just answer the question, Kingsize.' She aimed the gun at him with a gesture of certitude.

He said, 'The one that got the red gas-tank.'

She put her glass down on the bar, picked up her shades, stuck them on her face and walked toward the door. She was still holding the gun on Ronnie Bear. 'Don't follow me,' she said.

'You bitch,' he said. 'I'll get you.'

'Yeah yeah,' she said. 'Sure you will.'

She walked outside. She moved across the parking-lot to the cluster of bikes and she fired a single shot directly into the gas tank of Bear's Harley, which caught flame. Then she went to the rented Honda and got inside and drove to the exit of the lot, seeing in the rearview mirror bikers scurrying out of the bar into palls of thick black smoke. She backed up the Honda, reached out of the window, fired a second shot into the group of men, watched them throw themselves to the ground for protection. She wheeled around them, gun dangling from the open window. She saw Bear rise and lunge at the Honda in his rage and she accelerated a little, blowing dust up at him. He lost his balance and went down on his face and she circled him one last time, laughing, and then she headed back to the freeway at speed.

She drove fast for miles, drove until her sense of amusement had passed, until the exhilaration had gone out of her system. Fun, but fun always went away, even for Carly Phoenix, who needed new highs, new horizons. She needed challenges, not some half-assed encounter with an asshole in a roadside tavern, for God's sake. That wasn't enough. That wasn't even close to enough. No way. It was Pagan who kept coming back to her, her finger inside his mouth, the mounds of his closed eyelids, the wet surface of his tongue. It was Pagan who crowded her mind mile after mile.

She played the radio loud all the way to the outskirts of Dover. Sometimes when the sun glinted off the highway she had flashes of Capsicum, smoke drifting down Main Street, the gas station exploding. Dead, dreary Capsicum, arid and intolerable, the place where Carlotta's childhood lay trapped under the weight of tinder-dry fir trees and fallen cones that cracked when you stood on them during the long festering summers and the big fans that creaked round and round in the plantation house, where every shadowy room led to one in ever deeper shadow, a series of darkening boxes, the unoiled hub of a wheelchair squeaking, the flutter of her mother's gauzy dress against a wall, the dank webby smell of the black cellar where the old man sometimes sent her when she'd done something wrong – these details burst open in her head like fireworks on a night with no stars.

Sweating, she got out of the car at a gas station and used the pay phone. She dialled Chico's number in Virginia. He was a long time answering.

When he picked up, she said, 'Where were you? Watering your plants?'

'Something like that.'

'Got anything for me?'

'Could be,' he answered.

36

WASHINGTON

When the telephone rang in Pagan's room he answered
it at once. A man said, 'I'm downstairs in reception.
I've come from Langley.'

'Give me a minute,' Pagan said, and hung up. He
went inside the bathroom and dipped his face in what
was supposed to be cold water, but was actually
lukewarm. He looked at himself in the mirror. He had
a sense of appearing different, although he wasn't sure
in what way exactly. It was his own face that stared
back at him, and if changes had occurred in him they
hadn't taken place on the visible level. The same Frank
Pagan, but altered.

He drank a glass of water and remembered Foxie's
expression: *Basic biology*. But that didn't cut it. Biology
didn't begin to scratch the surface. There was no true
science of the heart. He thought: If I move and keep
moving, I won't have time to dwell on her. Focus.
Concentration. What had she said? *Don't stop to sift
through details*. He could still feel her, that was the
problem. She still adhered to him. He carried her
around like a photograph inside a locket that was a
little too heavy.

He retrieved his gun from under the bed, reloaded
the clip, inserted it. He stuck the Bernardelli in a

holster he wore at the base of his spine, then he put on a pale blue linen jacket that concealed the gun. He left the room, rode an elevator down into the reception area. A tall young man stepped forward to greet him.

'Frank Pagan? I'm Ralph Donovan.' He showed Pagan an identification card issued by the Central Intelligence Agency. 'Bob Naderson asked me to pick you up and deliver you to Langley.'

'Naderson said he'd call me himself,' Pagan said.

Donovan smiled. 'If you want to verify all this, why don't you ring him?'

Pagan looked at the young man. He was muscular and bland and his face suggested healthy pursuits – camping, fresh air, sixteen laps in a swimming-pool before breakfast, a couple of hours a week in the gym. It was a face without shadows. Pagan said, 'I'll take your word for it, Donovan.'

'Good. Car's just out front, Mr Pagan.'

Pagan followed Donovan outside. The car was a dark blue Buick. Donovan politely held the passenger door open for him. Pagan settled down inside the air-conditioned vehicle. Donovan got behind the wheel.

'So,' said Donovan. 'What do you make of our weather?'

'Hot,' Pagan replied.

Donovan smiled. 'There's a rumour of rain.'

Weather-chat. Pagan was comfortable with that. It was ordinary and manageable. He stared ahead through a congregation of tourist buses. People swarmed here from every corner of the Republic to pay their respects at an assortment of shrines. They came from all over the world, from countries where democracy was sometimes a deceptive concept manipulated by dictators and tribal chiefs, to peer at the great statues and pay tribute. He pondered the fact

327

that while these good people looked in awe at the Washington Monument or Capitol Hill, he was riding in a car driven by an employee of a clandestine agency, an organization the Founding Fathers could never have predicted. Public monuments, secret monoliths, the dichotomy at the core of these United States. Irony, if you were in the mood for it – but he wasn't, because he had a dichotomy in his own heart, and he couldn't deal with that one.

Donovan drove with a certain nonchalant competence. 'I don't take the regular route, in case you're wondering,' he remarked. 'It's usually clogged. More so this time of the year. It gets a little shabby from here on. But we contrive to hide all this from the merry tourists.'

The car was travelling grubby side-streets where topless bars were located. Girls Girls Girls!!! The Pussy Pit. The Peekaboo Lounge. Palace of Fuzz. The taverns were uninviting, darkened windows, unlit neon signs. Pagan always found something mildly depressing about unlit neon.

'You work directly for Bob Naderson?' he asked.

'You might say I'm a general gofer, Mr Pagan.'

'Meaning?'

Donovan shrugged and turned to glance at Pagan. 'I'm a floater, really.'

'You get moved around.'

'Shunted, more like. Department to department, one office to another, no regular abode. When a chauffeur's needed, I get the job. When a message has to be delivered, I'm usually the man. Unattached, you might say. It's OK. It gives me certain freedoms I might not have if I was tied down.'

'So you don't know why you're delivering me to Langley?'

'Mr Naderson's orders. I never ask questions, Mr Pagan. I do what I'm told to do. I like it that way. I'm not an ambitious sort of guy. I'm not what you'd call driven.'

Along a street of decrepit houses where porches sometimes stood at slanting angles, there were burned-out cars and boarded windows and For Sale signs. Dark faces brooded in the shadows of houses. On street corners dope deals were being transacted with an absence of subterfuge. Store windows were barred or sometimes totally hidden behind steel shutters. Here and there a figure could be seen lying on a sidewalk. Dead or doped or drunk, Pagan had no way of knowing. A city of memorials and crack dealers, monuments and vagrants.

'I don't know where we are,' Donovan said. 'But it sure ain't America. Sorry sight. All this hopelessness. Despair. It makes you think.'

'Every city has neighbourhoods like this,' Pagan remarked, as if to alleviate the apparent dismay in Donovan.

'Somehow it's worse when it's Washington. I mean, you don't expect the nation's capital to have this kind of shit going on. People come here because the city stands for an ideal. And as soon as you get off the beaten track – well, look around. Just look around.'

'Am I being chauffeured by an idealist?' Pagan asked.

'I believe in certain things, Mr Pagan. Trouble is, some of the things I happen to believe in are under fire. Guys selling dope openly on the streets – but where are the cops? And then you think of that dope coming across the country's borders, and you wonder what the DEA is doing. Whatever it is, it's not enough, otherwise you wouldn't have places like this, and you wouldn't see crack changing hands on street corners.'

Pagan noticed a small speck of saliva on the corner of Donovan's lips. The trouble with idealists was their naïvety. They expected the world to be one way, and when it wasn't, they bruised too easily. And when they were hurt, they frothed at the mouth. Like Donovan.

'You can't stop the flow of drugs,' Pagan said.

'You can try, though,' Donovan responded.

'What do you suggest? Seal off the borders?'

'Sure.'

'And after the borders, what next? The airports. The seaports. Wrap an electronic fence round the whole country?'

'Impractical,' Donovan said.

Impractical. It was clear to Pagan, whose suggestion of an electronic fence was meant to be interpreted as an impossible whimsy, that Donovan wasn't blessed with a sense of humour, at least not when it came to his idealism, his patriotism.

'We give too many visas to people who come here on shady business,' Donovan said. 'We get the dregs of the world washing up on our shores and we welcome them with open arms. Cubans. Haitians. You name it, we take them in.'

'The melting-pot,' said Pagan.

'The shitcan, you mean,' Donovan said. He banged the horn as a skinny kid materialized in front of the car with a glazed look on his face. The kid leaned away from the vehicle and Donovan braked.

'God-damn moron,' Donovan said, and stopped the car.

To Pagan's surprise, Donovan got out and grabbed the kid by the collar of his T-shirt and shook him vigorously. The kid was elsewhere, transported aloft on the narcotic of his choice, and for him the confrontation was probably just the bad-dream part of his trip.

330

A big white guy shaking him, jarring his bones, unreal. Pagan watched as Donovan dragged the kid to the sidewalk and dumped him in front of a stoop where a bunch of old men passed a bottle back and forth in a brown paper bag. Donovan launched a foot hard into the kid's ribs, then returned to the car.

'The rough approach,' Pagan said. 'Dangerous in a neighbourhood like this.'

'Dangerous,' Donovan said, as if the concept were alien to him. He looked at Pagan and smiled. 'Sometimes I get to the point where I have to . . . make a small gesture?'

A small gesture, Pagan thought. There was clearly a tiny screw not quite connected in Donovan's system. The way he'd grabbed the kid and shaken him as if he meant to force his eyes from their sockets, and that final needless crunching kick to the ribs. Random violence unsettled Pagan, who was beginning to wonder if Donovan's Aryan plausibility and bright demeanour didn't contain more than just a seed of darkness. Maybe they bred them like Donovan at Langley these days – unhappy patriots, malcontented idealists, candidates for some future American Reich to which nobody was permitted access unless they held certain untainted beliefs and could swear to them on old mildewed family Bibles hauled over on the *Mayflower*.

Donovan drove a little way before he said, 'I get pissed off, Mr Pagan.'

'I can tell.'

Donovan shook his head and sighed. 'It's not just dope. Dope's only a symptom.'

'Of what?'

'A far greater sickness,' Donovan said solemnly.

Pagan said nothing. He was losing touch with Ralph

Donovan. He stared through the windshield. The neighbourhood had deteriorated further, if that was possible, and now there was a series of unpaved streets and flattened houses and some kind of abandoned building project. A crane with shattered windows stood in the centre of a big empty lot, surrounded by bricks and tumbledown scaffolding. Shells of new houses had been erected but somewhere in the process of creation an abandonment had taken place – perhaps because somebody had run out of Federal funds or faith, or even both.

'This is typical,' said Donovan. 'A builder gets Federal money to slam up some new houses that are going to become slums as soon as they're occupied. But what happens is that the foundations get laid and a few walls go up and the contractor abandons the whole god-damn thing because it's too dangerous for his crew to work here – they get attacked, mugged, shot, name it. So the builder pulls out, claiming a lack of security, and his wallet's stuffed anyway, and the whole damn thing becomes a slum before anybody's even moved in – Ah, *Christ*.'

The car stalled, stopped. Donovan turned the key in the ignition a couple of times but the engine didn't fire.

'Shit,' he said.

'What's the problem?'

'I don't know what the particular problem is with this car, but I can tell you the *general* problem – inadequate maintenance, incompetent mechanics, a lack of professionalism. Fuck, fuck, fuck.'

Donovan got out of the car and opened the hood. Pagan sat for a time, the litany of Donovan's complaints ringing in his ears, and then when it became too hot and stuffy to stay in the car he opened the door and stepped out. He scanned the building site.

Deserted, forlorn, strangely still in the afternoon heat. He didn't like this place. He was sweating. This was the kind of weather that microwaved human brains. Maybe that was what had happened to Donovan – too many hours in clogged traffic, sucking too many fumes, working up a general despair at the condition of things. Drugs, bad mechanics, corrupt contractors, the waste of Government money, the incompetence of cops. The inside of Donovan's head had to be filled with all kinds of bad bagpipe music, laments.

Pagan walked to the front of the car. Donovan was concealed by the upraised hood, which resembled the big wing of a metal bird.

'Anything happening?' Pagan asked.

'Yeah,' said Donovan. 'Look what I found.'

He raised his face from the shadow of the hood and he was smiling. The sight of the gun in the young man's hand surprised Pagan, whose first inclination was to pass it off as a bad joke, or some irrational behaviour inspired by the weather, but Donovan's smile was lethally serious. There was nothing ambiguous in that expression.

'Why?' Pagan asked.

'I do what I'm told,' said Donovan.

'The gofer.'

'Right on the nail, Mr Pagan.'

'And you don't stop to ask, Ralph.'

'No, I never ask. I just get on with it.'

Pagan wondered about dying in a place like this. Shot, his body dragged and dumped behind a pile of bricks. Maybe not even that. Murders were commonplace around here. Maybe he'd just lie out in the open where he'd be seen and somebody might come by eventually and a call would be made to the cops. That could take days, by which time he'd be fly-fodder. He'd be crawling, infested. He didn't care for the notion. He didn't have time to waste dying. He'd been careless, taking Donovan at face value.

'Walk over here with me, Mr Pagan,' Donovan said. 'Let's take a look at where some of our Federal taxes have gone.'

They crossed the rutted dry lot, Donovan a pace or so behind, and moved toward the shadow of the crane. The ground sparkled with broken glass. Pagan stepped over planks of cut timber that had been vandalized, set alight and charred round the edges. The shells of the small houses suggested a theatrical set, and the sun was nothing more than a big bleak spotlight. The place was isolated. Pagan felt sweat gather around the loose collar of his shirt. A way out, he was thinking. A way out.

He stared at Donovan, who said, 'This is nothing personal, you understand.'

'That makes it OK, I suppose. I'd hate to think I'd offended you directly, Ralph.'

Donovan thought this funny and laughed a moment.

'Killing me is going to accomplish something, is that it, Ralph? I forgot, sorry, you can't answer. You just do what you're told. Who tells you, Ralph? Who is this somebody that dishes out the orders?'

Donovan stood directly under the giant yellow arm of the crane. A huge hook hung from the arm, like a claw. A bird rose out of the control cabin and flapped off wearily into the sun.

Donovan said, 'I wish you wouldn't ask questions, Mr Pagan. Anyway, what's the point in me answering them? It doesn't make a damn bit of difference to you now.'

Pagan looked beyond Donovan but saw no escape routes. Everything became distilled in the glimmer of

Donovan's gun: his whole life dwindled miserably to a dark hole the size of a human eyeball. 'I'm just curious, Ralph. That's all.' He tried to keep panic from his voice. But the deadpan manner, the artificial cool, was difficult to maintain in the circumstances.

'Step back about four feet,' Donovan said.

'You don't want my blood on you,' Pagan said.

'Dry-cleaning's a pain in the ass.'

Pagan took a few steps back and was seized by the sensation that he was posing for a photograph, moving himself into the correct angle for a camera.

'That's fine,' said Donovan. 'Stop where you are.'

Pagan looked up at the sun. The world seemed to him just then a place of dislocations. None of the parts fitted. Everything was out of joint. A dreaminess descended on him for a moment, as if he'd just swallowed morphine. He looked at Donovan, whose white shirt was a blur, a blaze.

Donovan raised the gun and pointed it. Pagan wasn't sure if he was meant to close his eyes or keep them open or whether somebody should step forward and blindfold him right now and perhaps stick a smoking cigarette between his lips. He held his breath and stared at the gun and considered his options, none of them viable. To rush Donovan was useless. To turn and run was futile. But to stand still and wait for death and just go out like a snuffed match – there had to be more to it than that. His mouth was a bone-dry cavity in his head. His eyes smarted from sweat.

He heard a crunching sound, something that didn't quite belong at an execution. He wasn't altogether sure where it came from, but it sounded like movement over broken stones. Donovan heard it too, and he half turned from Pagan, but he kept the gun in the firing position because he wasn't going to let his attention wander. The sound came again, and this time there were voices attached to it.

'Fucker come this way.'

'Car's back there.'

'He ain't far.'

'He gonna be one sorry sonofabitch.'

Pagan gazed at a high pile of gravel. Donovan, he noticed, looked slightly bewildered, his attention split between Pagan and the voices coming from the other side of the gravel mound.

'Gonna be one sorry mother,' a voice said.

'Gonna be, man.'

'Gonna wisht he don't come roun here, yeah.'

'Stompin on folks, what the fuck.'

'Yeah, yeah.'

The kid Donovan had assaulted appeared at the top of the pile. He held in his hand a length of lead pipe. Behind him, two others came in view – older, heavier, one carrying what looked like a Wildey automatic with a fourteen-inch barrel, the other a blunt little Uzi. Pagan experienced a distinct chill in the air, a pocket of cold gather in the shadow of the crane's arm. There was a curious imbalance about things all at once, Donovan unsure of his next move, the armed kids on the gravel summit staring down at him, and Pagan himself, a prisoner of shadow, spared his own execution – at least for the moment.

'That's the fucker,' said the small kid.

Donovan stepped back a few feet. He formed the apex of a murderous triangle, Pagan on one side, the gravel mound and the kids on the other. Pagan felt it coming, it was gathering in the air around him, the build-up of violence; it was like the dry claustrophobic heft of the atmosphere just before a thunderstorm.

Donovan said, 'You boys want to take your chances,

huh? You want to get hurt? I sure as hell know how to use this gun, but if you think you can take me, you're welcome to try.'

'Fuck white asshole!' The Uzi went off, a stuttering, manic sound, strangely flattened and impassionate. There was never any music in the weapons of death. Never a melody.

Dust was dug out of the ground around Donovan's feet and he danced a little to avoid the spray of gunfire. He shot the young kid dead with expert judgement, his arm extended and relaxed. Pagan edged out from under the shadow and Donovan, whose field of vision must have been extraordinary, caught a glimpse of him and, barely turning his head, fired off a shot that struck the steel base of the crane.

Pagan went down on the ground, rolling as he did so, tugging his gun from his holster. He fired at Donovan, missed, but at least he felt he'd declared his intentions sufficiently that the two kids left on the gravel mound would understand he wasn't on Donovan's side – if it came to anything as fine as that, that kind of hair-splitting, because once violence started it gathered its own senseless momentum.

He heard the Uzi stammer again and saw Donovan, still backing off, fire at the figures on the gravel, and they returned like with like, the Uzi rattling, the Wildey blasting. Donovan was struck in the shoulder and went down on one knee and continued to shoot and clipped the kid with the Wildey, who fell into the gravel and slithered a few feet, moaning. Pagan thought: you had to admire Donovan's mindless courage, the way he faced his assailants. But Donovan was bleeding from the shoulder, and it was bothering him that he had Pagan to one side and the kid with the Uzi to the other. He was effectively trapped, but he still kept shooting;

337

he'd shoot until there was nothing left in the chamber because he wasn't the kind of guy who understood there were limits to everything, including mortality.

Pagan saw the Uzi kick back into life. Donovan took a bullet in his shin and dropped face forward and fired at the one remaining kid on the gravel, and this time, with an accuracy that was uncanny, struck the kid in the neck. The kid didn't fall, didn't drop, instead he roared and charged down the gravel slope, rattling away with the automatic, energized by – by what? Encroaching darkness? A sense of his own life ebbing out of him?

Donovan was out of ammunition. His gun clicked uselessly. The Uzi went off in the kid's hand and Donovan's body shuddered with the impact of the bullets and then the kid was on top of him in a peculiar bloody embrace, and then there was silence, as if somebody had drawn a heavy curtain around the scene.

Pagan walked to the place where Donovan lay with the kid on his chest. He stood motionless for a while. Donovan's eyes were open, and his lips touched the dead kid's hair. The other figures on the gravel mound were silent, still. The scene transfixed Pagan; the aftermath of violence had an hypnotic effect. He stepped back and holstered his pistol; there was no need for it now. He raised his face when he heard a faint fluttering overhead and he saw the bird that had flown earlier out of the crane return to the broken window of the control cabin and, folding its wings, vanish inside.

He blinked as the sun hammered mercilessly down against him.

338

37

WASHINGTON

Max Skidelsky chopped stalks of celery with a quick cutting motion, then spread them to one side and started slicing bok-choi. The wok was beginning to heat up, so he dumped the vegetables in the oil. 'What's important here is timing, Jimmy. You fry the veggies in the oil too long and they lose all their goodness.'

Mallory watched the deft way Max handled the wok. He shook it with one hand and stirred the vegetables with a wooden spatula in the other. He sprinkled a touch of peanut oil over the concoction, tossed in a handful of pre-cooked shrimps at the last minute, gave everything one final stir, then spooned the food onto plates.

'Eat, Jimmy,' he said.

Mallory wasn't hungry. He'd been dragging nausea around with him all day and he'd been chewing on Swiss Crème Maalox, and his stomach felt like a vessel in which inchoate substances churned. He declined the chopsticks and picked up a fork and tasted the food, because he was too polite to turn it down.

'You look miserable,' Max said.

'No appetite, Max.'

'Why?'

'Why?' Mallory asked. He set down his fork and

placed his fingertips to his face. 'Maybe I'm coming down with something.'

'The bug of conscience?'

'Yeah. Maybe.'

'The trouble with conscience is you get sweet fuck all in return for your investment. It's like worry. It never solves anything.'

'It happens, though.'

Max held his chopsticks poised to his lips. 'When it comes to conscience, you fight it. You have a conscience attack, you ask yourself why. Why am I feeling this bad over – OK, the deaths of a certain psychiatrist and his under-age concubine, for example. So you ask yourself: was the act just one of meaningless destruction? Or did it have significance?'

'Then what?'

'Then you weigh the question. If it wasn't meaningless, then why are you having qualms about it? The shrink had to go. That was agreed. He was part of a meaningful design. And you made a decision to go along with that design, Jimmy, because you thought it was a good thing. The kid, well, she was in the wrong place at the wrong time and you're sorry about it, but you don't raise the dead by being sorry.'

'What if you think it's all unjustified? The shrink, the kid, the business in Capsicum, the whole agenda?'

Max put down his chopsticks. 'Is that what you think, Jimmy?'

'I didn't say that.'

Max Skidelsky got up from the table and went out of the kitchen and returned a few moments later with a stack of newspapers he tossed down in front of Mallory. 'Check them out, Jimmy. The *Washington Post*. The *New York Times*. The *Chicago Tribune*. On the front page of every one. Headlines. Carlotta everywhere. She's like a virus in the bloodstream of the whole country. People are panicked. Turn on your TV. Check Larry King. Check Dan Rather. Check *Nightline*. And it's her name you're going to hear. And by tonight they'll be busy dissecting the mind of a terrorist, and they'll be talking crap about how there might be some god-damn Oedipal element in the fact she killed her shrink and shot her own father. And that ought to make you feel good, Jimmy. Because you played a role in all that. You helped create those headlines. Believe it, Jimmy. *Believe.*'

Mallory didn't look at the papers. He heard an urgency in Max's voice, a fervour. How easy it was for Max to sway him. How simple. The voice insinuated itself into his head and it felt soothing. He wished he had Skidelsky's superb confidence.

Max rubbed Mallory's shoulder and said, 'It's not pleasant, Jimmy. I sympathize with that. Death leaves a bad taste. OK, so you have a conscience. And you haven't learned how to train it because there's some vestigial Christian guilt matrix inside you. But conscience is only a god-damn dog, Jimmy, and you control the leash. Don't forget that. Don't ever forget that. The dog doesn't wag your tail, pal.'

Mallory speared a shrimp on his fork and carried it to his mouth. He wondered about the black mongrel of conscience, a wilful creature. 'What about *your* conscience, Max?' he asked.

'I house-trained mine some years back. Now it doesn't shit in my head.'

Mallory chewed on the shrimp. It had a delicate ginger flavour.

'Eat,' said Skidelsky. 'Let's see enthusiasm. Never do anything half-hearted. Food, sex, work. Always give it everything you've got.'

Mallory was thinking about the girl who'd appeared in the doorway of Lannigan's bedroom. The image rose up like a bubble of trapped gas from the floor of a dank pond. The shrimp lodged at the back of his throat. He choked it down. Enthusiasm, he thought.

Once upon a time in his life he'd been enthusiastic about a lot of things – his work, his country, his marriage to Rosemary, the two kids. Rosemary, converted in middle age to weirdness, was long gone, taking the kids to San Francisco where she'd set up some kind of New Age art gallery and fallen in love with a spiritual guru who called himself Apis, after the sacred bull of Egypt, for Christ's sake. As for his work and his country – well, he was supposed to be working in a subterranean way toward the nation's betterment, but he had doubts about that. Serious ones. And they all distilled themselves in the memory of a kid's face in a doorway. He wanted Skidelsky to wave a magic wand and make his worries vanish.

Skidelsky finished eating, pushed his plate aside. He dabbed his lips with a napkin and said, 'Things of value take time to build, Jimmy. We Americans have been raised in a world of instant gratification. Want a burger? OK, you get one in a twinkling at a Burger King. No waiting. Life insurance? No sweat. A paramedic will call at your home within the hour and run some health tests. Car loan? Pick up the phone. This high-speed concept is a dangerous thing, because the quicker we do things the less quality they have. And after a while we don't notice any more. What we think is high-speed efficiency is actually the slipway to mediocrity, Jimmy.'

'The sleigh-ride,' Mallory said.

'The sleigh-ride, right.'

'And we're making things better,' Mallory said.

'Sure. But it takes time. Time, Jimmy. It's not a

matter of minutes. It's not a matter of hours. Even months. You signed on for the long haul.'

Mallory pushed his chair back from the table. He had the feeling that Skidelsky was about to go through the hand-bonding business and he wasn't in the mood to give Max his hand. He walked around the kitchen, which was all black and white tiles and blond butcher-block surfaces.

'I made a mistake,' Skidelsky said. 'I should never have asked you to go along with Donovan. I took you out of your environment and you couldn't cope. My fault.'

'If it was a test, I failed it,' Mallory said. 'Give me little jobs that require an eye for detail. Let me open bank accounts in foreign countries, Max. Let me copy documents or set up funny corporations. I'm a desk-man, face it. I don't belong out there . . .'

Skidelsky put plates in the sink. He turned and looked across the room at Mallory and frowned.

'I promise. No more fieldwork,' he said.

Mallory turned from the window. 'I can help in any other way you like. Just ask.'

'I know that, Jimmy.'

'Anything, anything except . . .'

'It's OK,' Max said.

'I understand – once you're in the Club, you don't get out again. You can't just resign your membership.'

'It would be problematic, sure.'

'I accept that. Just don't send me out again.'

'You have my word,' Max said. 'Give me your hand, Jimmy.'

Mallory stretched out his hand and sighed inwardly. Bonding-time again, he thought. He'd barely touched Max Skidelsky's fingers when there was the sound of the doorbell ringing. Skidelsky walked out of the

343

kitchen to answer it and Mallory felt a small relief that he wasn't going to be put through the strenuous business of the handgrip. Through the open doorway he saw Larry Quinn come inside the apartment.

Quinn entered the kitchen, followed by Skidelsky, and went directly to the refrigerator where he removed a bottle of Grolsch, which he opened at once and slugged from in a feverish manner.

'Hot out there,' Quinn said. He ran a hand across his forehead and moved to the table. He sat down, picking at the label on the big Grolsch bottle.

'So,' Skidelsky said. 'Cough it up, Larry.'

'I didn't think it showed,' said Quinn.

'It shows. Believe me.'

'I got two bits of news. Pasco's dead, one.'

Mallory said, 'Pasco's dead?'

Skidelsky shrugged. 'He's not important, Jimmy. He served a purpose.'

Served a purpose, Mallory thought. He remembered Pasco in the London hotel, the guy's scarred hands, the manic determination in his eyes. He remembered Pasco's head tilted to the side in concentration as he'd listened to his instructions. He'd come to like Pasco in a way. Certainly he'd pitied him. How could you be human and not pity somebody who'd been mistreated and abused like Pasco? *Served a purpose*, for God's sake. Sometimes he had to ask himself what Max had for a heart – a chamber of stainless steel, a vacuum bag? Or maybe nothing, nothing at all.

'The woman shot him, it seems,' Quinn said.

'Why am I not surprised? What about the money?' Skidelsky asked.

'I checked. It's still in the bank. Hardly touched. Pasco only took out five grand sterling.'

Skidelsky looked at Mallory. 'Jimmy, you better

make arrangements to transfer the funds back to Zurich. It's too much money to be lying around in an English bank.'

'Yes,' Mallory said. Transferring funds. Paperwork. His element. What he did best. Pasco's dead. He doesn't need the cash. The dead don't spend anything. The dead just lie around without expectations.

'Two,' Quinn said, and took another long pull from the lager.

'It's Donovan, isn't it?' Skidelsky asked.

'Yeah, it's Ralph,' said Quinn.

'You're going to tell me he fucked up.'

Quinn said, 'I don't know exactly how it happened, Max. But he got himself involved in a shoot-out.'

'A shoot-out?'

'The DC police report states that Donovan and three dead black guys were found on a building site.'

'Three dead black guys?'

'Yeah. Don't ask me what happened. The cops can't reconstruct it, and people in that neighbourhood don't confide in the law. Four corpses and no story. Beats me.'

'And Pagan?'

Larry Quinn shook his head. 'No sign, Max.'

'You checked his hotel?'

'He's not there.'

Skidelsky smiled unexpectedly. 'Interesting turn of events,' he said. He walked to the side of the kitchen where he studied a wall calendar.

'Interesting wouldn't be my first choice of word,' Quinn said.

Skidelsky stared at the calendar and said, 'Poole's asinine seminars begin tomorrow morning and they're scheduled to go on for three days.'

'And?' Quinn asked.

'If Pagan doesn't find and catch the woman in that time, we're home and dry.'

'If,' said Quinn.

'I don't like ifs. Conditionals don't belong in my kind of equation.' He turned from the calendar and said, 'We just find some other way to disable the Englishman, that's all.'

38

DOVER, DELAWARE

'Does he retrieve?' she asked.

The man in the stained blue dungarees said, 'Like there's no tomorrow.'

The woman watched the big fawn dog jump up and paw her cotton skirt. The animal's pink tongue hung out and vibrated. It was the kind of dog forever anxious to please, and the woman hated it at once.

She stroked the dog's neck, then looked at the man. 'How much?'

'Well, you saw I was asking fifty in the newspaper ad. That too much?'

The woman gave the impression of pondering this. She adjusted her glasses and looked around the yard at the back of the man's tumbledown house. There was a whole menagerie visible behind a maze of chicken-wire. Turkeys, a goose, a huddle of rabbits, a gaggle of parakeets, a fat gerbil labouring mindlessly inside a plastic wheel.

'You like animals,' she said.

'Yeah, but they multiply,' he said. 'The reason I gotta get rid of the dog is because I got half a dozen others back there and it's getting a mite overcrowded,' and he gestured with his head in the direction of kennels constructed out of wood and tar-paper. She noticed that he hadn't once taken his hands from his pockets since she'd arrived. He jiggled something in one of the pockets, perhaps a set of keys.

'I might come down to forty,' he said. 'I just want to think he's going to a good home, miss.'

'He's going to be well looked after,' she said. 'Guaranteed.'

'I had him four years now. It's a wrench.'

She searched the grass and found a stick and tossed it high in the air across the yard and the dog went after it with the kind of eagerness that can only be genetic.

'See,' said the man. 'Retrieves.'

The dog came back, stick in jaws. He dropped the stick and the woman patted his head. 'Forty, then,' she said.

'Okeydoke.'

She counted the money from her purse and the man asked, 'You live in Dover?'

'Up country a little way,' she said. She handed him four ten-dollar bills and he brought one plump hand out of his dungarees. She thought it resembled a small plucked pigeon ready for the oven. He stuffed the notes in his pocket.

'Dog's name is Roy,' he said. 'You might want to change that.'

'Roy's fine,' she said.

'I don't have a leash for him. If you like, I'll get some string.'

'Sure.'

He pulled a length of twine out of another pocket and made a noose, which he slipped round the dog's neck.

'Well, he's all yours, miss.'

348

She took the end of the string and tugged, and the dog cast a melancholy glance at the man, as if this transaction were a form of personal treachery.

'I'll walk you to your car,' the man said.

She tugged the string and the dog followed her out of the yard to where she'd parked the Honda in a side-street. The man came after, jiggling metal, whistling airily. She opened the back door of the car and the dog jumped in.

'You wouldn't know anyone in the market for a goose, would you?' the man asked.

'I don't think so,' she said, and she slid in behind the wheel.

'You hear anyone that does, you know where to send them.'

'Will do,' she said. 'Goodbye.'

The man nodded. He didn't look at the dog.

She drove away, reached the Dover city limits, parked outside a shopping-mall. She went inside, where the world was one of permanent fluorescence, and looked for a hardware store. She searched among the tools and instruments until she found what she wanted. She paid at the desk, left the mall, walked back to her car. The dog was standing with its paws pressed to the driver's window. She shooed the creature into the back of the car.

She drove a few miles, turned off the main highway and headed for a small inexpensive motel built from cinderblock. She parked outside room twenty-six and the dog followed her out of the car and into the room where it immediately went sniffing around, checking the territory, the rush of alien scents. Then, satisfied, it collapsed in a corner.

She opened a bag of dog food and poured some of it into a saucer and set it down in front of the dog and said, 'Chowtime, Roy.' The animal chewed at the substance with some slight suspicion.

The woman regarded herself in the mirror of the dressing-table. Cotton skirt, plain sleeveless blouse, hair pinned up and held back tightly. It was the face of a woman who would religiously walk her dog, a fussy kind of face, a little pinched perhaps, a solitary woman. Not exactly Kristen Hawkins, but a kindred spirit, an American edition. She strolled to the dog and kneeled beside it. She stroked the animal's keen big head for a time. She thought: Carlotta never had a pet as a kid, never a dog, cat, bird, anything. Nothing really lived in that big house. Nothing truly survived there.

She stood up, smoothed her skirt, picked up the telephone and dialled the number of The Madison in Washington, then asked to be put through to Frank Pagan's room, but there was no answer. Where was he? She'd expected him to be in his room waiting to hear from her, and the idea that he'd gone out annoyed her – as if he had no right to a life that wasn't connected to her in some way. She wondered where he'd gone, what he was doing at that precise moment. Looking for me, she thought – what else would he be doing?

She hung up, walked to the window, stared for a time at the forecourt of the motel. A yellow Ryder rental truck, a beat-up station-wagon, a VW bug. Stylish clientele. She raised her face and saw the sun declining in tracks of red and gold. Thirty minutes, she thought, then she'd get out of here. The dog padded across the floor and sat at her feet, turning its snout up, nudging the palm of her hand for attention. She stroked it, disliking the feel of fur against her skin. But she didn't intend to keep the animal long. Roy had a job to do, and that was it. That was the end of the story.

Where was Pagan?

She dialled the number again, and again there was no reply from his room. She took a slip of paper from her purse, looked at it, dialled another number in DC. This time she got an answering-machine. A man's voice said: *This is James Mallory. I can't come to the phone right now. Please leave a message.* She hung up. She gazed toward the dog and thought: Come on, Pagan, how good are you? Just how goddam good are you? She walked back to the window and stared impatiently into the sun which was sliding downward. Time to go. She couldn't hang around. Quickly, she packed her belongings, stuffed them inside a canvas bag, and then she left.

She drove with the dog in the back seat. A jet screamed above Dover Air Force Base, leaving a stream of grey vapour. She came off the main highway beyond the town of Lynch Heights. The sky was beginning to turn in slow stages from red to navy blue, and here and there an early star could be seen, pale intruders in the twilight.

The road narrowed the further she drove. She stopped in an isolated place, a shallow incline between two small hills, and took a map from the glove compartment, switched on the reading-light and studied the map a second, then when she'd memorized the turnings, she replaced it.

Although twilight was deepening, she didn't want to turn on her headlamps just yet. A sign ghosted in front of her, a wooden post to which was attached a board that bore the legend: *Property of the United States.* She ignored it and kept driving. She swung left. In the far distance a ship was visible on Delaware Bay, a sprinkling of lights.

351

Brown weeds grew profusely on either side of the narrow blacktop. She had a sense of travelling toward the core of darkness itself. A second sign loomed up and she had to flick on her low beams to read it. *Property of the United States. No Unauthorized Personnel Beyond This Point.* She kept going. There were no fences so far. No barriers. Only the signs. In the back, the dog was slumbering, wheezing in the throes of a canine dream, body quivering. What did dogs dream of? she wondered. What images came to trespass on their sleep? Cats, maybe. Fire hydrants. Or did they resurrect deeply buried ancestral dreams – hunting in packs, killing, bringing down prey in a flurry of ripped fur and blood?

She came to a third sign. *Property of the United States. Absolutely No Trespassing Beyond This Point. Danger.* Danger, she thought. She was used to that. Danger wasn't a word to deter her. In her world, the dictionary definitions of certain words were reversed. Danger wasn't a cautionary word. Danger attracted her. She stopped the car, got out, took her canvas bag from the back seat. She made a noose of twine and slipped it round the dog's neck, and then she began to walk.

She heard the jeep before she saw it, a groaning sound in the landscape. It came toward her, full beams blazing, and she blinked and stepped into the weeds at the side of the road, where she set the canvas bag down. The jeep stopped a few feet from her. The dog barked as two men climbed down from the vehicle. They were both squat men, matched like a pair of book-ends.

'You're on private property, lady,' one of them said. 'Didn't you see the signs?'

'Private property? I didn't know,' she said, and looked as if this information appalled her. 'I'm trespassing, then. I'm sorry. I was out walking my dog.'

'In the middle of nowhere?'

'I like quiet places,' she said. 'I didn't know I was breaking any laws.'

'Yeah, well, you are. Don't tell me you didn't see the signs.'

'I must have missed them, I guess.'

The two squat men gazed at her in the flare of the jeep's lamps. She wondered if there was some slight recognition dawning on them. A flicker. A face remembered from a newspaper photograph.

The second man, who so far hadn't spoken, asked, 'What's in that bag?'

She glanced down at the canvas bag in the weeds at her feet. 'Oh, just some stuff.'

'Stuff? What stuff?'

She held the leash with one hand and, bending, reached inside the canvas bag with the other. 'I'll show you,' she said.

'Wait,' the second man said. 'I'd prefer to do that myself, if you don't mind. Just take your hand away from the bag, lady.'

She said, 'Feel free.'

And she stood upright, turning with the gun in her hand. She didn't waste any time. Both men were perfectly outlined against the lamps of the jeep. Both were easy targets. She fired the gun twice before either of them could move. They fell together, matched in death as they had been in life. She reached inside the jeep and switched off the lights.

Then she continued to walk. She came to a wire fence which was about twelve feet high. Barbed wire had been strung around the top. A hundred yards away on the other side of the fence, six big satellite dishes were motionless and still, raised on stalks. They received signals from the sky, and these signals were fed into computers, then transformed and enlarged into images the human eye could understand. They monitored the world – troop movements, wars, storm systems, volcanic eruptions. At the press of a button they could produce close-ups, people walking on city streets, faces in the windows of houses, soldiers in tanks, lovers kissing in a park. She imagined she heard the darkening air rustle with the endless static of all this information. The sky was buzzing.

The dog had caught the scent of something, a passing rabbit, a skunk drifting nearby, a racoon; he was deeply agitated by sensed presences. She stroked the dog, made soothing sounds. The animal panted, leaped up against her in an unfettered display of affection.

'Good, Roy, good,' she said, and she made him sit still. She opened her canvas bag and removed the towel Chico had given her, rolled it open, and picked out one of the two plastic cylinders. In the palm of her hand it suggested a small plastic dildo. The other cylinder she returned to the bag. She took out the heavy-duty wire-cutters she'd bought in the hardware shop. She went down on her knees. This was the tricky moment because she didn't know if the fence was connected to a warning system. She cut the wire. Nothing happened. No bells, no alarms. Not yet. She twisted the cut strands back with some effort. A small opening. She was motionless a moment because she heard a sound – something she didn't immediately identify. A whirring. She saw one of the big dishes move. Then it was still again.

She took the plastic cylinder, twisted the cap on it, and looped it through the twine round the dog's neck and made certain it was secure. She found a stick, held it under the dog's snout, let the creature sniff it, become familiar with it – and then she raised her arm and tossed the stick as high and as far as she could over the fence. She released the dog and it bounded cheerfully through the opening in the wire. She immediately jammed the wire back into something akin to its original position, then she turned and ran back down the blacktop in the direction of her car. She didn't have much time. She was working on a very narrow margin.

When she was a few yards from the car she heard the sound of an alarm and she glanced back, seeing floodlights come on inside the compound. They illuminated the dishes with a stunning silvery-white light. As she opened her car door she was sure she heard a dog bark. She reversed quickly, a series of tight little manoeuvres, and then she drove at a reckless speed back down the road.

The station officer was a man called Lovett. When the electronic sensors detected an intruder inside the compound they immediately activated the floodlights and the alarm system. Lovett had complained a couple of times that the system was too sensitive, because it was sometimes triggered by nocturnal creatures that had burrowed under the fence – gophers, rabbits, a skunk one time. He'd asked for adjustments to be made, but so far nothing had been done. Budgetary reasons were usually given. Lovett accepted that his request to correct this nuisance was of low priority, but it needled him just the same.

He stepped out of the concrete building where the satellite controls and consoles were located. He stared across the compound. He carried a gun. Once, eight or nine years ago, some demented wannabee terrorist had avoided the guard patrol and actually climbed the wire, and although the intruder was basically a harmless nut mouthing anti-Government slogans, Lovett felt better knowing he had a gun in his possession.

He moved toward the dishes. He didn't see anything at once. The floodlights were blinding.

'What the hell is going on?'

Lovett turned. The man who emerged from what was jokingly referred to as the guest wing – actually a small prefabricated hut containing two single beds – was Kevin Grimes. Grimes, Mr Satellite himself, came here once or twice a month on a tour of inspection. An old Company man, Grimes was known in certain circles as The Grime Reaper – a weak play on the man's name, admittedly – but somehow appropriate, because he was a gloomy figure given to long monologues on the resurgence of communism, which he saw everywhere.

'Something set off the alarm, Kevin,' Lovett said.

'Obviously something set off the alarm,' said Grimes.

'I reported this to you once or twice before—'

'Yes yes,' Grimes said impatiently.

'But nothing was ever done about it,' said Lovett, politely turning a screw. 'The system needs some fine tuning. Badly.'

'Find out what happened,' Grimes said. 'Have a look round.'

The dog came rushing out of the darkness, skidding to a halt at Lovett's ankles.

'A god-damn dog,' said Grimes.

'There there,' Lovett said to the dog.

'How did a dog get inside?'

'Under the fence?' Lovett suggested.

Lovett examined the panting dog. It had a peculiar attachment to the string round its neck. Lovett reached out to touch it. It was a small cylindrical object and it had been knotted firmly in place.

'What have you brought for us, huh?' he asked the dog. 'What has this nice doggie brought for us?'

'What's going on, Lovett?' Grimes asked.

Lovett undid the knot, removed the cylinder. It was a moment before he understood what it was that he held in his hand, and when the pulse of recognition caused blood to rush to his head, it was a little too late.

39

WASHINGTON

Pagan had checked into a motel about a mile from the White House because The Madison was no longer a secure place for him. He wanted the safety of anonymity, and even if it meant denying himself access to his belongings – which he'd left at The Madison – then that was the way it would have to be. His clothes, toiletries, the little diary Zuboric had given him, none of these were important. As for the rented car, he could always get another one. The motel room was basic but clean, and the walls were covered with coloured photographs of the democratic shrines of the city.

He telephoned The Madison to check on his messages. There were three. Foxworth had called. And Artie Zuboric, who'd left a number for him to telephone. And a woman who said she'd call back. A woman, he thought. But nothing from Bob Naderson.

He sat on the edge of the bed for a few minutes, his hands on his knees, and he wondered about Ralph Donovan. Had Donovan's ID been genuine? If he was connected to the Agency, then why had he been sent out on a killing mission? Had Naderson despatched him to do the job? What did Naderson stand to gain from Pagan's demise? Silence? The betrayal of Pasco consigned finally to oblivion?

It was a possibility, but Pagan was disinclined to give it any weight. Naderson wasn't stupid enough to believe that by killing Pagan he'd bury the contorted history of Richard Pasco entirely. No, Naderson would think that this information would be known to other members of Special Branch – so what was the point in murdering one man, if others shared the knowledge? Such a murder would achieve absolutely nothing save the one thing Naderson presumably didn't want, which was to stir further curiosity inside Special Branch. Awkward questions would arise, and before long the matter would certainly rise to higher levels; it would reach Nimmo, and from there pass, like a hot charcoal, to the Home Secretary, and extend finally to the British Ambassador in Washington – and Naderson would surely have foreseen all these widening circles that would threaten to expose an old secret he didn't want revealed. So Pagan ruled him out.

Which left him with what? The idea that Donovan was acting alone? He closed his eyes and focused on the question, but it had a tendency to slip away from him the more he examined it. He thought about other puzzles – the possibility that names had been given to Pasco from a source inside the Agency, the fact that somebody was out there committing Carlotta-like atrocities. Fragments and shards, and they floated around inside his head like tiny reckless planets and he couldn't get them to orbit one another in a logical way. He had a feeling they were related in some essentially simple fashion – but he was missing a factor, and he wasn't sure what.

He picked up the phone and called Golden Square and was put through to Foxie.

'Where the devil have you been, Frank? I've been calling for hours.'

'Out and about,' said Pagan.

'The newspapers are filled with Carlotta's antics over there. What's she doing? Working overtime?'

'Don't believe everything you read in the papers, Foxie.'

'Nimmo's relieved, of course, that she's decided to transfer her activities elsewhere. He believes that the sheer weight of uniforms drove her out of the country. So he's feeling good about his policy of flooding the streets of our formerly green and pleasant land with policemen.'

'Let him believe what he likes. Has he been looking for me?'

'He's been making noises, yes.'

'And what did you say?'

'I feigned ignorance. I'm good at blank looks. He thinks you're pursuing a lead somewhere. Anyway, here's the thing. I've been doing a little background, and this might interest you, Frank. I started with Pasco's bank-book.'

'Very resourceful, Foxie,' Pagan said, thinking how he'd overlooked that, and wondering what else he might have failed to explore in his abrupt flight to America. *Mea culpa*.

'It gets interesting, Frank. The money, all five hundred thousand dollars of it, came from a company called Mongoose Enterprises. *Mongoose*, Frank? Ring any bells for you?'

'It was the name the CIA gave to its abortive project to assassinate Fidel Castro, if my memory serves.'

'Spot on. They were going to poison his cigars or some such thing. Mongoose is one of those ludicrous schemes the Agency was always dreaming up in the Fifties and Sixties. But the name set me thinking,'

Foxie said. 'I did a little digging, Frank. Mongoose has an office in Richmond, Virginia, so I ran a check on the company through the Virginia Corporations Commission.'

'And what did you find?' Pagan asked.

'I'm coming to that. I learned from the bank in London that the man who opened the account gave the name of Jason Mannering, allegedly a director of Mongoose Enterprises. Surprise surprise, he isn't listed with the Corporations Commission as an officer in the company. And the company address in Richmond is nothing more than one of those places people use as a mail-drop.'

'And?'

'The articles of incorporation of Mongoose Enterprises list only two directors. One is a man called James Mallory. And the other – listen to this – is listed as Richard Pasco. Since the corporation was only formed in May of this year, when Pasco was in the gulag, do you suppose they sent him papers to sign when he was a prisoner?'

'Hardly,' Pagan said.

'So what they did was use his name to set up a funny company,' Foxie said.

'He'd find that droll, I'm sure,' Pagan said.

'Droll indeed. So Mongoose, of which Pasco is an unwitting director, opens a bank account for him in London, courtesy of a man called Jason Mannering, who isn't a director, although he tells the bank manager he is. Which leaves us with Mallory.'

'Don't tell me. Mallory's a dead-end.'

'No, no, that's the sheer joy of it, Frank. Mallory isn't a dead-end at all. Mallory is apparently a living breathing actual human being, and I have an address for him, courtesy of the Corporations Commission, where I had the good fortune to speak to a very helpful have-a-nice-day young lady named Barbara who liked my accent and said if I was ever in the neighbourhood she'd like to meet me.'

'You get a gold star, Foxie,' Pagan said. 'Give me the address.'

'Number 4 Roundtower Apartments, Glastonbury Street, Washington. My own feeling is that James Mallory is probably also Jason Mannering.'

'He might have had the foresight to change his initials,' Pagan said and wrote down the address.

'And the name Mongoose – good lord, that's like hanging out a flag.'

'The Agency was never over-endowed in the imagination department,' Pagan said. 'I've changed hotels, by the way. If you need to get in touch with me, I'm at two oh two, eight six three, nine nine seven seven, extension three nine.'

'What happened to The Madison?'

'Too expensive,' Pagan said. He heard an unexpected little sound, a tap on his window, and he turned his face quickly. A few soft drops of rain slid down the glass.

'You still there, Frank?' Foxie asked.

'I'm still here.'

'You'll check on this Mallory, I take it.'

'I'll check . . . And Foxie, listen. I appreciate.'

'Promote me when you come back, Frank. Look after yourself.'

Pagan hung up, wandered to the window, stared out at the soft rain falling in the night, the way it drizzled down through street lamps. Mongoose, he thought. An old absurdity. It had to be some kind of in-joke to name a company Mongoose. But who was the joker? Who was the one with the sense of humour? He watched the rain a moment and then reluctantly called the number for Artie Zuboric, whose mood was vile.

'Where the fuck are you, Pagan? I been phoning you for hours.'

'I've been sightseeing,' Pagan said. 'Interesting town.'

'Yeah, yeah, monuments I don't want to hear about. I'm a weary man, Pagan. I'm beat. My bones are aching. Last thing I need is to be hound-dogging you. Where are you anyway?'

'At a pay phone,' Pagan said.

'Where?'

'I don't know this city well enough to be sure, Artie.'

'Bullshit, Pagan. You're dodging me, that's what you're doing. And I don't like that. If you're working on something, and you're not telling me what it is, I'll come down on your head like a ton of reinforced concrete.'

'I'm being good, Artie. I've been keeping my little logbook up-to-date for you.'

'Fuck the logbook, Pagan.'

'You mean I don't *need* to keep it? After all the time I spent recording my movements, you tell me you're not *interested*?'

'I hate sarcasm, Pagan. I hate that patronizing tone in your voice. Listen, I got enough on my plate right now without having to deal with you.'

Pagan listened to the lovely liquid sound of rain upon glass and said, 'No impending arrests, Artie? No signs? No clues?'

'You think I'd tell you?'

'In other words, nothing.'

Zuboric was quiet a moment. 'We got thousands of guys out there beating the bushes, Pagan. Plus, the phones don't quit ringing. The public's squealing like a pig with a spear up its kazoo.'

'It's bedlam,' Pagan said. 'I sympathize. I've been there.'

'Bedlam. Worse than bedlam. What I feel like is some god-damn rat forced through one of them lab mazes, only the corridors don't go anywhere except into walls, and so you need to go back the way you came, which doesn't do a bit of fucking good because you only come to another wall. So what makes her all this difficult to find, Pagan? Huh? You're the expert. You tell me. She got some deal with the devil, something like that? Or has she discovered the secret of invisibility, huh?'

'You're stressed, Artie.'

'Yeah, I'm stressed. I'm beyond stressed. See, I can't figure out her trick, Pagan. I can't get inside her head.'

'Even if you could, you wouldn't be able to read what's written there. It's not in any language known to man.'

Zuboric sighed. 'She's everywhere, Pagan. If I'm to believe these reported sightings, she's like something straight outta quantum physics, because she's been seen simultaneously in Albuquerque, New Mexico, and Baltimore, Maryland. Oh, and Alaska too.'

Pagan said, 'It's the effect she has on the public. They want to see her, so they see her.'

'Listen, I'm hanging up, I got people climbing all over me, this place is a god-damn zoo,' Zuboric said. 'I suggest you go back to your hotel and do nothing, and if the urge to go sightseeing comes over you again, resist it. I don't want some crazy Englishman running loose. Follow me?'

'I follow, Artie.' Pagan put the phone down.

The rain was slow and easy outside, coming down through lamps like the silvery strands of an intricate, shifting web. He watched it gather in shallow pools on the roofs of cars parked in the lot. He picked up the telephone and dialled Naderson's number from memory, and the old man answered on the third or fourth ring.

'Ah, Frank Pagan, you were on my mind,' he said.

'Did you speak to Poole?'

'Yes. We talked.'

'Did you tell him I think he's in danger?'

'Of course I did,' Naderson said.

'Have you both taken precautions?'

'We have, Frank. You may be assured on that score.'

Precautions, Pagan thought. He hoped they were stout ones. He hoped they were bomb-proof. Fat chance. 'What about the names?' Pagan asked. 'Have you made any progress?'

Naderson was quiet for a short time. Pagan imagined him sitting inside his atrium, surrounded by floating greenery, the photographs aligned on the wicker table. 'I think we have that one under control, Frank.'

'How?'

'Really, Frank, I'm not at liberty to discuss Agency business with you.'

'I understand that. I thought that in the circumstances you might be a little more co-operative, Bob. After all, I was the one who came to you, I was the one who warned you. I didn't have to do that, I could have turned my back. I could have ignored you completely.'

'Yes, you could have done,' said Naderson.

'I think a little tit for tat might be in order, Bob.'

Naderson issued a long sigh. 'You're pressuring me, Frank.'

'Yes. I know I am.'

'I'm a little too old for pressure.'

'Look, Bob. Whatever you say, it's between you and me. It's off the record. I can promise you that.'

'Your word?'

'Completely.'

'Is an Englishman's word as sound as it used to be?' Naderson asked. 'Or is that an outmoded concept in this day and age?'

'I can't talk for my fellow countrymen, Bob. I can only speak for myself. You have my word.'

Naderson was quiet for a time before he said, 'Certain individuals are being questioned, Frank. These are people with access to the Executive Director's files.'

'Can you name them for me?'

'Two secretaries. Both have been on the Executive Director's staff for the past four years. One has been with the Agency for fourteen years, the other six. I don't see what function it would serve to give you their names, though.'

'A favour, Bob. Please.'

'You've almost come to the end of your favours,' Naderson said. 'They're both women. One is called Wanda Loeb, the other Gilda McNamara. Those names mean anything to you, Frank?'

'No,' Pagan said. 'Are they the only candidates?'

'As far as the Executive Director is concerned, they are.'

'What about *you*, Bob? Does either of these women strike you as likely to plunder Poole's private files for gain?'

Naderson was silent a moment. Then he said, 'No, not really.'

'You're holding something back, Bob. What is it?'

'I think I've said as much as I'm going to say,' Naderson remarked. 'Anything else would be subjective and indiscreet.'

'You believe there might be a better candidate than either of these women.'

'I have nothing more to add, Frank. Let's leave it that way.'

There was a note of finality in the way Naderson said this. Pagan caught a reflection of himself in the dark rainy window. 'One last thing, Bob. Does the name Ralph Donovan mean anything to you?'

'Should it?'

'You didn't send him to my hotel?'

'I haven't sent anyone to your hotel, Frank. Why?'

'Then somebody misrepresented you,' Pagan said.

'Why?'

'I'd love to find out why,' Pagan said. 'He had Agency ID.'

'Which might have been fake.'

'Maybe.'

'Even if it was genuine, it doesn't follow that I'd know this Donovan personally. There are thousands of people in the Agency, Frank. I can't keep track any more. Sometimes I think I'm getting a little too old for this murky business. Once upon a time life used to be different. Things were clearer in the old days. You knew the enemy. You knew where you stood. You knew the risks and you ran them and be damned. Now, everything's muddy. Everything's cloudy. The view from the promontory isn't what it used to be.'

The view from the promontory, Pagan thought. He assumed this was Naderson's way of referring to the moral high ground, when the angels congregated over Langley, and God was one hundred per cent on your team, and 'The Star-Spangled Banner' had the status of a psalm, and all the dark brooding enemy forces were gathered on other continents.

'This Carlotta,' the old man said. 'If she were

simply a mercenary, perhaps she'd be easier to understand.'

'But she's not.'

'I just learned that somebody blew up a satellite station tonight, one of our places in Delaware. Does that sound like her handiwork?'

'Yes, it sounds like her,' Pagan said.

'Totally destroyed the place, I understand.'

A satellite station in Delaware, an Agency installation. It fitted what Pagan believed was her agenda. He looked into the darkness and imagined her out there somewhere in the rain. He had the unsettling feeling that she was nearby, radiating a kind of energy he could sense.

Naderson said, 'I'm leaving here tonight and going away for a few days, Frank, to a very safe place. I doubt if we'll need to talk again. I wish you well.'

'I wish you the same,' Pagan said.

Naderson hung up. Pagan held the receiver a moment before he set it down. Then he descended into the lobby, where he asked the desk clerk about car rentals.

40

WASHINGTON

There were about seventy of them in total and they fanned separately across the city and the suburbs. They checked hotels and motels. They reported to Max Skidelsky every hour because that was the way Max wanted it. They asked the same questions where-ever they went. *Has a man called Frank Pagan checked in here?* If this question was answered in the negative, they'd been instructed to pose the more general question: *Has a man with an English accent checked in during the day?* And then, if they had to, they described Pagan according to the details they'd been given by Skidelsky. It was legwork and it was tedious, and more than a few of them reflected on the fact that while they were out driving in the rainy night, Max was sitting in his dry apartment by the telephone.

It was a thought that certainly occurred to Mallory as he went from motel to motel. It wasn't one he entertained for long, because the routine task was somehow comforting, and it negated the need to think about Ralph Donovan, or Pasco, or the girl murdered at Lannigan's. He just had to plod through the night. He just had to ask his questions, and leave, and then drive to the next motel in the sector of the city he'd been assigned.

Max had been military in his planning – dividing a map of Washington into sectors, telephoning Artichoke personnel wherever they could be located, bringing them into play. You had to admire Max and the way he'd arranged the sweep through the city, the big map spread out on the kitchen table, the red felt-tipped pen in his hand inscribing segments even as he issued commands over the phone. What impressed Mallory most was the amount of manpower available to Max and how widespread Artichoke had to be, certainly larger and better organized than Mallory had ever truly imagined. It was as if some deep tap root, carefully cultivated by Skidelsky, generously tended, ran unseen under the soil of the Agency – a plant that had not yet quite flowered, but one vibrant with energy.

Mallory watched his windshield wipers go back and forth. His brief was simple. Locate Pagan, call Skidelsky. He was to take no action himself. Max had been emphatic about that. Just a phone call. Leave the real fieldwork to somebody else. Gladly, Mallory thought.

He was driving on Pennsylvania Avenue now. Until recently, motorists had been able to drive past the front of the White House, but because of the number of assaults made on the Presidential mansion in the past year, a pedestrian precinct had been constructed as a security measure. Consequently, Mallory was obliged to take a detour to his next stop – a place called The Capitol City Motor Lodge, which turned out to be your basic motel charging foreign tourists inflated prices.

He turned into the driveway, parked, went inside the lobby. He noticed that signs were written in English, Japanese, German and Arabic. He approached the desk where the clerk, a lean man with a lazy eye that drifted in an unco-ordinated manner in its socket, surveyed him with nonchalance.

Mallory produced his ID card and the clerk's manner instantly changed to one of attentiveness. 'I'm looking for a man called Frank Pagan,' Mallory said.

'English guy?'

Mallory, who had so far been to fifteen motels without success, was surprised. 'He's *here*?'

'He was. You just missed him,' said the clerk.

'By how much?'

'Twenty minutes. He asked me about car rentals. So I arranged an Avis for him.'

'Twenty minutes,' Mallory said.

'Yeah. You want the auto details?' The clerk looked around for the paperwork and placed it in front of Mallory. 'Compact Buick. The licence plate number's on the rental agreement. What's he done, this Pagan? I know, I know, you can't tell me, right? It's some kind of national security thing, right?'

'You might say,' Mallory remarked. He copied the car details from the rental form.

'He didn't have any luggage, you know,' the clerk said. 'Which I thought pretty odd. And he didn't pay with a credit card either, which is odder still.'

'Right,' Mallory said. He was in no mood to be engaged in conversation with this desk clerk or anyone else for that matter. He just wanted to go home. 'I need to use your phone.'

'Go in my office. It's more private back there,' said the clerk.

'Thanks.'

Mallory closed the door of the clerk's office and dialled Skidelsky's number. Busy. He sat back in the chair and felt weary. The day had been long and dreadful and kept coming back at him, like a pocket of malodorous gas. You're doing all this for your country. Believe. Keep the faith. He looked at his hands and thought how unfamiliar they seemed all at once, like appendages sliced from a stranger and tacked onto his arms. Fatigue bred illusions.

He tried Max again, and this time the phone was picked up.

Mallory said, 'I have some news. He rented a car, Max.'

'Where are you?'

'A place called The Capitol City Motor Lodge. He left here about twenty minutes ago.'

'Give me details,' Max said.

Mallory read out what Max needed to know. Year and make of the car, registration number.

'You've done good, Jimmy.'

'I got lucky.'

'Sometimes we make our own luck,' Skidelsky said. 'Here's what I want you to do now. Go home. Run a nice long bath. Get some sleep.'

'That's it?'

'That's it. I promised you no more fieldwork. I like to think I keep my promises, Jimmy. You've done enough. I'll call you tomorrow.'

Mallory put the telephone down. Nice long bath. Sleep. He could go for that. He left the office, thanked the clerk, stepped out into the rainy night which was steamy and tropical, the sky oppressive as a leaden weight, and he walked to his car. He could smell thunder in the air, a storm rolling in from the Atlantic, and he wondered if it might cleanse his memory and emotions as surely as it would cleanse the dry streets and the rock-hard landscape of the country.

He drove north through the city until he came to the suburb where he lived. His apartment was small, but since Rosemary and the kids had gone, what did he need with space? Too many rooms just meant more square feet to patrol during his insomniac nights.

He slipped his key in the lock, turned on the light, stepped inside the living-room, shut the door and sighed as if he were expelling everything toxic from his system. He moved toward the liquor cabinet, thinking a screwdriver might go down quite nicely—

'James Mallory? Or is it Jason Mannering?'

Mallory stopped halfway across the floor. He felt rigid, muscles locked, his heartbeat rushed. The man was sitting in an armchair beside the fireplace. His hair, dark streaked with threads of grey, was short and unruly. There was no expression on his face.

'Which name do you prefer?' the man asked.

The accent was English, Mallory guessed London.

'You're Pagan,' he said.

'I'm Pagan.'

41

WASHINGTON

She reached the outskirts of the city and immediately encountered a traffic jam caused by an accident in the rain. There were the usual grim attendants on such scenes, ambulances and fire-trucks and cop-cars, paramedics and firemen. Ahead, she could see two trucks turned on their sides and the road littered with cigarettes, cartons of them, some that had broken open in the collision, thousands of paper cylinders soaking up the rain.

She tapped her hand on the steering-wheel. She was impatient and uneasy. There were too many cops gathered in one place for her liking. She considered the notion of somehow trying to weave her way through the jam, but the lanes ahead were blocked. Stuck, no option but to wait.

She switched on the radio, scanned the channels, turned it off again. The world was full of noise, too many call-in shows, rednecks babbling in the ether, every half-drunk moron sitting in a broken-down trailer park had a half-assed opinion on drugs, sex, abortion, immigration control, racism.

She stared through the windshield. A crane had lumbered onto the scene and was being deployed to shift the trucks. She saw a long chain descend from the sky, metal links made red and blue by the lights of cop-cars. She rolled down her window; the interior was steamy.

A cop was standing a few yards from her car. She hadn't noticed him. He was a young man and his uniform was wet. 'Bad,' he said.

'Looks that way,' she said.

The cop's gun hung lopsided against his thigh. 'The rain,' he said. 'They travel too fast in the rain. Slick surfaces. Next thing . . .' He turned his face and looked at her but his expression revealed no little flash of recognition. 'They'll get this mess cleaned up in a few minutes,' he added. 'You in a hurry?'

'Not particularly,' she said.

He stepped a little nearer to the car. She thought about the canvas bag on the floor behind her seat. She had the strangely compelling urge to introduce herself, to say *I'm the one you're all looking for*, as if she wanted to test fate and win. She imagined how the young cop might react – reaching for his gun, crouching at the knees as he went for his holster. But it wasn't going to happen that way. She was just a woman locked in a traffic jam, somebody he'd engaged in a few moments of idle conversation. Maybe one day he'd see a photograph of her and he'd remember this short encounter, and he'd feel a little rush of a half-forgotten familiarity, and he'd wonder. But he'd never know for sure.

The crane cranked, the chain creaked.

'You'll be moving soon enough,' the cop said.

'My husband's probably worrying about me,' she said. She found herself thinking about Pagan, wondering if his ultimate destination was the same as her own, whether their futures would collide in the rain. She wondered if he had what it took to keep up with her, if she might have left him a more direct trail to follow – but no, if he needed too much assistance, then he wasn't worthy of her, and she'd misjudged him.

She didn't think she had. She'd know soon enough. But first there was the man called James Mallory.

42

WASHINGTON

Pagan said, 'I have a gun, but I prefer not to use it. Is that clear?'

Mallory struggled to gather the unravelling strands of himself. He reached the liquor cabinet. He was trembling. Pagan produced the weapon from somewhere. One second it wasn't to be seen, the next it was in the palm of his hand, a conjuring trick. Mallory laid his fingertips on the metal frame of the cabinet and received an unexpected electric shock. Stung, he gasped and pulled his hand back.

'It's the static in your carpet,' Pagan said in a matter-of-fact way – like a guest, somebody Mallory had invited into his home. 'It builds up. You touch metal – and whack, the electricity goes straight through you.'

Mallory said, 'I need a drink.'

'Don't let me stop you.'

Mallory opened a bottle of Absolut and poured a shot and slugged it back and shut his eyes.

Pagan said, 'You were just a little careless, Mallory. You used one name in London when you opened Pasco's bank account, then another in Virginia in the articles of incorporation. Not very smart – unless, of course, you happen to have some deep-rooted desire to be found out. Do you, Mallory?'

Mallory poured another drink. He couldn't keep his god-damn hand steady. *A deep-rooted desire to be found out.* He had to wonder about that, he had to give that one a lot of thought; but it meant exploring the hidden channels of his motives and the crypts of his conscience, and he wasn't in the mood for deep self-analysis. He'd come to a place where all he wanted was a general numbing of his doubts.

'Talk to me,' Pagan said.

'What is there to talk about?' Mallory said.

'I have a few questions.'

'Maybe I don't have the answers you want.' Mallory heard a curious little throaty quality in his own voice, a thickness.

Pagan wandered the room. He was looking at a photograph Mallory had of the kids, snapped when they'd been very small.

'Yours?' Pagan asked.

Mallory nodded and gazed down into the surface of his drink. A deep-rooted desire to be found out, he thought. Maybe it was more than that. Maybe it was an urge to liberate himself from the deadly trappings of his membership of The Artichoke Club. Maybe it was something as simple and as complicated as freedom. He didn't know. He'd become detached from the essence of himself. He was smudged round the edges, like a bad charcoal drawing.

'Nice-looking kids,' Pagan said. 'They live with you?'

'California, with their mother.'

'Too bad. A marital breakdown,' Pagan said.

'You could say.' Mallory felt emotional all at once. He didn't think about the kids any more. They'd vanished in the void of divorce only to be beamed back down in faraway California with a new daddy, and that made him sad. Some things you didn't think about

378

because they only choked your heart. 'You're not here to talk about my marriage, Pagan.'

'No, I'm not.'

Mallory looked at the Englishman. He was an inch or so over six feet, and lean, and gave the impression of a man who hadn't totally surrendered his humanity in the course of his work. If you looked closely, you might see a quality of sympathy around the eyes. Mallory wondered if he was simply imagining this, if it was something he'd constructed around the genuine way Pagan had said the words *too bad* when he'd been looking at the photograph of the kids.

'Tell me about Pasco,' Pagan said.

Mallory didn't reply. He could play this silently, acting dumb and innocent. He thought about Max and wondered how far he was prepared to go to protect him and his secrets. He wondered what Max would do if he was the one in this situation.

Pagan said, 'I don't want to get brutal, Mallory. I have a good side, and I have a bad side, and I genuinely prefer the former, because the latter is ugly and consumes too much energy. Talk to me about Pasco.'

'What is it you don't know, Pagan?'

Pagan shrugged. 'You put him in touch with Carlotta, didn't you?'

Mallory said, 'Boy, you're guessing. You're dickering around, Pagan. This is a fishing expedition.'

Pagan passed the gun from one hand to the other, making a little arc of silver. Mallory wondered if he was meant to construe this gesture as a threat, a reminder of where the balance of power lay.

Pagan took a step across the room and said, 'I don't mind fishing, Mallory. Let's just say Carlotta comes on the scene and we'll forget the mechanics of it for now. OK, she's on stage, and her role is that of helping

Pasco. Carlotta doesn't object to this in principle. After all, there's some destruction involved, and that's what she does best, and besides she doesn't feel a great deal of affection for any kind of law-enforcement agency, Special Branch, the FBI, the Agency, whatever. The trouble is, Pasco's an encumbrance she doesn't need.'

Mallory poured himself another measure of vodka. His hand was steady now. He looked at Pagan and said nothing.

Pagan sat on the arm of the sofa, the gun dangling from his fingers. 'But she likes Pasco's agenda in general. The idea of coming back to America after all these years and making loud noises, this really gets her motor ticking over. But now I run into a problem, Mallory. There are loud noises, sure, but some of them don't originate with her. And this baffles me. Capsicum, North Carolina. The shrink, Lannigan. Big noises, granted – except they're not Carlotta's. So who's making them?'

Mallory thought of the kid in Lannigan's house. The painted nymph. She was going to wander again and again into his dreams, he knew that. He was going to carry her around for God knows how long. She was going to haunt him. He felt the vodka create a warm funnel in his stomach, but that warmth didn't take the chill off his memory. He'd need part of his brain removed to achieve the kind of amnesia he needed. He raised his face from his drink and looked back at Pagan and he felt the urge to explain – but then Skidelsky rose in his mind, a demon in a fashionable linen suit, and a vast disturbing shadow fell across him.

'Pagan,' he said. 'Take my advice. Drop it. Just drop it.'

'And what? Go back to London? Forget everything?'

'Go anywhere you like—'

'I can't do that, Mallory.'

Mallory drew the cuff of his jacket across his lips. 'There are guys out there looking for you, Pagan. And they're not hunting you because they want to give you the good news that your rich uncle in Honolulu just died and left you his entire estate. They don't want you getting near the woman.'

'Why?'

'Pagan, leave it,' Mallory said. 'Leave it alone.'

'They want the woman for themselves,' Pagan said.

Mallory nodded almost imperceptibly. He had the feeling that in this one tiny gesture he'd given away more than he ever intended.

'Who are these people, Mallory?'

Mallory said nothing. He was conscious of how treachery was formed in layers, strata. He'd betrayed the Agency by aligning himself with Max Skidelsky. And now he was approaching another level, where he had the choice of betraying Skidelsky too. The trouble with betrayal was what it did to you, the bruises it inflicted on you, the way it blew a shifting unpredictable tempest through your own values. *What values, Jimmy?* he wondered. Do you have any left? His thoughts cluttered his head. He had collapses going on inside him. He felt dizzy. He listened to the rain fall in the shrubbery outside. The cleansing rain.

He glanced at Pagan. 'In your shoes, Pagan, I'd walk away.'

'You're not wearing my shoes,' Pagan said.

'I'm thankful for any small mercy that comes my way.'

Pagan rose, stepped across the room, and for a second Mallory had the feeling he was about to be struck. Nothing too savage, a quick punch in the gut, a flick of the pistol across his mouth, but Pagan didn't touch him. 'My patience isn't endless, Mallory. It has limits, and I'm approaching them, and I don't honestly like the idea of losing it entirely, believe me.'

Mallory wandered to the sofa, out of Pagan's range, and sat down, looked inside his glass. What did it matter to him if this stubborn Englishman went out and got himself killed by Skidelsky's people? What was one more death anyway? *She stands in the doorway, that young face painted, the ridiculous prophylactic in her fingers, and she looks so damned innocent, so disturbingly innocent, and young enough to be your own fucking daughter, and now she's a nightmare you have to carry around.*

He gazed at the photograph of his lost kids. Carrie would be thirteen now, Cindy eleven. He imagined what it would be like to sit down with them one day and tell them about his life and the things he'd done and see their expressions. How would they look at him? With understanding or condemnation? He doubted if he'd ever see them again anyhow, so the conjecture was purely a dry academic exercise.

He drew a hand across his face in a weary manner. He said quietly, 'My wife complained I gave too much of myself to my work. And she was right, Pagan. I was always going overseas, I was gone too long too often, and everything just evaporated in my absences. I'd come home to a house of strangers, and I'd feel . . . I guess the word is alienated. It's a sad story, and it's banal. Happens all the time.'

Pagan was silent, tapping the barrel of his gun against the palm of his hand. Mallory couldn't read his expression. The grey eyes were unresponsive.

'They'd send me to Paris. Rome. Athens. Istanbul. Anywhere you'd find old operatives from the former Soviet bloc. Guys with hot secrets to sell. Documents they wanted to trade in exchange for US residency. All these guys with pathetic expressions. Trouble is, while I was away strange things were going on behind my back, and I wasn't paying close attention. My wife found a replacement, my marriage collapsed, and my country was falling to pieces. And one day I came home to an empty house and a sick nation.'

'The abandoned husband, the disillusioned patriot,' Pagan remarked.

'That sums it up, Pagan.' Mallory turned his face to Pagan, a quick little movement of the neck. He felt a small burst of hostility toward Pagan suddenly. Why should he tell this stranger anything? The guy was intruding on his life. 'Christ, Pagan. Why don't you just do yourself a favour and walk straight out of here? Forget you ever saw me.'

'I think I'll linger,' Pagan said. He moved a little closer to the sofa. He gave Mallory the impression now of a man who was holding himself in check, energies only just repressed, coils about to unwind.

Pagan said, 'Besides, I'm interested in disillusioned patriots. How do they compensate?'

How do they compensate? Mallory forced a weak smile. His feeling of animosity dispersed as if it were a vapour. He heard voices inside his head, a clamour of them, Skidelsky's, his ex-wife's, a kid crying out in a bedroom doorway – there was displacement going on inside his skull, discordant voices echoing in an empty auditorium. He got up and walked back to the liquor cabinet and filled his glass. 'There's no real compensation, Pagan. I thought there might be. I guess I figured it all the wrong way. I'm not sure. Even now, I'm not sure.'

'Tell me how you figured it, Mallory.'

Mallory ran a hand through his hair. Vodka was

getting in the way of his thinking. Unfinished sentences floated in and out of his mind, explanations, justifications, things beyond the reach of his language. 'I'm not a bad man, Pagan. That's how I assess myself. I'm not what you'd call a bad man. I just happen to be involved in . . .'

'In what?'

Mallory paused. The precipice, he thought. The place where, without benefit of either parachute or safety-net, he could jump. Skidelsky's face formed in his imagination. A warning frown behind the glasses, those clear eyes penetrating. What did he owe Max Skidelsky anyway? Put it into words, what did he owe? Skidelsky had filled certain gaps in his life. Skidelsky had given him a fragile sense of belonging to something. Max's dreams were infectious, but none of them were real. He created illusions. He was setting the country right, and you wanted to believe him, god damn it, but he was a quack revivalist in a big tent making cripples think they could walk without crutches, except they could only ever manage a few halting steps before they collapsed, but that was enough for some people to believe in miracles. It was all deception, and Mallory was just another gullible cripple fooled and fuelled by a huckster's enthusiasm.

'See, my trouble is I could never really see how the means justified the end. The others could. They managed the moral arithmetic of it all. Me, I always had problems with the numbers. Right from the start.'

'Tell me about the numbers,' Pagan said.

'Some people had a good look round, Pagan. And they just didn't like what they saw. They didn't like the general drift of the country. They didn't like the lack of focus. They didn't like the way pessimism had replaced belief, the inability of cops to control the streets, the wholesale spread of guns, the cheapness of human life – the whole uphill struggle, the grind of keeping law and order, the breakdown in domestic security and intelligence that is supposed to be the reponsibility of the FBI.'

Pagan said, 'These people – colleagues of yours?'

Mallory sipped his drink. He imagined himself sitting in a confessional, unloading all the trash in his system. But the price of atonement was higher than a few god-damn Hail Marys and a bunch of rosaries. He'd done wrong, he'd been carried along in the rush of Skidelsky's raw intensity, but a stronger man would never have allowed that to happen in the first place. Another kind of man would have challenged Skidelsky's strategies. Another kind of man would have tried to wrestle the gun out of Ralph Donovan's hand. And another kind of man would have drawn a line and said *I don't go beyond this point*.

'I'm weak, Pagan,' he said. 'Not wicked. Just weak.'

'We're all a little weak,' Pagan remarked.

'Yeah, we're all weak. We're only human, right? Yourself included. They say you have a thing about this woman. Is that your weakness, Pagan? Or is that just gossip?'

Pagan didn't answer the question. But Mallory didn't need it answered. He stared into Pagan's face and sensed some form of inner flinching, as if he'd touched an open sore in the man. Mallory heard himself laugh, an abrupt little hawk of a sound, a vodka sound. There was no mirth in it. He felt himself sliding down a slope of shale into a place of solitude and inexpressible bitterness – and, what was worse, he had the feeling that this was the place where he really belonged. The bottom of a chute. A locked coal cellar.

'This is hard for me, Pagan. Damn hard. You don't know.'

'Take your time,' Pagan said.

Mallory paused. This was betrayal, he thought. But he was moving into a realm where it frankly didn't matter to him. He couldn't differentiate one kind of treachery from another. They all smelled bad. He had the vague feeling that if he spoke to Pagan he'd be throwing off his guilt and could somehow go back to that point in the roadway of his life where he'd taken a wrong turning.

'We decided we could do a better job,' he said slowly. 'I know how fucking arrogant that assumption is, but that's what we decided. The Agency has a sophisticated system in place, we have highly-trained individuals who are underemployed, and the Agency is being pushed out into the cold and left to rot.'

'Because you have no role to play these days,' Pagan said. It wasn't a suggestion, more a statement of fact.

'Exactly. No role to play, because we're pretty much limited to external matters, and all the while the nation is turning inwards. Who gives a shit about what happens in Bosnia or Rwanda anyway? Your average American wants a world where he doesn't have to lock his car at night and turn his god-damn house into a fortress, he doesn't care about a few Serbs and Croats and a bunch of starving Africans. Not exactly praise-worthy, maybe . . . But the domestic scene was off limits to the Agency. OK, we had a foothold in it, but it wasn't much, because the Feds guard their home territory like pit-bulls. And the Agency, instead of turning its attention to the concerns of the nation, which we're well-equipped to do . . . we just play old-fashioned games at Langley, Pagan. That's all we do.'

Pagan was all attention. 'You needed to undermine the FBI.'

'Yeah, we needed that for starters.'

'To make them look incompetent.'

'Yeah. Incapable. Utterly incapable.'

'And you felt the woman could do that for you.'

'Can you think of a better candidate? She's evaded them for years.'

'So your people blew up Capsicum. You arranged the murder of the shrink. All to get Carlotta firmly back in the national focus. She's out there doing her thing, and the Feds are clumsily panting after her. And they're *seen* to be panting, which is even better.'

'That was part of the scheme.'

Pagan was silent a moment, absorbing this information. From Mallory's angle of perception, the Englishman looked imposingly cool. You couldn't imagine him being flustered. You couldn't see his feathers ruffled. And yet the scuttlebutt had it that the woman was under his skin and had infiltrated his system like a rogue cell. We're all weak, Mallory thought. Amen to that. He rose and went back in the direction of the Absolut and noticed he was weaving just slightly as he moved.

'There's more,' Pagan said.

Mallory poured another drink. 'Yeah, there's a twist or two,' he said. 'If the Feds couldn't capture the woman, we could. Capture or kill, it doesn't matter. The Agency lives. The Agency is capable of bagging big game, even on the domestic front. The Agency can outsmart the FBI.'

'Presumptuous,' Pagan said.

'We lived on presumptions, Pagan. We *dined* out on them. Don't you understand that?'

'How do you intend to capture her?'

Mallory, by now half drunk and enjoying the sensation, winked. Vodka was a great provider of bravado. Fuck Skidelsky. Fuck Pagan. Mallory wanted only peace and quiet. 'Sorry, buddy. I've gone as far as I can go,' he said.

Suddenly Pagan moved. He moved quicker than Mallory's retarded eye could follow. The glass was swept out of his hand and Pagan clutched the lapels of his jacket and forced him down on the sofa. Pagan was above him, looking down, his face grim.

'Go a little further for me, Mallory,' he said. 'You've got my attention.'

Mallory struggled to rise, but Pagan had him pinned to the sofa. He was stronger than he looked. His hands were locked tight around Mallory's wrists. Mallory struggled briefly, tried to turn this way and that, then subsided with a grunt of exasperation.

'Go on,' Pagan said.

Mallory stared up past Pagan's face, seeing where the overhead light threw a pale ring against the ceiling. 'The rough stuff,' he said. 'I thought you were a civilized guy.'

'That's a veneer, Mallory. I wouldn't trust it. Speak to me.'

Mallory shut his eyes. He had the thought that his life was a disaster area, ripped through by typhoons and twisters, whole streets of his world swept away on a rancid foaming tide. His inner landscape depressed him completely. He licked his dry lips and opened his eyes and looked up into Pagan's face.

'Speak to me,' Pagan said again.

43

WASHINGTON

Max Skidelsky said, 'I don't like to ask, Larry.'

Larry Quinn said, 'I know that.'

'I wouldn't ask if I had another alternative.'

'I know that too.'

'I like the man personally,' Skidelsky said. He spread his hands in a gesture of futility. 'He's a nice guy.'

'I've always thought so,' Quinn said.

'But sometimes you need to do a little house-cleaning. Sometimes you need to change the water in the flower vase because it's starting to offend you,' Skidelsky said. 'Are you up for it, Larry?'

'Do I look like a hitman? No, I'm not really up for it.'

'I understand that. I sympathize. You have reservations.'

Larry Quinn, his black hair glossy under the spot-lights recessed in the ceiling, shrugged his shoulders slightly. 'I didn't say I wouldn't do it, Max. I'll do it. I just wanted you to know how I feel about it, that's all.'

Skidelsky laid a hand on Quinn's shoulder and squeezed it. 'I think he's going to be a burden over the long haul, Larry. A nice guy, like you say. I'd be the last to dispute that. But soft-centred.'

'Like a chocolate liqueur,' Quinn remarked.

Skidelsky smiled. 'I asked too much of him, Larry. I put him through a big test and I don't like the results. Maybe it's better to find these things out now, instead of further down the road.'

'Yeah. OK. I'll go, I'll go.' Quinn looked reluctant. When he turned to move, he did so sluggishly.

'You know where he lives?' Max asked.

Quinn said, 'Glastonbury Street. I've been in his apartment. The place depresses me.'

He listened to Larry Quinn leave the apartment and then turned his face back to the telephone on his kitchen table and willed the thing to ring. But he had long ago learned that when you were waiting for your phone to ring, time assumed an elastic quality, seconds stretched slowly into minutes, minutes expanded laboriously into hours. He had about seventy men and women rummaging through the city looking for a Buick with a certain licence-plate number and so far none of them had called in to say they'd seen it. He could have done with more people at his disposal, but the others that might have been available to him were already in Roanoke, waiting in hotel rooms for his call.

He bit on a fingernail, an uncharacteristic gesture of tension. As long as Pagan was out there, the chance existed that he'd locate the woman, especially if she took it into her head to find a way to contact him because she just happened to be in a mood to play some of her weird mind games. And that couldn't be allowed to happen.

The phone suddenly rang – *at last*, he thought – and he reached for it immediately. The man on the other end of the line was Jacob Turk, a disaffected black Skidelsky had recruited from the Office of Logistics at Langley.

'I see him, Max.'

'Where is he?'

'He's headed for Interstate 95.' There was a measure of fuzz on Jacob Turk's mobile phone.

'Great. Keep in touch. I'm leaving now.'

44

WASHINGTON

She stepped out of her car and moved toward the shrubs that grew in the forecourt of the apartment complex. The night was wild and a wind blew bloated rain-clouds across an intermittent moon. She crossed the forecourt, paused under the branches of a cherry tree. She waited, checked the area for human presence, saw nothing. Apartment windows were lit here and there – it was a shabby place, twenty years old or more, and without a security guard. Easy for her.

She moved out from under the cherry tree and headed toward the building and found the door she was looking for. A rusted iron FOUR hung askew upon the wall. She touched the door handle, laying her hand on it gently, fully expecting it to be locked. But it wasn't. In a world of electronic security systems and deadbolt locks, a world of paranoia, she was immediately suspicious. She hesitated.

She could step inside, Chico's gun in her hand, and she could confront Mallory and make him explain the one thing that still rang an unharmonious chord in her – and that was Pasco's insistence that she strike at the camp in the southern part of Virginia. *If you asked me to single any one thing out, I'd have to say the training-camp near Roanoke would be my number one priority.*

That's the one I'd really like to get. I'd like to see that place demolished. I'd like to see it just blown sky fucking high. She understood his hatred of the place, sure – but it was the manner of his delivery that had triggered uneasiness inside her. He'd been too strident, too eager. He'd pushed the idea with just a little too much effort. She wondered if she was supposed to walk into something there. Was that the reason for Pasco's pushiness? If there was a set-up, was that the place for it?

The idea that somebody was trying to manipulate her didn't spook her; it had a contrary effect – it elated her, excited her. But there was a definite advantage in being forewarned, in knowing what you might expect to find when you reached your destination.

She felt rain fall against her blouse, soak through the cotton to her skin. It was warm rain and the dark was cloying with humidity. She had to move. She went forward toward the door and twisted the handle and entered the room with the gun in her hand.

A young black-haired man in a long blue raincoat stood in the middle of the room, bent over something he was reading on the table. He turned at once, his expression one of surprise. She fired her gun as soon as she saw the weapon in his fist. Without thinking. Without hesitation. He went clattering backward into a liquor cabinet and it toppled under his weight and bottles crashed on the floor around him. He fell with a stricken look. He lay amongst broken glass.

She immediately stepped over him and went through the rest of the apartment – an empty bathroom, a fastidiously clean kitchen, then a bedroom where a lamp burned in a feeble manner beside the bed. The figure who lay on the bed was a middle-aged man fully dressed in a grey suit. His silver hair was neatly combed, parted to one side.

The gunshot wound had been inflicted in his chest. Blood soaked his shirt. Pulpy pieces of his shattered heart were visible through the untidy gash in his chest and she saw the discoloured pinkness of an exposed rib-bone. She didn't pause, she searched his pockets, found a wallet. The wallet contained a Central Intelligence Agency ID card with the dead man's name: James Mallory.

Mallory. He was beyond her reach now. He was beyond speech. She kept the card, tossed the wallet aside – they'd find her fingerprints when they investigated the murder, but what did that matter? It was only fuel to her reputation – and then she returned to the room where the other man lay. He smelled of spilled booze and fresh blood.

She frisked him hastily. His wallet contained a raft of credit cards, Diner's, Amex Platinum, Visa, Mastercard, each imprisoned inside a plastic window. She also found his ID. CIA. Lawrence F. Quinn. She studied his picture a second – long-jawed, thin lips, stern features. She picked up his gun, a Mitchell 45 Signature with a custom-made silencer. She'd keep the gun.

Lawrence Quinn had come here and killed Mallory, because—

Because of what? She pondered this question a moment. What had Galkin said? *One faction wants the power that another faction has.* An internecine war. A struggle for control. Was that why Mallory had been killed – because he was on the opposing side to Lawrence F. Quinn? She remembered Quinn's position as she'd entered the room, the way he'd been inclined over a table, reading. She walked to the table and saw several sheets of quality paper, some of them crumpled into balls. An uncapped fountain-pen lay nearby.

The sheets were drafts of a letter that the writer had been composing with difficulty. Words were crossed out, sentences abandoned. She started to read, found it muddled, but it was apparently the work of a man contemplating suicide and trying to leave behind him a few phrases of farewell. He'd obviously laboured hard over what he'd written; too hard, she thought. Certainly hard enough to give himself time to reconsider the feasibility of suicide. And the handwriting was wild and uneven, as if the pen had been held by a drunk.

My dear friend, I have come to the realization that – and the rest of this phrase was obliterated and a revision inserted. *I have come to the conclusion I don't belong . . .* And again: *I don't see any other way out, I've betrayed you, betrayed myself . . .* She scanned the self-pitying phrases and read: *I have had a visit from our English friend and I told him . . .*

Our English friend, she thought. Her interest quickened.

The remainder of the sentence had been scrawled over with furious energy and was illegible. She picked up another sheet and read: *I couldn't keep it to myself, try to understand that. I was never the correct material for you. I know you tried to make me feel I belonged, and I appreciate that, but I don't have the stomach for it, the heart, whatever you call it.* She saw Mallory's signature at the bottom of this page. It was spidery and slanted downward, and surrounded by ink-blots.

She picked up one of the crumpled sheets and smoothed it out. Another unfinished draft. *I never intended to sell you, try to understand that, but I had no choice. I suppose from the very beginning I was playing out of my league, and when Pagan came, I told him about Roanoke, he didn't have to push me too hard . . .*

Pagan.

She stood very still. She listened to the rain rattle against the windows. The night had a random quality about it, a recklessness. *Pagan had been here.* How long ago? An hour? Less? She tried to imagine him in this room, perhaps standing where she now stood herself.

He'd come here, and he'd talked to Mallory, and Mallory had mentioned Roanoke, and then sat down to compose a suicide note, scribble his farewells to some unnamed friend because he felt – what – the weight of a treachery? Then he'd abandoned his letter writing and, perhaps drunk and indecisive and panicked by the chilly idea of self-elimination, perhaps undergoing a change of heart, had stumbled through to his bed – where Lawrence Quinn had found and killed him. It was as much of a reconstruction as she could make.

Pagan, she thought.

He'd come here. He'd sifted through the dross and found his way to Mallory. She thought: I knew you wouldn't disappoint me in the end, Frank.

45

VIRGINIA

Pagan couldn't see more than a few yards in front of the car. The rain had increased and the night sky collapsed. Along the freeway cars and trucks had pulled over to the side, drivers blinded by the relentless downpour. Pagan sat hunched forward, concentrating on the road, which he saw only in brief glimpses. The deluge was beyond the capacity of the wipers. You didn't need a car in this kind of weather. What you needed was an ark.

He kept going, feeling every so often the effect of aquaplaning, the car skidding over the slick surface of road. He struggled with the wheel when the vehicle slithered in the direction of an exit ramp. He pulled over at a filling-station and studied his map. The last sign he'd seen was for Charlottesville. He had a long way to go.

Once, when the tumult became impossible, he pulled over to the hard shoulder, listening to the rain sizzle like sleet on the roof. He rolled his window down an inch because the inside of the car was stuffy, and he smelled the sharp acidic scent of dry land suddenly saturated. He heard water fluming violently down inclines in the earth. Out of the western sky came an eruption of lightning followed by the deep bass of thunder. He was impatient with the elements and with himself. He had to keep moving.

The rain kept battering at his windshield. At one point he felt he was driving through a very narrow funnel of darkness. He thought of Mallory – that whole pathetic situation, the way Mallory had collapsed under the weight of his own dilemma. *I believed it was the right thing, Pagan.*

The right thing, Pagan thought. The so-called Artichoke Club and its devious scheme for correcting what it perceived as social wrongs, all the corruptions and erosions within the system – a solution that involved treachery and violence and murder. You couldn't construct a secure society on the basis of bloodshed. You couldn't construct a secure society period. The whole world, in Pagan's view, was in disorder.

By his own admission, Mallory had been sucked in by the man he called Max Skidelsky, who seemed to Pagan a major piece of nasty work – Assistant to Christopher Poole, plotting away below the surface of the Agency, hiding in the cracks, gathering together his private army of foot soldiers and informers and assassins, like Donovan. Skidelsky held Mallory in thrall. Even when James Mallory had finally broken down in wet-eyed inebriation and told Pagan what he wanted to know, he'd talked about Skidelsky as if the man were some kind of visionary. *I still want to believe, Pagan, that's the worst of it. Even now, when I know it's totally wrong, I still want to believe. Max is right, you understand, only his methods are fucked.* And Mallory had wiped his face with the cuff of his jacket, and hung his head in the fashion of a man who has betrayed something he believes precious. *Only his methods are fucked,* Pagan thought. More than his methods, Mallory. Start with his basic premise and take it from there.

She goes down to Roanoke and that's where she gets it, Mallory had said.

Just like that? Pagan asked.

Place is going to be crawling, she can't get away. There are people down there with orders to shoot on sight if they have to. Dead or alive, it doesn't matter. The Agency gets the credit.

She can get away, believe me, Mallory.

Not this time. She gets in easily enough, she gets just enough space to do the job, and then she finds she can't get out again.

The job? Pagan had asked.

The job, the demolition work.

Pagan peered out into the streaming wet night. He was doing fifteen miles an hour, sometimes ten. The rain came harder and he had to pull once again to the side of the freeway. Mallory's voice echoed inside his head, as persistent as the rain. The demolition work, the job, he thought. And he wondered if Carlotta was even now making her way through this aquatic landscape toward the ultimate destination.

He thought, *I want her.* The sheer force of this unexpected thought, which struck him as almost childish in its wilfulness, astonished him. *I want her. I deserve to get her. I've been after her too long to let anyone else have her.* And all the rest, as she'd once said to him, was background noise.

The helicopter came in over the trees and dropped toward a circle of light in the grass. Christopher Poole, who sat up front with the pilot, said, 'Admirable how you can fly in this awful weather.'

The pilot said, 'You can fly a machine like this in most kinds of weather, sir. Discounting hurricanes, of course.' He smiled.

'Of course,' Poole said, and turned his face rather stiffly to look at Bob Naderson in the back. 'Are you holding up, Bob?'

'Fine, just fine,' Naderson said. He was uncomfortable, very much so. His stomach couldn't take this kind of trip.

'Choppy,' Poole said.

'Just a little.'

The helicopter descended through thrashing rain. It struck the ground with only a slight shudder. The blades began to slow.

Poole said, 'It's going to be pleasant to see some familiar old faces, Bob.'

Naderson agreed.

'I'm looking forward to it,' Poole went on. 'It'll be something of a tonic. Take our minds off this, this recent unpleasantness . . .' He gestured loosely with his hand.

'Yes,' Naderson said. He thought about the two secretaries who were presently under suspicion. Each had denied giving anyone information from the Executive Director's private files. Naderson was inclined to believe them. He was inclined to think that the culprit was somebody closer to Christopher Poole's heart. But he couldn't say so, because that was tantamount to questioning the old man's judgement – territory into which Naderson wasn't prepared to go. Besides, he owed Poole for a ten-year-old favour. He owed his freedom, possibly his life, to Poole.

Both men climbed down from the chopper. A woman in a heavy wax coat of the kind favoured in equestrian circles stood under an umbrella just beyond the light. Poole ducked his face beneath the spokes of the umbrella and kissed the woman on the side of her face and said, 'Joan. It's been months.'

'Months? Your memory's slipping. More like a year, Christopher,' Joan Dunne said. 'And here's Bob.' She offered her plump little cheek to Naderson, who kissed it, but only briefly, because he'd never much cared for the woman.

She said, 'Let's get inside out of this horrible rain. There's hot punch waiting.'

They entered a wooden building that was commonly called The Lodge. Joan Dunne, a tiny woman with a face Bob Naderson had once referred to as resembling a bloated chihuahua, shook drips from the umbrella. 'Come into the lounge, both of you. Put your bags down. I'll have somebody take them up to your rooms. Follow me.'

Joan Dunne was bossy. She'd spent her life being bossy. She'd bossed hundreds of young trainees who'd passed through this place, instilling fear in them – fear of sexually-transmitted diseases, foreign agents, blackmail, compromising situations.

'This way, come along,' she said. 'Don't dilly-dally. The punch will get cold.'

The lounge was large, wood-panelled. The heads of stuffed animals peered down into the room. Around a fire, which had been lit despite the clamminess of the air, sat a large group of men and women. Poole made his way into the group, shaking hands, bussing and being bussed, his head held at that characteristic stiff angle.

Naderson, who lingered on the fringes, recognized most of the others. Guy Backus, Assistant Director of Training. Marge Habbs, Director of Foreign Broadcast Information Service. The red beefy face of Ted Hollander, Chief of Special Operations Division. Angus Scott, Director of the Office of European Analysis. Billy Dearkins the Third, no less, Chief of Staff Evaluation. Alex Schwab, with his ill-fitting toupee,

Chief of Management and Analysis Support Staff. A gathering of chiefs, Naderson thought. There were about fifty in all, senior people drawn from different sections of the Agency. The Office of Security. The Office of Imagery Analysis. Communications. Central Reference. Global Issues. Development and Engineering. SIGINT Operations. These people wouldn't encounter one another often in the normal course of things – and so Poole had brought them together for this series of seminars to bounce around constructive ideas concerning the Agency's destiny.

As Naderson scanned the group he was struck by the rather bleak fact that the ageing process had touched everyone maliciously – the proliferation of white hair, baldness, paunches and, in the case of Ted Hollander, a walking-stick. It was depressing. He realized he was looking forward to retirement, two months away. He had a general sense of having outlived his usefulness. His world was long gone. He'd retire quietly, and raise his organic vegetables, and every now and then perhaps he'd think of the life he'd left, and maybe he'd remember the price that had been paid for his liberty.

Marge Habbs emerged from the crowd and linked an arm through his. 'With all of us down here, what I want to know is – who's minding the god-damn store?'

Naderson said, 'It makes you wonder.'

Marge Habbs pinched Naderson's arm. 'And how are you anyway, Bobby?'

'Struggling along,' he said.

Marge Habbs wore very heavy make-up. She drew Bob Naderson toward her and lowered her voice confidentially. 'Tell me, Bob. You've got Chris Poole's ear. Is this ship being scuttled? Or are we to run on a skeleton crew?'

'It's too soon to tell,' Naderson said.

'This man in the White House,' she said. 'He doesn't respect the Agency. Nor the Agency's traditions.'

'Amen to that,' Naderson said.

'Fuck democracy, I say. If the people vote that kind of man into office.'

'If you run across a better system, let me know, Marge.'

'You're far too serious,' and she poked him in fun with a fingertip.

He looked at her a moment. 'What's the security like here?'

'Security? You worried about something, Bobby?'

'Just curious.'

'This is The Lodge, for God's sake. If you're not safe here, you're not safe anywhere.'

Naderson reflected on this. There would be guards all around the place. There would be an electronic detection system. He sighed, tried to relax.

In the background Joan Dunne was making a speech. She was standing up on a chair but she still looked diminutive. 'I want to welcome you all officially to The Lodge. Some of you have never been here before. Most of you, I'd say, came to the Company *long* before The Lodge was functioning.'

There was a general little round of self-deprecatory laughter. Naderson thought he detected uneasiness in it.

'Anyway,' Joan Dunne was saying. 'Business begins tomorrow at ten a.m. Breakfast will be served between eight and nine thirty in the dining-room. You've all been allocated rooms in The Lodge. Due to lack of space, some of you will have to double up. But not, ha ha, on a mixed basis. We don't have any trainees in residence this week – so their rooms are available to us. Christopher Poole, where are you? Do you want to say a few words before we retire for the evening?'

Poole, who liked the spotlight every so often, spoke in a firm voice. 'I seriously hope something beneficial will come out of these seminars. I don't have to tell you all that we're going through some troubled times. But we've had troubled times before, and we've survived them, and we'll do so again. To our health. To the Agency. Long may we flourish.'

He sipped from his cup, then raised it aloft, and everyone in the lounge did likewise. There was, Naderson thought, an air of forced cheer about all this, like that of people celebrating Christmas Eve in a bomb shelter during an air-raid.

The rain didn't matter to her. She was caught up in its majestic power. She drove without caution. She overtook slow-moving trucks and cars that crawled carefully. When lightning lit the sky in the distance she found the sight uplifting. The night pulsated. There was urgency in the storm, and urgency in herself.

46

VIRGINIA

Pagan sat in a truck-stop eight miles from Roanoke and quickly drank black coffee. With a paper napkin he made an opening in the steamed-up window and gazed out at the parking-lot. The rain kept hammering, and visibility was bad and oily puddles trapped the blue neon sign of the truck-stop in a sequence of disturbed reflections.

His head ached; driving in this kind of weather required hard concentration and wakefulness. He drained the coffee, then spread before him on the table the rough little sketch Mallory had made for him. Ten miles before Roanoke he was to follow a sign for a place by the name of Trout. *It's a few cabins and a bait shop*, Mallory had said. *You don't want to blink*. A mile beyond Trout he'd come to another sign pointing to a community called Goode. Before he reached Goode he'd see a signpost for Camp Ladyfair, his ultimate destination. *Two miles along a bad road and there you are. There won't be any security. At least not going in.* Camp Ladyfair, he thought. An innocuous name. It might have been a summer camp for kids.

He rose and walked to the cashier and paid his bill. He purchased a bottle of aspirin and swallowed two with a glass of water. Then he turned up the collar of his jacket and stood in the doorway, gazing in the direction of his parked car some twenty or thirty yards away. He made a dash for it through the blitz.

Max Skidelsky answered the mobile phone in his car.

Jacob Turk said, 'I've lost him, Max.'

'Fuck,' Max said.

'I don't know how it happened. I can't see shit most of the time. It's a nightmare. He must have come off the freeway somewhere.'

'Where are you exactly?'

'About twenty miles out of Roanoke on 81. Where are you?'

'Not far behind. Near Lexington.'

'What do you want me to do?'

'Just keep going, Jake. If you see him, get back to me. If you don't, you know where you're going anyway.'

'Gotcha,' said Jacob Turk.

Skidelsky replaced the mobile phone unit. He looked at the clock on his dashboard. 04:53. He drove with his shoulders hunched forward. The sparse traffic heading slowly in the opposite direction glared against his glasses. He thought of the ancient ones gathered at The Lodge, living in the past, reminiscing even as they were allegedly trying to look into the future. A waste of time and breath.

He picked up the phone and punched in a number and said, 'Time to move,' and he hung up again, thinking of the thirty or so people who waited in different hotels in Roanoke, imagining them stirring out of their beds, drinking quick cups of coffee, snatching a doughnut maybe, then making their way separately and quietly to the community of Trout, where they'd assemble and wait for action.

He turned on the radio as he drove. There was country music for a while, and then news of an explosion the night before in Delaware, and although the details were scant the announcer said that the place was believed to have been 'a military installation', a vague term that suggested to Skidelsky government censorship, prompted, of course, by the connivers inside the FBI, who still wanted to play down the terrorist element, even though the whole of America knew Carlotta was at liberty in their midst.

All right! Max slapped the dash open-handed. She'd done the business in Delaware. And that left the camp. He worried a moment about her unpredictability, but if she'd been to the satellite installation then the camp would be next on her agenda, and she'd want to do it fast, on the back of her work in Delaware, because he understood the way she worked, how she liked the cumulative effect of her actions, one devastation following another – as if she were a magician trying to top one trick immediately with another even more mystifying.

The bug was Pagan. Pagan, who was somewhere in this dreary wet landscape, somewhere close. Pagan, who could only be in this general vicinity because he too was headed for The Lodge, which was a nuisance – but not one Skidelsky was going to fret over too much.

He wondered how Pagan had found out about the camp. It didn't matter now. He wondered about Larry Quinn, and why Larry hadn't reported back. But these considerations were intrusions, and he couldn't give them headroom, because in the long run they weren't hugely important. He was focused and on the move, he was all compressed energy, he was a young man whose numbers were about to come up on the lottery.

And like all people who know they are winners, he didn't entertain the possibility of defeat.

He took a cassette from the glove compartment and stuck it in the player. Christopher Poole's voice issued through the speakers. *One, the woman is unlikely to return to this country. Two, I can't imagine her singling out Agency personnel as targets. If she has destructive grudges, they're directed at the Bureau.* Max had quite a collection of Poole's little speeches on tape, and later, when the smoke had cleared, he intended to use them to edify influential parties in Congress who might be horrified to learn that the Executive Director, God rest his soul, had been so dreadfully out of touch with the realities of the world. They'd understand then why the Agency had drifted into impotence, and why it required an instant transfusion of new blood. There would be a sizeable number of vacancies to be filled soon enough.

She parked her car off the road in a concealed place between pine trees and, canvas bag in hand, she got out. She was dressed in black leather jacket and jeans and her hair was slicked back. She was Carly Phoenix again, and she was comfortable with the identity. She walked under the trees. The whole landscape was dense and secretive, scented with wet pine needles. Rain fell still, but it was slowing. She listened to the rush of small streams.

She opened the canvas bag and took out her one remaining cylinder and put it in the pocket of her jacket. She had Quinn's gun in her hand. She abandoned the canvas bag under a clump of ferns and moved between the trees and the ground underfoot became muddy in places and sucked at her leather boots. Now and again she paused and listened for sounds not associated with the rain. But she detected nothing.

She felt a remarkable calm descend on her; it was that lull before action, that quiet chamber inside which she withdrew. The place where she collected herself. She moved slowly and easily down the slope, sometimes pausing to push aside an overhanging branch, sometimes stopping to attune her ear because she was still listening for foreign sounds.

Darkness was beginning to splinter, a crack here, an opening there. Dawn would come in flat grey brush strokes. There would be no sunlight. Rain-clouds were low in the sky. She remembered Pasco's description – one central building known as The Lodge, and a couple of outbuildings, one a shooting-range, the other a lecture hall and library. Beyond these were two tennis courts, a softball pitch, and a swimming-pool. But The Lodge was the heart of Camp Ladyfair. It lay in a hollow and could be seen from above as soon as you were clear of the trees.

She kept moving through the pines. An owl floated past her. Bats, their radar short-circuited by rain, made mazy patterns overhead. The trees began to thin. She found herself on a low ridge half a mile above a huge wooden house. The Lodge. No windows were lit.

She could make out the two surrounding buildings and the edge of a tennis court. The place was silent and seemingly deserted and for a time she was reluctant to begin the descent down the gentle slope, because it was *too* silent. There was no visible security, no dogs, no wire fences, just the exposed house. Why were there no guards? No sentries? No patrol vehicles? The place had the feel of a vacation home left empty, a weekend retreat with nobody in it.

She stood under a tree and watched, waiting for

something, a movement, a sign of life. She could go down the slope undetected, she was sure of that – if she kept low; if she hunched her way through the wild shrubbery that grew there, it wouldn't be difficult in this dark grey light to reach The Lodge. But she didn't move. She turned her face and looked the length of the ridge. Silent. Nothing. Just trees, just the slow ineluctable progress of light. No sense of anyone hidden in the pines.

She gazed down once again at The Lodge.

A porch-light went on and a man appeared, his white hair startling. He stretched his arms and appeared to yawn, but he was too far away for her to tell. He walked to the edge of the porch and put one hand out as if to test the temperature of the rain, then he pulled the hand back to his side. He wore striped pyjamas and a robe. He scratched his head and went back indoors.

She continued to watch. She thought of Pagan, wondered where he was. If he was close by. If he was only a mile or so away, zoning in on her. She considered the situation. She weighed the notion of making her way down the slope. Her damp clothes adhered to her flesh, and her jeans stuck to her thighs and a solitary drop of drizzle slid between her breasts. She smiled. There were no uncertainties in Carly Phoenix's world. No doubts and misgivings. She was the kind of woman who'd always go all the way, and even a little further.

She edged forward and began, in a zigzagging manner, to go down the slope. The rain was recharging itself, and by the time she was halfway down the slope it was blowing hard against her face and black mud slushed round the soles of her boots.

*   *   *

The rustic sign simply said: *Camp Ladyfair*. Nothing else. There was no gate, no barrier poles. Pagan turned his car into the narrow driveway, which ran between tall pine trees. A few yards further and he encountered another sign. *Lodge. Half a mile.*

His windshield wipers creaked back and forth, clawing away rain and pine needles that had been washed out of the trees. He understood that if he drove the car too close to The Lodge he'd alert somebody, bring attention to himself, so he parked the Buick on the grass verge at the side of the road and he got out, and instead of following the road he went into the trees, which creaked in the downpour like the masts of sailing-ships.

He was wet through within moments, but he didn't feel it, because he was concentrating on the woman and nothing else, and the possibility that she was here to do what Mallory had called the demolition work. And if she was here, the only thing that mattered to him was getting to her before anyone else.

A compulsion in the rain, and he knew it – but sometimes compulsions overwhelmed judgements, and it didn't matter if you understood that they were indicators of weaknesses in yourself. You could only follow their dictates. And that, that was what he was doing as he slid under the high trees and moved beneath branches and dawn finally broke through, a frayed dawn the colour of old iron, and uncompromisingly drab.

The woman had been watching the landscape through binoculars for hours. She rarely altered her position. If her muscles were stiff, it didn't matter so long as she didn't take her eyes off the ridge and the surrounding area. She hadn't slept. Sometimes she poured coffee from a vacuum flask to keep herself alert. But she was a tough old bird, and she always had been. The cardigan and sensible tweed skirt might have fooled some people into thinking otherwise. But she knew.

She listened to the silences of the big house, which were sometimes punctuated by the creak of a floorboard or wind in the eaves. It was too bad about The Lodge, because she'd become attached to it over the years, but change was change, and sometimes it was painful, and you had to go through it anyway. Like labour. Her wrists ached and her eyes hurt, but she had deep reservoirs of resolve and stubbornness and self-control.

She shifted her position just slightly, elbows propped on the window-ledge.

There, she thought. On the ridge. And moving. Moving down into the shrubbery, wild berry bushes, stunted crab-apples, the thickets and thorns. The camouflage was good – but not good enough for somebody with her keen eyesight. She punched a number on her phone and said, 'She's coming. Get your people in place.'

On the other end of the line, Max Skidelsky said, 'Bless you. You're terrific.'

'Just remember me at the appropriate time and I'll be happy,' she said.

'You better get out of there fast.'

'I'm out the door,' she said.

'Later.' Max Skidelsky cut the connection.

Joan Dunne, who hadn't undressed for bed, left her room. She made her way toward the back staircase, and descended through the house. She passed the closed doorways of rooms where people snored, dreaming their fossilized dreams. She thought the place had the feel of a large museum containing relics of

412

an extinct species. She put on her raincoat and left The Lodge by the back door and walked quickly in the direction of the tennis courts and from there headed toward the wet open fields beyond.

Later, she could tell people she'd taken an early morning stroll, and so she'd survived by a stroke of good fortune. But, hell, she was a survivor from way back. She always had been. It was a question of knowing which way the wind was blowing, that was all. And Max Skidelsky, who was blowing a whole new gale of his own through the structure of things, had made a promise to return her to a suitably senior position at Langley. She was weary, finally, of being stuck in this backwater, and of generations of trainees who only reminded you of your own passing years.

She walked and walked in her wellington boots. She wanted to be very far away when it happened. For a tough old bird, she still had a residue of sensitivity left.

In front of The Lodge was an open area, a lawn studded with a bright array of flowers. It was too exposed. She decided she'd approach the building at an angle and so she moved toward the indoor shooting-range, which was located about fifty yards from the main house. She went quickly, because the light was growing stronger despite the clouds and the rain, and she didn't want to increase the risk of being observed. From the shooting-range, she could reach The Lodge sideways, and thus avoid the porch and the entrance.

She lingered motionless until she felt sure that the house wasn't going to spring suddenly to life, and then she broke cover and ran to the side of The Lodge where plants grew in plastic containers. She went down on her knees, took the cylinder from her pocket, gave the cap a half-twist, then placed the device in one of the containers.

Goodbye, rhododendron.

Goodbye, Lodge.

Goodbye.

She figured she had five minutes to get clear, but she wasn't sure, because sometimes the timing-mechanism on these Czech devices was erratic. Given time and equipment, she would have constructed one of her own.

She stared a second at the cylinder in the soil and then she turned and ran back toward the shooting-range. From there it was her intention to go back up the ridge to the safety of the trees. She moved quickly in the direction of the shrubbery.

Pagan became aware of two things simultaneously. Behind him, he heard the movements of people stepping slowly through the trees, the occasional whisper; and he saw Carlotta, in black leather jacket and jeans, hurry away from The Lodge and run in the direction of the upward slope. His attention was divided between what lay at his back and the sight of Carlotta about four hundred yards to his left.

He glanced round, disconcerted.

Although they wore camouflage jackets and caps, the people fanning out between the trees were noticeable from where he stood, a distance of some two hundred yards. In the grey light they were spectral.

They carried rifles.

It was, he realized, a trap. It was, as Mallory had said, easy to get in; but there was no way of getting out.

If she reached the slope and tried to make it to the tree line, she would be gunned down. Pagan had

414

the urge to break free from the stand of pines that concealed him and sprint across the open spaces toward Carlotta – to achieve what? To warn her? To save her for himself? But he'd be shot down too. He had no doubt about that. He didn't know how many armed people were making their way through the trees. He'd counted more than a dozen in the last thirty seconds, but in places where he couldn't see there were probably more. It was obvious that their goal was to string themselves out across the ridge, and when Carlotta came in plain view—

Open season, he thought.

The end. The end of all his searching, his running. The end of his quest. Why didn't he feel what he should have felt? Why was there no elation? Why this throbbing dull sensation in his head? Because she'd been taken away from him. Because he couldn't take her back to London. Because she would never stand trial. Instead, she'd be gunned down in the soft mud of this place.

He watched her move. She ran with an easy lovely grace. Once, she turned her head and looked back at The Lodge, and Pagan remembered the reason she'd come here, and he swung his face toward the large gloomy wooden edifice, which reminded him of something that belonged in the Black Forest. And he knew – it was only going to be a matter of seconds.

He imagined he heard a clock tick. He saw Carlotta begin toward the slope. He heard the footsteps of the others in the trees, the assassination squad. He stared at The Lodge. He felt it even before it happened.

The explosion was brutal and fiery. Flames rapidly rose up the side of the wooden structure. Windows shattered, slates flew violently from the roof, the chimneys were blasted. The smoke, hideous and dense, blew out into the rain, at first with enormous speed and then slowing and rolling across the lawn like a thick and misleadingly gentle fog. Flames spread through the house with the obscene haste of a prairie fire. There was a secondary explosion almost immediately – perhaps a fuel tank, a gas line. This one rocked the house on its foundation and even greater fumes spewed up into the grey dawn and suddenly all geography was obscured, all spatial relationships demolished, and the landscape was reduced to flame and smoke, and the house became a concatenation of lesser explosions as glass blew out of frames and doors were forced from walls and timbers groaned in the roof and the porch collapsed.

Pagan ran then, rushing from the concealment of the trees and going toward the smoke-clogged lawn with his jacket drawn across his mouth for protection from the fumes; he ran into the blind drifting mess of toxic smoke because the assassination squad couldn't see him, and he stumbled in the direction of the slope. The smoke was everywhere, a large dun-coloured cover penetrated but not dispersed by rain. He could barely see the incline. Shrubs and bushes were ghostly shapes. He saw Carlotta moving away from him in the course of her ascent, shrouded in the same fog that enveloped him. Half-seen, she was more of a phantom than she'd ever been. She seemed to belong to the smoke, as if she were a creation of it.

He called her name.

She turned once, smiled, kept going away from him. The smoke was drifting up the ridge, thinning as it reached the tree line. If she went any further, she'd be seen by the gunmen in the trees.

He gasped for air, waved a hand uselessly in front of his face as if to create a pocket of oxygen for himself, he coughed, his lungs hurt, there was pressure in his head. But he kept running despite all this. He kept running because he had to get to her. She turned and lazily fired her gun at him – an act she performed so casually he knew she had no intention of striking him. There was barely any sound from the weapon. It was silenced.

Suddenly, as if she sensed the danger that lay up there in the trees, she changed direction. She knows, Pagan thought. She knows what waits for her up there, and he marvelled at her instincts, that finely-tuned instrument of her intuition. She was running *back* toward the burning house, away from those who carried guns along the ridge. Pagan turned too, and went after her, pursuing her past the house where the heat blasted him and he felt as if the skin were peeling from his face, past tennis courts, a swimming-pool, a softball field, and then into muddy meadows. He had his gun in his hand but he knew he wouldn't use it. Not yet. She kept going, Pagan kept running. He was gaining on her, but the effort was costing him. Drained, muscles aching, he chased her into a place where the meadows yielded to deciduous trees, oaks, birches, elms, a whole pastoral corner the smoke didn't reach. The rain fell cleanly here. Nearby, a stream ran through a gulley in the land. He called her name a couple of times, but she didn't stop. She didn't acknowledge him. He ploughed mud underfoot as he chased. He didn't know how long he could keep this up. He wasn't sure he could win this race. And she knew it, she knew his uncertainty; this was part of the same teasing game she'd always played.

Then she stopped dead. Just like that.

For a second Pagan thought she was either going to change direction on him again, or else turn with her gun, and it would all come down to some absurd duel in the rain, and he didn't want that.

But then he realized why she'd stopped.

A young man in steel-framed glasses appeared suddenly from between the trees. He held a shotgun under his arm. His thick fair hair was matted, flattened against his skull. His raincoat glistened. Pagan, some yards behind Carlotta, came to a halt and stared at the young man, who moved a few paces forward.

'Well,' he said. 'Two for the price of one.'

Pagan wiped rain from his face with his hand.

The young man looked first at Carlotta and then at Pagan and said, 'This is tidy. This I like. We haven't met. But I know you. I know both of you.' He smiled. The smile was dangerous, Pagan thought. It was as if the young man were lit from within by a light source from a cold corner of his heart.

'Max Skidelsky,' the young man said.

Pagan lowered his head, looked down at the mud, the way puddles squelched under his shoes. Skidelsky, visionary, saviour. 'Mallory's friend,' Pagan said.

'Ah. You met Mallory. So you know.'

'I know what Mallory told me,' Pagan said.

Skidelsky said, 'Economical little plan. This lovely woman gets rid of a whole bunch of our deadheads in one shot. And we get the woman.'

'It's murder, no matter how you dress it up,' Pagan said.

'Murder? Call it mercy killing, Pagan. The Agency was turning into an old folks' home, for Christ's sake. Too many dodderers. Too many Neanderthals. If they won't go out to pasture when they should, then I say let's give them a helping hand. Let's get the show back on the god-damn road.'

Pagan had the feeling there was an imbalance in

Skidelsky. Not exactly madness, not that, but an intelligence impaled upon a spike of brutality and wild ambition. Something had gone wrong inside Max Skidelsky's gyroscope and it was spinning in a contrary way. The plan Mallory had explained – what was that but the product of a mind in disarray? Demoralize the FBI. Strengthen the Agency. Root out the old plants and discard them. Make it a force again. Give it a purpose. And woven into this general tapestry of things was Carlotta, who stood with her face turned toward Pagan. It was an odd moment, Pagan thought; he and Carlotta faced by a common enemy. A curious twist of events, another kind of intimacy he didn't want.

Skidelsky looked at Carlotta. 'Thank you, kind lady. Thank you for all your help. You didn't know you were being so constructive with your services, did you?'

She said nothing. Pagan had the feeling she considered Skidelsky no more than a temporary intruder in the situation that existed between her and himself. She stood with her hands at her sides, her gun dangling from her fingers.

Skidelsky said, 'Both of you. Put your weapons down. On the ground.'

'And then what?' Pagan asked.

'Then it's night-time,' said Skidelsky.

Carlotta said, 'You expect us to toss our guns down?'

'It doesn't matter one way or another in the end,' Skidelsky said.

'OK,' and she threw the gun to the ground. Her voice was jaunty and bright. 'Nice set-up you arranged. I have to admire you for that.'

Skidelsky glanced at the weapon, as if it were familiar to him.

Carlotta said, 'Belonged to a certain Lawrence Quinn. An Agency guy. You know him?'

'That's Larry's gun?'

'Lawrence. Larry. Whoever.'

'I don't have to ask what happened to Larry, I guess.' Skidelsky looked at Pagan, and Pagan went through the odd etiquette of dropping his pistol. He was conscious of Carlotta from the corner of his eye, her casual stance, her hands at her sides, the way her long fingers were loose and relaxed.

She smiled at Pagan. 'Funny kind of ending, babe.'

Babe, he thought. She kills, and she calls me babe.

And we die together, babe.

Skidelsky held the shotgun forward. Raindrops accumulated on his lenses. Carlotta put her hands on her hips, a gesture of defiance, of boldness, as if she meant to provoke Skidelsky at the very end.

'Stand side by side,' Skidelsky said.

'Makes your job easier,' Carlotta said.

'You've made my job easier all along, lady. Why change it now?'

She moved toward Pagan. Her arm brushed his. He felt something against his hip, the motion of her hand, and then he realized she was working the hidden hand furtively toward her pocket, that she wasn't quite ready to give up her life here and now.

He stared at the shotgun, at Skidelsky's spectacles, the smudges of rain on glass, pondering ways to stall the man, to give Carlotta time to do whatever it was she had in mind – but he didn't need to; her movement was secretive and swift and faster than Skidelsky, who carelessly hadn't considered the possibility that she carried a second weapon, could have followed. She whipped the gun out of her pocket and in a continuation of the same motion fired a single shot.

It struck Max Skidelsky in the glasses, and his shotgun went off and he dropped as if he'd been sandbagged – and Pagan, fast to respond, quick to realize he'd been given an unexpected new lease of life, grabbed the woman's hand, and twisted it back hard, and crushed her fingers so that she had to release the gun, and then shoved her away.

The gun fell from her hand.

He bent to pick up the weapon without taking his eyes from her. 'Thanks,' he said.

She smiled. She simply smiled.

'Now what?' she asked.

47

CAMP LADYFAIR, VIRGINIA

'You're coming back with me to London.' He heard in his voice a lack of conviction. The gun he pointed at her felt insubstantial, a weightless object.

'Just like that. After I saved your life.'

'Just like that,' he said.

'No gratitude, Frank.' She shrugged. 'If I don't agree, what will you do? Shoot me in cold blood?' Her tone was flippant. She stood with her legs slightly apart. Dull light reflected from the folds of her open leather jacket like small pools. Her wet T-shirt stuck to her skin.

'Well?' she asked. 'The great Frank Pagan – what will he do? Will he shoot down the reluctant Carlotta? Does he have what it takes?'

He understood he was being provoked. He wondered if he could be callous enough to kill the woman where she stood. She took a step toward him. He looked slightly away from her, conscious of Skidelsky lying some yards off in the grass.

'Back to London,' she said. 'Generally, the amenities in gaols leave much to be desired. I'm fussy who I shower with. Plus I might find myself rooming with some fat butch sweaty bitch. I don't see my future behind bars.'

'You have no future,' he said.

She came closer. He was aware of a number of perceptions – rain on his face, pallid light, the woman's proximity to him; especially that, her nearness, the quietness of her breath.

She stood about two feet away from him. He was tense. The dawn was filled with the relics of violence. Pagan wondered if the woman sensed his tension, if she saw his nervousness.

'It's a long way to London, Frank,' she said.

'We'll get there.'

'I love that determination in your voice. *We'll get there*. You don't exactly sound confident. OK. Fine. Take me. I'm not armed. It's a piece of cake, Frank. London here we come. Pagan returns with notorious terrorist. Headlines and glory.'

Pagan gazed at her. What he couldn't understand was this ready acquiescence; nothing was ever simple when it came to her. He half-expected her to reach out and try to disarm him, but she didn't. She tucked her thumbs in the belt of her jeans and smiled at him, and her expression made him wary.

'Got cuffs?' she asked.

He shook his head. 'Walk in front of me. Slowly.'

'No cuffs? Pity. I like the idea of being shackled to you. The intimacy of bondage.'

'Just walk, Carlotta. We'll walk to where I left my car, and we'll take our time, and if the posse's gone we'll drive away.'

They walked through the trees. After a few minutes, she turned and looked at him. She tossed her head back a little and smiled at him in a secretive way and he was plummeted back into the hotel room in Washington, into that crucible of memory, remembering how she'd aroused him. Other women had excited him, inflamed him – but not like this one, not like Carlotta. Not even, God help him, Roxanne. She'd divined the secret heart of how to pleasure him. There was a core to him, and she knew where to find it, how to massage it. But he couldn't dwell on this baffling chemistry, he had to ignore it and get on with his life, the return of the woman to London and to justice, three thousand miles from here. Justice, and perhaps peace in himself, an end to turmoil, a return to what might pass as sound mental health.

'Walk,' he said.

'Carry me,' she said.

'*Carry you?*'

'Why not?'

'You're out of your mind.' He forced a laugh.

'Funny, I seem to have developed a cramp in my leg,' she said.

'Bullshit. Walk. Just walk.'

'You're scared, Pagan. You can't bring yourself to touch me. You can't predict how you're going to react. But I can. Because I know what you are.'

What you are, he thought. What exactly was that? He saw her fingertip run lazily up and down the zip of her leather jacket. He remembered how she'd undone her jeans, the way her hand had vanished down inside white lace. He despised the direction of his thoughts, the way these images assaulted him. Be careful, he thought. Be careful and keep moving, you can't afford to be still.

'So. Are you going to carry me or not?' she asked. The smile was knowing, intimate as a caress.

'Just walk,' he said. She was right: he couldn't touch her. He couldn't run the risk of contact.

'Such cruelty,' she said.

He made a motion with the gun and she began to

walk a few paces ahead of him. But she stopped again. 'What makes you think you can get me out of the States? Some people here want me as badly as you, Pagan. In a different kind of way, if you understand my meaning.'

Matters of jurisdiction didn't concern him right then, and he chose to ignore the way she played on the word *want*. 'Just keep moving,' he said.

'You're thinking about the hotel room, Pagan. You're thinking of what might have been. You're wondering what you might have missed. You're wondering what it would really be like to fuck me. That's what you're thinking.'

He didn't speak. He concentrated on the quiet sounds of water sliding from leaves.

'You're watching me, Pagan. You can't take your eyes off me. I can feel you. I can feel all this pent-up shit inside you. I don't even have to look at you to feel it. You're ready to explode.'

'Wrong,' he said.

'Sure I'm wrong.' She balanced herself on one leg and bent the other, reaching down to scratch the back of her leg. 'Don't worry. I don't have a gun stashed inside my boot.'

Her balance was a delicate thing. He wondered what she'd be like if the sickness could be drained out of her, if her love of destruction could somehow be leeched from her system. A pointless consideration. She was beyond redemption. She didn't want absolution or understanding. These were concepts she mocked. Human life was derisory, and frail, ultimately worthless. He wondered, as he'd done before, at the contrariness of nature, at how someone so murderous as Carlotta could be so beautiful. Why wasn't she disfigured in some way? Why wasn't she ugly?

When would he ever see that her loveliness was a travesty?

She straightened her leg. She tucked her thumbs back in her belt, fingers splayed near her groin. The gesture, she knew, was provocative. She stared at him. His face was lined with tension. How easy it was to get to him. She had the urge to go down on her knees in the mud and draw him inside her mouth and suck him and feel him flood her throat and experience his passion and release. She wanted to hear him groan as he came. She wanted to expose his vulnerability.

She had to act soon. She moved a little closer to him, and he stepped back.

'We're all alone. We don't need to let the moment pass,' she said.

'The moment passed in the hotel room,' he said. 'The moment's gone.'

'I don't think so.' She stretched out her hand, reached for his sleeve. He backed off again. 'You're running away from me, Pagan. You don't have to do that.'

He considered the fragility of distance. He saw her hand fall an inch or so short of his sleeve. You're taking her back to London, he thought. Anything else isn't a consideration. He heard the trees stirred by slowing rain. In the weak light of dawn her face was rendered soft and curiously youthful; if he hadn't known better he might have considered her features those of an innocent girl. He had to keep reminding himself of who she was and what she'd done. He had to keep remembering, an act of silent incantation. *Carlotta, Carlotta. She's Carlotta.*

He saw her hand go up to his face, felt the palm against his cheek. He didn't move this time. He wasn't going to back off. He wouldn't give her that satisfaction. It was a matter of concentration, pretending he felt nothing. He kept his grip on the gun.

He felt her fingertips touch the lobe of his ear, then she drew her index finger to the corner of his mouth and parted his lips and touched the tip of his tongue, then worked the finger gently inside his mouth, along his gums. Just as she'd done in the hotel.

There was an instant when he realized he could still pull free, but it passed like a match terrifyingly snuffed out. He was drifting away from himself. He saw her face come close to his. The kiss when it happened was as shocking as stained glass shattering, more than a collision of lips and tongues; it was a connection taking place at a level beyond consciousness, a place he'd never been. He was swimming through mist. There was an ocean in his head. He had his own tides running in full spate. The kiss scared, brutalized, aroused him. He was aware of her wet hair, the intense scent of her damp flesh, her breath on his flesh, her fingers working at the buckle of his belt. She was saying his name as a lover might, giving it secret inflections, personal resonances. *This is Carlotta*, he thought, and the recognition had the fleeting urgency of a feline creature scurrying into darkness after prey, and then it was gone. It was all madness, and he was dissolving into it.

He couldn't help himself, he pushed her leather jacket back from her shoulders, pulled her T-shirt up over her breasts, there was no way out of this, no direction but forward. Clutching one another frantically, they sank together down into the mud. She had his cock in the palm of her hand and he was hard. There were transformations here, identities lost, lust stripped you down until there was nothing of you left but the overpowering need to be inside the woman. He

427

dragged her jeans down over her hips, unconscious of the wet earth on which he lay, unaware of the discomfort of mud, the way it pressed against his skin. She tore open the buttons of his shirt with one rough gesture and he ripped aside her underwear. She tugged his jeans down and all the while she kept saying his name as if it were a word designed to trigger an hypnotic trance. Rain dripped from leaves, mud adhered to their bodies, sucked at them, yielded under them when they rolled over together. He stared down into her face and she said, '*Give it to me, Frank. Give it to me hard. Hurt me, fuck me until I bleed.*'

Yes, he thought. Until you bleed. This was beyond lust. Lust was too simple. This was a marriage of blind physical impulse and retribution, as if by bringing her the pain she wanted he was in some way avenging all the dead, as if by hurting her he might cancel out the destruction she'd caused. Until you bleed. He saw streaks of mud on her face and throat and breasts, felt his knees sink into soft saturated dirt, felt her fingers, grainy with particles of soil, reach down and guide him inside the private warmth of herself. His head was filled with bright flashes. She moved, rolled, straddled him, face thrown back slightly, mouth open. She was wild and unfettered and he felt as if windows long shut tight in himself had been opened and daylight poured through and she was saying *Harder than that, harder, harder.* He thrust his hips upward, staring into her face and seeing absences in her eyes, and then her hands were rubbing his bare chest with wet earth as if she were drawing patterns in his skin, pictures of a primeval sort, tribal marks, mystic ideographs inscribed on the walls of hidden caves. He caught her wrists, forced her body underneath his own, heard the way his breathing quickened, felt the fuse of orgasm begin to burn far

428

inside him. It was the release of all releases, scorching, and even as he began to soar he understood at one level of himself there was a price to pay, an aftermath to face, the crash of his damaged self—

But she'd moved. She'd shifted out from under him. She'd slid away from his body. He ejaculated into the void of wet earth, and he was attacked by despair, understanding he'd been fooled, this was another of her games, another way of humiliating him. He saw her hand fumble toward the gun he'd let slip in his insanity and he lunged on his knees toward her, and before she could reach the gun he clubbed her fiercely across the wrist. He grabbed her, pinned her in the mud, struck her again and again and again with his knuckles until her mouth bled and the taut skin of her cheek-bones had split. He wanted to kill her. He wanted to beat her until she was dead. He wanted to crush all the life out of her. He battered her face and head more times than he could count and he stopped only when his knuckles hurt and he wondered what he was turning into, what kind of metamorphosis had gone on, how profound was the erosion that had reduced him to mindless savagery.

He watched blood slither across her lips, run beneath her chin to her neck and create a tiny rivulet slicking between her naked breasts. He was breathless, weary, empty. He was conscious of a strange frontier where sex and violence met, a border town where odd kinships were forged and unruly alliances made. And she'd led him to this place, she'd taken him there, she'd shown him the squalid territory where she lived her life.

This is me, Pagan. *This is Carlotta.*

He fumbled around in the dirt until he located the gun, then sat hunched in the gloomy silence of

429

self-reproach. The leaves still dripped. The stream was still running. The landscape murmured. The light was forlorn. His hands hurt, but that was only a superficial pain.

She licked blood and dirt from her fingertips. '*Welcome to my world, Pagan,*' she said, and although she spoke in a muffled way through swollen lips she managed to infuse her voice with a tiny note of triumph.

He moved toward her. He found it from somewhere deep inside himself, leftover rage, a fresh upsurge of anger that rushed to his head like a dense pall of hot smoke, and he raised his hand high in the air and brought the gun down hard into the soft little hollow at the base of her neck, and she slumped to one side, her face pressed into the mud, her bloodied lips open.

Shaking, straining with effort, he reached down and gripped her under the shoulders and dragged her unconscious body across grass and through trees. He hauled her this way for what seemed a very long time, and he stopped only when he realized that he was drained of energy and that some essential part of himself was lost for all time in the wet hostility of this landscape.

48

LONDON

Summer had gone. Early October, autumn descending in its languid way: the parks of London were browning and melancholy. A hibernatory mood gripped Pagan. He stayed inside his flat with the curtains drawn and sipped malt whisky. He didn't feel a need to play his music. He developed a fondness for silence. He'd submitted a report to Nimmo, and then shut himself away.

He hadn't been able to get Carlotta out of the United States because a stubborn airline ticket-clerk wasn't pleased with the fact that she lacked a passport and, moreover, obviously wasn't in a terrific shape to travel, and Pagan's belligerent attitude had only exacerbated the situation. The clerk called the FBI and, after an argumentative scene, Carlotta was handcuffed and led away by stern-faced men in charcoal suits. She was their property now.

The FBI had her in the end. Despite everything. Despite Skidelsky's ambitions.

She was incarcerated, and had refused any form of legal representation. At her trial, a hastily-arranged affair, a three-day circus, she had pleaded guilty to all the charges the FBI could bring against her. Pagan had read in a newspaper that she'd spurned the attentions of lawyers from the American Civil Liberties Union, that she refused to give interviews, that she was resigned to the death sentence the judge had passed. This didn't sound like her. This acquiescence, this passive attitude, this embrace of her own execution. He didn't trust this Carlotta, brooding in her cell. He couldn't imagine her going silently to her death.

But he wanted to forget, which was the hard part.

Nimmo was caught between the need to congratulate Pagan in the press: *How wonderful that a British policeman tracked her down*, and to rail against him in private: *She is ours and I don't give a damn what the FBI think and you shouldn't have surrendered her so easily*. A jurisdictional feud: Pagan didn't need it.

He liked to sit in the living-room and watch daylight fade beyond the curtains. The world was a permanent dusk. There was a lull all through his life, a cessation of curiosity. A graph of his existence would have shown an abrupt plunge, then the flat unbroken line of a silent heart.

He had days when he looked at himself in the mirror and failed to recognize his reflection. He didn't shave. His telephone rang unanswered. He thought too often of the woman, who paraded in and out of his memory as if he had no means of filtering his own recollections. At night he sometimes remembered the smell of mud.

One afternoon, Foxie came to the flat. 'When can we expect you to emerge from this bizarre little cocoon?' he asked with forced cheer.

Pagan said, 'When I'm ready.'

'And when will that be?'

Pagan shrugged the question off.

'It doesn't do any good to sit around, Frank. What the hell is wrong with you anyway?'

'I caught the woman,' Pagan said.

'And that depresses you?'

'No, that doesn't depress me, Foxie.'

'Do you want to explain?'

Pagan clutched a tumbler of whisky and wandered around the room. 'I can't explain.'

'What are you hiding, Frank?'

'I don't know if I'm hiding anything,' Pagan said.

'You know what I think? You should pull yourself together and get back into the fray of things. Forget whatever it is that's bothering you and get on with your bloody life.'

'The cheer-leader speaks.'

'You're a hero, Frank. You caught the wicked witch. You did what nobody else could do. Start with that. Build on that. Get a bloody grip.'

'Get a grip on what, Foxie?'

'Everything.'

Too vague, Pagan thought.

Foxie's expression was one of concern. He observed Pagan wander the room. More than the stubble on the jaw, the pallor of the skin, something intangible had changed in the man. Call it spirit. Fire. It just wasn't there. Foxie had the feeling he was in the company of a counterfeit, a stand-in for the real thing. He wondered what had happened when Frank had finally captured the woman, what had taken place between them. Whatever it was, it had cut deeply into the fabric of Pagan.

Foxie tried to think of something that might lure Frank out of this strange, disaffected mood and back into the world. He said, 'You might be interested to know that the FBI has compiled a confidential report on this Skidelsky character, a copy of which was sent to Special Branch. It appears he had ambitious plans that extended beyond his drastic and rather extravagant idea of reforming the Agency. The Feds have uncovered a stack of documents that suggest he intended to use what you might call the "post-holocaust Agency" as a platform for a general reconstruction of law enforcement in America. He foresaw a time when the Agency would have ultimate control over all police and FBI activities. He had wide-ranging and somewhat sinister plans to put in place a vast network of domestic surveillance, using only Agency personnel – whose numbers, naturally, would have to be boosted enormously if such a spying operation was to be successful . . . Apparently he'd even speculated about the eventuality of the Agency controlling the daily decision-making processes at the Pentagon. One would have to say he was a man of no small ambition, Frank.'

Foxie paused, waited for a reaction from Pagan, but saw no sign, no flicker of interest. He simply stared inside his whisky glass.

'Of course, the FBI could have invented some of this stuff,' Foxie said. 'The blacker they paint Skidelsky, the better they look. A dangerous power-seeker, an egomaniac, unhinged and unbalanced . . . Besides, they're also claiming that they were responsible for his death. The woman isn't mentioned in the report. Nor are you.'

Pagan raised his face and said, 'It all seems so far away, Foxie. Far away, long ago.'

Foxie sighed and, seeing that further communication was useless because Pagan wasn't about to emerge from his baffling place of retreat, went toward the door. Before he left he grasped Pagan's hand and said, 'Phone me if you need me.'

Alone, Pagan slumped in his armchair. He was stricken by the feeling that nothing existed out there in the world. Not Nimmo, not Foxworth, not Golden

Square. And Carlotta – maybe Carlotta was just a creature he'd conjured up out of the dark realms of his imagination, from those caverns where, like guano, the undesirable elements in himself collected.

Three days later, Pagan drove his Camaro out of London and headed south. Marcia Burr had telephoned to invite him down to Sussex; an afternoon in the country will do you the world of good, she'd said. As if he were an invalid. As if he were tubercular. He ignored the motorways, kept to the old back roads. The landscape was beginning to decay. He felt he carried the change of seasons inside himself. What was it? he wondered. What was this dying fall he experienced? Depression? Guilt? He'd caught the wicked witch, but at what price to himself? How did you make such an accounting anyway?

He drove to Lewes, asked directions at a post office for Marcia's cottage, then headed out of the town, passing thatched houses, cosy pubs, a tangle of narrow streets.

The cottage was situated in a quiet country lane. It was surrounded by roses and bramble bushes. Blackbirds crowded the trees, rooks scavenged in harvested fields. A ragged scarecrow stood askew in barren ground.

Pagan parked the car. Marcia Burr was standing in the open doorway of the house, a tiny whitewashed dwelling with trellises pressed against walls, windowboxes, fresh-painted frames. Bucolic tranquillity.

'I heard your car,' she said. She wore a two-piece suit, brown cardigan and pleated skirt, and her hair was pinned back by tortoiseshell clasps. Pagan embraced her briefly, then followed her into the tiny sitting-room where cakes had been laid out on a table.

The walls were painted a pale yellow; wooden beams, blackened by time, criss-crossed the ceiling.

'I'll pour tea,' she said.

Pagan sat.

'I'm glad you came down, Frank.' She slid a cup toward him. 'You look dreadful. No colour in your face. And those circles under your eyes . . . Aren't you sleeping well?'

'I sleep too long,' he said. Which was true. Sometimes twelve hours, even more. Waking was an effort. His sleep was usually dreamless, placid. He reached for the china cup and picked it up. The tea was unexpectedly fragrant.

He surveyed the room. There was a menagerie of small glass animals on a shelf. An antique hunting horn hung on the wall. A cluster of framed photographs.

'I baked the cakes myself,' she said. 'Try one.'

He chose a confection decorated with a chocolate leaf and tasted it. 'Good, very good,' he said.

'I have a lot of time these days for trying out new recipes.'

Pagan tasted his tea again. It was like drinking the liquid essence of flowers. He pretended to enjoy it. 'Are you happy down here?' he asked. He wasn't in the mood for conversation. But he felt obliged to force it along.

'I'm fine, Frank. Really. Some days . . . There are ups and downs.' She smiled at him. She patted his knee. 'But what about you? You're to be congratulated. You found the woman.'

'Yes,' he said.

'I don't know all the details, of course,' Marcia Burr said. She fidgeted with her pearls a second. 'I understand she's being held in a maximum-security prison in the States. Are these places really secure, Frank?'

Pagan let the question drift unanswered. Secure, he thought. Secure was only a word; words carried no guarantees.

'She's going to die in the electric chair,' he said.

'She deserves to die, Frank.' There was an uncharacteristic venom in Marcia's voice.

He gazed at the leaded windows and imagined he was staring through the glass of an execution chamber and seeing Carlotta strapped to an electric chair. *She deserves to die.* His mind drifted to Burr, to the unanswered question that had troubled him all along – Pasco's unhindered passage through Heathrow, Burr's favour for Christopher Poole, the condemnation of an innocent man.

He wiped crumbs inside a paper napkin. He finished his tea. Why did he feel so uncomfortable? he wondered. Maybe it was just his own unsociable mood. Maybe it was because Marcia reminded him of Martin, and he didn't need reminders. He looked at her face, which was turned just slightly away from him, and downcast.

'Do you really think she'll die?' she asked. 'Or is she plotting some last-minute escape?'

'I've wondered about that,' he said. And he had. Time and again the possibility of Carlotta's escape had entered his mind. The idea that she was planning something, that she had a scheme for avoiding her execution, a stunning stroke of magic pulled off at the very end, another mystifying disappearance.

He said, 'Maybe she wants to die. Maybe she's done everything she ever wanted to do and there's nothing else that interests her.'

'Do you believe that?'

'I don't know what I believe,' he said. 'She may want to die the way she lived. A piece of theatre. A flash of electricity. Publicity.'

Marcia fiddled with her pearls again in an anxious way. 'Was it difficult?' she asked.

'Difficult?'

'To catch her.'

He made a vague gesture with his hand, then got up from his chair and walked to the shelf where the glass zoo was located. He picked up a small transparent panda and turned it over in his fingers. 'It was difficult enough,' he said.

Marcia said, 'I collect those little creatures.' She stood alongside him. 'I've had some of them ever since I was a child.'

Pagan's eye passed over the glassy gathering. The workmanship was exquisite. The animals trapped light, which seemed to instil them with a kind of life. He felt Marcia Burr's hand close over his own and he turned his face toward her. Something unsaid hung in the narrow space between them.

'Martin was a decent human being, Frank.'

'I know.'

'He always tried to do the right thing. Always.'

Why was she saying this? he wondered.

'Sometimes he had conflicts,' she said.

'You're trying to tell me something, Marcia.'

She removed her hand. She twisted her face away from him. Pagan carefully replaced the small glass panda, setting it down between a bear and a giraffe. He heard Marcia pull a handkerchief from the sleeve of her cardigan. She raised it to her lips.

'What is it?' he asked. 'What's on your mind, Marcia?'

She made no answer. She reached for the teapot, filled her cup. Then she sat down, her face expressionless. Pagan waited, but still she said nothing. The room seemed intolerably small and cramped to him right then. He looked at the glass animals, let his eye drift along the collection of photographs. Martin was depicted in most of them. In one, he wore naval uniform and looked impossibly youthful. In another he stood with his arm linked through Marcia's; Marcia must have been in her mid-twenties, Burr at least forty. The shot had been taken on a pebbled beach. A rough sea, stilled for all time by the camera, was visible in the background.

Pagan raised a hand, touched the frame, and was about to turn his attention back to Marcia when he stopped.

He was cold suddenly. There was ice in his bones. He took a photograph down from the shelf and stared at it for a long time and then he moved to the table where he laid the picture down in front of Marcia. He didn't know what to say. His synapses were flawed. He couldn't make the connections he needed to make. Marcia didn't even glance at the photograph he'd set down before her.

He remembered the atrium stuffed with herbs, the scents of marjoram and thyme and basil. He remembered Bob Naderson. And he remembered this same image enclosed in a frame on the wicker table: Naderson with his arm round a girl's waist. Naderson and the girl smiling.

Pagan saw it now. The girl was Marcia.

He felt a serious displacement of himself. He hovered at Marcia's shoulder. The room was layered with silences. Awkwardness, puzzlement, the mysterious hush of the past, of hidden relationships.

She covered the picture with the flat of her hand.

'Martin didn't have a choice, you see. He did what I wanted him to do. He felt an obligation, Frank.'

Pagan watched her trace a line with the tip of her finger over the face of Bob Naderson. The glass was slightly dusty and the motion of her nail left a trail resembling a faded scar across Naderson's forehead. She extended the line, linking her face with Naderson's; a connection made in a thin layer of dust. Pagan walked to the window, looked across the slope of lawn that ended in hedgerow.

'An obligation,' he said. Of blood, he thought. Of family. How could Martin have refused to help? How could he have turned down his wife's request?

'He didn't like it, Frank. But what would you have done in the same circumstances? What would you have done if it had been *your* wife's father that was being held in Moscow and you didn't know what was going to happen to him? How would you have acted if it had been somebody close to you?'

How would he have acted? He tried to imagine how he might have felt if Roxanne, say, had been in peril, if she'd been seized and held against her will in a place where he couldn't reach her. He'd have done the same as Martin, he thought. He'd have done whatever it took to get Roxanne back, even if it meant turning a blind eye to what you knew was an injustice, even if it meant sacrificing another person. Love wasn't all sweetness and sharing; it had its own ruthlessness.

He looked at Marcia Burr. Her eyes watered.

'He never truly forgave me,' she said. 'That's what makes it so awful. He never forgave me for influencing him, and he never quite forgot. He always said it was water under the bridge, but I knew how he really felt.' She stood up, fidgeted with cups and saucers. She stopped, her body rigid. She suddenly swept the cake stand to the floor. Tears ran across her cheeks, gathered at the corners of her mouth.

Pagan knew he couldn't comfort her. He felt powerless and clumsy. Bob Naderson's daughter. How Burr must have struggled with the decision to sacrifice Richard Pasco. How hard he must have warred with himself. Any decision he made was certain to be the wrong one; it had been that kind of situation, a conflict between duty and family, between law and love. And Burr had chosen family. Ten years ago he'd chosen the freedom of his wife's father.

The room was too small for Pagan suddenly. It crowded him. He had the beginnings of a headache. Marcia came toward him, touched his arm. 'I caused Martin pain,' she said. 'And in the end I caused his death.'

'You couldn't have predicted it,' he said. 'You can't blame yourself.'

'I tell myself that,' she said, and her voice was thin. 'I tell myself that all the time. If I hadn't convinced him, if I hadn't tried to sway him . . .'

'It's a waste of time to think that way.' He placed a hand across his forehead, which was warm, slightly fevered. What he needed was movement, an open road, the blur of speed.

Marcia lowered her hand to her side. 'And my father . . .'

Pagan thought of rain and floodlights.

She said, 'I had a visit from a couple of friendly men from the American Embassy. They never tell you the whole story. Only the bare facts. Never the details. The woman was quote unquote involved in the explosion that took Bob Naderson's life, very sorry, is there anything we can do to help, and so on. *Involved.* Don't you like that word, Frank?'

441

Marcia stepped away from him and looked down at the broken cakes on the carpet, the inverted cake stand. She appeared to concentrate on the crumbs as if by force of will she might restore them to shape. Then she pressed a foot into one of the dented cakes and ground it vigorously into the rug. 'She deserves to die, she deserves to die.' She said this over and over, as if repetition were a means of exorcizing her sadness.

Pagan moved toward the door and opened it. He gazed out at his parked car. 'I'll leave,' he said.

Marcia Burr didn't look at him. She continued the grinding motion. She was still determinedly pulverizing the crumbs as he stepped outside and drew the door shut behind him. He walked to his car, paused, listened to the hard cawing of rooks in a nearby field. Their shrill cries suggested words in a language he didn't know.

He stayed inside the flat in Holland Park for days after the visit to Lewes. The weather changed. The sky turned cloudy, the green bleached out of the park across from his flat. The area was no longer populated at night by dopers. In daytime it was patrolled by solitary figures walking dogs. Flowers died. He continued to sleep for a dozen hours at a stretch. Consciousness was undesirable.

He spent time walking from room to room, or fingering Roxanne's collection of books. He'd developed a deep need to reassure himself that she'd existed, that once upon a time he'd shared his life with somebody else, that he'd loved, that he was more than the creature of dark violent needs that had emerged in Virginia. It was as if remembrance of Roxanne would expunge Carlotta completely from his system. A victory of the dead over the living.

His loneliness was acute; you could cut yourself on the sharp edge of such solitude. He experienced the odd sensation that he was beginning to fade, that he was yielding to shadow, that the shadow ultimately would give way to nothing, and that anyone who came to the apartment to look for him would find no trace, not a bone, a lock of hair, nothing. No evidence he'd ever existed, he'd ever been married, that a life had been lived in these rooms. He supposed his condition, for want of a better name, was one of despair, but it was a deeper furrow than any he'd ever known before. And he couldn't find a way out of it, couldn't scratch his way to the surface, back to life and light.

On the day Carlotta was scheduled to die, he decided the hollowness of the apartment was finally unbearable. He forced himself to shave and dress and go out. He drove through the streets of Notting Hill. The sun was gone and the sky the colour of a battleship. He understood where he was headed, and although there was an inevitability about his destination he wondered why he felt the desire.

It had been a long time since he'd come this way. Once or twice in the past year he'd considered visiting the place, but he'd always rejected the prospect. What was there to see?

He parked his car in a quiet street of austere Victorian houses and stepped out and made his way in the direction of the wrought-iron gates, noticing that they'd recently been painted. They were black and waxy. He passed through, listening to his feet crunch on the gravel pathway. He paused a second because he'd forgotten the way. He stood under an elm, hesitant. In the distance grey-white smoke rose from a tall dark chimney, as if it were pollution from a foundry.

The place he wanted was close to that chimney, he remembered.

He began to walk, quickly at first, but he slowed the closer he got to his destination. He plucked a handful of wild flowers, held them delicately in his hand because they shed their petals easily. A bouquet of wild flowers: a token. He kept going, seeing here and there stalks of uncut grass grow in tangled clumps, a proliferation of weed and nettle in disarray. The whole area had an illusory stillness about it, an uneasy serenity that affected him: I shouldn't have come here, he thought. But you had to because – because you need to anchor yourself in your past, you need a memory of how you used to be.

The wild flower petals drifted from his fingers and fell across his coat. He didn't feel the echo of grief he'd expected. He experienced an odd calm as he approached the stone, which was plain and unassuming. A patch of lichen grew against the surface. Tall grass obscured the name. He kneeled, pushed the stalks aside, laid the disintegrating wild flowers against the stone. He looked at Roxanne's name. The dates of her living and her dying. The brevity of her time. He read the epitaph, one word: *Missed*. He imagined Roxanne taking shape in front of him, delicate and strong, her expression sympathetic: a heartbreaking phantom. He reached out and touched the indented letters. He thought: I love you.

It was only then he noticed the writing at the base of the stone, the letters painted carefully below Roxanne's name. He closed his eyes. Even here, he thought. He felt a hammer rise and fall inside his skull. He looked at the words and he imagined her coming here and sitting in the long grass with a paintbrush in her hand, her lips pressed together in concentration;

he imagined her fingers, perhaps stained with streaks of red paint, working the brush against the stone.

I'll always be around, Frank, she'd written. *Look for me.*

I'll always be around, Frank. He wondered how many months had passed since she'd written these words. She'd known he'd come to this spot sooner or later, that he'd find these words, that this desecration would devastate him. From her place of incarceration more than three thousand miles away, she was still trying to manipulate him.

No, he thought. *God-damn you.* No more. This is where you draw the line. In this place of the dead. This is where it ends. Here. Now. Buried and forgotten. A memory extinguished, an anguish annihilated. No more. And he pictured her being strapped in an electric chair, guards watching her closely, a priest mumbling useless platitudes. He imagined her head and hands and ankles tethered to the lethal chair, the impassive faces of observers looking at her through a window as she was bound. He imagined a switch pulled and the voltage coursing through her body, the stiffening of her muscles, the eventual slump of her head. There would be no last-minute escape. No astounding stunt. She was going out in fire. The electricity was all around him. The air was suddenly charged with it. He could hear it crackle nearby. He could almost feel it rush through his own body as if, at the very last, the simple act of an executioner throwing a switch three thousand miles away had liberated him finally from his own imprisonment.

He got to his feet and the stalks he'd parted with his hands regrouped with all the forceful elasticity of nature and he stepped away from the stone, and in a rich outbreak of liberating anger he said aloud, '*No, you won't, you won't ever be around again, you're going to burn, you fucking bitch.*' And, his heart beating hard, he gazed in the direction of the smoke that rose in wisps of cloud from the chimney of the crematorium, up and up into the sky like final messages left by departing souls.

He clenched his hands and walked away, his stride that of a man sensing the possibilities of reinvigoration, a man freed from a time of wreckage and mourning. He'd come back and he'd scrub the paint from the stone and he'd begin to live again in ways he couldn't yet predict.

Look for me, he thought. No, never, never again.

THE END

JIGSAW
by Campbell Armstrong

The spirit of *Jig* lives on . . .

On a bitter winter evening a bomb explodes in a crowded London underground train. People are senselessly slaughtered. Who planted the murderous device? And why?

A few hours later in a Mayfair flat a young prostitute is brutally killed and an enigmatic message written in blood is left in her room. It is addressed to Frank Pagan, counter-terrorist specialist, and it draws him into the most terrifying case of his career.

Pagan finds himself pitted against two extraordinary adversaries: the lethal Carlotta, a woman whose appetite for blood is matched only by Pagan's hunger for justice – and the ghost of Jig, his most famous antagonist, whose death has given birth to new demons . . .

From London to New York, Berlin to Venice, *Jigsaw* weaves a breathtaking story of conspiracy and power, passion and betrayal – a magnificent follow-up to Campbell Armstrong's worldwide bestseller *Jig*.

'Armstrong creates electric tension'
Daily Telegraph

'Campbell Armstrong has outdone both Frederick Forsyth and Ken Follett with *Jigsaw*. *Jigsaw* features a villain to die for, plus the most unusual and haunting romance I've encountered in a thriller'
James Patterson, author of *Along Came a Spider*

'Armstrong has created a thriller where the sex is sexy, the horror horrific, and the plot is, as it should be, the skeleton for a well fleshed-out piece of storytelling'
The Times

0 552 14168 2

A SELECTED LIST OF FINE WRITING
AVAILABLE FROM CORGI BOOKS

14168 2	**JIGSAW**	*Campbell Armstrong*	£4.99
13947 5	**SUNDAY MORNING**	*Ray Connolly*	£4.99
14227 1	**SHADOWS ON A WALL**	*Ray Connolly*	£5.99
14353 7	**BREAKHEART HILL**	*Thomas H. Cook*	£5.99
14518 1	**THE CHATHAM SCHOOL AFFAIR**	*Thomas H. Cook*	£5.99
13827 4	**SPOILS OF WAR**	*Peter Driscoll*	£4.99
14377 4	**THE HORSE WHISPERER**	*Nicholas Evans*	£5.99
13275 9	**THE NEGOTIATOR**	*Frederick Forsyth*	£5.99
13823 1	**THE DECEIVER**	*Frederick Forsyth*	£5.99
12140 1	**NO COMEBACKS**	*Frederick Forsyth*	£4.99
13990 4	**THE FIST OF GOD**	*Frederick Forsyth*	£5.99
14293 X	**RED, RED ROBIN**	*Stephen Gallagher*	£5.99
14472 X	**CONFESSOR**	*John Gardner*	£5.99
14223 9	**BORROWED TIME**	*Robert Goddard*	£5.99
13840 1	**CLOSED CIRCLE**	*Robert Goddard*	£5.99
13697 2	**AIRPORT**	*Arthur Hailey*	£4.99
13678 6	**THE EVENING NEWS**	*Arthur Hailey*	£5.99
13696 4	**OVERLOAD**	*Arthur Hailey*	£4.99
13698 0	**STRONG MEDICINE**	*Arthur Hailey*	£5.99
07583 3	**NO MEAN CITY**	*A. McArthur & H. Kingsley Long*	£4.99
14249 2	**VIRGINS AND MARTYRS**	*Simon Maginn*	£4.99
14250 6	**A SICKNESS OF THE SOUL**	*Simon Maginn*	£4.99
14389 8	**HAYWIRE**	*James Mills*	£5.99
14327 8	**THE ENGLISHMAN WHO WENT UP A HILL BUT CAME DOWN A MOUNTAIN**	*Christopher Monger*	£4.99
14136 4	**THE WALPOLE ORANGE**	*Frank Muir*	£4.99
14392 8	**CASINO**	*Nicholas Pileggi*	£5.99
13094 X	**WISEGUY**	*Nicholas Pileggi*	£5.99
14143 7	**A SIMPLE PLAN**	*Scott Smith*	£4.99
10565 1	**TRINITY**	*Leon Uris*	£5.99